Lesley Eames is an author of historical sagas, her preferred writing place being the kitchen due to its proximity to the kettle. Lesley loves tea, as do many of her characters. Having previously written sagas set around the time of the First World War and into the Roaring Twenties, she has ventured into the Second World War period with her fifth book, *The Wartime Bookshop*.

Originally from the northwest of England (Manchester), Lesley's home is now Hertfordshire where *The Wartime Bookshop's* fictional village of Churchwood is set. Along her journey as a writer, Lesley has been thrilled to have had ninety short stories published and to have enjoyed success in competitions in genres as varied as crime writing and writing for children. She is particularly honoured to have won the Festival of Romance New Talent Award, the Romantic Novelists' Association's Elizabeth Goudge Cup and to have been twice shortlisted in the UK Romantic Novel Awards (RONAs).

THE WARTIME BOOKSHOP

Book 1: Beginnings

Lesley Eames

PENGUIN BOOKS

TRANSWORLD PUBLISHERS
Penguin Random House, One Embassy Gardens,
8 Viaduct Gardens, London SW11 7BW
www.penguin.co.uk

Transworld is part of the Penguin Random House group of companies
whose addresses can be found at global.penguinrandomhouse.com

Penguin
Random House
UK

First published in Great Britain in 2022 by Bantam
an imprint of Transworld Publishers
Penguin paperback edition published 2022

A CIP catalogue record for this book
is available from the British Library.

ISBN
9781529177350

Typeset in New Baskerville ITC Pro by Jouve (UK), Milton Keynes.
Printed and bound in Great Britain by Clays Ltd, Elcograf S.p.A.

The authorized representative in the EEA is Penguin Random House Ireland,
Morrison Chambers, 32 Nassau Street, Dublin D02 YH68.

Penguin Random House is committed to a sustainable future
for our business, our readers and our planet. This book is made
from Forest Stewardship Council® certified paper.

For my precious daughters,
Olivia and Isobel, who fill my life with joy.

CHAPTER ONE

Alice

Only two weeks had passed since Alice Lovell's move to Churchwood, and with her injured hand making the simplest task slow and uncomfortable, she'd spent most of that time unpacking instead of getting to know the village's other residents. Even so, she'd learned enough for her steps to falter as she neared the shops and saw the bulldog-like figure of Naomi Harrington up ahead.

Mrs Harrington was a woman who clearly loved to take charge so already Alice thought of her as Churchwood's social sergeant major, though perhaps she'd prefer to be likened to a more senior rank – colonel, brigadier or even major general perhaps. Middle-aged and wealthy, she had an air of authority in both her bearing and her dress. Today's outfit was typical: a cream blouse and tweed suit in a countryside brown that resembled military khaki covering what was doubtless a sturdy corset. A matching hat sporting a small feather like regimental insignia completed the picture.

As befitted a person of power, she was accompanied by a second in command, though Marjorie Plym was her physical opposite. Tall and lanky, Miss Plym had shoulders that drooped like the curve of a question mark. Her dull grey coat and hat drooped, too, and she had none of Mrs Harrington's forcefulness. In fact, Alice suspected Miss Plym of being rather silly.

Judging from the clipboard Miss Plym was holding to her skinny bosom, Alice guessed that the two women were on the watch for passers-by to recruit to some sort of project. It might be the sort of project that would do good in the world but, much as Alice wanted to do good – and find friends, too – she recoiled from the thought of being bullied into a situation she might find awkward and even humiliating, given the state of her hand.

Hoping she hadn't been spotted, Alice turned to the nearest shop window, intending to linger until the women had moved away or were so busy recruiting someone else that she could sidle past unnoticed. The window belonged to the cobbler and contained only a dull display of shoe polishes, brushes and laces, but Alice remained there anyway, reading an advertisement about the durability of Hexton's leather soles until she noticed the cobbler nodding at her through the glass as though encouraging her to step inside. Embarrassed at having no business for him, Alice turned away – and saw that Mrs Harrington had not only spotted her but appeared to be waiting for her.

Sighing, Alice walked on, quickening her pace to give the impression that she had no time for chatting, though she still nodded politely. 'Mrs Harrington. Miss Plym.'

Naomi Harrington wasn't to be thwarted so easily. 'Just the person.'

Oh, heavens. Just the person for what? Reluctantly, Alice came to a halt.

'First-aid classes,' Mrs Harrington explained. 'With a war on, many of our doctors and nurses are going to be busy looking after our servicemen overseas or in hospitals here at home. Looking after injured civilians too. We owe it to King and country to make as few demands on the medically qualified as possible. That means ensuring we have the skills to look after ourselves and each other.'

Alice's dismay must have shown on her face because Mrs Harrington frowned. 'The enemy may not have attacked us here in Britain yet, Miss Lovell, but it can only be a matter of time. You weren't born when the 1914 war was raging, but I have clear memories of the devastation wrought by the bombs dropped by those dreadful Zeppelins and Gotha aeroplanes. The injuries and loss of life were terrible. Modern aeroplanes are likely to bring even more destruction.'

'I don't doubt it.'

Alice had no argument with Mrs Harrington's account of the earlier war, or with her prediction that the current conflict might prove to be even more tragic. As for learning basic nursing and first aid, Alice was in favour of it, even in peacetime. But she foresaw that two requests were about to be made of her, and she dreaded them both.

The first request came swiftly.

'Perhaps your father might lead the classes as he's a doctor?'

'My father is retired,' Alice pointed out gently.

3

'We all have to do our duty in wartime.'

'My father spent three years caring for British troops in France in the last war. Now he needs his retirement.'

It was the wrong thing to say. Miss Plym's plain features sprang to attention, doubtless at the scent of juicy gossip about a breakdown in Dr Lovell's mental wellbeing. Alice had realized as early as her second day in Churchwood that Miss Plym was a gossipmonger after walking into the grocer's shop and finding her there with another customer. No more than a minute or two had passed before Miss Plym had sidled up behind Alice, nudged the other customer with her elbow, then nodded towards Alice's injured hand as though asking, 'I wonder what could have happened to make such a mess?'

Alice had seen it all reflected in a glass display case. Even now, the woman was torn between searching Alice's face for clues about her father and sliding her gaze downwards for a better look at the injury.

'What I meant to say is that my father feels he should leave things to younger men,' Alice corrected. 'Younger men with knowledge of modern medical practices.'

'But—'

'My father wouldn't wish to instruct people in old ways when there are better – perhaps safer – ways of doing things.'

Mrs Harrington looked startled, as though it hadn't occurred to her that medical matters might become outdated. But then uncertainty crept into her face. Did she suspect that Alice was fobbing her off with an excuse? If so, her instincts were sound because the reason Dr Lovell would refuse to lead the classes had nothing to do with safety.

'I've spent almost forty years at the beck and call of patients,' he'd told Alice more than once. 'I've had them knocking on my door and telephoning at all hours, and I've dragged myself out of bed to attend to them on more nights than I can remember. Half of them were malingerers too. I've earned this retirement.'

He also needed an escape from a war that he could scarcely believe was happening so soon after the last conflict. Alice doubted that Churchwood would take a sympathetic view of his position, though, and, while he wouldn't care what Churchwood thought of him, Alice cared on his behalf. It distressed her to think of him being regarded with disapproval by Mrs Harrington and her cronies, especially as the day might come when, contrary to his current expectations, he found that he actually craved the companionship of his neighbours or needed their help.

Besides, it wasn't only Archibald Lovell who'd moved to Churchwood. Alice had to forge some sort of life here too. Certainly, she needed something to lift her spirits.

The first-aid classes weren't the answer, though. Her hand just wasn't up to fixing dressings and bandages, especially not with a curious audience looking on. Anticipating that Mrs Harrington's second request would be Alice's presence at the classes, she began to back away. 'I imagine the Red Cross will be able to provide an instructor who's up to date with best practices. Good afternoon, Mrs Harrington. Miss Plym.'

Alice turned to walk on but, once again, Mrs Harrington wasn't to be thwarted.

'I hope *you'll* join the classes?' she called. 'A doctor's daughter could be useful, and the classes will bring your own skills up to date.'

Could Alice pretend she hadn't heard? Not convincingly. She hadn't gone nearly far enough. She turned back slowly, trying to conjure an excuse about being needed at home. 'My father—'

'Surely he won't object to *you* taking part?' Mrs Harrington looked ready to denounce Dr Lovell as a traitor.

Instantly Alice felt protective of him. 'Of course not, but—'

'Put Miss Lovell's name on our list, Marjorie.'

Alice fumed silently as Miss Plym wrote on her clipboard then hugged it to her chest with a look of smug triumph. But the next moment Miss Plym stiffened in almost comical outrage.

Glancing around to see what had brought about this extraordinary reaction, Alice saw a pony and trap ease to the kerb. The driver was a young woman of a similar age to Alice – around nineteen or so. 'Wait there, Pete,' the girl commanded the pony.

Putting the reins down, she jumped to the ground. She was tall with an elastic grace, and radiated the sort of healthy energy that Alice could only dream of. But she was dressed like a scarecrow in what appeared to be cast-off men's clothes: an ancient jacket held together by patches, a checked shirt with the collar missing, filthy breeches that were almost worn through at the knees, and overlarge boots.

Only the girl's hair conceded her femininity. The

colour of coppery-brown horse chestnuts, it was unfashionably long and plaited into a careless braid down her back. Escaped tendrils floated around her face. It was a striking face, especially with those bold, dark eyes, but it was also smeared with dirt. As for the girl's hands . . . Alice caught a glimpse of blackened fingernails.

The girl mounted the pavement with animal ease and sent a taunting look in their direction. 'Ladies,' she said, but she didn't stop.

She headed for the grocer's shop instead. Just before entering, she rubbed her palms down her thighs as though to clean off some of the dirt. Without water, it seemed likely that she was merely redistributing it.

'Humph.' The distaste in Mrs Harrington's expression deepened the starburst wrinkles around her mouth and eyes. 'Churchwood is a respectable place, Miss Lovell, but every town and village has its problem families. Ours is the Fletcher family, but we don't let its members upset our way of life. We'll keep you informed about the classes.'

Alice managed another faint smile, continued to the baker's to buy bread and then set off on the short walk home.

Churchwood was very different from London, where Alice and her father had lived before. In London a person was never far from bustle. There were shops, offices and other businesses by the thousand, millions of homes and an abundance of theatres, hotels and restaurants. Streets were busy with pedestrians, and traffic was intense with cars, double-decker buses and trains jostling above the ground while more trains sped through tunnels beneath it.

Here there was quietness. Churchwood was a village – not a tiny village, but not quite a town either – set among a patchwork of gently rolling fields and hedgerows. The centre comprised a triangular-shaped village green with a war memorial and wooden benches in the centre. Facing it on one side were St Luke's Church, the Vicarage, the Sunday School Hall and the elementary school. Facing it on the other sides were pretty cottages and shops: grocer, greengrocer, baker, butcher, chemist, cobbler, Post Office-cum-newsagent and one small shop run by a married couple who offered hairdressing on the ground floor and a barber's business upstairs.

More cottages and houses occupied the surrounding roads and lanes, but other businesses were few. There were two pubs, a flour mill and a basket-weaving concern. Also a family venture in which two middle-aged brothers combined shoeing horses with blacksmithing work while their sons turned their hands to repairing tractors and other vehicles. The surrounding land was given over to farming, with a few acres being tended by a market gardener called Mr Makepiece.

A small bus lumbered through the village now and then to take residents to and from surrounding towns but there was no train station and no library either. Dr Lovell might have hundreds of books but Alice's own collection was modest so the lack of a library was a blow.

The Lovells' new home was along Churchwood Way, the main thoroughfare through the village, but on the outskirts. It neighboured Naomi Harrington's property, Foxfield, but was separated from it by

Brimbles Lane. Beyond Foxfield there was only Mr Makepiece's market garden.

The new house was as different from their old one as London was from Churchwood. A tall, white-painted villa in the middle of an elegant terrace in leafy Highbury, the London house had served as Dr Lovell's consulting rooms as well as a home. This house was a cottage, low-built and relatively small.

It was picturesque enough, with casement windows criss-crossed with silver lead and an old oak door around which roses would grow in summer. But it wasn't a convenient place to live. The three bedrooms had sloping ceilings, which made them cramped, and although there was a lovely drawing room with French windows opening on to the rear garden, Alice's father was using that as his study, leaving only a small dining room and kitchen for other uses. The cottage was also damp and, having been uninhabited since the death of the owner a year previously, had been iced up inside and out on their arrival just before Christmas.

Alice hadn't complained. Her father had looked forward to his retirement for many years and she hadn't the heart to diminish his joy in it. 'Of course you must take the drawing room as your study,' she'd said. 'You need the space for your books and desk, and it'll be lovely for you to open the French windows in summer.'

She'd also felt she had no right to expect better accommodation for herself after being such a burden to him over the past year. The surgery on her hand had cost him dearly and he'd also had to pay someone to cover the duties she'd no longer been able to fulfil as his receptionist, secretary and house-keeper. Alice was doing her best to recover strength and movement, even if she could do nothing about her hand's appearance, but healing was proving to be a slow business.

Letting herself into the kitchen, she put away the bread she'd bought then went to inform her father that she was home again. Not that he'd have remembered she'd gone out. Standing by the open door of the drawing room, she watched him for a moment, feeling a burst of love as he studied one of his books with a beam of delight.

Like Alice, he was fair-haired, blue-eyed and short. But where she was neat and slender – too slender, perhaps – he was a rounded, cherubic little man with hair like a fuzzy halo. This sweet appearance had helped him in his medical practice because it had created an impression of a sympathetic man who'd mollycoddle patients through their ailments, real or imagined.

It had been a misleading impression. As a doctor, Archibald Lovell had been kind and thorough, but while he'd been sympathetic to genuine distress, he'd had little understanding of his patients' other emotional needs. 'Nothing wrong with you,' Alice had heard him tell Mrs Pinsent, a woman who was feeling neglected by her husband and in need of some fuss.

'Fit as a fiddle,' he'd told Miss Andrews, who relied on a delicate constitution to make her interesting to her friends.

'Perhaps a tonic?' Miss Andrews had suggested.

'A waste of money,' he'd declared, not appearing to realize that Miss Andrews would consider it to be

10

money well spent if she could tell her friends that her doctor was insisting on paying close attention to her fragile state of health.

He was the same with over-protective parents. 'What little Johnnie needs is to run about in fresh air,' he'd told Mrs Paget, who'd promptly clutched little Johnnie to her bosom.

'Surely not, Doctor? Not when he's so delicate!'

The appeal of the cherubic appearance tended to fade when the Mrs Pinsents, Miss Andrewses and Mrs Pagets of Highbury realized that Dr Lovell took a robust approach to medical matters. In time those patients would drift away to more sympathetic doctors.

Fortunately, there had always been enough genuine patients – and new malingerers – to keep Dr Lovell in business, even if his practice hadn't been the most successful in Highbury. Alice knew enough of his financial situation to understand that, in retirement, his style of living was destined to be modest. It would require careful management if he were to continue to buy the sorts of books he loved and perhaps to travel occasionally when the war was over. It made her even more determined to ask little for herself while doing all that she could to achieve independence.

'Cup of tea?' she offered now.

Her father looked up from his book, blinking as though surprised to find himself in Churchwood instead of the historic Greece he'd been reading about. 'Oh, hello, my dear.'

'Tea?' she repeated.

'Splendid, splendid.'

11

'This room is taking shape.' Alice glanced around at the shelves of books, though the truth was that progress was slow, because every time her father picked up a book, he was unable to resist opening it and reading at least the first few pages.

Still, he had all the time in the world to devote to his unpacking now he was no longer working. 'Isn't it?' he said, his smile joyful.

There were literally hundreds of books, mostly on ancient civilizations. Studying them was to be the delight of his retirement and would have been the delight of his life if the need to pay bills hadn't made that impossible.

His gaze drifted back to his book and within seconds he looked so engrossed that Alice wondered if he'd forgotten she was even in the room.

'The man who lives on the moon was on the village green,' she ventured. 'He'd come down for a visit and brought his wife and sixteen children.'

'Splendid, splendid.'

Alice sighed and rolled her eyes. 'I'll put the kettle on.'

The kitchen was poky but there was just enough room in the middle for a small square table and four chairs. Alice put a tray on the table then prepared the teapot and cups.

Hearing the second post of the day drop through the letter box, she went out to the hall to investigate. She found one letter addressed to her father – probably a bill relating to the house move – and another addressed to herself that brought a small jolt to her heart.

She stared at it for a moment before taking both letters into the kitchen, leaving hers on the table unopened and placing her father's bill on his tray. When the tea was ready, she took the tray in to him, the once-simple task of carrying it having become a tricky business since her accident. Her damaged hand wasn't strong enough to hold the handle normally any more. Instead, Alice had to ease one end of the tray over the edge of the table so she could balance it on her wrist. Even that was uncomfortable, but she was determined to persist instead of asking her father for help. If discomfort was the price for independence, Alice would happily pay it.

'Tea and a letter,' she announced, making a mental note to ask about the bill later to ensure it wasn't overlooked. Her father had a habit of losing correspondence among his notes and Alice had no wish to be pursued by debt collectors.

Returning to the kitchen, she poured tea for herself then sat at the little table to contemplate her own letter again. She hadn't needed the Yorkshire postmark to confirm the sender. She'd recognized the handwriting immediately: written on a thick, creamy envelope of excellent quality, it was tall, straight and confident, like the man who'd penned it. She traced the name he'd written – *Miss A. Lovell* – wondering at the thoughts that had passed through his mind as he'd wielded his pen.

Then she tutted at herself; there was nothing to be gained by delay. Slicing into the envelope with a knife, she pulled out a sheet of cream paper.

It had been written from the military camp where

Daniel was currently stationed. He'd served in the Officer Training Corps at school and university but hadn't gone into the regular army afterwards. Instead, he'd become a part-time territorial soldier, but that still meant he'd been called up on the outbreak of war. Most territorials were already in France with the British Expeditionary Force. Doubtless it was only a matter of time before Daniel joined them.

Dear Alice,

Happy New Year! I hope you and your father are keeping well and settling down in Churchwood. Moving house is an exhausting business but I trust you've now found places for all of your possessions and are pleased with your new home. It's a relief to me to know you're in Hertfordshire as I suspect it'll be much safer than London when the bombing starts.

Has Dr Lovell begun his studies? I hope he isn't drowning under books and papers!

I may not be in Yorkshire for the scenery, but it's a beautiful county, even at this time of year. I'd like to see more of it but have other plans for the leave I hope to be granted soon. My family expect me to spend some time with them but I also have a godmother in St Albans who'd like to see me as she hasn't been well. I believe Churchwood is only ten or so miles from her house so I might be able to call on you, too, to see how you're getting on. I believe you're no longer on the telephone so I can't let you know if or when I'm coming but please don't hesitate to send me on my way if I arrive at an inconvenient moment.

Fond regards,

Daniel x

A picture of Daniel's face floated into Alice's mind. Dark-haired, dark-eyed, fresh-faced, handsome . . . A rush of conflicting emotions followed – excitement at the thought of seeing him again, but sorrow, too, because she knew he'd be visiting for the wrong reasons.

CHAPTER TWO

Kate

Frost had frozen the ground overnight, and it wasn't softening as the day progressed. It was the frostiest winter in more than forty years, according to the newspaper Kenny had brought home from the Wheatsheaf last night. Still, it would take more than frost to stop Kate working, hard work having been her close acquaintance for as long as she could remember. She thrust the blade of the spade into the ground, forced it deeper with her foot and heaved the earth aside. Satisfied that she was making reasonable progress, she allowed her thoughts to drift back to the first-aid classes, a subject that had been flitting in and out of her head ever since she'd heard Mrs Harrington and Miss Plym talking about them down in the village.

No one had asked Kate to take part. Not that she could have spared the time – and not that she wanted to be involved anyway. As if! Kate scowled as she imagined the whispers that would fly around the room if she dared attend.

'One of the Fletchers . . .'

'So uncouth!'

'I heard those boys were fighting in the Wheatsheaf again . . .'

There'd be sideways looks at her men's clothes and

16

filthy fingernails, too. Frowns, curled lips, sniffs of disgust . . .

Those gossipy women should try keeping their fingernails clean after working in soil every day. They should try taking baths in front of the kitchen fire, too, when Ernie and the boys were likely to walk in at any moment, not understanding the concept of privacy. Or choosing not to understand it.

She let out a bark of laughter at the thought of snobbish Naomi Harrington and her silly friend Marjorie Plym trying to bathe at Brimbles Farm, though there wasn't much mirth behind the laughter. Then Kate wondered if the young woman she'd seen outside the grocer's shop would attend the class. A doctor's daughter, according to a conversation Kate had overheard. A slight little thing who'd be useless with a spade in frosty earth, but doubtless Churchwood was welcoming her to its bosom. She was neat, ladylike and – if appearances were any indication – respectable.

Was there more to the girl than that, though? Kate had been struck by the intelligence in those pale eyes. The lack of condemnation too. But that was probably only because the girl hadn't heard about the Fletchers' reputation yet. It wouldn't be long before Churchwood dripped its poison into her ear.

Kate paused to stretch her back. Enough digging for one day. The boys would be wanting their tea and wouldn't hesitate to complain if they had to wait for it. She shook the worst of the dirt from the spade, returned it to the barn and headed for the farmhouse.

Outside the kitchen door she used the boot scraper and stepped inside. Having no other shoes, and certainly no carpet slippers, she kept her boots on but washed her hands at the sink using water she'd left warming over the kitchen fire for the purpose. She scrubbed at her fingernails in vain; then she set the kettle to boil again, prepared the ancient brown teapot and carved bread.

Her father arrived first, trailing mud all over the floor. 'Tea won't be long,' Kate told him, and he grunted something she took to mean acceptance.

He walked to the sink and washed his hands carelessly, splashing the surroundings with dirt and smearing more dirt over the towel before throwing himself into a chair at the kitchen table. He was a thin man with a weasel's narrow face and a fox's cunning. His hair was thin and greasy, his teeth terrible.

Kenny, the eldest son at twenty-five, appeared next, bringing more mud into the kitchen. Chestnut-haired like Kate, he could have been a good-looking man had his expression been less sour. 'Where's the tea?' he demanded.

'It's coming!' Kate snapped.

Vinnie, the second brother, soon followed. A younger version of their father in appearance, Vinnie was sly and mean. Kate imagined it gave him pleasure to see the dirt he was tracking in.

A moment later the kitchen door burst open again and the twins entered. Frank 'n' Fred were twenty-one and orange-haired, with a habit of trailing destruction via their pointless energy. More mud dirtied the floor.

Not one of the Fletcher boys troubled themselves with handwashing.

Kate placed the teapot on the table and poured cups for each of them. There were no saucers. Too many had been broken over the years, and none of the Fletcher men cared for social niceties anyway.

'I want my bread toasted,' Vinnie announced.

'You know where the toasting fork is.' Kate was in no mood to indulge him.

He sent her a surly look, which left her in no doubt that something spiteful would follow. A smear of butter on a chair, perhaps, or a spillage of tea on the floor. That was Vinnie.

She placed the plate of bread on the table along with butter and a jar of jam. Filthy hands grabbed for the bread, the twins aiming for the same slice. 'Beat you to it!' Frank crowed.

'Liar!' Fred accused. 'I got it first.'

Predictably, they jumped up to fight. The twins were always swift to fight, swift to make up and swift to fight again.

No one took any notice. Ernie, as they all called their father, simply moved his cup closer to him, and Kenny asked Vinnie about the condition of the fence around Two-Acre Field.

Within seconds the disputed slice of bread was in rags. 'You have it,' Frank said, tossing a crust at Fred.

'No, you have it.' Fred tossed the crust back.

There were crumbs all over the table and floor, but both twins simply sat down and reached for fresh slices.

Kate drank her own tea standing by the window so she wouldn't have to look at the mess.

'*How* much?' she heard her father say, and she guessed he'd joined the conversation about the fence.

Ernie was a skinflint who kept a tight rein on family finances. The boys received beer money every

Wednesday night, but Kate was given nothing for herself. The only money that passed through her hands was for groceries and she was expected not only to make it go far but also to account for every penny. Each item she bought – and the price she paid – had to be noted in Ernie's cash book and he studied it with merciless intensity.

'What's this?' he'd ask. 'How could it have cost ninepence?'

Kate would have to justify why she hadn't managed to get the item for eightpence, though sometimes she suspected he challenged her simply to make her afraid of spending a farthing more than necessary.

The one time she'd tried to sneak a personal purchase through the cash book he'd jumped straight on it. 'Soap? We never pay this much for soap.'

'I bought two bars,' Kate explained, but that wasn't enough for Ernie.

'Show me,' he insisted, and Kate had been left with no option but to produce the bar of scented soap she'd bought for herself. 'The coal-tar soap hurts my hands,' she'd explained. 'It's because they're in water so often. Washing clothes, washing dishes, washing vegetables . . .'

'Take the fancy stuff back and don't waste my money again or I'll tan your hide with my belt. Hurts your hands? Who do think you are? Some kind of fine lady? You're a farmer's daughter, and don't you forget it.'

The boys returned to work after ten minutes or so, leaving Kate to clean up the kitchen. More work awaited her but instead of hastening to it she decided to take a rare five minutes for herself. She climbed the narrow staircase and tugged her boots off outside the door to the smallest bedroom where she slept. Kate liked to keep the room clean and tidy so stepped inside in her socks.

There was space for only a narrow bed and a chest of drawers. Kate sat on the bed, opened the bottom drawer and ran her fingers over the contents. They were her late mother's things, rescued from a box in the barn several years ago.

Mary Fletcher had died when her daughter was only a few months old, and Kate had no memories of her. Even so, Kate liked to think about the sort of woman her mother might have been.

She certainly hadn't been the sort of woman to wear men's breeches. Folded neatly into the drawer were two of Mary's old dresses. Both were home-made, as money had doubtless been tight, but both reflected the taste of a woman who liked to be pretty – a lace-edged collar decorating one dress and ribbon decorating the other.

There was a hairbrush, too, and a small tin that had once held humbugs but in which Mary had stored hairpins. As well, there was a necklace of blue beads, a handkerchief bearing an embroidered M, and a tray cloth that Mary appeared to have stitched herself.

Closing the drawer again, Kate turned her attention to her late mother's books, which stood on top of the chest. There were only two storybooks – *The Tale of Benjamin Bunny* by Beatrix Potter and *The Railway Children* by E. Nesbit. Had Mary pictured herself reading them to her daughter? The third and final book was a bible in which Mary had noted the births of all four of her children. The handwriting looked painstaking, as though it had been a matter of pride to write *Kenneth Ernest Fletcher*, *Vincent George Fletcher*, *Francis Paul Fletcher*, *Frederick James Fletcher* and, finally, *Katherine Louise Fletcher*.

Would Mary have been appalled at the way her motherless daughter had been brought up? Kate imagined so.

A neighbouring farmer's wife had come in to help in the early years after Mary's death, but following frequent arguments with Ernie, Mrs Abel had refused to set foot on Brimbles Farm ever again. She'd moved away soon afterwards.

After her departure, Kate had run wild for several years. Ernie cared little for education, and Kate could easily have avoided going to school for much of that time if she'd wanted to, but she'd loved learning and the magical world that books opened up for her. Her teacher, Miss Gibson, had been full of praise and even called at the farm to tell Ernie that his clever daughter deserved every encouragement. Far from being impressed, Ernie had told poor Miss Gibson that she had no business trespassing on his farm and interfering in his family. He'd insisted she get off his land before he kicked her off.

Kate's attendance had gradually declined after that. One reason was that the older she grew, the more she was expected to help at home. The other reason was that she'd become increasingly self-conscious about her none-too-clean appearance and ragged clothes. About her family's bad reputation too. School had become an ordeal of mean looks and whispers, and often Kate preferred to stay away. At least the chickens and cows on the farm didn't sneer at her.

There'd been no question of Kate staying at school a day longer than the law required anyway and no question of her getting a job elsewhere. 'You'll stay here and do your duty, girl,' Ernie had insisted.

Girl. Ernie and the boys called her a girl only when it suited them. By their reckoning girls owed obedience to their fathers and brothers and were obliged to keep house for them. Without payment, of course, because girls had no need of beer money.

Yet when it came to digging, planting, chopping firewood and mending the roof, Kate was expected to work as hard as a boy and she'd been mocked mercilessly the one time she'd asked for a dress.

'Heard this, Ernie?' Vinnie had said. 'Our Kate fancies herself a fine lady.'

Ernie had looked her up and down with a scowl. 'Then she's a fool.'

'A fool who needs to know her place,' Vinnie had agreed, and he'd flicked ash from his cigarette on to the floor with spiteful relish. 'That's your place, our Kate. Cleaning up after your betters.'

'I'd rather be a fool than a nasty piece of work like you,' Kate had retorted.

She'd said no more about a dress – she went nowhere a dress would be appropriate anyway – but while she sometimes considered cutting her hair to a more practical length she kept it long. Old-fashioned her braid might be, but cutting it would have felt like defeat.

Kate could see nothing on her horizon but Brimbles Farm and work, yet she still nursed a vague hope that the world might one day open up to her, if only in a small way. Desperate to know more of life beyond the Fletchers' patch of land, she fell upon the discarded newspapers the Fletcher men sometimes brought home from the Wheatsheaf and read them hungrily. There was no wireless at home, so newspapers were the only way she learned about all sorts of things – the maiden voyage of HMS *Queen Mary* to New York, a musical called *Me and My Girl* opening in London, the death of thirty miners in a disaster at Holditch Colliery, a typhoid outbreak in Croydon, men marching from Jarrow to protest against unemployment and poverty . . .

Would she have known about the death of old King George V if she hadn't read about it in a newspaper? Would she have learned that the Prince of Wales had succeeded his father only to abdicate to marry an American divorcee called Wallis Simpson? Probably not.

Propped next to her late mother's bible was a photograph of Mary and Ernie standing side by side. Kate didn't know when the picture had been taken, but they both looked young. Picking the photograph up, she studied Mary's sweet smile then slid her gaze to Ernie. He'd screwed his eyes up against the sun, so it was impossible to gauge if he'd been surly even then or made bitter by the premature loss of his wife. Might he have been a better person – and a better father – if Mary had lived?

The sound of Ernie's voice out in the farmyard jolted Kate from her thoughts. Speculation about what might have been was pointless. Kate had to live with how things were and, right now, there was work to be done.

CHAPTER THREE

Alice

Alice's mood was gloomy as she walked to the first-aid class on Wednesday morning. 'Eleven o'clock sharp at the Sunday School Hall,' Mrs Harrington had said when she and her crony Miss Plym had called at the cottage a few mornings previously.

Unable to think of an excuse for staying away, Alice had murmured vague thanks, grateful only for the fact that, having opened the door holding a feather duster, she hadn't been expected to invite the callers in – disappointing Miss Plym, who'd still tried to peer over Alice's shoulder into the hall.

Ever since then Alice had been trying to counter the gloom by telling herself that the classes might actually offer benefits:

1. She might learn something new that she could use to help a sick or injured person one day. Heaven knew Alice needed to feel useful.
2. She might meet new friends. Heaven knew Alice needed to ease her loneliness too.
3. She'd be representing her father as well as herself and preserving their reputations in the eyes of Churchwood society.

The classes still felt like an ordeal and Alice paused to brace herself when she reached the hall. She breathed in deeply, raised her chin and entered.

Churchwood's women had rallied to the cause enthusiastically – or maybe been bullied to support it. There had to be twenty of them present: young, middle-aged, old . . . Disappointingly, the Fletcher girl wasn't amongst them. Not that Alice had expected to see her, but the girl had roused her curiosity.

'Come in, Miss Lovell,' Mrs Harrington called, clicking her fingers at her crony. 'Register, Marjorie.'

Miss Plym marked something on her clipboard, presumably a tick against Alice's name. 'You've brought your gas mask?' she asked. 'Naomi says we all have to remember our gas masks.'

Alice held up the cardboard box that contained her mask and Miss Plym marked another tick on the clipboard.

Chairs had been set out in three rows. Alice took a seat at the back and moments later their instructor, Dr Phillips, was introduced. He was considerably older than Dr Lovell, making Alice wonder if she should expect an acerbic comment from Mrs Harrington – but perhaps pride would keep her silent. She hadn't struck Alice as the sort of woman who'd readily admit to having been fobbed off.

Dr Phillips began to talk about first aid in general. Alice learned nothing new but felt that she'd be fine if the classes continued in the same style. She suspected that practical exercises would follow, though, and she was right. Dr Phillips moved on to demonstrate bandaging an injured arm and Mrs Harrington announced that the women were to divide into groups to attempt this procedure for themselves. But first there was to be a tea break.

By apparent pre-arrangement, two women passed through a door at the side of the hall. One then opened a hatch to reveal a small room fitted out with a stove, kettles and the usual institutional cups and saucers.

'Tea for our instructor, please, Marjorie,' Mrs Harrington ordered, and she passed over a coin with which to pay for it.

A queue began to form. Alice toyed with the idea of not bothering with tea. The fingers of her bad hand would cramp if required to hold a saucer for long and couldn't be trusted to control the cup. But she didn't want to give the impression that she begrudged spending however many pennies village convention dictated to be the appropriate price.

She joined the queue, hoping she might find a place to rest her saucer while she drank. Conversations were going on around her. 'I took tea at Foxfield last week,' one woman said, her voice airy with triumph.

'Mrs Harrington invited me to lunch,' her companion crowed, clearly enjoying the superior privilege.

Another woman looked jealous of both of them.

Foxfield wasn't beautiful, precisely. In Alice's opinion, there was something awkward about the red-brick Victorian architecture, possibly due to later additions spoiling the proportions. But it was the grandest house in Churchwood, with lovely gardens extending all around it. An invitation to Foxfield was obviously prized amongst Churchwood's womenfolk. Perhaps amongst Churchwood's menfolk too.

Alice had seen a man she'd taken to be Mr Harrington while out on one of her daily walks. He'd been getting into a sleek and expensive-looking car that had been parked on Foxfield's gravel drive. The distance between them had been too great for detailed observation, but she'd registered him as taller and thinner than his wife with a handsome though austere face. Looks could be deceiving, though, as she knew from her father's cherubic appearance. Perhaps Mr Harrington was a sociable man around a dining table. A perfect host, in fact.

The queue for tea shuffled forward and Alice caught the word Foxfield in another conversation. The speaker made it sound like hallowed ground, but before Alice could hear more, the woman immediately in front of her turned with a friendly smile. 'You're the doctor's daughter.'

Alice smiled back and kept her voice gentle as she said, 'Retired doctor. My father doesn't practise any more.' The sooner the people of Churchwood realized they couldn't rely on Dr Lovell for help with their ailments the better. 'I'm Alice Lovell.'

The woman introduced herself as Janet Collins and the friend who stood beside her as Betty Oldroyd. Both had to be twenty years older than Alice but they were kind and welcoming. They asked how she was finding Churchwood and Alice praised it warmly.

The conversation broke off when Janet and Betty reached the front of the queue. They both put silver threepenny coins in the saucer that had been set out to receive contributions, so Alice put a silver threepence in too. Someone had put a shilling in. Mrs

Harrington, probably. There was a sixpence in there too, and also a farthing.

Janet and Betty waited for Alice to receive her tea then drew her into a group of other women. 'This is Alice Lovell, the doctor's daughter,' Janet said.

'Retired doctor,' Alice added swiftly.

Names washed over her as the other women were introduced. There was an Annie, an Agnes, a Margaret, a Ruth and a Pamela, who seemed to be Ruth's daughter. Pamela wasn't much older than Alice in years but she was already a mother of two and appeared to feel she had more in common with the older women.

'You're from London?' Annie asked, and soon Alice was answering questions about the effect of the war on the country's capital city.

Yes, it had been sad to see little children labelled up and departing for the countryside as evacuees, though some had since returned home as the predicted air raids hadn't yet materialized. Yes, white lines had been painted down the middle of streets to guide people on their way during the blackouts. Yes, trenches had been dug in London parks and anti-aircraft guns mounted. Yes, there were worries about food supplies and prices . . .

Someone clapped their hands for attention. Mrs Harrington, of course. 'Ladies, we're about to resume. Please return your cups to the kitchen.'

Everyone drifted towards the hatch, Alice included. She'd barely touched her tea because there'd been no surface nearby on which to rest the saucer. She hoped her full cup wouldn't be noticed amongst the sea of other cups but one of the women in the kitchen held a hand out for it. 'Sorry to have wasted your lovely tea,' Alice said hastily. 'I'm afraid I was too busy talking to drink it. People are so friendly here.'

Hastening away again, her stomach clenched at the thought of the practical exercises that lay ahead. Janet and Betty invited her to make a group of three and Alice volunteered to play the role of patient, offering her good arm for the exercise while burying her injured hand in the folds of her skirt.

Betty took the first turn at bandaging. 'Lucky I never wanted to be a nurse,' she said, laughing at her not very neat handiwork.

Janet fared better and was faster, too. Too fast for Alice's liking as she'd hoped the class might end before her turn came to attempt bandaging. Regretfully, there was plenty of time. 'I'll be the patient,' Janet said, sitting in the chair Alice had reluctantly vacated.

Alice picked up the bandage and got to work but it was hopeless. Anxiety or plain bad luck had her injured fingers cramping the moment she used them and matters only worsened when Mrs Harrington and Dr Phillips came to observe. 'Miss Lovell is a doctor's daughter,' Mrs Harrington informed him.

'Is that so?' he murmured, his soft voice making it impossible for Alice to gauge whether he was surprised by her incompetence or sympathetic because her injury was on view for all to see.

Either way, Alice felt the sting of humiliation. 'I apologize. I'm not sure I can . . .'

'Perhaps you'd be more comfortable acting as the patient,' Dr Phillips suggested, but of course Alice had already done that.

'Giving guidance to others would be useful, too,' Mrs

Harrington said, but Alice stood unmoving until Mrs Harrington and the doctor walked away.

'An accident, was it, dear?' Betty asked.

'Yes, an accident.' Alice didn't elaborate.

She burned inside for the rest of the class but clung to self-control long enough to thank Dr Phillips and Mrs Harrington at the end and smile goodbyes to Betty and Janet. Once through the door, she raced towards home before anyone could draw her into conversation.

What was it about her hand that so upset her? The ugliness? Alice had never considered herself to be vain, having no great opinion of her slight figure, pale hair and unremarkable face. But she was human and the scars were . . . Well, they were ugly.

Even so, the ugliness contributed in only a small way to her distress. Much more concerning was the fact that the injury had taken away her independence. Before the accident Alice had been busy and capable. An illness suffered shortly after giving birth had weakened her kind and gentle mother's heart so Alice had grown up self-sufficient. Ten years later that weak heart had taken Ellen Lovell's life and Alice had been left with even more responsibilities.

Much as she'd grieved for her mother, there'd been no hardship involved in running the house. Alice loved to organize. She'd managed the administration side of her father's medical practice from the age of sixteen too, having taught herself to type while still at school. Accounts and correspondence, ordering supplies, making appointments, looking after patients who came for consultations . . . Alice had taken the work in her stride.

She had no idea how she could achieve independence now. Before the accident she'd thought she might stay to work in London when her father retired, especially as he had hopes of travelling to the homes of the ancient civilizations he wished to study. But she hadn't seen a way to support herself while one of her hands was so disabled. Now she'd moved to Churchwood, the prospect of finding employment looked even bleaker.

There was a third reason the injury upset her so much, a third reason that grieved her more than the other two combined: the accident had changed her relationship with Daniel Irvine irrevocably.

Still, Alice couldn't regret having put herself in harm's way. It meant she'd saved the life of a child and how could she regret that? Even so, the thought of attending more classes appalled her. She needed to be busy elsewhere if she were to have a valid excuse for avoiding them. But busy doing what?

Stratton House was several times larger than Foxfield but offered no threat to Mrs Harrington's position as Queen Bee of Churchwood, as it stood aloof from the village. Even by taking a shortcut along Brimbles Lane and the overgrown bridle path the lane eventually became, the hospital was two miles away. The journey by road looked closer to five miles according to the map. Besides, while it had once been the grand country seat of landed gentry, Alice understood it had lain empty for years before being taken over for use as a military hospital at the start of the war.

It was a handsome building. Constructed from grey stone in the Palladian style, a raised terrace sat in the centre, reached by steps on each side. From the terrace, pillars rose to support a balcony with tall windows behind it, and more tall windows reached to the left and right of the three-storey building.

The word that floated into Alice's mind was imposing. Intimidating, even. But nothing ventured, nothing gained, and she was desperate.

Approaching on foot, her shoes crunching on the gravel drive, Alice wondered if she should find a less official-looking entrance than the enormous double doors on the terrace, but perhaps entering by another door would mean intruding into private areas. She mounted the steps to the terrace and, seeing that the central doors had been left ajar, stepped tentatively between them, looking around as her eyes adjusted to the relative shade. The hall was large with a grand staircase, wood-panelled walls and tiled floor.

A middle-aged porter sat behind a desk. 'How can I be of assistance, miss?' he asked.

'I'm here to ask if the hospital needs volunteers.'

'The volunteer being you?'

'If I can be useful.'

'Well, let's see who might . . . Morning, Dr Trent.'

Alice glanced around to see a tall, grey-haired man smiling at her curiously. He had merry eyes. 'I trust you're being attended to?' he asked. 'Miss . . . er . . .?'

'Lovell. Alice Lovell.'

'She's here to see if she can help,' the porter explained.

'You're a nurse?' the doctor asked.

'No, but I wondered if I might volunteer in some other capacity.'

33

'How jolly decent of you.'

'The thing is, I'm not fully fit.' She gestured to her hand with a grimace.

The doctor's expression turned compassionate – which she understood but couldn't welcome as she hated to be pitied – and then became conspiratorial instead. This puzzled her until he lifted a foot and stamped it down again. 'False,' he explained. 'Lost the original in the Somme campaign of '16 so we're two old crocks together, eh, Miss Lovell?'

Old crocks? The description made Alice wince but she could see that he'd meant it kindly so hid her dismay behind a smile.

'In a place this size there must be something you can do,' he continued; then he brightened as a woman walked purposefully through the hall. 'Let's hand you over to Matron here.'

He beckoned her over. She was much older than Alice. Brisk, and clearly busy. 'Young lady wants to volunteer,' Dr Trent told her.

'I see.' The matron looked torn, as though she admired the offer in theory but hadn't the time to manage a volunteer. 'You'd better come with me,' she told Alice.

Dr Trent beamed paternally. Alice thanked him – the porter, too – then hastened after the matron, who was already marching along the right-hand corridor at speed.

'You have a nursing background?' the matron asked.

'Not exactly. My father was a doctor in general practice but—'

'Back into bed, Private Haynes!' The matron sped towards a patient who'd wandered into the corridor.

'Just taking a look around, missis.'

'I'm not your missis or anyone else's. I'll be addressed as Matron, thank you very much. And, until you're fitter, the only thing you'll be looking at is the ceiling. From your bed.'

They entered a ward; once a gracious reception room, it now contained two rows of metal-framed beds, which looked incongruous set against lavish wooden panelling and the remains of chandeliers. A nurse in the grey dress and scarlet trimmings of Queen Alexandra's military nurses hurried over, clearly agitated at the prospect of being told off for letting a patient escape. 'My apologies, Matron. I only turned my back for a minute . . .'

'A nurse needs eyes in the back of her head.'

'Yes, Matron.' The nurse drew Private Haynes away.

'Now, where were we, Miss Lovell?'

'I want to help, but—'

'Come to the office. We haven't had a volunteer before. You need to understand that patients aren't here to be gawped at or gossiped about.'

'Of course not. As I said, I may not be medically trained but my father was a doctor and I worked as both his secretary and his receptionist. I'm used to treating patients with confidentiality.'

'What is it, Nurse Evans?'

Another nurse had approached. 'Corporal Smith is asking for more pain relief.'

'I'll speak to the doctor.'

'The thing is—' Alice began, needing to explain her physical limitations since Dr Trent hadn't mentioned them.

But a third nurse called from the door. 'Telephone call for you, Matron.'

'Thank you.' The matron took two steps forward before turning back to Alice. 'You may not be medically trained, Miss Lovell, but I imagine you know more about medical matters than most. Or think you do. A little knowledge can be a dangerous thing, however, so don't be tempted to intervene with the nursing. Please make yourself useful while I'm gone. But don't get in the way.'

The matron bustled off, leaving Alice standing in the ward with her coat still on and her bag hanging from her arm. She sent an anxious smile around the room, hoping to catch the eye of a patient who might welcome help. When Private Haynes sat up in bed, she started towards him gratefully. But he simply stared straight through her as though frozen; then he vomited over the side of the bed.

A passing nurse was carrying a tray of teacups. 'Take this, please,' she instructed, thrusting the tray in Alice's direction.

Alice took it automatically and the nurse rushed to Private Haynes's side. Feeling her injured fingers cramp, Alice looked around in panic for somewhere to deposit the tray. A table and two chairs stood at the end of the ward. Fingers screeching pain, Alice headed for the table at speed but before she could reach it her fingers gave up the fight and the tea tray crashed to the floor.

CHAPTER FOUR

Naomi

Naomi was looking through the notes she'd made of the first-aid class when she heard Alexander's car approaching along the drive. A glance through the window gave her a glimpse of the Daimler's black roof. It was clean and shiny because every time Alexander handed the car over to Sykes, the Foxfield gardener-handyman, he insisted on it being washed. Setting the notes aside, Naomi rang the bell to alert the maid to the master's arrival and sat up, prepared to greet her husband with a smile.

She'd left the door to the sitting room open to encourage him to look in on her. This wasn't the grand drawing room but the place where she sat when alone or with close acquaintances. It was also the place where she made her plans for Churchwood's improvement.

Suki's quick little steps sounded on the parquet flooring of the hall. A moment later the front door opened, and Suki spoke. 'Good evening, sir. Mrs Harrington is in the sitting room if you'd like . . .'

The words trailed off as Alexander's firmer treads headed towards his study. The study door opened and then closed again. There was no sound from Suki so Naomi guessed the little maid was hovering in the hall, wondering what was best to be done. Snatching her notes back up, Naomi was attempting to look engrossed in them when Suki appeared in the doorway.

'Is there anything I can fetch for you, madam?' Suki asked.

Naomi made a show of dragging her gaze up from important matters. 'Thank you, but I don't think so. I'll ring to let you know about drinks and dinner. Mr Harrington has a great deal of work to get through tonight so may prefer a tray.'

'Very well, madam.'

Relieved to be alone again, Naomi slumped in her chair. After a moment or two she noticed that Basil was watching her, his expression mournful. Basil wasn't a handsome dog. English bulldogs in general were too sturdy, too big around the head and jowls to qualify as pretty, but Basil was even sturdier and more jowly than most of his breed. He reminded Naomi of herself, and she wasn't the only one to have noticed the similarity.

'Hard to know which one is the bulldog,' she'd heard a man jest as she'd walked Basil past the Wheat-sheaf one day.

The jester's friends had responded to the comment with raucous laughter. Naomi hadn't deigned to show she'd even heard it.

Sending Basil a smile now, she got up and checked her appearance in the mirror above the fireplace. Neat was the best she expected, and neat was the best she got.

Leaving the sitting room, she knocked on the study door and then stepped inside. 'I thought I heard the car,' she said. 'How was your day, dear?'

'Busy.' Alexander was taking papers from his case.

He was a stockbroker, and he worked hard. At least twice each week he overnighted at the flat in London, and he still worked during the evenings he spent at Foxfield. Even on Saturdays and Sundays he was often away, golfing with clients or wining and dining them.

'Cocktail?' she offered.

'Thank you, but I'll manage.' He nodded towards a tray of decanters and crystal glasses.

'About dinner . . .'

'A tray will suit me best.'

'Of course.' She returned to the door.

'Naomi?'

'Yes, dear?' She turned eagerly.

'I have papers for you to sign.'

He spread them on the desk and passed her a pen. It was the pen she'd given him for Christmas three or four years ago but for his own use he still appeared to prefer a silver pen he'd bought for himself. 'Sign here,' he said, pointing. 'And here.'

'What are they? The papers.'

'Investment changes. You want me to get the best return on your money, don't you?' He looked up, a frown cutting between his ice-blue eyes. Was he growing irritated?

'Of course,' Naomi assured him hastily. 'You know I don't mean—'

'Well, then.'

Naomi signed the papers and returned the pen. 'I'll organize a tray for you.'

Back in the sitting room she rang for Suki, gave the dinner instructions and then sat staring into space as she reminded herself for what felt like the millionth time that she shouldn't mind Alexander working so hard. After all, it proved he was keen to earn his own money instead of sitting back and living off her modest fortune as other men might have done. It proved he'd married her for love, in fact, which was something she'd never expected.

Naomi had been seventeen when her father sold his business. Tuggs Tonics claimed to relieve all sorts of maladies, from baldness to biliousness, though in reality, Naomi had long suspected, they mostly relieved gullible purchasers of their money. Still, someone had seen enough potential in the business to pay handsomely for it.

A widower who now had both time and a certain amount of wealth at his disposal, Cedric Tuggs had set out to launch himself and his daughter into County society. To Naomi the experience had been a form of torture. Tongue-tied and awkward at the best of times, it had mortified her to witness her father strutting around, oblivious of the disgust on people's faces when they saw him eating peas off his knife, witnessed him belching or heard him boasting about money, a subject that genteel people appeared to consider indelicate. Naomi had burned with shame the evening he'd walked up to a complete stranger and asked how much the man had paid for his suit before bragging about the price he'd negotiated for his own clothes. 'There's no one sharper than Cedric Tuggs when it comes to drivin' a bargain,' he'd said.

Tormented by many such incidents, the fear that she was considered equally uncouth had worsened Naomi's usual self-consciousness into near-paralysis. Even with the bloom of youth on her cheeks she hadn't been pretty, and she'd known that her fussy way of dressing lacked taste and elegance. But to Cedric, every frill, every bow and every piece of jewellery she wore announced to the world that he was a man to be reckoned with.

'Put them sapphires on, love,' he'd urge. 'That ruby brooch an' all. Show the world that Cedric Tuggs 'as made somefink of 'isself.'

Much of the time she'd found herself sitting alone at balls and parties. It had been humiliating, but not half as humiliating as dancing with men who'd been thrust forward by avaricious parents, or those with their own obvious financial ambitions.

'Tuggs may be a repellent little man but think of the money, Ralph,' she'd heard one father telling his son.

'Money isn't everything,' the son had replied, but his father had shown no patience with that philosophy.

'You can keep the man at a distance.'

'Maybe so, but what about the daughter? You can't really want to see me married to a girl with no charm and no breeding who looks like—'

'How many times do I have to explain that we're on our uppers, Ralph? If you don't marry money soon, we'll be ruined.'

Ralph had sighed in acceptance of his fate and headed towards Naomi with the obvious intention of asking her to dance. She'd got up and walked away before he could speak and avoided him for the rest of the night.

Not all of her dance partners had been motivated by money. Some had been driven by pity. Older men, mostly, the sight of a young girl sitting alone clearly stirring their paternal instincts enough for them to spare five minutes or so to give her a twirl around the dance floor. Inevitably, Naomi's complete absence of charm had driven them away again after a single dance. 'You must excuse me now, my dear. These old bones can't keep up with young things like you . . .'

Alexander had been different. The night she'd met him Naomi had fled into the garden after another embarrassing experience with a dance partner who'd obviously steeled himself to overlook her plainness and focus on Cedric's pounds, shillings and pence. She'd come upon a fishpond with a raised wall around it and sat on the edge to trail her fingers in the chilly water, hoping it would cool her scalding humiliation.

Alexander had been walking past when he'd pulled up short at the sight of her. 'Oh! I beg your pardon. I didn't know anyone was here.'

Naomi hadn't known what to say.

'Are you quite well?' he'd asked. 'Would you like me to fetch someone? Or bring you a glass of water? I could brave the harridans in the kitchen if you'd prefer tea?'

'No, thank you. I'm just . . . I needed some air.'

'As did I. So we're both absent without leave.' He'd smiled, and even in the darkness she'd seen that there was a twinkle in his eyes. Then a different thought had appeared to strike him. 'But perhaps I'm intruding?'

'No,' Naomi had assured him, glad to know she wasn't the only person who needed to escape the party, though she was curious as to why this man should feel that need.

She'd noticed him earlier. Tall, fair and debonair, he'd spun his partners around with skill and all the appearance of being at ease, but perhaps he was simply better than Naomi at pretending to enjoy himself.

'May I?' He'd gestured at the wall.

'Of course.'

He'd sat next to her but kept a respectful distance between them. Stretched out in front of him, his legs had looked long and lean, and she'd been glad that her dumpy appendages were concealed beneath her dress. Time had passed. A minute. Two. Perhaps three. 'You're very restful,' he'd said then.

'Restful?' Awkward would have felt a more accurate description.

'You're not arch like many of the girls I have to dance with at these gatherings. Not pert and knowing and simpering. And I imagine you don't show off to your friends when you've bagged a partner.'

Naomi had no friends except for a girl from school who'd moved back to Ireland.

'I'm sorry,' he'd said then. 'Do I sound arrogant? I don't mean to suggest that I'm sought after as a partner. I only mean to say that it's pleasant to sit with a girl who's natural. Who isn't putting on airs.'

'I don't know how to be any other way,' Naomi had admitted. 'It doesn't make me very successful at these gatherings, as you called them.'

'Some people consider it a triumph to dance every dance. I find it tedious.'

'It's certainly pleasanter out here than in that ballroom,' Naomi had agreed.

'But regretfully your absence is bound to be noticed soon and people can be poisonous when it comes to a young lady's reputation. Let me walk you back inside.'

He'd got to his feet, offered his arm and walked her across the terrace towards the ballroom's French windows. 'You know, there's one way we can both avoid irksome partners,' he'd said.

'Oh?'

'We can dance with each other. Forgive me if that's an unwelcome suggestion, though.'

'It isn't. Unwelcome, I mean.' It would be a huge relief, in fact.

'Then will you do me the honour of dancing with me, Miss . . . I don't know your name.'

'It's Tuggs.'

'Tubbs? I had a nanny called Miss Tubbs.'

'Tuggs,' Naomi had corrected. 'Naomi Tuggs. My father is Cedric Tuggs.' If this man was going to take fright at her connection to Cedric, the sooner the better. 'Of Tuggs Tonics.'

'I don't think I'm familiar with them.'

'You haven't missed out.'

He'd laughed at that. 'I'm Alexander Harrington.'

They'd danced a waltz; then he'd been the one to take her into the supper room when dinner was announced, remaining with her even when her father joined them.

'Naomi is a pretty name,' Alexander had commented when the evening drew to a close.

It was the only pretty thing about her, but Alexander still asked to see her again and only four months after that night in the garden they'd become engaged. It had been a sweet proposal, complete with a red rose, though Alexander had also been endearingly frank. 'I need to be honest with you,' he'd said. 'I know how my proposal might look to nasty, suspicious people.'

Naomi hadn't understood.

'It might look as though I want you for your money,' he'd explained. 'I have no capital of my own, you see. The family fortunes were healthy once but . . . no longer.'

'You didn't know about my money when you first courted me,' Naomi had pointed out.

'That's right. I didn't. I only hope your father will remember that when I ask for his blessing.'

Fortunately, Cedric had been bowled over by Alexander's crisp, aristocratic accent and elegant appearance. 'I'll still be the boss of the family and control the old purse strings,' Cedric had told Naomi. 'Besides, 'e's a stockbroker so should earn a decent wage of his own. Fancy! A stockbroker in the family!'

But just a few weeks later, Cedric had died unexpectedly and Alexander had insisted on bringing the wedding date forward. 'You shouldn't be alone,' he'd said.

Which was ironic really, as she'd often been alone during their marriage, even when – like now – Alexander was in the house.

Fighting back against the low mood that was settling over her, Naomi returned to her first-aid notes and found herself thinking about the doctor's daughter. There was something about her that interested Naomi. Was it fanciful to suspect that beneath her gentle appearance the girl had inner strength and integrity?

Shame about that injured hand, of course, but life

laid down challenges to everyone. An injured hand for one person. Childlessness to another.

Naomi's stomach squeezed painfully, but she'd learned long ago that the trick with adversity was to rise above it and stay useful. Squaring her shoulders, she turned her focus back to her list of first-aiders and decided she'd keep Janet Collins and Betty Old-royd apart at the next class. They chatted too much.

CHAPTER FIVE

Alice

If her bedroom had been larger, Alice would have paced the floor as she tried to reach a decision. Instead, she stood at the window, staring out at spindly winter trees but taking care to avoid fogging the glass with her breath. She'd already wiped condensation from the cottage's windows that morning. From some, she'd wiped away ice.

Her first visit to the hospital had gone badly but was that a good enough reason not to try again? Alice cringed every time she remembered dropping that tray. Not all of the cups and saucers had smashed but several had. She'd apologized again and again until she'd realized she must be getting on the nerves of the matron, who'd returned to investigate the commotion. 'I think you'd better leave clearing up to us,' the matron had finally said, as Alice darted about collecting shards of crockery.

Us meaning the professionals, Alice supposed. Not bumbling amateurs like her.

At that moment, a patient had called out, 'Nurse! Nurse!' while another had groaned loudly.

'Perhaps I should come back another day when you're not so busy,' Alice had suggested.

'Good idea,' the matron had agreed, walking away and probably hoping that Alice wouldn't bother.

Returning would be embarrassing but Alice thought of those poor men lying in their beds in that big room and felt a tug of sympathy for them. After all, they'd fallen sick or been injured in the service of their country. *Her* country. It would be cowardly not even to explore the possibility of making their lives a little better. Did Alice want to be a coward? Certainly not.

There. Decision made. Moving rapidly for fear that cowardice might still win out, Alice went downstairs, put on her outer clothes and bade goodbye to her father. She strode to the hospital quickly, dodging icy puddles and encouraging herself with the thought that if she managed to find a niche at Stratton House, she would not only have an excuse for avoiding Mrs Harrington's first-aid classes, but also something to tell Daniel that would make her appear busy and useful instead of pathetic and in need of rescue.

She marched straight up the steps to the tall double doors of Stratton House. Once again they were open, though only by a narrow crack. There was a grand-looking bell beside the doors but she was hardly a grand visitor and had no wish to bring anyone rushing to her assistance. She opened the door a little wider and saw the porter on duty at his desk again. 'May I come in?' she questioned, and he beckoned her inside.

'Here to volunteer again, are you, miss?' he asked, and Alice hoped that he recognized her because he had a good memory for faces rather than because he'd heard that she'd been a disaster.

'If I can be of any use.'

'Well, let's see . . .'

He made a telephone call – Alice guessed to the matron – explaining that she was here. 'I'll do that,' he said at the end.

Do what? Tell Alice that volunteers were no longer required, or at least not hopeless ones like her?

'You're to go to Matron's office,' he said. 'Follow the corridor over there and it's on the left.'

'Thank you.' Alice smiled tightly and set off, shoulders braced.

The door to the office stood open. The matron was on the telephone again, so Alice remained in the corridor until her conversation ended. 'Come in!' the matron called then.

Alice hastened inside. 'I'm here to volunteer again. I know I made a hash of things last time, but I hope to do better. I should have made it clear that I can't do much in the way of lifting or carrying unless it can be done one-handed, but I don't mind what else I do. I could write letters for any patients who need help with that sort of thing. Read letters to them too, if—'

'Corporal Attercliffe,' the matron said.

'I'm sorry?'

'Start with Corporal Attercliffe. Half-blind now, poor chap. What did you say your name was?'

'Alice Lovell.'

The matron wrote the name in a notebook. 'Address?'

Alice told her.

'Referee?'

'You want a reference?'

'Sickness and injury make patients vulnerable, Miss Lovell. We need to ensure their protection.'

'Of course.' Alice gave details of a Mr Clifford, a

dentist who'd had a consulting room next door to her father's in London.

'We only have two wards open at present,' the matron informed her then. 'It would be nice to think that we won't need more, but the fighting has barely started yet. Being realistic, we expect to open several wards over the course of the war. Stratton House was chosen because of its size and because its location makes it an unlikely casualty of air raids. Most of the patients have injuries that will require lengthy recovery times so they'll be here for weeks if not months. Eventually, we'll have more patients with combat wounds but what we have now are mostly patients who've been injured while training, travelling – some were heading for France when they were caught in that train crash you might have read about – or by other mischance. These men were still serving their country so deserve every respect.'

'Of course,' Alice repeated.

'Not that you'll enquire into the nature of their injuries or their lives. You're here to support them, not interrogate them. Neither will you talk about individual patients outside of the hospital. As for interference in medical matters . . .'

'Strictly forbidden.'

'Quite so.'

The matron issued a few more prohibitions then led Alice along the corridor to another large room that had been turned into Ward Two.

'Do you have pen and paper?' the matron asked.

'Yes, and envelopes too.' Alice had packed them into her bag before setting out, determined to have something useful to offer.

They arrived at the bedside of a man with bandages across his eyes. A very young man, Alice guessed, who raised his head from the pillow at their approach. It must be unnerving to hear footsteps and be unable to identify who was making them. 'Miss Lovell is here to write a letter for you, Corporal Attercliffe,' the matron told him. 'If that's what you'd like?'

'That'd be grand, Matron. It *is* Matron, isn't it? I recognize your voice.'

Corporal Attercliffe smiled proudly when she confirmed it but there was a tremble beneath the smile. He was putting on a show of good cheer but emotionally he was fragile. Alice felt a tug of compassion for him. If she could improve his life by even a little bit, she'd do it gladly.

'One more thing,' the matron told Alice. 'Sitting on beds isn't allowed.'

Alice flushed but once again said, 'Of course.'

'Bring the letter to my office when you've finished. I suggest you find yourself a chair.' With that she bustled away.

Alice looked around and saw wooden chairs at the end of the ward. Leaving her bag behind she hooked her arms under a chair back and managed to get it to Corporal Attercliffe's bedside. 'I'm Alice Lovell,' she told him, sitting down. 'You can call me Alice.'

'Don't let Matron hear you say that. A stickler for doing things proper is Matron.'

'Then I'll call you Corporal.'

'The name's Jimmy between you and me.'

What she could see of his face twitched but then he raised a hand to his bandages. 'That was supposed to be a wink,' he said, and there was sadness in his voice

51

because either he hadn't managed to perform the action or he realized she couldn't have seen it.

'Isn't winking against Matron's rules?' Alice asked and was pleased to see the downward turn of his mouth reverse into a grin.

'Probably.'

'Well, Corporal Jimmy, would you like me to write a letter for you?'

'Yes, please. To my old mum, if that's all right? I got a letter from her yesterday. It's over there. Somewhere.' He gestured towards the narrow cupboard at the side of his bed. 'You couldn't read it for me, could you? A nurse read it for me yesterday but too quickly.'

Alice found the letter and drew it out of the envelope.

8 Smithwick Terrace
Leeds

Dear Jimmy,
Well, lad, it were a shock to hear you'd been injured. Proper worried, we were. But we've come round to thinking that mebbe it's a good thing as it means you are safe from the fighting. As long as you get well, of course. Write and let us know more about that sort of thing and when you think you might come home. I have a tin of salmon put by – yes, salmon! – and I'm saving it for your homecoming tea. You'll enjoy it in a sandwich.

We're all well here. Dad cleared out the understairs cupboard so we can go in there in the event of an air raid as we haven't been given one of those Anderson shelters to put up in the back garden yet. It means the stuff that was under the stairs is spread around the house and, as you know, this house isn't a mansion. Still, it's a chance to sort through it. We shouldn't be hoarding stuff we don't need, though this war means we may have to make do and mend more than ever before.

Dad is busy at the mill in the daytime and talking about taking his turn as a fire warden one or two evenings each week. He's got the allotment to keep him busy too and he's looking at how we can turn our back garden into a vegetable patch. We need to grow as much as we can now they've started to bring in rationing.

Cathy and Joyce are doing well at school. Cathy talks of becoming a nurse but she's plenty of time to decide. Joyce wants a job in a fashion shop when she leaves school but there may not be any fashion shops left if this war goes on.

Well, Jimmy, this letter writing has fair worn me out and the ironing is waiting so it's time for me to finish. Keep your spirits up and let us know how you're getting on.

With love from your mother, father and little sisters. Here's a kiss from each of us – xxxx

Alice read it out twice, taking her time so Jimmy could savour every word. 'What would you like me to write in reply?' she asked then.

'*Dearest Mother,*' he dictated. '*There's no need to worry about me as I'm being well looked after. I don't know when I'll be allowed home but I'm looking forward to eating that salmon and seeing you all.*'

After that beginning, his mouth opened only to close again.

'Might your mother appreciate knowing more about what the doctors have told you?' Alice suggested gently.

'No need to worry the old folks until I know what I'm facing. The doctors have done what they can and now it's one of those wait-and-see things. Or not see if . . . if it's bad.'

Alice caught the bleakness behind the words. How courageous he was in trying to shield his family from what might be devastating news. 'Perhaps you might mention something about Stratton House. I can describe it for you, if you like? Or you could say something about your fellow patients.'

'I could!' Jimmy agreed. He raised his voice, flapping an arm in the direction of the man in a nearby bed. 'I could tell the folks that Sid over there has the loudest snore in the hospital. In the world, mebbe.'

'You can talk,' Sid shot back. 'You're a champion snorer too.'

Other men joined in the banter and it was settled that Sid had the loudest snore but Jimmy wasn't far behind.

'If you've got time, miss, I wouldn't mind help with a letter to my folks,' Sid said when Jimmy's letter was finished.

Sid had injured his writing arm.

Alice helped him with a letter to his parents, the grandmother who lived with them and his three bossy older sisters. 'Write that I'm looking forward to one of Mum's treacle tarts,' he said. 'The food here could be worse – it's better than army rations – but it isn't a patch on Mum's home cooking.'

After Sid's letter Alice wrote one for a private called

John who had to lie flat on his back, which made writing difficult, and another for a private called Timmy who had no injury that prevented him from writing as far as Alice could see but perhaps wanted attention.

It wasn't a bad start to her volunteering. Alice was pleased, and if there'd been any curiosity about her hand, these brave soldiers had hidden it well. She'd felt less self-conscious about it here, perhaps because their bodies were broken too.

The smell of cooked food reached her. Lunch must be arriving, and she didn't want to be in the way while it was served.

'You'll come back another day?' Jimmy Attercliffe asked.

'If you like.'

'We do like. Don't we, chaps?'

There was a chorus of agreement.

'Is there anything I can do before I leave? Fetch books for you or something like that?' Conscious that Jimmy couldn't see to read, she added. 'You could read out loud to each other.'

'Books?' Sid made a scoffing sound. 'Rare as blue moons in here.'

Alice was surprised. 'Don't you want books?'

''Course we do. But we can't magic 'em out of the air.'

Alice was thoughtful as she made her way back to the matron's office where she handed the letters over. 'The men said there aren't many books here. Would you object if I brought a few from home?'

'Not at all.' The matron barely looked up from her paperwork. She made an impatient sound – something in the paperwork had annoyed her – then she got up and headed for the door. 'Good day, Miss Lovell.'

Alice walked home feeling better than she'd felt in a long time. She'd been useful today, and she might be useful again.

Her father was in his study, still working on arranging his book collection. 'Splendid,' he said when Alice told him about her morning.

'I thought we might loan the patients some of our books,' she suggested.

'Loan our books?' He'd spent years building up his precious collection and many of the books had been expensive. He was a kind man, though. 'If you really think the patients will be interested . . .'

Alice studied his shelves and realized that the patients probably wouldn't be riveted by the likes of *Medicine in the Hellenistic Age* or *The Byzantine Empire: A Scholar's Guide.* The books were too big and heavy for invalids to manage anyway. Besides, she hadn't the heart to take her father's books.

'I think my books might be more appropriate,' she said, and left him looking relieved.

She warmed soup for their lunch and then studied her own book collection. Perhaps she was making assumptions about what would appeal to the patients, but she decided to discount those books that were aimed at girls – *Little Women* and *Anne of Green Gables* – and concentrate on adventure stories instead. She set ten aside.

What were the chances of getting them back after she'd loaned them to the patients? She couldn't afford to replace them, so she wrote her name on the flyleaf of each book in the hope that at least some of them would find their way back to her. If they didn't, she'd have lost them to a worthy cause.

She slipped a note through Naomi Harrington's door the following morning, explaining that she was unlikely to be able to attend many first-aid classes in future, and set out for Stratton House in the afternoon. With her injured hand making carrying difficult, she'd placed the books in a large canvas bag, which she slung over her shoulder. It was too heavy for comfort but she was keen to benefit as many patients as possible as soon as possible.

She hadn't gone more than half a mile before she had to stop and rest her shoulder. She tried clutching the bag to her chest but after a while that was uncomfortable, too. Stopping again, Alice heaved the bag back over her shoulder but the strap broke and it fell to the ground, spilling books on to the icy, rutted lane.

The sounds of a horse's hooves and jangling harness reached her from behind. Someone was coming. Alice scrambled to pick up the books before they could be crushed into the mud.

CHAPTER SIX

Kate

Kate eased the cart to a halt and looked down at the doctor's daughter as she tried to stuff a book into a bag. She appeared to be struggling and no wonder. She had an injured hand. 'I'm sorry I'm blocking your way,' she said. 'If you wouldn't mind waiting just a moment . . .'

Kate jumped down from the cart. 'Want some help?' She kept her distance in case she received a sneer in response. The doctor's daughter had probably heard all about the wild Fletcher family by now.

But it appeared that she hadn't, because she smiled and said, 'Thank you.'

Kate crouched down beside her. 'I'll hold the bag, shall I?'

The girl passed it over and Kate held it open, hoping she wasn't putting dirty finger marks on the canvas.

A feeling close to hunger gusted through her as she tried to read the book titles. *The Call of the Wild, The Hound of the Baskervilles, Kidnapped . . .*

'You like books?' the girl asked.

Kate turned defensive. 'They're all right.'

'I love books. There's so much to be found between the covers – knowledge, adventure, surprises, emotions, escape . . . They make me think about life outside my own small pocket of the world, too.'

Kate said nothing, though she was in complete agreement.

'You're welcome to borrow a book.'

'No, I couldn't.' It could only be a matter of time before the doctor's daughter *did* hear about the Fletchers and came to regret her kind offer.

'I'm lending them out anyway. To the patients at Stratton House. You could return it to me when you've finished it. I live at—'

'The Linnets.'

'I suppose new people stand out in a place like this. You're Miss Fletcher, I believe?'

Kate blinked. 'You know I'm a Fletcher?'

'I heard it mentioned.'

'Not in a nice way.'

The girl's mouth curved in a smile – half-amused and half-rueful – and the blue eyes that had appeared so earnest before danced merrily. Clearly, there was indeed more to the doctor's daughter than a neat and respectable young woman. 'I like to make up my own mind about people,' she said. 'Besides, I'm not sure my family's reputation is likely to be considered stainless either.'

Kate was intrigued.

'My father is a retired doctor but he's here to hide from people and I fear Churchwood is going to be disappointed in him, Mrs Harrington especially.'

'That old crone!'

'I imagine she means well.'

'You'll imagine nothing of the sort if she starts looking down that snooty nose at you.'

'Perhaps not. I'm Alice, by the way. Alice Lovell.'

'Kate.'

'Are you going to borrow a book, Kate? You'll be lightening my load a little if you do.'

'How would I return it?'

'You could come to The Linnets and swap it for another book.'

'Your father won't want me treading farm dirt into your house.'

'I want my father to meet people. It isn't good for him to hide away all the time. Besides, he's so swept up in the pleasure of retirement that he wouldn't notice if you came in dressed as Father Christmas and scattered reindeer droppings.'

Kate couldn't help smiling. 'All right,' she said. 'Thank you.'

She chose *The Call of the Wild* as she liked the idea of a wolf story.

'One favour deserves another,' Kate said then. 'Let me give you a ride to the hospital. The handle on this bag won't mend without stitching and maybe not even then.'

'I don't want to be a bother.'

'Stratton House is no distance.' It wasn't, though Ernie and her brothers wouldn't like it if they saw her being friendly to a stranger.

Kate put the bag of books into the cart and turned back to Alice, wondering if she should help the girl to climb up, but Alice managed fine. It wasn't as though she had much weight to heave up, being a slight little thing.

'On, Pete,' Kate called to the pony and, as the cart

lurched forward, Alice clung to the side. 'Not used to carts?' Kate guessed.

'Trains, buses and – very occasionally – taxis are more in my experience.'

'You've come from London?'

'An area called Highbury. Do you know London?'

'Never been,' Kate admitted. 'I've never travelled further than a few miles from Churchwood in any direction.' How unsophisticated she must sound! An ignorant country bumpkin.

'I haven't travelled much either, but we can both travel to all sorts of places through the pages of books. Paris, Australia, the North Pole . . .'

Kate would enjoy that very much, but it wouldn't be enough. She longed to forge a life away from Brimbles Farm one day, but with no money and only hand-me-downs to wear it was impossible to see how that could happen. Ever. Just as her father and brothers intended, of course. But Alice was trying to cheer Kate up and it would be churlish not to respond to her kindness.

'We can ride Arab stallions, sail the oceans and soar through the sky in aeroplanes,' Kate said, joining in the fantasies.

'I'm not sure I'd like to go in an aeroplane,' Alice confided.

'You'd love it once you got up there. Just think of the view.'

'That would indeed be spectacular.'

They reached the entrance to Stratton House, and Kate hesitated. She didn't like to go further while looking such a mess but the drive was long and Alice would struggle with the broken bag. Nudging the pony on again, Kate steered the cart between the gateposts and took it close to the front steps. Jumping down again, she carried the bag to the tall, forbidding doors and handed it to Alice. Surely someone inside the hospital would help her now?

'I don't know how I'd have managed without you,' Alice said.

'You've repaid me already by lending me the book.'

Kate shuffled her feet. She knew the social graces that were expected in shops – words like please, thank you and goodbye. But was anything different expected when you parted from someone who wasn't a friend but who'd behaved with friendliness? Kate had only vague memories of playing with other children in her early days at school and since then there'd been no one.

Alice took the lead and smiled. 'You've been a life-saver, Kate. I'm looking forward to hearing your opinion of the book.'

Alice heaved the bag up with her good hand and slipped through the doors.

Kate returned to the cart and steered Pete towards Brimbles Farm, the borrowed book on the seat next to her. She'd have to smuggle it up to her room as she knew instinctively that Ernie would be livid that she'd met Alice. For as long as she could remember he'd hated her talking to anyone outside the family.

'Get over here now,' he'd bawled when he'd seen her talking to some picnickers as a child.

'In the house,' he'd told her when a family had walked up to the farm to ask for directions.

'Stay in the cart and speak to no one,' he'd

instructed when she'd accompanied him into the village one day.

'Stick to your own kind,' he'd insisted, time and again, her own kind being Ernie and her brothers.

Even now he kept a close eye on the time she took to run errands in the village and demanded explanations if she was away longer than expected.

Besides, there was every chance of Ernie or her brothers stubbing cigarettes out on the book's cover, or leaving wet rings on it from their teacups. Vinnie might even ruin the book deliberately.

It was incredible how a day that had started the same as thousands of others could turn around suddenly and become quite different. Kate realized she was smiling. She had a book to read – a book! – and she'd met Alice Lovell. Not that she and Alice could ever be friends in the sense of spending time together, but to know that they could share smiles and nods in passing, and perhaps even exchange the occasional word . . . It might not sound much to some people, but to Kate it was a huge step forward.

CHAPTER SEVEN

Alice

'All gone?' Private Meadows asked.

This was Alice's fourth visit to the hospital and, though her books were circulating, there weren't enough for all the patients. 'All gone for today,' she confirmed.

He took the disappointment with good-humoured acceptance. 'Don't worry about me, miss. I have letters to read.' Smiling, he held up two envelopes.

Stevie always had a smile for Alice. She was trying hard to avoid having favourites among the patients, but it was impossible not to warm to Stevie Meadows. He was a sweet, golden-haired boy who remained sunny-natured despite the accident that had cost him a foot.

'I still reckon I'm lucky when you weigh things up,' he'd told her the first time they spoke. 'I've got the best family a chap could have and a sweetheart who's sticking by me. Her name's Esme. Look.' He'd held out a photograph. 'Isn't she lovely?'

Esme was a fair-haired girl with a smile as sweet as Stevie's. 'She certainly is,' Alice had agreed.

'We met when we were five and I knew even then that she was the girl for me. I've also got a champion boss at the factory where I've worked since I turned fourteen.

Mr Hargreaves says he'll give me a sitting-down sort of job if I can't stand for long, though I'm hoping they'll give me some sort of peg leg so I can walk again.'

'I'm pleased you can count your blessings.'

'Doesn't do to mope,' he'd said. 'The future won't be quite the way I expected, but it'll still be good.'

Alice was full of admiration for him. 'Letters from home?' she asked now.

'One from my mum and one from Esme.'

'That's wonderful. Here's hoping I have a book for you soon.'

'I'll keep my fingers crossed, but don't worry if you haven't one to bring.'

The man in the neighbouring bed grunted. 'Expect nothing from the world and you won't be disappointed,' he said. 'That's all the world's got to give. Disappointment.'

If Stevie was a favourite, Jake Turner was a challenge. Whether he'd been born a cynic or made one by experience, Alice couldn't know. He'd lost both of his legs, judging by the cradle that supported his bedcovers, and he was a miserable man with dark, saturnine looks to match. Alice hadn't seen him smile once, but the loss of his legs must have been a terrible blow to him and who knew what other misfortunes he might be suffering?

She smiled at Stevie then went on to ask if any patients wanted her to write letters for them. She wrote two for the men in this ward before moving on to the other ward.

'Any books?' a patient asked, and a quick glance around showed that other men were looking at her hopefully too.

Oh dear. Alice explained that no books were available just now but they should make their way around the hospital in time. There was a general slump of frustration.

Later, as Alice walked home through the chilly afternoon, her thoughts remained on the poor soldiers at Stratton House, bored and in pain with nothing to distract them. She couldn't magic more books into existence, but it occurred to her that there might be something she could do to raise the spirits of Jimmy Attercliffe and perhaps a few more of the men. The moment she got home she'd—

'Oh, I'm sorry!' Alice realized she'd startled an old lady.

There were woods on both sides of Brimbles Lane at this point. On the Foxfield side there was also a lake. The woman had been staring down at it but now she'd whirled around, her eyes wide with alarm.

'I didn't mean to disturb you,' Alice added, but the woman had already scurried away, her cheerful blue coat at odds with the frown that had settled on her lined face as the first shock receded.

It was unlikely that she'd feared being robbed on such a little-used lane as this, especially when the weather was so cold that the trees and bushes were white with frost. Perhaps she'd resented the interruption to her peace and quiet or perhaps she'd felt foolish at reacting so dramatically. Whatever her reason, Alice wouldn't hold it against her. There was often more to people than first met the eye. Kate Fletcher was a prime example. She'd shown a much warmer side when she'd helped Alice with the books, those striking eyes gleaming with intelligence and kindness. Even Naomi Harrington's bossy manner might hide inner softness.

Nearing home, Alice felt tension tighten her body as she wondered if Daniel might have called. Once inside she headed straight for her father's study. 'Any visitors today?' she asked, hoping she sounded casual.

'Are we expecting visitors?'

'I just wondered if anyone had called. Sorry if I disturbed you.'

Much as she tried to avoid feeding her attraction to Daniel, Alice would be devastated to miss him. It was frustrating not knowing when or even if he'd call. With notice, she could prepare to greet him with the same calm friendliness she'd show to any acquaintance from the past. But if she were to be taken by surprise, Alice feared she might give away her feelings before she got herself under control. A single, joyful look was all it would take.

Up in her room, she decided to sacrifice another two novels to the patients and also looked out a compendium edition of *Your Fireside Friend* that had sat in her father's waiting room for patients to read while they awaited their consultations. Alice's father had often run late. He might not have tolerated malingering or fussing, but if a patient needed extra time, that patient got it.

The *Fireside Friend* contained short stories and features about travels, history, traditions and riddles. It was a weighty volume but Alice hoped she'd be able to carry it to Stratton House without mishap.

She returned to the hospital the following afternoon, wishing she could give one of the novels to Stevie Meadows, but other men claimed them first.

'I don't mind waiting,' Stevie told her, and Jake Turner in the next bed snorted.

Alice wrote a couple of letters for patients and then approached poor, sightless Jimmy Attercliffe, the first patient she'd helped.

'Would you like me to read a story out loud?' she asked. 'An adventure story, perhaps?'

'Yes, please, miss. There's not much adventuring going on here.'

Alice took *Your Fireside Friend* from her bag and settled down to read 'The 9.15 to Brighton'.

'*London was thick with fog that November night . . .*'

'Could you speak a bit louder?' Stevie called. He was a few beds along from Jimmy. 'I'd like to hear the story, too.'

'Me as well,' another nearby patient said.

'As long as I won't be disturbing anyone . . .'

Jake Turner humphed but neither he nor anyone else voiced an actual objection.

'Very well.' Alice raised her voice a little.

' "Harcourt first saw the man outside Victoria Station one foggy November evening. There was nothing about his clothes to draw attention as homburg hats and fawn-coloured raincoats were common, but he lit a cigarette as Harcourt drew near, and the match flickered light across a thin face, narrow moustache and hard, furtive eyes. As though aware of Harcourt's scrutiny, the man turned and walked away." '

Alice glanced up to gauge if her audience looked interested. It did.

' "Harcourt entered the station, bought his ticket and boarded the 9.15 train to Brighton. In three days' time he was due to give evidence in court that should lead to the conviction and imprisonment of a gang of counterfeiters. As a respectable employee of the Fleet Bank, he knew it was his duty to give evidence, but fearing for his safety in the meantime, he was travelling into Sussex to be the guest of a friend." '

Another glance assured Alice that she still had the patients' attention. In fact, the ward had fallen silent.

The rest of the story detailed the appearance of the furtive man, a fight in the carriage, Harcourt jumping from the train to flee along the tracks and the would-be assassin giving chase with a revolver. Finally, Harcourt hid behind a scarecrow in a nearby field. He waited for the villain to run past, knocked him unconscious with a rock, tied him up with his belt, and ran to the nearest village and telephoned the police.

' "Wednesday came and Harcourt duly gave evidence in court. "Guilty," the foreman of the jury declared.

'Harcourt was thrilled to be awarded a medal for bravery and also a financial reward, which he thought he might use as a deposit on a small house. Not in Sussex, though. It would be a long time before Harcourt took the 9.15 to Brighton again." '

Alice was surprised when a round of applause broke out. 'Miss?' a patient at the other end of the ward called. 'That sounded grand but we couldn't hear it properly down here. Any chance you could come closer and read it again?'

Alice was happy to oblige and received another round of applause just as Matron came in.

'Good day, Miss Lovell,' she said, nodding.

Was it a nod of approval or was that too much to hope? Alice decided to feel pleased anyway, but as she walked home – daylight fading and coldness pinching her fingers even through her gloves – she pondered the book shortage again. Reading stories out loud was all very well, but it occupied only a few minutes of the patients' time. They needed books that could entertain them for hours.

Unfortunately, Alice couldn't afford to buy any books. She might have acted as her father's secretary in London – a job that, in another practice, would normally pay two or three pounds a week – but, knowing he was saving for his retirement as well as providing her with bed and board, she'd insisted that ten shillings a week was more than enough for her needs.

Small as the wage was, it had still allowed her to enjoy some of the pleasures of London, from sight-seeing to egg on toast in a Lyons Corner House on Saturday afternoons. She'd also been able to save a few pounds into a Post Office savings account. But ever since the accident, she'd been treating those savings as emergency funds only.

'Take what you need for your own use out of the housekeeping money,' her father had urged after she'd stopped earning, but Alice took as little as possible, feeling it wouldn't be right to deplete his modest retirement funds more than necessary.

Alice slowed as she reached the lake, concerned to avoid startling the woman in the blue coat again. There was no sign of her, though, which was unsurprising considering twilight was falling and ice was crunching in the puddles underfoot.

It was no evening to be outdoors and Alice was relieved to draw close to the cottage, though she tensed as she wondered once again if Daniel had called.

Her breath suddenly caught in her throat. Someone was standing by the porch.

CHAPTER EIGHT

Kate

'I didn't mean to frighten you,' Kate said.

'You didn't.' Alice moved forward again. 'I thought you might be someone else, that's all.'

She didn't explain who that someone else might be. Clearly, it was someone important, though whether important in a good or bad way Kate had no way of knowing.

'I've come to return the book.'

'Thank you. Come in and meet my father.'

'Best not. I've come from the farm in all my mess.'

'You can wipe your boots on the mat. Besides, I want to hear what you thought of the book and what you'd like to read next.'

Kate was torn. When she'd rushed through her jobs on the farm to make time for this visit, she'd intended only to hand the book over and go straight home. In fact, before Alice had arrived, she'd been looking for a place to leave it so she wouldn't need to knock on the door. Even now she was aware of the clock ticking. As ever, jobs awaited her at home and there'd be complaints if she left them undone.

But she also craved Alice's company and was curious about the way she lived, especially when she opened the door and allowed Kate an enticing glimpse inside the cottage.

'Don't let the cold creep in,' Alice urged.

Kate wiped her feet and stepped into the hall, closing the door behind her. The hall was dominated by a cupboard, presumably for coats, which was too large for the space available for it. An armchair took up more space. 'Our house in London was bigger – our furniture fitted better there,' Alice explained.

At least the Lovells' furniture was cared for, unlike the scuffed, scratched and damaged furniture on Brimbles Farm.

'Come and meet my father,' Alice repeated.

'No, I—'

Too late. Alice had knocked on a door, leaving Kate to chew on her lip in frustration. Doubtless the doctor would look at her with amazement and disgust. Afterwards, he'd take Alice to task. 'Really, my dear, I like you to be polite to everyone, but inviting such a yokel into our home . . . I'm afraid it won't do. You'll oblige me by confining invitations to more suitable girls in future.'

Well, so be it. As Alice opened the door Kate raised her chin and fixed a look of defiant indifference to her face.

'This is my friend, Kate Fletcher,' Alice said.

Friend? Kate felt a burst of pleasure at that, though perhaps it would only incense Dr Lovell further. 'Over my dead body!' he'd probably say.

She stepped into the room only to be taken aback by the number of books. They were on shelves, on the desk and even in stacks on the floor. What a joy! What a paradise! But what of their owner?

He was sitting behind the desk, a small, round man, rather like the cherub that was carved on a gravestone in the churchyard. Not that she expected him to behave with cherub-like sweetness.

'Splendid,' he said.

Splendid? Perhaps he had poor eyesight and hadn't seen her properly. His spectacles were on the desk.

'I'll bring you some tea,' Alice told him.

Kate felt obliged to say something before she followed Alice. She settled for, 'It's nice to meet you.' How clumsy she must sound!

'Likewise, my dear.'

Still puzzled, Kate backed out of the room.

Alice led her into the kitchen. 'Sit down,' she invited, gesturing to one of the chairs by a little table. 'This room isn't big enough for two people to stand without getting in each other's way.'

It was less than half the size of the kitchen at Brimbles Farm. Shabby too, but with pretty touches in the form of clean, fresh curtains, sparkling china and pot plants. An old Pye wireless sat on the smaller of the two window ledges.

'Your father doesn't see well?' Kate asked.

'He wears glasses for reading. Oh.' Alice had guessed why Kate was asking. 'My father is a good man. Just unlikely to live up to Churchwood's expectations.'

'Naomi Harrington's expectations,' Kate corrected. 'She beats the drum and the rest of Churchwood marches behind her.'

Kate had been on the receiving end of Mrs Harrington's disapproval all her life: disgusted looks, judgemental sniffs, steps to the side as though to avoid contamination . . . Occasional comments, too.

Like the time Kate had accidentally trodden wet mud over the grocer's shop floor and Mrs Harrington had said loudly, 'I'm afraid you need to mop this floor, Mrs Miles. Not all of your customers have the courtesy to wipe their feet.'

As if Kate had done it on purpose!

Even worse had been the time Mrs Harrington had nodded towards Mrs Hutchings's basket and said, 'I shouldn't leave your purse on show like that. Not now.'

Not now Kate had walked into the shop and might steal it.

Never having suffered such unfairness, Alice only shrugged. She'd make up her own mind, Kate supposed, which was actually a good thing. After all, Alice's independent thinking was the reason Kate was sitting here now.

Alice set two cups on the table and one cup on a tray. They were delicate china cups, patterned with flowers and sitting on saucers with silver teaspoons beside them. She set out matching plates, too, her movements neat and self-contained even as she worked mostly one-handed.

Kate took care not to stare at Alice's damaged hand but couldn't help noticing the scarring. Was the injury responsible for the sadness Kate sensed in Alice? And was it Alice's sadness that had made her sympathetic to Kate's?

Perhaps. But Alice was strong-minded despite being a little thing. Intelligent, too.

'Fruit cake,' she said, taking a tin from a shelf. 'I doubt there'll be many more of these, so let's treasure every crumb.'

Kate ran her hands over her pockets. Wanting to repay Alice for the loan of the book, she'd taken four apples from their straw beds in the loft, thinking they might make a welcome gift. Would they appear paltry, though?

There was only one way to find out. She placed the apples on the table. 'I thought you might like them, but if you're awash with apples—'

'No! I'm delighted to take them if you're sure you can spare them?'

'Of course.' Kate would have liked to add that she had plenty of apples at her disposal but the truth was that she'd taken a chance sneaking out even four. Ernie would be furious if he found out.

Alice filled the teapot. 'We can leave the tea to brew for a moment. Shall we pop upstairs so you can choose another book?'

'If you're sure . . .'

'Of course. How did you find *The Call of the Wild*?'

'I loved it. Imagine taking a dog sled out in the wilds of Alaska.'

'It would be cold but just think how pristine white the snow would be. And how bright the stars overhead. There's no need to take your boots off.'

Kate had untied the string that was holding them fastened in lieu of proper laces. 'I prefer it.' She was keen to show that she had some standards.

Alice led her up to a small bedroom with a sloping ceiling. Again, the furniture was overlarge but Alice had made the room attractive with an embroidered eiderdown, a set of silver-backed hairbrushes, framed photographs and sweet china trinket trays.

A narrow bookcase supported several shelves. There

were blank spaces where books had been removed, presumably to go to the hospital. Alice returned *The Call of the Wild* to a shelf and took out another book. '*Little Women*,' she said. 'It's a different sort of book but I think you might enjoy it, especially the character of Jo. She's a spirited young woman. Just like you.'

Kate hadn't thought of herself as spirited. Angry and frustrated, certainly. Perhaps aggressive at times, too.

'You can try another book if you don't like the sound of this one.'

'I do like the sound of it. Thank you.'

Kate's curiosity got the better of her and Alice caught her in what was meant to be a covert study of the photographs. 'My family,' she said.

There was a picture of Alice as a young child, a little doll-like creature who looked neat even then. Another photograph taken a year or two later showed her walking on a beach with the doctor and a woman Kate took to be Alice's mother. A third photograph showed the woman in close-up. She looked pleasant but her face lacked Alice's character.

'Your mother?' Kate ventured to ask.

'She died when I was ten.'

'My mother died when I was even younger.'

They shared a look of mutual sympathy then returned downstairs where Alice poured the tea. It seemed she'd perfected her technique for lifting the tray, balancing one end on her damaged wrist.

Kate longed to help but sensed that Alice prized her independence. Kate still got up to open the kitchen door; then she knocked on the doctor's door and opened it. She stood back so Alice could enter and returned to the kitchen to avoid embarrassment if the doctor assumed Alice was alone and said something disapproving about her visitor.

'Did the patients at the hospital like the books you took?' Kate asked when Alice returned.

'Very much so.' Alice ate her cake with ladylike nibbles, and Kate tried to copy her, thinking with distaste of teatime on the farm, which was devoid of anything approaching good manners. Food shoved into mouths, crumbs all over the floor . . .

Alice told Kate about writing letters for the patients, reading stories out loud and chatting to the men as well as distributing books. 'It sounds as though you're doing a wonderful thing there,' Kate told her.

'I'm not sure about wonderful but I think I'm beginning to meet a need. The problem is that I haven't enough books to go round so many of the men have nothing to do all day except brood.'

Kate couldn't imagine having nothing to do. Work awaited her even now, and the thought of it served as a reminder that her absence from the farm might be discovered at any moment. But she could understand how troubles might weigh all the more heavily on a person's shoulders when there was nothing to take attention away from them.

'I still have some books upstairs, as you saw,' Alice continued, 'but most date from my childhood or they're too . . . female.' She smiled. 'It would take a brave man to read *A Little Princess* in a ward full of strapping men.'

If the men on the wards were anything like Kate's brothers – Vinnie, especially – the mockery would be merciless.

'Unfortunately, I don't think my father's books will appeal either. And I don't have the money to buy more.'

'I don't have any money at all,' Kate admitted, wanting to make it clear that she couldn't contribute a brass farthing to any book purchases.

'Perhaps you might help me another way?' Alice suggested.

Kate tensed, fearing she might be asked for a favour she had neither the time nor power to grant. Besides, Kate's involvement in any scheme was more likely to doom it to failure than promote its success, given Churchwood's poor opinion of her.

'I'm thinking of appealing to other Churchwood residents to donate books,' Alice explained. 'I have in mind a poster outside the Sunday School Hall, announcing that I'll be receiving books in the hall on a Saturday morning. People could drop them off while out shopping, provided the vicar agrees.'

Kate nodded, unsure of the role Alice wanted her to play.

'Perhaps you could receive the books with me?' Alice said.

'I couldn't spare the time to sit in the hall,' Kate said hastily. 'There's virtually no break from farm work.' Neither could she bear the thought of being a sitting duck for sneers and gossip.

'It was just an idea.'

Kate chewed her lip. Might she help Alice another way? 'I could take you and the books to the hospital in the cart.' Kate wouldn't be allowed to take the cart without good reason so she'd have to ensure she had another errand to run.

'To use one of my father's favourite words, that would be splendid.'

Then Kate had another thought – a different way to help Alice, perhaps. 'Do you grow vegetables here?' she asked.

'No, but I've been thinking about it with the Dig for Victory campaign in the news now rationing's starting to bite.'

'Not to mention shortages and higher prices.' Ernie wasn't pleased about that, and doubtless he'd scrutinize Kate's spending on groceries even more closely. 'I could help you to clear a patch of ground.'

'That would be kind.'

'I'm used to heavy work.' Alice looked as though her horticultural skills extended only to dead-heading roses and arranging flowers in vases. Besides, she might struggle to garden with her injury. 'It's almost dark now. I'll come back another day but it'll depend on when I can slip away.'

Kate had stayed much longer than planned and was feeling twitchy about what was happening on the farm.

'Let me cut you another slice of cake to take home,' Alice said, and insisted on wrapping the cake in a cotton napkin despite Kate's protests.

Kate slid the cake into the pocket of her men's jacket along with *Little Women*. 'Thank you. And good luck with the book appeal.'

'I could call at the farm to let you know if the vicar gives permission,' Alice suggested then.

Kate was horrified. Not just at the thought of sweet Alice being exposed to the surly Fletcher men but also because Ernie wanted Kate on the farm, labouring unpaid in the fields and in the house, instead of open to other influences that might feed her discontent. The moment he learned about Alice Lovell would be the moment he and her brothers got to work to crush Kate's spirit and make it impossible for her to set foot off Fletcher property.

Kate's feelings must have shown on her face because Alice added tactfully, 'But perhaps a visit wouldn't be convenient with the farm being so busy.'

'It's always busy,' Kate confirmed gratefully.

'Don't let that stop you from calling in here whenever you're passing.'

Kate walked home briskly but entered the kitchen to find Ernie and Kenny already there. 'Where've you been?' Ernie demanded.

'Getting some air. I need fresh air with the way you and the boys fug up the house with your foul cigarettes.'

As if on cue, Ernie struck a match and lit a Woodbine. Kate rolled her eyes and hung her jacket up, trying to look casual, but her thoughts were on the book and cake in her pocket. They were her secrets, and she couldn't wait to enjoy them.

CHAPTER NINE

Naomi

'I take it you approve, Mrs Harrington?'

The Reverend Septimus Barnes's long, thin fingers hovered in front of the poster as though ready to tear it down should Naomi voice displeasure.

BOOKS WANTED, the poster announced.

> *The patients at Stratton House are in need of books to read. Are you able to donate one or more books to them? I shall be in the Sunday School Hall on Saturday 3rd February between 9 a.m. and 1 p.m. to receive any book donations or to give more information.*
> *Thank you.*
> *Alice Lovell, The Linnets*

'It sounds a useful sort of project in principle,' Naomi admitted. 'I'll have a talk with Miss Lovell about it.'

'Quite right.' The reverend nodded. 'I've no doubt that Miss Lovell is well intentioned, but a young head must always benefit from your wiser counsel. Did I mention how much I enjoyed tea at Foxfield last week?'

'You did.' Several times.

'It's always a pleasure to enjoy charming company in pleasant surroundings.'

'It was good of you to come.'

'I'll always make time for your gatherings, Mrs Harrington.'

Naomi knew it all too well. An ageing widower with overlong white hair and an eagerness to please, Septimus Barnes was a worthy enough man. But his liking for fine food and wine meant he was constantly angling for invitations. It made him ever so slightly tiresome.

She smiled thinly. 'Good day to you, Vicar.'

She set off for home, though he remained dipping and dancing at her side for several yards before she finally shook him off. Glad to be alone at last, Naomi turned her thoughts to Alice Lovell. It was surprising that she should have launched the book appeal without discussing it first, but Naomi was ready to make allowances. The girl was new to the village and still learning Churchwood ways. It was to her credit that she wanted to help the patients at Stratton House and Naomi was perfectly willing to take the girl under her wing to ensure the project succeeded.

Marjorie might not like it, as she had a tendency to be jealous, but Naomi would smooth her friend's ruffled feathers somehow. Like Septimus Barnes, Marjorie was one of Naomi's staunchest allies but she too could be tiresome. Alice Lovell might be a breath of fresh air.

Calling at The Linnets, Naomi was pleased to find Alice at home. 'I wonder if you might spare me five minutes of your time?'

Was that hesitation in the girl's face? Perhaps she

was busy. But the expression was gone in an instant, replaced by something that looked like determination. Even challenge. 'I have a visitor, but you're welcome to join us,' she said.

'Perhaps another time might—'

'Please come in, Mrs Harrington.'

Naomi was led into a cluttered hall followed by a cluttered dining room but her attention was snatched from the furnishings by the presence of that dreadful Fletcher girl standing by the window, her clothes as appalling and her eyes as insolent as ever.

'Well, really!' The words were out before Naomi could even think of holding them in.

'Do you know Miss Fletcher?' Alice asked calmly. 'Kate, this is Mrs Harrington. Please sit, both of you.'

Alice glided into a chair with ladylike elegance. The Fletcher girl sat, too, but carelessly, as though she enjoyed provoking Naomi's disapproval.

Naomi sat on the edge of another seat. 'Thank you, but I only need a quick word. I saw your poster appealing for books.'

'Oh?' Alice's face brightened.

'It's a promising idea. I'll be happy to put a committee together so we can take it forward properly.'

'A committee?' Alice blinked in apparent surprise.

'With my connections we can—'

The Fletcher girl snorted. 'This is Alice's project,' she said. In other words, it was nothing to do with Naomi.

Ignoring her, Naomi pressed on. 'I'll gladly chair the committee, so you don't need to worry about that.'

Another snort from the Fletcher girl.

'I appreciate the offer, but I'm not sure a committee is needed just yet,' Alice said.

Her voice was gentle but it still felt to Naomi like a slap in the face. Harsh and painful. Feeling an urgent need to leave, she rose to her feet. 'I'm sorry for disturbing you.'

'Please don't think I'm ungrateful. It's just that—'

'Good day to you, Miss Lovell.' Naomi hastened through the small hall, opened the front door herself and stepped outside.

'Please, Mrs Harringon,' Alice called, but Naomi walked on.

She turned for home but realized she was too agitated to face the staff back at Foxfield. Too agitated to face anyone. Turning again, she walked along Brimbles Lane and around the back of the lake to the quiet path that bordered Bert Makepiece's smallholding. Here she walked up and down, trying to calm herself.

How dare that Fletcher girl sneer at her? And how dare Alice Lovell reject Naomi's offer of help so . . . so *bluntly*? Naomi had expected no better from Kate Fletcher, but from the doctor's daughter . . .

Naomi realized she was crying, which was absurd. Feeling annoyed was one thing. But upset to the point of tears? At the rude behaviour of two silly girls? She dashed the tears away with the back of her hand but more tears fell to replace them.

What was the matter with her? Naomi didn't have to go far in her thoughts to find the answer. She'd felt belittled. Ridiculed. Embarrassed. And despite the passing of the years and the success of the life she'd built in Churchwood, she'd been Naomi Tuggs again.

Plain, dumpy Naomi Tuggs, crushed by the humiliation of knowing she was a graceless bore who wasn't wanted. Who was despised, in fact.

But she was forty-five now. She'd left Naomi Tuggs behind more than a quarter of a century ago.

Or had she? Not entirely. She'd never forgotten the sting of those days, and every so often she felt the old insecurities creeping back before she managed to get a hold on them again, keeping herself busy with lists and organization. She'd never been driven to tears before, though, so why now?

Was she reaching the age when changes in her body would leave her at the mercy of sudden and overwhelming emotions? The change of life was only ever mentioned in whispers accompanied by knowing looks. 'It's her age,' someone would murmur of a middle-aged woman who appeared to be overwrought. 'It's the change.'

The words would be met with understanding nods and sometimes rueful comments too. 'Happens to us all,' or, 'Something to look forward to.'

It grieved Naomi to think that her body might be closing down without ever producing a child. She'd given up hope of a child long ago, of course, and so had Alexander; it had been years since he'd approached her in an intimate way. Even so, to think that she might be withering inside . . .

The scene in The Linnets dining room loomed in her mind. Naomi had always known the Fletchers were a bad lot but she'd gone to the cottage with every intention of liking the doctor's daughter and befriending her. Yet Alice had wanted nothing to do with her.

Naomi's shoulders rounded over as a sob broke out. It was ridiculous to feel overpowered like this. Naomi needed to get a grip on herself. She forced her head up again, blinked rapidly and sniffed.

'Looks like you're having a spot of bother, Mrs H.'

Naomi whirled around to see Bert Makepiece watching her over a hedge. She blinked some more and swallowed hard. 'Something blew into my eye,' she said stiffly.

'Something blew into both of your eyes from the look of 'em.'

'The breeze threw up some grit.'

'It's a windy day all right.'

It was one of those chill winter days when nothing moved and time seemed frozen. 'Whatever hurt my eyes seems to have cleared away now,' Naomi said, desperate to regain self-control. 'Thank you for concerning yourself with my welfare, Mr Makepiece, but don't let me keep you from your work. I'm going home now.'

'Off you go then, Mrs H. I hope your staff won't be *too* worried when they see the state of you.'

Naomi bristled at that. Bert Makepiece had never been one to bow and scrape to her but neither had he spoken with such easy familiarity before. What was it about today that was making people address her without the respect she'd worked so hard to earn? She supposed she'd never given Mr Makepiece cause to speak to her disrespectfully before because she'd never given him cause to think she was weak. To look weak before him now was frustrating.

Yet he had a point about her appearance. She must look blotchy and tear-stained, and arriving home in such a state would indeed have her staff wondering about her. She opened her handbag in search of a handkerchief.

'I've got water and a mirror indoors,' he told her.

Was he suggesting that she should visit his house? It would hardly be the most salubrious place, judging from his appearance, as no one could describe Bert Makepiece as smart. He was a big shambling man whose clothes were limp and faded with age. Sometimes they were even held together by garden twine. But using his water and mirror to tidy herself might be the lesser of two evils.

'Won't take more than a few minutes,' he said. 'Gate's just along there.'

He set off in the direction he'd indicated. After a moment Naomi followed. By the time she caught him up, he was holding the gate open.

She'd visited the smallholding before to order Christmas foliage and other flowers but on those occasions she'd arrived through the main front gate and hadn't gone much further. Entering this way took her to the rear of the property. How neat it was with its carefully tended growing beds and well-maintained greenhouses. Clearly, Bert's care went into his business rather than his clothes.

He led the way into a kitchen, though a drawing room would surely have been a more appropriate place in which to entertain Mrs Alexander Harrington. She was willing to allow that he probably meant no offence, though.

The kitchen was large, surprisingly clean and almost as neat as the growing beds, even if it was old-fashioned. The paper on the walls was dull with age while the painted cupboards, stove and table had probably been in place for decades. Two armchairs placed on each side of the hearth looked to be of similar vintage though they were mostly covered by hand-knitted blankets that could have been the work of long-dead Mrs Makepiece. Beside them were small tables, one of which bore seed catalogues. Against the far wall stood a dresser with plates, bowls, cups and saucers on the shelves. Not china, but simple pottery in a mix of flower patterns. There was nothing of style or elegance about the room, yet it had an air of comfort and ease.

A cat dozed on a rug in front of the fire. It raised its head to blink sleepily at Naomi before relaxing again as though it had seen nothing of interest.

'Water,' Bert said, gesturing towards the sink. 'Mirror.'

The mirror was a small, plain square, hanging from the window frame on a length of wire.

'Do you need a towel?' he asked.

'My handkerchief will suffice.'

Naomi dampened it and patted her face. She really did look dreadful, her eyes swollen and rimmed with redness. How shaming to appear so before this man. The patting did no good, so she dampened another corner of the handkerchief and tried again.

'Kettle's on,' Mr Makepiece announced.

Was he expecting her to keep him company over a cup of tea? No, it was too much.

Turning to decline the offer, Naomi caught sight of the cat again, yawning and kneading the rug as though clawing itself deeper into comfort. The fire burned brightly, too. And she really wasn't ready to face her staff at home.

'Grit all gone?' he asked.

Was he mocking her? Probably. It was ungentle-manly of him, but she could hardly criticize him for using a story she'd invented. 'Yes, thank you.'

'Sit yourself down then.'

The armchair with the seed catalogues nearby was probably where he normally sat. Naomi took the other chair, feeling self-conscious in this homely kitchen. At Foxfield the kitchen was for the staff.

'Here you are. Nice and strong. Bracing after an upset.'

He set a cup and saucer beside her and then sat down heavily. 'So what brought on the grit attack?' he enquired.

Naomi bristled. It was none of his business.

'Or is the right question: *who* brought it on?'

'I don't understand you, Mr Makepiece.'

'I think you do, Mrs H.'

'Harrington. I prefer to be called Mrs Harrington.'

'Is that right? Me, I don't care what folk call me. Bert, Mr Makepiece, sir or the King of England. We're all just people behind the fancy feathers we put on to fool the world.'

Was she using her title – Mrs Harrington of Foxfield – to fool the world? Surely addressing a per-son correctly was simply a matter of respect? Preferring not to think too hard about it, she took a sip of tea. It was hot, strong and flavoursome.

'So,' he said again, 'someone upset you.'

She wanted to tell him to mind his own business. But she was sitting in his kitchen, drinking his tea and taking advantage of his hospitality in order to spare herself from sparking gossip at home. The best thing might be to throw him a bone. Just a small one.

'I wouldn't say that she upset me exactly, but that awful Fletcher girl was rude.'

'Rude?'

'She sneered at me.'

He nodded thoughtfully. 'You've never sneered at her, I suppose?'

Naomi blinked in surprise. Surely he could see the difference? 'The Fletchers are a terrible family, Mr Makepiece.'

'Some of the Fletchers are bad 'uns,' he conceded. 'But the girl . . . She's always been civil to me.'

'Then you've received better treatment from her than I.'

'Perhaps because I haven't been so quick to judge.'

'She's insolent.'

'Doesn't doff her cap to Mrs Harrington of Foxfield. Is that it?'

'Don't be absurd.'

'Seems to me she's being judged because of her family. Not because of the person she is. If she puts up a bit of a defence, then I say a show of spirit is to her credit. Better than being broken. But you're used to the Fletchers so I don't reckon it was their girl who brought you so low.'

Naomi said nothing. She'd been seduced by the comfort of this cosy kitchen but now she wanted to be gone.

'Was it the other one?' he asked. 'The doctor's daughter? I saw Kate Fletcher calling at the cottage so perhaps they're friends.'

'Thank you for your hospitality, Mr Makepiece, but it's time I was on my way.'

'Hit the nail on the head, have I?'

She put her cup down, though it was still half full, and heaved her stocky body up.

'Seems to me there's nothing wrong with a couple of young 'uns making friends. If they don't want interference from older folk . . . well, it's only natural, especially if those older folk jump in with their boots on and bark out orders.'

'Good day to you, Mr Makepiece. Thank you for the tea.'

'You're welcome.'

Naomi walked home briskly as though trying to outrun her thoughts, which, annoyingly, kept replaying what Bert Makepiece had said. It had felt more like a lecture than a conversation. Really, that man needed to learn to keep his nose out of matters that didn't concern him.

Reaching the house, she handed her coat and hat to little Suki. 'It's a fine day so I made the most of it by walking around the lake,' Naomi said to explain her lateness.

'I'll bring hot tea straight away to warm you up.' Suki was a sweet girl.

Tea would remind Naomi of Mr Makepiece. Not an encounter she wished to dwell upon. She opened her mouth to say tea wouldn't be necessary but a departure from routine might have Suki wondering if all was well with her employer. 'Lovely,' she said.

'Miss Plym is here,' Suki added then.

Naomi's spirits dipped further at the thought of Marjorie's mindless chatter but she fixed a smile in place and stepped into the small sitting room. 'Marjorie, how nice to see you.'

'I've called to ask what you think of Alice Lovell's

book appeal. I saw the poster outside the Sunday School Hall. Have you seen it?'

'I gave it a glance.'

'Yes?' Marjorie waited for the verdict.

'I don't feel it's something I need to concern myself with,' Naomi told her. 'There are enough demands on my time already, especially as I've decided to organize parcels for the Red Cross to deliver to prisoners of war. I suggest we start listing what we might need.'

Keeping busy. That was the ticket.

CHAPTER TEN

Alice

'You're not still worried?' Kate asked.

Alice looked up from her digging. She had neither Kate's strength nor her technique but was still making progress. 'I'd like to know Mrs Harrington isn't offended.'

'I told you before, she's too thick-skinned for that.'

'Everyone has feelings, Kate.'

'If snobby Naomi Harrington has feelings, she's getting a taste of her own medicine. She never hesitates to stamp over other people.'

Alice guessed that Kate had her own bruised sensibilities in mind and couldn't blame her for being bitter. Even so . . .

'She went off in a huff because she couldn't get her own way,' Kate insisted, but Alice wasn't entirely convinced, especially as Mrs Harrington hadn't made eye contact with her when they'd passed each other in the street. It was possible that, busy talking to another woman, Mrs Harrington hadn't noticed Alice, but equally she might have chosen not to notice her.

Despite the certainty with which Kate had spoken, a look at her face made Alice wonder if doubts had begun to stir in her friend's mind too. Not wanting to add to Kate's troubles if that were the case, Alice changed the subject. 'This vegetable patch is coming along nicely.'

They'd marked off a section of the overgrown, winter-sleeping garden and got to work clearing and digging over the ground. Now they had a patch of brown earth instead of green grass and brambles, and there was a rich loamy smell in the air. 'Bert Makepiece's smallholding is the place for seeds and stuff,' Kate told her. 'He'll give you advice too. I'd go along with you but it's hard to get away and I think my time's better spent on digging.'

'I appreciate your help.'

Kate grinned. 'Even though I've ruined your shoes?'

Alice looked down at her feet. Not having working boots, she was wearing her oldest shoes and they were caked in mud. There were smears of mud on her lisle stockings too. Kate's clothes might be big and ugly, but they were far more practical than Alice's old skirt, blouse and cardigan.

Kate pushed a stray tendril of hair from her eyes. It really was glorious hair, especially at this time when the setting sun brought out its coppery depths and glossiness. Kate worked for a few minutes longer and then announced that she needed to get home. Declining Alice's invitation to wash or drink tea, she left by the side gate and pounded along Brimbles Lane at speed.

Alone in the garden, Alice watched a blackbird snatch a worm from the earth. The bird stared at her as though challenging her to steal the trophy before flying away with the worm in its beak. Nature in the raw.

Alice shivered. The day was cooling fast but she didn't want to risk dirtying her coat. She continued digging, thinking about Naomi Harrington but coming to no conclusions, and then turning her mind to another of Kate's suggestions.

'Chickens,' she'd said. 'You have plenty of space for them and you'll be glad of the eggs, especially if the war makes them hard to come by. Bert Makepiece should be able to start you off with a couple of hens.'

'Goodness, I'll be quite the little farmer.'

'Maybe one or two fruit trees would be useful too. An apple. A pear . . .'

It would be sensible to plan for shortages. After all, the last conflict had lasted for four years and who knew how hard rationing might bite in this second war?

'Your father won't object to the garden being taken over?'

Alice had smiled. 'My father is only interested in gardens that existed thousands of years ago.'

It was lovely having Kate to help but Alice didn't want to become a burden to her. She wanted—

Alice heard a sound behind her and turned to investigate. Had Kate forgotten something?

But it wasn't Kate who stood by the house. Alice felt blood drain from her face then pound in her ears.

'Your father let me in,' Daniel said.

Alice could only stare at him. At the crisp, dark hair that was shorter now he was a soldier, but which still flopped a little over his smooth forehead. At the gleam in his warm brown eyes and smile. At the tall, fresh-faced healthiness of him in his army greatcoat and loosely hanging scarf.

'You've been busy,' he observed, nodding at the turned earth.

Alice came back to life though her head was

reeling. To be caught unawares and looking a fright in a limp grey flannel skirt, a cardigan that drooped almost as much as one of Miss Plym's and an ancient scarf of her father's . . . Alice was human enough to feel mortified, even if she had no intention of trying to attract him. 'Hello, Daniel.'

There. She'd spoken. And her voice had sounded normal. Almost.

He walked towards her, his strides long and loose. 'You have colour in your cheeks. It suits you.'

Alice felt her cheeks flush even more. Despite her good intentions, longing was bubbling up inside her at the softness of his voice. The frustration of it made her want to stamp her foot. Or cry. But she swallowed and tried to recapture at least the appearance of normality. 'You've come from your godmother's?'

'Mmm.' He looked back at the vegetable patch. 'Digging for victory?'

'That's the idea.'

'Not easy work.'

Was he referring to her injury? Alice's cheeks flamed again, this time with a mix of frustration and regret. 'Not easy, no. But I'm enjoying it, and I'm making progress.'

He shrugged out of his coat and wrapped it around her shoulders. Alice tried to ignore the fact that it was warm from his body. He held out his hand for the spade. 'May I?'

'You can't dig in your uniform!'

'Yes, I can.'

'I was finishing up anyway. The light's fading and—'

'I'll enjoy the exercise.'

Was that true? It was impossible for Alice to judge.

Ever since the accident, Daniel had done whatever he could to try to compensate her for the injury he so clearly felt responsible for. In the early days he'd offered money for her surgery, volunteered to take her to hospital appointments and asked to pay for the extra help her father needed due to Alice's incapacity – a part-time secretary to type his letters in the months before his retirement, and extra hours for their charlady. Much to Alice's relief, her father had declined all such offers. 'Good of you, dear boy, but quite unnecessary,' he'd insisted.

But gradually, as it had become clear that the injury had compromised her ability to support herself – certainly in the foreseeable future – she'd begun to suspect that Daniel saw her as his long-term responsibility and planned to rescue her by marrying her.

Not that he'd said so yet, but he was too kind to let her know that his proposal would be motivated by guilt rather than love. Instead, he'd begun to work his way towards it via an appearance of courtship, though the war was rather getting in the way.

To Alice the idea of a marriage based on pity was unbearable. She might love Daniel, but it had become apparent before the accident that all he felt for her was friendship. Unwilling to sacrifice her dignity and his happiness on the altar of misplaced guilt, Alice was doing everything she could to keep him at arm's length before he declared his intentions and humiliated them both.

'Please,' he added now, and Alice saw no way to refuse that wouldn't look churlish or strange.

She handed the spade over and stepped back.

'Your boots will get filthy,' she warned, in a last attempt to dissuade him.

'They'll clean up.'

He heaved over frozen earth as though it weighed nothing. Soon his athletic physique found a rhythm and he worked fluently.

'My father must want his tea,' she said when she could bear to watch no longer. 'It's almost dark, too.'

Daniel glanced at the sky. 'Why don't you make tea while I finish out here?' he suggested, and Alice was glad to escape.

Her father probably hadn't even noticed the absence of tea but she prepared a tray for him and set out cups and saucers for Daniel and herself. There was a little cake left so Alice cut three slices – regular-sized for her father, wider for Daniel and thinner for herself.

It wasn't long before Daniel appeared at the door, a picture of vitality. 'I've looked out a newspaper,' Alice told him, focusing on practicalities. 'You can use it to scrape the worst of the mud off your boots. I have shoe polish and brushes too.' She passed them over.

'That cake looks good.' He grinned, showing even white teeth, then took the newspaper and cleaning kit outside, closing the door to keep the heat in the kitchen. Alice heard him working on his boots with brisk energy. She took her father's tea in to him but delayed pouring the other cups until Daniel returned.

'All done,' he reported.

'I hope your boots aren't ruined.'

'They're army boots. They'll be fine.'

'We can take our tea into the dining room.' There was no fire in there but if she kept the door from the kitchen open . . .

'This kitchen looks cosy enough for me.'

He sat at the little table and Alice sat, too, though it would do her bruised heart no good to be so close to him. She poured the tea then passed over a cup, saucer and plate of cake.

Daniel smiled his thanks and nibbled at the cake. 'Tasty. You didn't—'

'Make it? No.' She couldn't manage a heavy mixing bowl.

Daniel must have realized it because regret drained the smile from his face.

'I didn't make this cake but I'm going to make one soon,' she added quickly, hoping to head off any discussion of her hand.

It didn't work. 'I have to ask,' he said, and there was no need for him to elaborate.

'I'm healing well and doing more every day,' she said. 'I can peel vegetables now so I'm managing to cook.' It took a long time because her hand cramped if she held anything for more than a few seconds but she was determined to persevere.

'Any pain still?'

'None to speak of.'

If only she could tell him she was able to earn her own living again so had no need of rescue. Casting around for a different way of showing she was managing without him, she settled on Kate. 'A friend who lives on a farm is advising me about the vegetable patch. She suggests I grow potatoes, carrots and onions. Beans, too. If I do well with those crops, I may try others.'

'I'm glad you've found a friend.' Daniel's voice was soft again. 'I was relieved when I heard you were leaving London, but I've been worried about you moving to a village where you know no one.'

'I like being somewhere new and I'm far from bored. There's a military hospital not far from here. I visit the patients to write letters for them, read stories, and—'

Alice broke off, deciding she wouldn't tell him about her book appeal. Much as she wanted books for the patients, she didn't want Daniel distracted from his duties and trying to appease his guilt by encouraging everyone he knew to donate books. He needed to focus on staying safe and she needed to focus on living without him. Besides, he'd feel even sorrier for her if her appeal met with only a lukewarm response in the village.

'I've been taking first-aid classes, too,' she finished. One class anyway.

'I imagine you could *lead* the classes,' Daniel said. 'You've been steeped in medical matters all your life.'

'We can all learn something new.'

'Indeed.' He hesitated; then he said, 'I imagine there are few opportunities for work around here.'

They were back on the subject she didn't want to discuss. 'I'm enjoying having the time to settle into Churchwood. Even when I was at school I worked for my father during the evenings and holidays. It's nice to take a break. But enough of me. How are you finding army life?'

His expression turned sombre in a different way and Alice felt dread stir inside her.

'You're being sent overseas,' she guessed.

'To France.'

'I'm sorry.'

'I've been luckier than most in spending the last months in England, and it wouldn't feel right for me to leave all the fighting to other chaps.'

Daniel might have trained in warfare at school, university and army camp but in civilian life he was an engineer working in racing-car design, not a fighter. Alice hated the thought of him being sent into action, but no one with sense actually *wanted* the person they loved to go to war. It was a price that had to be paid to save their country – and others – from tyranny.

Daniel's hand lay on the table. Alice fought the urge to snatch it up and kiss it. 'When are you leaving?'

'In a few days' time, I imagine.'

A moment of quietness followed until Alice roused herself, fearing the atmosphere was growing too personal. 'My friend Kate suggested I keep chickens for their eggs,' she said, scrambling on to a safer topic.

'Good idea. You'll need a coop to protect them from foxes. I could come back tomorrow and build one for you.'

Not such a safe topic, after all. The more Alice saw of Daniel, the more he'd torture her fragile emotions. But once he left for France he'd be putting his life on the line and she might never see him again. The thought of that was even more agonizing. 'Won't your godmother mind?' she asked, putting up token resistance.

'She's told me she doesn't want me under her feet *all* of the time. She needs to rest.'

'You needn't feel obliged to come. Kate will help.'

'I'd like to help too.'

So she'd see him again. The knowledge was bittersweet.

'Your father appears to have settled into retirement well,' Daniel said then, 'though I didn't keep him talking for long. I imagine he prefers to spend his time reading about men in togas than talking to flesh-and-blood motor designers.' He smiled again.

'I'm glad he has time for his interests at last.' It was on the tip of her tongue to add that she hoped he wouldn't become too hermit-like but she bit it back in case it gave Daniel another reason to worry.

A different thought struck her. Was Daniel expecting an invitation to stay for something to eat? 'You're welcome to join us for dinner, though it won't be anything special.'

'Unfortunately, my godmother is expecting me. I'm lingering because it's cosy in here, but I really must go.'

He got up and shrugged back into his coat. 'I'm afraid there's mud on your trousers,' Alice said.

'It'll sponge off. I'll be better prepared for hard labour tomorrow.'

He walked into the hall. 'I've already disturbed your father once so I won't do so again.'

Alice opened the door and saw a car in the lane. 'Luckily I had some petrol stored,' he explained.

Swooping down, he kissed her cheek. It was a brief kiss but Alice's breath caught in her throat and she stepped back before his closeness could overwhelm her.

Daniel must have assumed she was shivering because of the wintry air. 'Go inside,' he urged. 'Keep warm.'

'Thanks for your help with the digging.'

'My pleasure.'

Alice closed the door but stood at the window long after the car had moved out of sight, knowing she'd see Daniel again tomorrow and wondering how it was possible to feel dismay and joy at the same time.

CHAPTER ELEVEN

Kate

Kate, as always when squeezing in a secret visit to Alice, was rushing. If she'd been walking more slowly she might have heard voices and crept away again. There was something she wanted to talk to Alice about – something that was gnawing at her peace of mind – but she'd have left it to another day if she'd known her friend already had a visitor.

As it was, Kate practically flew into the garden of The Linnets only to pull up short at the sight of a man hammering nails into wood while Alice held the wood steady. There was no way of retreating unseen now.

'You're busy. I'll come back another time,' she said.

'Don't go,' Alice urged. 'Daniel, this is the friend I mentioned. Kate Fletcher.'

There was that word again. *Friend.* It was a lovely, warm sort of word but this man must surely think it an odd way for Alice to refer to a scruffy bumpkin.

He was far from a bumpkin: tall, good-looking and smart. Kate was no expert on men's clothing – or women's clothing, come to that – but even she could see that, despite their obvious age, there was quality in the cut of his trousers and the wool of his olive-green sweater. But if he was horrified by Kate, he hid it well. He even smiled at her.

'This is Daniel Irvine,' Alice continued. 'His parents live near to my father's old house in London.'

Daniel waited, as though wondering if Alice might have more to say about him. When nothing came, he stepped towards Kate. She realized he was offering a hand for her to shake and panicked at the thought of her rough, work-worn fingers. But, once again, if he felt any disgust, he hid it well.

'It's good to meet you,' he said.

Kate mumbled something back.

'We're making a coop for the chickens,' Alice explained. 'Mr Makepiece was able to supply materials, and he should have some chickens for me soon.'

'That's good to hear, but I don't want to get in the way so—'

'Please stay,' Alice urged, and Kate wondered if she'd heard a note of desperation in Alice's voice.

There was no obvious reason for it. Daniel had been laughing when Kate arrived, and it had been the sort of laughter that was rich in warmth and humour.

'We might finish today if you help,' Alice added.

'All right, but I can't stay long.'

Daniel was an efficient worker, which surprised her as his clothes suggested he worked in an office or a bank. Kate tried to make up for her own dreadful appearance by being equally efficient.

'Alice tells me you live on a farm,' Daniel said.

'That's right.' Kate supposed good manners required her to ask about his home too. 'You live in London?'

'Near Oxford, actually. It's closer to where I work at Della-Hux. We make racing cars.'

Kate had never been in a car in her life so had nothing to say on the subject but working with cars would explain his deftness and quickness. It was strange to be there between Daniel and Alice. Both were perfectly friendly but there were undercurrents. Once Kate caught him looking at Alice's injured hand and there was no mistaking the distress that flickered across his handsome face. It wasn't revulsion, though, because whenever he looked Alice in the face his eyes softened.

Another time Kate caught Alice looking sad before she used a smile to cover it. Something was going on between these two people though both appeared to be making heroic efforts to pretend all was well.

'Have you been back to Stratton House?' Kate asked Alice after a while, not wishing to appear either struck dumb with stupidity or surly.

'I went this morning. I wrote some letters and read some stories. The men seemed to enjoy them.'

'I've been hearing about Alice's volunteering,' Daniel said.

Maybe he could help her by donating some books. Alice might have felt she couldn't ask but there was no reason Kate shouldn't mention the book shortage. 'The problem is, there aren't enough—'

'—hours in the day,' Alice finished, cutting her off.

Kate blinked in surprise but Alice wouldn't meet her gaze.

'You're doing what you can,' Daniel told Alice and, again, there was a soft glow in his dark eyes. 'That's the important thing.'

They were old friends who appeared to like each other, so the tension between them felt odd to Kate. Unless one of them wanted romance and the other didn't.

Kate had no experience of romance, either as a participant or an observer. If her parents had shared any tenderness, she'd been too young to witness it, while none of her brothers had ever shown interest in any girl except Joanie, the barmaid at the Wheat-sheaf, and they only spoke of her in vulgar terms. Kate had seen couples link arms in the street occasionally, and she'd once heard a boy call, 'Hello, gorgeous,' to a passing girl. It wasn't much to go on, but some sort of romantic mismatch was the only explanation Kate could imagine.

What sort of mismatch, though? Did Daniel like Alice more than she liked him, or was it the other way round? Kate couldn't decide, and anyway she could be wrong in assuming that romantic feelings were at work. Old friends could have all sorts of misunder-standings or disagreements.

'I need to go,' Kate said eventually.

'You won't stay for a cup of tea?' Alice asked. 'Dan-iel brought a beautiful fruit cake.'

'Not today.'

'I'll walk you out.'

Daniel told Kate it had been a pleasure to meet her. Kate murmured something back then set off for the gate, Alice beside her. Perhaps now Kate might manage a private word with Alice.

'Thanks for all your help,' Alice said.

'I don't suppose you've seen Mrs Harrington?' Despite all Kate had said about the woman's lack of feelings, Alice's concerns had taken root inside her too and she couldn't shake off the worry that they might have upset her.

'I saw her in the village yesterday, but she was rushing and didn't stop to talk.'

'Rushing or avoiding?'

Alice grimaced. 'I suspect the latter, though I can't be sure. I've decided to go to the first-aid class on Wednesday. She can't avoid me there. I just want to be sure she isn't offended.'

'It's my fault if she *is* upset.'

'We both turned down her offer of help.'

'Yes, but you did it politely and I . . . didn't.'

'Don't worry. She may just be in a huff, as you called it, or she might have forgotten all about it. She seems to be the sort of woman who keeps busy.'

Kate was tempted to reply that Mrs Harrington was busy enough judging other people, but wasn't that the sort of attitude that had caused this problem in the first place?

Kate's thoughts returned to Daniel. 'Having your friend here got the chicken coop made quickly,' she commented, but her hope that Alice might say more about him was disappointed.

'Having you here helped, too,' Alice said, and that seemed to be the end of it.

Kate's most spiteful brother, Vinnie, was in the farmyard when Kate raced in. 'Been shirking, I see,' he said, clearly relishing the thought of getting her into trouble.

'A quick walk, that's all. Anyway, I saw you shirking, too.'

She'd seen him in Five Acre Field when she'd set out for Alice's house. He'd been working but Kate had a shrewd idea that he'd have slacked off sooner or later.

'Just a ciggie break.'

'Ah, but it wasn't just one ciggie, was it? Several ciggies, I reckon.'

She must have guessed correctly because he scowled and spat at her feet before loping off into the barn.

Kate went inside and started cooking dinner, having prepared the meat and vegetables earlier. The kitchen erupted into its usual filthy chaos as Ernie and her brothers arrived but Kate let the annoyance wash over her. She had other things on her mind. What was the story of Daniel Irvine? Why didn't Alice want him to know about her book appeal? And if Mrs Harrington really was offended, would she sabotage that book appeal out of spite?

CHAPTER TWELVE

Alice

'Any books today?' sunny Stevie Meadows asked.

'Hopefully soon,' Alice told him.

'Ah, well. I'm lucky to have more letters from home.' He grinned. 'My mum's promising to make my favourite dumplings when I get back and my dad's growing rhubarb because he knows I love it in a crumble. My sisters are little treasures, too. They're saving their pocket money to treat me to a film and fish-and-chip supper, and my gran's knitting me a new jumper.'

'And Esme?'

His sweet face softened. 'Look what she sent.' He held up a newspaper cutting, which featured a photograph of a riverbank. 'This is our favourite place for walks. I'm planning to propose there as soon as I can get down on one knee.'

Jake Turner made a scornful sound and turned his back.

'I think that's romantic,' Alice told Stevie.

Other patients were more obviously disappointed about the lack of books. 'I can read another story out loud if you'd care to listen?' she offered.

'A story will be grand, miss,' one said, and others nodded.

She placed her chair where her voice would reach to

all of them without the need to shout. Concerned not to disturb any patients who were resting – or annoy Jake Turner unduly – Alice intended to read the story three times, at the top, in the middle and at the bottom of the ward.

'I thought I'd read "Simkins and Stanley" today. It's about a man and a dog. A rather clever dog.' No one appeared to think she'd chosen badly. '*Simkins and his dog, Stanley, were inseparable,*' she began. '*Wherever Simkins went, Stanley went too, much to the exasperation of Mrs Simkins. "That dog is—"*'

Alice broke off as a wail from the other end of the ward erupted into the quietness. A man was thrashing in his bed and a nurse rushed past to help him. 'It was just a dream, Private Matthews,' she soothed.

'The poor chap's ship was torpedoed,' Stevie Meadows explained. 'He dreams about being caught below decks as water rushed in, then getting out only to find the sea ablaze around him. Oil, you see?'

Alice did see and shuddered at the thought of it.

She caught the eye of the nurse as she walked back up the ward. 'Would it be better if I left?'

'I think Private Matthews will feel worse if you leave. He won't like to think he's to blame.'

Alice nodded and started again with 'Simkins and Stanley'. This time she read until the end.

'I wish I had a dog that found money,' a patient commented.

'Me and all,' another said. 'Might give the missis one less thing to moan about.'

'If I had more money, I'd buy a house for Esme and me,' Stevie said. 'We'll be happy living with my parents and sisters for a while, though. We're not greedy.'

Jake Turner pulled a pillow over his head.

Alice moved to the middle of the ward and read the story again. By the time she reached the end where Private Matthews lay, he was awake but miserable. Supposing he was embarrassed, too, Alice didn't single him out for attention but he was in her thoughts and she hoped he took at least a little pleasure from the story.

She spent an hour in the other ward before deciding it was time to head home. She was walking along the corridor when a middle-aged man and woman emerged from Stevie's ward. Alice assumed they were parents visiting an injured son, especially when the woman began to cry into a handkerchief.

Her husband eased an arm around her shoulder. 'There, there, Connie. Don't take on.'

'How can I help it when Jake's so bad?'

These must be Jake Turner's parents.

'He's alive,' Mr Turner pointed out.

'Yes, but how's he going to cope? How's he going to work?'

'He'll have a wheelchair, and maybe tin legs too, in time. And he still has the use of his arms.'

'He'll never manage carpentry again.'

'Maybe not, but there are other jobs.'

'You know carpentry wasn't just a job to Jake. It was a passion. He'll never play football again or tramp over the moors. He'll never do any of the things he loved most.'

'Our boy will find a different way of living, you'll see.'

'Without a wife? Without children?'

'We don't know that for certain. Just because Judy didn't feel able to—'

'Horrible girl! What happened to *in sickness and in health?*'

'She couldn't do the *sickness* part, I suppose. But that's not to say there isn't another girl who'll see the best in our boy.'

They reached the entrance hall and passed through the doors to the outside world – a changed world for their son. Alice felt a rush of sympathy for dour Jake Turner. His misery clearly extended beyond the loss of his legs.

Tom the porter caught Alice's eye. They'd become friends. 'There'll be many more families like that before this war's over,' he predicted.

'I'd like to think you're wrong, Tom.'

'But you know I'm right. More's the pity.'

Alice thought about Jake on the way home. It must be grim to have to listen to Stevie's happy plans when his own had come to nothing. Not that Stevie was insensitive to Jake's feelings. Probably he knew nothing about them because Jake kept them to himself.

She thought about Private Matthews and his nightmares, too. Then she tried to achieve some perspective on her own situation. Counting her blessings was nothing new for Alice. She'd been doing it all her life.

Her injury had hit her hard, but even though her hand would never be as good as new, it was still of some use and the scars would improve over time. More importantly, she could go wherever she liked, whenever she liked. All things considered, there were far worse misfortunes than an injured hand.

Of course, like Jake Turner, Alice was also nursing a bruised heart, but it wasn't because Daniel had let her down. On the contrary, he was trying to look after her. It was just her bad luck that she felt more for him than he felt for her.

Pictures of him snapped through her mind like photographs. His fingers running through that thick, dark hair; his smiles and laughter; his kindness to her father and Kate . . . The memories set up a physical ache inside Alice's heart. She *hurt*.

He'd called on her for a third time that morning. 'Who knows how long it'll be before I can visit again?' he'd said.

They'd gone for a walk but she'd made sure he hadn't got close enough to touch her, even accidentally. And when she'd thought he might link his arm with hers she'd darted off to inspect the snowdrops that were peeping out of hedgerows like hesitant fairies.

He'd stayed for a cup of tea before leaving. 'Alice,' he'd begun, reaching a hand towards her.

Pretending not to see it, she'd jumped up, saying, 'You must say goodbye to my father.'

She'd fetched him from his study and her father had stood in the kitchen, his hair dishevelled and his glasses halfway down his nose. 'Good luck,' he'd said, shaking Daniel's hand. 'Plenty of men came through the first war so don't feel despondent.'

'Thank you, sir.'

Had Daniel wished for a chance to be alone with her? Alice had avoided catching his eye, and when her father made to return to his study, she'd linked his arm to anchor him to her side instead.

'I hope you'll write?' Daniel had said.

'If that's what you'd like.' Alice had tried to speak casually.

'I would,' he'd told her firmly, looking as though

he wanted to say more but was held back by the presence of her father.

Which was exactly what Alice had intended. She'd tugged her father to the door and they'd both stood waving until Daniel had driven off.

Afterwards, her father had returned to his study and Alice had gone up to her room, feeling drained. It had taken all of her self-control to stop herself from clutching Daniel close to savour the touch, the warmth and the clean, fresh scent of him. It was good that she'd resisted, but she'd still cried herself into exhaustion.

Should she write to Daniel as he'd asked? Alice was torn. A clean break was doubtless wisest. But the war was changing things. Unable to bear the suspense of not knowing how it was affecting him, she decided on a compromise. If Daniel wrote to her, then she'd write back, but her letters would make it clear that she was getting on with her busy life so had no need of rescue. In time, Daniel might understand that, and her bruised heart might heal.

'Get back here now!'

The voice jolted Alice out of her memories. It was a female voice, raised high in irritation, but Alice couldn't see the owner, owing to a curve in the lane. With her gaze focused ahead, Alice was taken by surprise when a boy suddenly burst out of the trees beside her. 'Whoa!' she said as they collided.

Hands on his shoulders, she steadied him. He was about seven or so, dark-haired and dark-eyed, and he looked more than a little wary of her. 'It's all right,' she assured him. 'No harm done.'

'Samuel! Come here this minute!'

A woman had rounded the bend. Tall, straight and slender, her dark hair was drawn off her face with immaculate neatness under a stylish hat. Her dark green coat was beautifully tailored and her feet were shod in smart shoes with heels that were remarkably high considering the icy weather. With an elegant matching handbag, she looked as though she should be gracing Mayfair or another of London's more fashionable areas instead of rural Churchwood where practical clothes and sturdy footwear were the norm.

'Come here, Samuel,' she repeated. 'Stop bothering the lady.'

'I've no objection to children behaving like children,' Alice assured her, smiling. 'Where can children run about if not in the woods?'

'Hmm.'

It appeared that this smart woman *did* find children's behaviour objectionable. Older than Alice by several years, she drew on a cigarette with a desperate air as though her nerves were coiled tightly enough to snap. Two other children crept out of the woods and all three stood watching Alice with solemn, distrustful eyes.

'Good day to you,' the woman said pointedly – a none-too-subtle hint to Alice to move on.

Alice did so, smiling at the children as she passed. They didn't smile back.

Three children were clearly a handful but there was something about their serious faces that touched Alice and brought a sharp stab of pain as she thought of the children she'd never have with Daniel. Would she ever have children with anyone? It was impossible to imagine loving another man.

Closing off the thought, she spent the rest of the

walk with her mind on her book appeal and the pleasure the books would bring to the patients.

Only a hedgerow separated the lane from Naomi Harrington's Foxfield. At this time of year the trees and bushes were skeletal and, glancing through them, Alice saw Mrs Harrington walking up her drive. Alice waved but no answering wave came. Perhaps Mrs Harrington hadn't seen her.

It was the same at church on Sunday morning. Alice tried to catch Mrs Harrington's eye to send her a smile but Mrs Harrington was always looking elsewhere. Alice was glad she'd decided to attend the next first-aid class. Hopefully, it would put her mind at rest.

It didn't. Alice arrived early, hoping to snatch a few words with Mrs Harrington about the weather or anything at all so she could test the older woman's manner, but several others arrived early, too. 'Come in, ladies. Please take seats so we can begin promptly,' Mrs Harrington called, her gaze merely skating over them before turning to welcome Dr Phillips.

As soon as the tea break was announced Alice moved swiftly towards her quarry only for Mrs Harrington to race along the opposite side of the room calling, 'I'd like a word, Mrs Hutchings!'

After Mrs Hutchings she spent a moment with Mrs Roberts and then returned to Dr Phillips as Marjorie Plym carried tea to them. Frustrated again, Alice joined the queue for tea.

'How have you been, dear?' Janet Collins asked, and Alice remained with her and Betty for the remainder of the break.

'I saw your poster asking for books for them poor

devils up at the hospital,' Betty said, lowering her voice.

'The patients need them badly.'

'I'm afraid I haven't any books to give, not being much of a reader. I enjoy good stories as much as anyone, but I like to hear them read over the wireless while I get on with my knitting. Anyway, I just want you to know the reason I can't help is because I've no books. It isn't for any other reason.' She stiffened suddenly. 'Oh, hello, Miss Plym.'

'Pardon me for interrupting. I just want to tell Miss Lovell that I saw her young man calling on her and I so admire the fact that he's serving his country. I did see him in uniform, didn't I?'

'Our visitor was indeed wearing a uniform but he isn't my young man. He's the son of an old neighbour of my father's.'

Miss Plym nodded but clearly preferred her romantic interpretation; it made for better-quality gossip. Doubtless it would soon be all over Churchwood that Alice had a young man.

'We need to press on, ladies,' Mrs Harrington called.

The class followed the same pattern as before – a talk before the break and practical exercises afterwards. 'You stick with me,' Janet told Alice as they divided into groups. 'Betty has to move to another group. Her Highness thinks we talk too much if we're together.'

Alice was glad to have kind Janet at her side as they attempted to splint broken legs. Being teamed with two other women, Alice was able to play the patient three times.

'You haven't had your go at splinting,' one woman said as the clock ticked towards the end of the session.

'She doesn't need it,' Janet answered swiftly. 'Being a doctor's daughter, she could probably run these classes for us. Isn't that right, Alice?'

She winked as she spoke. How kind she was.

Mrs Harrington and Dr Phillips went from group to group, inspecting the handiwork and adding guidance where necessary, but spent barely a minute with Alice's group. 'Very nice, Mrs Palfrey,' Dr Phillips said, after a brief inspection of Alice's splinted leg, then Mrs Harrington ushered him onwards without meeting Alice's eye.

When the class ended Alice said some goodbyes then lingered until only Mrs Harrington, Dr Phillips and Miss Plym remained.

'You're joining us for lunch?' Mrs Harrington asked Dr Phillips as Alice approached. 'I have some rather fine sherry.'

'A glass of sherry will be most welcome.'

Alice coughed. 'I'm sorry to intrude but I'd like to thank you for the class.' She included both Mrs Harrington and Dr Phillips in the thanks.

'You see, Doctor?' Mrs Harrington said, still without looking at Alice. 'All our ladies appreciate your classes. Don't forget the bandages, Marjorie!' She walked away as though to ensure Miss Plym followed instructions.

Alice was left with nothing to do except go home. She was in no doubt now that she'd caused offence and, if she wanted to put things right, she'd have to confront Churchwood's Queen Bee in her own hive.

CHAPTER THIRTEEN

Naomi

Naomi was in the small sitting room when the doorbell rang. She raised her head from her notes to look out of the window but was too late to see who'd approached. Not Marjorie, she hoped. Marjorie was a dear friend but two hours of her silliness over lunch with Dr Phillips had been quite enough for one day.

Especially this day. Alexander had telephoned earlier to say he'd be staying in London again. 'I'll have to stay in town all week if I can't get more petrol coupons, of course,' he'd said.

Was it really inevitable? Churchwood might not have a railway station but other husbands took buses or rode bicycles to train stations in nearby towns. It was hard to picture someone as dignified as Alexander riding a bicycle or sitting on a public bus but people had to be flexible in wartime and surely a little discomfort was a small price for a man to pay in order to spend more time at home with his wife?

Suki's footsteps sounded in the hall as she went to answer the door. Naomi strained to pick up the visitor's voice but all she could hear was an indistinct murmur. Then Suki knocked on Naomi's door and opened it. 'Miss Lovell to see you, madam.'

Naomi hadn't expected this. She got to her feet,

annoyed at herself for feeling flustered and unprepared. Alice was no more than a girl, after all, while Naomi was a woman of maturity and standing. Besides, Naomi thought she'd done rather a good job of showing she was far too busy to concern herself with the unpleasantness of two young women.

Perhaps Alice was here about something else.

'Thank you for seeing me,' she said as she entered.

As always, Naomi was struck by the girl's quiet self-possession and tried to meet it with some poise of her own. 'Come in, Miss Lovell. You'll take a cup of tea?'

'I don't want to be any trouble.'

'No trouble, I assure you.' Naomi let out a little laugh to suggest it would take more than an unexpected visitor to discompose the mistress of Foxfield. 'Tea, please, Suki.'

'Yes, madam.'

'I hope you enjoyed the first-aid class this morning,' Naomi continued, eager to take control. 'We should always be open to learning, no matter how much we think we know.'

'Indeed. I hoped to have a private word with you at the class but it wasn't to be, so here I am.' Alice became serious. 'I'm afraid I offended you when you offered to help with the book appeal.'

'Offended me?' Naomi laughed again but she could feel her face heating up. How direct this girl was. 'Goodness me, no. I've barely given your little venture another thought. I've always been a busy woman, Miss Lovell, and with a war on I'm busier than ever. The first-aid classes, collecting for Red Cross parcels . . .'

'It's been preying on my mind that you might have thought me ungrateful. Even rude.'

'*You* weren't rude, Miss Lovell.' Still smarting from the memory, Naomi couldn't resist making a dig at the Fletcher creature.

'You're referring to Kate,' Alice guessed. 'She's worried, too. She would have come here today but she had to work on the farm.'

'How convenient.'

Alice sprang to her friend's defence. 'It's true. Kate struggles to get any time away from her work. And it's farm work that puts food on our tables. You may not see much to admire in Kate, Mrs Harrington, but I see some excellent qualities.'

'She's lucky to have you as her champion.'

'I'm lucky to have her as my friend. I wonder if you've ever stopped to think of what life must be like for Kate on Brimbles Farm?'

Naomi bridled at that. It had been bad enough hearing Bert Makepiece speak out of turn. If she hadn't felt so out of sorts that day she'd have given him a dressing-down. To be expected to listen to a lecture from this slip of a girl . . . in Naomi's own home, too . . . It was unacceptable.

Alice's mouth suddenly twisted and humour flared in her eyes, lighting up her pretty face. 'Now you definitely think I'm being rude.'

There was something honest and fearless about this girl. She must have suffered in life – like Naomi she'd lost her mother and there was the injury to her hand, too – yet she bore her misfortunes with dignity.

'I'm sorry,' Alice said. 'I've no wish to upset you, but I do wish you'd consider Kate's position with more . . .'

What? Naomi suspected she'd been about to add

123

the word *kindness* but that would imply that Naomi was *un*kind.

'Open-mindedness,' Alice finished. 'With imagination, too. Kate didn't ask to be born a Fletcher. She didn't ask for a father who keeps her so short of money she hasn't any clothes that didn't belong to her brothers first. She didn't ask for brothers who go around swearing and fighting.'

'But she does choose how she conducts herself,' Naomi pointed out, feeling pleased by her answer though it didn't knock Alice off balance.

'Kate has spirit, I'll grant you. Imagine you had a family that embarrassed you and brought shame on you.'

Naomi's imagination didn't have to work hard to summon Cedric Tuggs to mind. How she'd squirmed when out and about in his company! Even everyday visits to shops or restaurants had been fraught with mortification. 'We'll have the best wine you've got and don't try to pass off any old rubbish as the best,' was typical of the things he'd say. 'No one gets one over on Cedric Tuggs.'

Even now the memories made her shudder. Yet Naomi's father had loved her. She'd never had cause to doubt that. He'd showered her with gifts and compliments and told her she was the belle of every ball, though nothing could have been further from the truth. Was Kate Fletcher loved by her family? It sounded doubtful.

'Kate puts on an act of not caring what people think of her but I'm sure she cares deeply,' Alice continued. 'Many people put on acts in front of others to hide their true feelings.'

A picture of Bert Makepiece's face popped into Naomi's mind. 'You'd know all about putting on acts in front of folk, Mrs H.,' she imagined him saying. 'Isn't that what you're doing right this minute, pretending you didn't care how the young 'uns treated you?'

Alice hadn't finished yet. 'I think it's to Kate's credit that she hasn't let her spirit be broken.'

As a girl, Naomi's spirit had been crushed. She'd dreaded going out with Cedric and she'd hidden away from people as much as possible, in cloakrooms, behind pillars, in back rows and even – the time she'd met Alexander – in a hostess's garden. Alexander had rescued her. It was just a pity he was so busy with his work.

Naomi returned her thoughts to the present. 'You defend your friend passionately, Miss Lovell, but I'm sure you'll allow others to have their own opinions.'

She'd intended it as neither defeat nor challenge, but Alice looked disappointed in her. Naomi didn't understand why that should matter but it did. Still, there was nothing she could do to remedy the situation.

'Where's our tea, I wonder?' she said, wishing she hadn't invited Alice to stay, if it meant spending more time under the cloud of her disapproval. 'Ah, here's Suki.'

Naomi was glad to be able to fuss over the tea things while she thought of a new topic of conversation. She opened her mouth to comment on Dr Phillips only to fear that she might appear to be implying a criticism of Alice's father. She opened it again to talk about the Red Cross parcels only to fear that she might look as though she was trying to outdo Alice's book project. She certainly wasn't going to ask Alice about the young man Marjorie had apparently seen, though Naomi was curious about the sort of man who would attract this clever and self-possessed girl. She fell back on the staple of British conversation: the weather. From there it was an easy step to the forthcoming spring.

'It'll be nice to see new growth in gardens after the bareness of winter,' she said. 'There's usually a pretty display of daffodils at The Linnets.'

'They're beginning to poke up through the soil.'

'Primroses, too. Then there'll be bluebells and, towards summer, you should have roses.'

'I'm looking forward to seeing what's there,' Alice said, 'though I've made part of the rear garden into a vegetable patch.'

Suspecting that the Fletcher girl had had a hand in this, Naomi shifted the conversation on to rationing. 'Only petrol, sugar, butter and bacon so far, but what'll be next, I wonder?'

She felt drained when Alice got up to leave, though she hadn't lingered long.

'It was good of you to call,' Naomi said, aiming for a gracious tone.

'It felt the right thing to do.'

Still seeking to appear magnanimous, Naomi saw Alice to the door in person instead of ringing for Suki. They exchanged final pleasantries; then Naomi returned to the sitting room, sat down heavily and thought back over Alice's visit, especially the final look Alice had given her. It had been uncertain, as though the girl was unsure if she'd actually succeeded in clearing the air.

Had she? Naomi was willing to concede that Alice hadn't intended any offence in rejecting her offer of help. What was it Bert Makepiece had said? Something about it being natural for two young girls to want a project of their own. Perhaps he was right. Even so . . .

Was it the change of life that was making Naomi so sensitive? She felt hurt and humiliated and . . . well, worried. She'd worked hard to build her life in Churchwood and had believed herself to be respected and admired. But the foundations of that life appeared to be crumbling, leaving old certainties teetering on the edge. Alice Lovell, Kate Fletcher, Bert Makepiece . . . They'd made her feel like the old Naomi Tuggs again: awkward, unwanted, and fearing that people fawned over her only because of her wealth and not because they actually liked her.

Basil lumbered over and butted her fingers with his face. She stroked his neck the way she knew he liked. 'You're a true friend, Basil,' Naomi told him. 'Maybe my only real friend.'

After a moment her thoughts returned to Kate Fletcher. If the girl's life really was terribly tough, it was to her credit that she went about with her head held high. In her shoes – her men's boots, rather – Naomi was sure she'd have skulked away from public gaze. Perhaps courage was what Alice and Kate had in common. But did any of that excuse the Fletcher girl's insolence?

A wave of impatience swept over Naomi. She was growing maudlin and that was no way to deal with the change of life. She rang for Suki to clear the tea things; then she picked up the list of the items she'd collected for Red Cross parcels. Tinned pilchards, potted meats, toffees, soap . . . If the Red Cross didn't want them all, the poor certainly would.

CHAPTER FOURTEEN

Kate

Vinnie was outraged. 'What do you mean, they didn't have any Woodbines?'

'I mean they're out of stock. In case you hadn't noticed, there's a war on and supplies are being disrupted.' She rolled her eyes to signal that he was an idiot. Then she paused before adding, 'They expect more supplies by tomorrow, so I'll go back then. I'll collect those mended buckets at the same time.'

'Got enough ciggies to tide you over?' Ernie asked Vinnie.

'I suppose so.'

With that, the conversation ended. Kate moved to the window and stared out at the farmyard, breathing deeply to steady her fast-beating heart.

The grocer had plenty of Woodbines but tomorrow was Saturday and she needed an excuse to leave the farm and transport the books that – with luck – would be donated to Alice. She also needed a reason for taking the pony and trap so she'd delayed collecting the buckets from the blacksmith, too. So far so good. Kate would simply have to hope that none of the Fletcher men wandered into the grocer's and saw cigarettes aplenty.

What would she say if that happened? Certainly not

the truth. The family would put an end to her friendship with Alice the moment they heard of it. No, she'd say she'd taken a leaf out of Vinnie's book and pretended there were no cigarettes just to spite him. After all, he'd spilt tea over a pile of shirts she'd washed and folded yesterday. He was due some retaliation.

The Fletcher men returned to work and Kate leapt into action, washing cups and wiping the table. The floor was covered in mud but she'd already swept it twice that day and she had something more important in mind – sneaking out to see Alice for the first time in several days. Shrugging into her jacket, she returned to the window to check that no one was in the farmyard; then she slipped through the kitchen door, glancing this way and that in case Ernie or one of her brothers appeared.

As usual when visiting Alice, she avoided the main track down to the lane and wove her way through the orchard, hoping the trees might give her some cover. She reached the lane and strode out briskly. It was a pity Alice didn't live nearer; even at a fast pace it took Kate more than fifteen minutes to walk there and the same time to walk back.

She reached the lake, then the back of the Foxfield gardens, and her conscience prickled again. Naomi Harrington had deserved to be taken down a peg or two but actually upsetting her was feeling like a step too far. Kate might not like Naomi Harrington, but she liked herself even less for being unkind. It had brought her down to Vinnie's level.

It had also made Alice worry. 'I'm going to try to clear the air,' Alice had announced. 'I'll visit her, but I'm not expecting you to come with me.'

129

'If anyone should clear the air with her, it's me,' Kate said. 'I'm the one who upset her. I don't suppose she'll let me into the house, but I can try talking to her at her door.'

'You have to work. I'll visit on behalf of both of us.'

Kate hadn't felt happy about leaving her friend with the responsibility for what was likely to be an uncomfortable conversation but at least Alice would be given a chance to speak. Kate might be ordered off Harrington property before she'd opened her mouth.

Now Kate was eager to hear how Alice had got on. Not wanting to disturb the doctor or tread mud through the house, Kate had got into the habit of entering The Linnets by the garden gate on Brimbles Lane. Alice wasn't outside so Kate knocked on the kitchen door. When Alice answered, Kate scanned her face anxiously. She saw no sign of tears but Alice's smile was weary, which suggested . . . what, exactly?

'Come in,' Alice invited.

Kate hesitated. It had rained and her boots were even muddier than usual. But she didn't want Alice to have to come out into the cold. Kate stepped inside but remained near the door. 'Did Mrs Harrington see you?'

'She wasn't given a choice – her maid let me in. I explained that we hadn't intended to cause offence and Mrs Harrington told me she'd been far too busy to give us another thought.'

'You didn't believe her?'

'No, but I hope we can at least be polite to each other when our paths cross now.'

'If she's polite to me, it'll be for the first time.' Bitterness rose up in Kate but she pushed it down again. 'It was brave of you to see the dragon in her lair.'

130

'Not brave. Just the right thing to do.'

Even doing the right thing took courage.

Kate changed the subject. 'Any news on the chickens?'

'Mr Makepiece should have some for me soon. Can you stay for a while?'

'Not today. I need to get the vegetables ready for tonight's stew. I wanted to do it earlier but got called out to mend our own chicken coop.'

'Can you still help me with the books tomorrow?'

'I have a plan for taking the pony and trap out, but I can't promise a particular time. You finish collecting books at one, don't you?'

'That's the advertised time.'

'I'll get there as close to one as I can. I've brought *Little Women* back.' Kate took it from the inside pocket of her jacket. 'It was as good as you said, though I have to admit to crying when Beth died.'

'Me too,' Alice said. 'I've another book for you here.' It was *Jane Eyre*. 'Jane has some of your qualities and the story is all about triumph over adversity.'

'Thank you.' Simple, everyday words but Alice's books – and even more her friendship – were like the sun bursting through on Kate's life. 'Good luck tomorrow.'

'I just hope people realize the difference books will make to the patients and give generously.'

Kate let herself out through the garden gate. The sight of Mrs Harrington and her bulldog in the garden of Foxfield pulled her up momentarily. Then, to her surprise, Mrs Harrington acknowledged Kate with a nod. At least it looked like a nod. From this distance – and with the bony sticks of trees and bushes in the way – it was impossible to be sure she hadn't just moved her head to look at something. Kate nodded back but went on her way, thinking she'd need more evidence than a dipped head to believe that miracles were happening in Churchwood. Still, if anyone could bring them about it was Alice.

'If any of you want anything from the village, tell me now because I'm only going once,' Kate said the following morning, pitching her voice at truculent to give the impression that she'd rather not go to the village at all.

She was desperate to go, of course, but the merest sniff of her real intention would find her kept on the farm.

When no one bothered to reply she made a disgusted sound. Then, hiding her triumph under a sigh, she put on her jacket and left the farmhouse kitchen to harness Pete to the cart. She collected the mended buckets from the blacksmith, handing over the money Ernie had given her – the exact money so she couldn't be tempted to siphon any off for her own use – and continued to the grocer's for Vinnie's Woodbines.

A woman was coming out as Kate reached the door. Mrs Giddins, or was it Gubbins? Seeing Kate, she shrank away in distaste but Kate managed to catch the door before it triggered the bell. No one appeared to notice her walk in.

'No, I'm not giving any books,' Marjorie Plym was saying to a group of other women. 'Naomi says we have our own projects to keep us busy so we should leave book collecting to Miss Lovell. It isn't as though

Miss Lovell seems to appreciate Churchwood society, is it? Have you heard that she allows that awful Fletcher girl to visit? Yes, straight from the farm in all her dirt.'

One of the women spotted Kate and gasped.

Oblivious, Miss Plym continued: 'Miss Lovell may look respectable, but clearly she—'

Someone elbowed Miss Plym in the ribs.

She began to protest but then she too saw Kate. 'Oh!' she said, turning a far from fetching shade of puce before starting to simper. 'I didn't mean—'

'Yes, you did.' Kate strode up to the counter, scattering the women as she went. 'You won't mind if I jump to the head of the queue? Seeing as I've come straight from the farm in all my dirt, as you so kindly described it.'

'Well, I—'

'A pack of Woodbines, please.' Kate slapped Vinnie's money down on the countertop; then she snatched up the cigarettes and turned to face the women. 'Alice Lovell is worth more than you nasty lot put together.'

With that, she left the shop. Alice was a good person who'd befriended Kate out of kindness and who was trying to make the world a little bit better for men who were suffering in the cause of keeping Churchwood safe. Surely there were some decent people in Churchwood who'd understand that and support her book appeal?

Racked with guilt at having brought troubles down on Alice, Kate leapt into the cart and urged Pete to quicken as they headed for the Sunday School Hall.

CHAPTER FIFTEEN

Naomi

Naomi was taking a turn around her garden with Basil that afternoon when she saw Bert Makepiece's shabby truck draw up outside The Linnets. She stepped behind a tree and watched as he swung out of the cab and shuffled to the back of the truck to take out . . . chickens! Three of them, by the look of it. So, Alice Lovell was going to keep hens. Why not? It made sense with a war on.

He passed through the side gate into the Lovells' garden and Naomi stepped away from the tree to see how the first daffodils were coming along. When she heard the Lovells' gate open again she turned her back so she could pretend to be unaware of Bert Makepiece's presence.

Unfortunately, Basil had other ideas and trotted off towards the hedgerow that bordered Brimbles Lane. Hastening after him, she realized Bert Makepiece was standing just behind one of the shorter bushes as though waiting for her. She nodded in what she considered to be a gracious acknowledgement of his existence – more than he deserved after the over-familiar way he'd spoken to her the last time they'd met – but he continued to stand there.

What did the man want now? Naomi decided she

wouldn't let him take the upper hand this time. She was feeling much stronger in herself today. After all, she'd behaved with dignity towards Alice Lovell. She'd nodded at the Fletcher creature, too. And tonight she was hosting a dinner party at Foxfield: pleasant guests, excellent wines, the best food that could be procured in wartime without resort to the black market of which Naomi disapproved vehemently, and – best of all – Alexander's company.

She'd been letting the winter blues paint her marriage with a touch of wistfulness recently. A shared evening together with everything carefully chosen to gratify him would be just the tonic they needed. After all, Alexander had enjoyed dinner parties in the early years of their marriage. They'd brought out his charm and made her feel more appreciated by him. But he worked hard – relentlessly hard – and spent many an evening and weekend entertaining clients so it was no wonder he'd grown irritable over the years. Tonight there'd be no clients present so he'd be able to relax in the company of guests who shared his interests. And in enjoying the evening, he'd be reminded of how he could enjoy Naomi's company, too.

'You're looking pleased with yourself today, Mrs H.,' Bert said.

What had happened to *Good afternoon, Mrs Harrington*?

'I'm well, thank you.'

'That would be the sort of well that means happy, would it?'

'Certainly.'

He nodded, but it didn't look to be a satisfied nod. It looked thoughtful and almost . . . disappointed.

Annoyance swept over her. Naomi had tried hard to build herself back up and here was Bert Makepiece – no more than a casual acquaintance who didn't even move in her circle – making her doubt herself again. She wanted to bid him good day and walk away with her head held high before he could reduce her mood to crumbs, but she couldn't help it. She had to ask . . .

'Is there any reason I shouldn't be happy?'

'Well, now, I'd say that depends on the type of person you are, Mrs H. Me, I wouldn't be happy after wrecking a young 'un's hopes of helping men who've served their country with honour. But we're all different, aren't we?'

'I've no idea what you're talking about.'

'Young Alice.' He gestured back at The Linnets. 'You told folk to steer clear of her book collecting.'

'I did no such thing!'

'Maybe not directly. But through your lapdog . . .'

Naomi was confused. Her dog was Basil, a bulldog. He couldn't possibly—

Ah. 'What's Marjorie been saying?'

'She's been keeping herself busy telling folk you don't approve of Miss Lovell and her book collecting.'

'I simply told her we shouldn't interfere! Or words to that effect.'

'It's *how* we say words that gets their true meaning across.'

Naomi's conscience nudged her. Shoved her almost off her feet, in fact. When she'd spoken to Marjorie, her pride had been smarting and she'd been hurting, too. Was it all that surprising that Marjorie – never a clever woman – would have taken those feelings for disapproval, especially as Naomi had tried to hide them behind stiff indifference?

'I'll have you know I actually donated some books to Miss Lovell,' Naomi said, trying to fight back. She'd given the books to Suki to take over to The Linnets.

'I saw 'em. Five books, was it? Maybe six? Very welcome, I'm sure. But the young 'un needs a lot more books than that. She needs all of Churchwood behind her.'

'I'm not all of Churchwood, Mr Makepiece. But I'll have a word with Marjorie to correct any misunderstanding. Now you must excuse me. We have guests coming for dinner and I need to prepare. Good day to you.'

Naomi walked away without looking back, though she felt he was watching her – and judging her – for all the time it took her to reach the house. She went into the dining room to check the arrangement of the table but mostly to have a moment to herself so she could recover her happier mood.

Suki came in. 'Sorry, madam, I didn't realize you were here.'

'I thought I'd check the flowers.' Naomi moved the central arrangement of purple cyclamen, ivy and evergreens a half-inch to the right. 'It's a pity there isn't much of a choice of flowers at this time of year but these cyclamen look well enough.'

'Very pretty, madam.'

Naomi could sense little Suki watching her with concern. 'You've made a good job of the table, Suki. I think I'll have a short rest before I get ready.'

'Shall I bring you some tea, madam?'

'That would be kind.'

Naomi went out to the hall and paused by the door to Alexander's study. Hearing nothing, she headed up the wide, curving staircase to her room. It was an impressively large room with heavy brocade curtains at the window, a Persian carpet underfoot, magnificent walnut wardrobes and dressing table, and a bed bearing a heavy silk-covered eiderdown.

Naomi stared at the bed and felt another pang of wistfulness. It had been considerate of Alexander to tell her he'd sleep in a spare room to avoid disturbing her when he worked into the small hours, but those nights had gradually become so frequent that he hadn't set foot inside this room for many years. Still, it didn't mean they were actually unhappy together and couldn't grow closer.

Naomi took off her shoes and got on to the bed, plumping up the pillows to support her back. She reached for her book, a romance she'd looked out the morning she'd been choosing books to donate to Alice Lovell. Naomi enjoyed romances but they tended to leave her feeling oddly sad, so she'd avoided them in recent years. This morning she'd thought she'd try one again. She turned to the beginning but her concentration wandered before she'd read the first paragraph.

She drank the tea Suki brought then sat back to rest her eyes only to find her conversation with Bert Makepiece gnawing at her peace of mind. After a while she heard Alexander come upstairs, his footsteps brisk. Naomi sat forward, wondering if he'd look in on her, but he walked on to what had once been a spare room but was now known as Mr Harrington's room.

Marjorie would be coming tonight, of course, but Naomi would seat her as far from Alexander as possible because he found her irritating. Naomi couldn't blame him. Marjorie was a silly woman with an even sillier laugh, but while Naomi could see Marjorie's redeeming qualities, Alexander couldn't see past the traits that annoyed him. He had no patience with the vicar's fawning ways either, so she'd seat Septimus Barnes away from him too. Her other guests would entertain Alexander: the Carmichaels, who had a country house near St Albans, and the Fanshawes, who lived in a village six or seven miles from Churchwood. Both Mr Carmichael and Mr Fanshawe worked in finance in London, and both were golfers like Alexander. Surely he'd find enjoyment in their company?

Naomi bathed and took care with her appearance as she dressed for the evening. Her new corset had arrived and tonight she was to wear it for the first time. It had come in a beautiful pale pink box with the name 'The House of Madame Elodie' running across it in swirling letters. A pale pink ribbon held the box closed. Naomi untied it and parted the tissue paper inside to reveal the corset itself.

The Harmony corset had been available in pink, white or peach. She'd opted for peach, thinking that pink was more suited to younger women while white was no different to what she already had. *Transform your silhouette*, the advertisement had promised, so Naomi set to work to do just that, hoping Alexander might notice and feel a revival of interest in her. Harmony was a step-in corset that pulled up instead of fastening around the body with hooks and eyes, but she'd barely got it above her ankles before she suspected she had an insurmountable challenge on her hands.

She huffed and puffed, tugged and heaved, undoing the fresh feeling her bath had given her. After several minutes she'd got the corset up to her knees but already it was crushing her thighs together. She persevered for a while longer but it was hopeless and Naomi feared that, even if she got the corset into position, there was every danger of being unable to get out of it, especially as it would be squashing the breath from her. Disappointed, she peeled it off again – still no easy feat – and wrapped it back in the tissue paper ready to return it to the House of Madame Elodie and reclaim the guinea she'd paid.

She fastened on one of her old corsets, finished dressing and looked in the mirror. There was no transformation of her silhouette. Naomi looked as stocky and bulldoggish as ever.

But her dress was an attractive shade of blue velvet, her hair was neat in its chignon and the pearls she wore around her neck were rather fine. Naomi had bought them herself after trading in two of the gaudier pieces her father had bought.

'What beautiful pearls!' Marjorie had once declared. 'A gift from Mr Harrington?'

Naomi had pretended she hadn't heard the question. There was no harm in letting Churchwood think that Alexander spoiled his wife.

Naomi went downstairs early, hoping Alexander would join her for a cocktail before the guests appeared, but he didn't come down until the door knocker announced the first arrivals. He looked bad-tempered but his face cleared as soon as the guests were shown in. 'Delighted you could come,' he said, shaking hands with Mr Carmichael, then saying something charming to Mrs Carmichael that had her silvery laughter tinkling around the room.

Marjorie arrived next, her faded green 'dining out' dress drooping as always. Naomi steered her to the other side of the drawing room. Should she mention Alice Lovell's book appeal? Not now. Marjorie might cry if she thought she was being criticized and Alexander would be more irritated with her than ever. Naomi kept Marjorie by her side until Septimus Barnes was announced then handed her over to the vicar.

Alexander gave every sign of being delighted with the Carmichaels and Fanshawes, and even managed to bid Marjorie and Septimus a gracious farewell when the party broke up.

'What a lovely evening,' Naomi said. 'I hope Giles Carmichael amused you? Roger Fanshawe too.'

'Giles Carmichael is a bore and Roger Fanshawe is a fool,' Alexander snapped, dropping his charm like an actor who'd walked offstage after performing to an audience he despised.

'But the golfing conversation . . .'

'Tedious,' he said, heading for the door. 'I'm leaving for London early in the morning. I won't disturb you.'

CHAPTER SIXTEEN

Alice

Alice needed to think, and, hoping a walk might help, she wrapped up warmly against the winter chill and headed along the lane to the lake.

Churchwood had disappointed her. In a small village like this, it was natural that one forceful person could make a big impression on everyone else – especially if she happened to be the village's chief organizer and owned the house to which social invitations were coveted – but Alice had hoped the residents of Churchwood would have proven to be stronger-willed than that.

Why couldn't they be more like Kate? Or Bert Makepiece, Janet Collins and Betty Oldroyd? What was it Betty had said when she'd explained why she wouldn't be donating books? Something about the reason being lack of books rather than anything else. Clearly, the *anything else* had been Naomi Harrington.

Alice had suspected that she hadn't quite cleared the air between them, but for Mrs Harrington to sabotage a project that would help men who'd been injured in the service of their country was . . . well, it was appalling.

Kate had been furious when, dark eyes flashing, she'd burst into the Sunday School Hall where Alice had been waiting for book donations. 'So much for worrying about that woman's feelings! Naomi Harrington doesn't have any feelings. Apart from spite and pride.'

She'd reported on Marjorie Plym's conversation in the grocer's shop.

'That explains why I've been sitting here all by myself,' Alice had said.

'Has no one given books?'

'Three people called in. An old gentleman gave these two.'

Kate had grimaced at the sight of stained covers and brown-edged pages, some of which had come loose.

'I'm sure he meant well,' Alice had said. 'A woman brought in this book, which is just the sort of thing I need.' It was an Agatha Christie crime story. 'And Mr Makepiece brought in some old seed catalogues.'

'Seed catalogues?' Kate had been unimpressed.

'He thought some patients could find them soothing, and actually, I think he's right. Men who like gardening might enjoy thinking about what they can plant in their gardens or allotments once they're home.'

'I suppose so. But that's all you've got?'

'Better than nothing.' Still, a huge disappointment.

'What will you do next?' Kate had asked then. 'What *can* you do?'

'I don't know yet. But I'm not giving up.'

'Good for you.'

'I'm sorry I dragged you away from the farm unnecessarily. I don't need to go to Stratton House today with so few books to carry. I can take them next time I visit.'

'At least let me take you home.'

Kate had dropped Alice at the cottage. 'There's a box on your doorstep,' she'd pointed out.

Alice had found five books inside, all of which would be welcome at the hospital.

'Someone was too afraid of incurring Mrs Harrington's wrath to donate them in public, I suppose,' Kate had surmised, before heading back to the farm.

Bert Makepiece had shaken his head when he'd called with Alice's chickens and heard about the failure of the appeal. 'It's a crying shame, young Alice, but I hope you won't give up.'

'I won't. Now, please introduce me to these feathery ladies.'

The chickens didn't have names, so Alice had decided on Audrey, Constance and Louisa for no reason other than that the names suited them, Audrey being tall and thin, Constance being matronly and Louisa being rather pretty.

Bert had given her advice on looking after them; then he departed, saying, 'Any problems, you know where to find me.'

Reaching the lake now, Alice noticed the woman in the blue coat whom she'd startled the other day. But she was on the far bank on this occasion and unlikely to be disturbed by the presence of another so Alice turned her thoughts back to books. Having criticized Mrs Harrington for letting wounded pride sabotage the book appeal, Alice was determined that she wouldn't let her own pride get in the way of helping the patients. Should she admit defeat and ask Mrs Harrington to chair a committee, after all?

No, it was too late for that. Having already spoken badly of the project, Mrs Harrington could hardly reverse her opinion without making it obvious that her motive in sabotaging the appeal had been to manipulate her way into taking it over.

Alice would have to find more books herself, but she had no ideas as to how.

Instead, she took out the letter she'd received from Daniel the previous morning and had read numerous times already.

Dear Alice,

It was wonderful to see you and terribly hard to have to leave but duty called. It was good to meet Kate, too. She seems a useful young woman. Terrific with a hammer! It's such a relief to me to know you've found a friend.

I had a safe but choppy journey across the Channel. The accommodation here isn't plush but it isn't much worse than a dormitory at school. The food is of a similar standard, too. Imagine soggy cabbage and gristly meat of uncertain origin and you'll get the idea. I'm with a decent set of men, though, and that's more important.

How are you? Still visiting the hospital? It must cheer the patients immensely to see you and hear you reading stories.

Have the chickens arrived? Is the vegetable patch thriving?

Sorry about all the questions but I'm eager to hear your news!

Do write soon, Alice. I'll be looking out for your reply. I want to hear what you're doing but I also

*want to know your feelings so please don't keep them
from me.*
Fond regards,
Daniel x

Her gaze lingered on the kiss he'd added and she couldn't suppress a sigh.

Alice had first met Daniel a little over two years ago. With Christmas approaching, she'd been queuing in a bookshop to pay for *In Search of the Aztecs*, a gift for her father, and feeling proud because she was paying for an expensive book out of her earnings. Unfortunately, a woman at the front of the queue was asking the sales assistant question after question, apparently oblivious to the queue building up behind her.

'Those Aztecs lived five hundred years ago,' someone said softly from just behind her shoulder. 'The way this queue is moving – or rather not moving – it'll be another five hundred years before anyone gets to read about them.'

Alice glanced round to see Daniel grinning at her. Not that she knew his name then. He was waiting to pay for a children's book: *The Story of Babar the Little Elephant*. She answered in the same spirit. 'The way this queue is moving – or rather not moving – the child you're buying *Babar* for will have outgrown it before he gets to see it.'

'He'll be an old man,' Daniel agreed, 'with stooped shoulders and a walking stick.'

'Not forgetting whiskers in his nose.'

At seventeen, Alice had never exchanged jokes and banter with a young man before. She'd received the occasional admiring look in the street, endured overfamiliar winks from the coalman's assistant, and even been invited to the cinema by a young man who'd brought his grandfather to see Dr Lovell, though she'd declined the invitation, pleading a need to keep a professional distance from patients and their families. The truth was that while the young man was pleasant, she'd felt no stir of romantic interest in him.

Daniel was different. She was too inexperienced to gauge if he was flirting or simply having fun, but he made her feel exhilarated and she was disappointed to part from him when she finally paid for her book and left the shop.

Several weeks passed, then one Saturday afternoon he fell into step beside her as she was walking home after fetching her father's shoes from the cobbler's. 'Was *In Search of the Aztecs* appreciated?' he asked, his dark eyes merry.

Pleasure burst inside her at the sight of him. He'd remembered the title of the book she'd bought, too. How flattering! 'My father was delighted with it. Was *Babar the Little Elephant* appreciated?'

'My nephew adored it, though it began to pall on me after he asked me to read it to him for the twelfth time.'

'A nephew must be fun.'

'I have two nephews so twice the fun – when they're not climbing on me and wiping sticky fingers in my hair. Yesterday, I went out with a half-eaten pear drop stuck to the back of my head. I wondered why people were giving me odd looks.'

Alice laughed then felt another pang of regret as she realized she'd already reached home.

'You live here?' he asked, looking up at the tall, white-painted terraced house.

'I do.' She wondered why he sounded surprised.

'My parents have moved into the house four doors along,' he explained.

It was Alice's turn to be surprised. Excited too – until she realized he hadn't said that he'd moved in with them. 'You don't live there?'

'I live near Oxford, though I'm about to go to America for six months.'

Six months? She forced a smile. 'That'll be an adventure.'

'I hope so, but it's a working trip rather than a holiday. I'm going to study American racing cars.'

At that moment her father had emerged for his daily walk and Daniel stepped away as though to save her from any awkwardness. 'It was nice to see you again.'

'Enjoy America.'

Alice went to greet her father but her thoughts were racing. Had Daniel walked away, too? Was he regretting that they hadn't talked for longer? Or was his mind already full of other things?

By the time she looked around again Daniel had gone.

Over the months that followed, Alice often glanced towards the house four doors along. The couple who lived there were both tall and trimly built like him. They were smart, too. One evening Alice saw them getting into a taxi, his mother in dark blue satin, white gloves and sparkling jewels while his father wore a dark evening suit and white silk scarf.

For all their smartness Alice formed an impression

of warm-hearted people. They linked arms when they walked, greeted people politely, were quick to thank taxi drivers and delivery men, and openly adored their grandchildren.

Alice had worked out that Daniel's sister was the mother of his nephews. She too was dark-haired and trim, and, judging from her frequent visits, presumably lived nearby. The boys were young – the eldest around three and the other a baby.

When six months had passed, Alice grew excited at the thought of seeing Daniel again, though she had constantly to remind herself that she'd only met him twice and had no reason to think he had any particular interest in her. Being four or five years older, he might have thought her entertaining enough to fill a few minutes of his time but too young to mean more than that.

Another two months passed and she saw no sign of him. She supposed he must have forgotten all about her and told herself she was a fool to feel so disappointed.

Then one Friday morning she answered the door expecting to see her father's next patient on the step. But the visitor wasn't Mrs Arbuthnot and her spoilt Pekingese dog Princess. It was Daniel. His dark eyes and smile caused Alice's heartbeat to skitter, and for a moment she was speechless.

'Good morning, Miss Lovell,' he said. 'I hope you remember me?'

Alice could only gape at him. Time apart hadn't exaggerated his handsomeness and the humour dancing in those brown eyes. Neither had it exaggerated the strength of the attraction she felt.

'You don't remember me? That's disappointing, but I hope—'

'I do remember you! I'm just surprised to see you.' Alice could feel heat in her cheeks. She hoped she wasn't blushing.

'My return was delayed, but now I'm here to say hello.'

He stood aside as Mrs Arbuthnot came up the steps carrying Princess. He bowed politely and said, 'Nice dog,' though after she'd moved inside he pulled a face at Alice because Princess was a snappy, bad-tempered thing.

'I can see you're busy and I don't want to get in your bad books by being in the way,' he said. 'Might you take pity on a newly returned traveller by joining me on a walk tomorrow? We could have lunch. Or tea. Or dinner, come to that.'

'Aren't your parents expecting you to spend time with them?'

'I timed my return badly. They already have engagements for tomorrow. So . . .?'

Princess barked. 'I have to go in,' Alice said, concerned that the yapping might disturb her father's current consultation.

'Tomorrow?'

'I'm working in the morning and I don't know what time I'll finish.'

Princess's barking grew louder.

'Go,' Daniel said. 'We'll continue this conversation another time.'

He turned and jogged down the steps, glancing back to wave before moving out of sight. Instantly, Alice wished she could call him back. She feared

150

she'd given the impression of not wanting to go out with him. But it was too late now.

'Good of you to bother with me,' Mrs Arbuthnot said when Alice came in. The awful Princess had stopped barking, presumably because her owner had stopped encouraging her now she had Alice's attention.

'Unexpected caller,' Alice explained.

'Is that what they call flirting these days?'

'I don't even know that man's name.' It was the truth even if it wasn't the whole truth. 'Please take a seat. I'm sure my father will be ready for you soon.'

'Humph.'

Alice sat at her desk to type a letter for her father. She arranged two sheets of notepaper with a carbon paper sandwiched between them to make a file copy then fed them into her typewriter and set to work. Within seconds she'd made several mistakes but continued typing anyway, not wishing to confirm Mrs Arbuthnot's impression of her as a silly, incompetent girl when she was usually so accurate. It was just that her mind was fizzing from Daniel's reappearance.

Had he flirted with her as Mrs Arbuthnot had suggested? Or had he simply been friendly? Flirting felt premature so Alice settled on friendliness, though she saw no reason why it couldn't lead to something more if both parties wished it.

Had she missed her chance, though? Perhaps it was only because Daniel had found himself at a loose end that he'd remembered Alice living only four doors away. Even now he might be telephoning some other acquaintance to arrange to fill his day.

On the other hand, he'd gone to the trouble of

discovering her name. Or had he? He might simply have deduced it from the brass plate beside the front door that advertised Dr Archibald Lovell's consulting rooms.

It was after seven in the evening when the last patient left and she went downstairs to the basement kitchen to prepare dinner, feeling despondent because Daniel hadn't called. When the doorbell sounded she raced upstairs to find him back on the doorstep.

'Now I'm probably interrupting your dinner,' he said.

'No, it's fine.' This time she'd give him no reason to think she might be indifferent.

'Dare I hope you'll take pity on me and come out with me tomorrow?'

'I'd like that.' Alice's cheeks warmed again. 'As long as you don't mind waiting until mid-afternoon? My father tends to overrun when he sees his patients. He's very thorough.'

'Would three o'clock be too early?'

'Three should be perfect.'

They took the bus to Hyde Park, Daniel explaining that he'd left his car in Oxford. It was a fine summer's day, and they circled the Serpentine, watching the children launching toy boats across the water, before heading for Kensington Gardens.

Daniel suddenly stopped in his tracks.

'What is it?' Alice hoped she hadn't bored him.

'It just occurred to me that you must have skipped lunch if you finished work shortly before we came out.'

'I didn't mind.' It had been worth the sacrifice to

spend time with the man she knew by now to be Daniel Irvine.

'I shan't be responsible for your collapse from hunger. Let's find a tea shop.'

They found the Copper Kettle amongst the Bayswater streets. 'Choose something substantial,' Daniel urged as they studied menu cards.

Alice ordered tomato soup and, pressed by Daniel, a slice of toasted cheese. 'I'll have toasted cheese, too, please,' he told the waitress, and Alice liked him for the friendly respect in his smile.

She didn't warm to people who regarded others as inferior, people like some of her father's patients, who appeared to think that even a modest amount of wealth entitled them to put on airs.

Conversation with Daniel had been easy so far as there'd always been something to observe in the ever-changing scenery. Sitting face to face across a small table was different. Alice felt self-conscious. 'Did you enjoy America?' she asked, eager to appear relaxed.

'Very much. I was lucky to be given the chance. The company I work for was set up by Harry Dellamore and Luke Huxtable. You might have heard of them.'

'I'm afraid I've never followed motor racing.'

'They were legends for their driving a few years ago. So was Harry's wife, Lydia. Anyway, Harry and Luke – Hux, as everyone calls him – are Americans and have a branch of their business in the States. I learned a lot from seeing what they're doing over there and watching cars perform on different tracks.'

'Were you working all of the time?'

'Not quite. I made sure I took in some sights – Niagara Falls, the Empire State Building, the White House down in Washington DC . . . I had a few days in Maine, too. Gorgeous scenery.'

'You weren't tempted to stay?'

'I love to travel, but I also love to come home. Besides, I don't want to find myself trapped thousands of miles away if the situation in Europe bursts open.'

'You think there'll be a war?'

'There's no doubt the situation in Germany is looking ugly but I'm not giving up hope that Hitler might have second thoughts. If he doesn't . . .' Daniel shook his head as though imagining the horror that would be unleashed but then he shrugged as if to dislodge those dark thoughts and changed to a brighter subject. 'I've told you about my job. Will you tell me about yours?'

Alice was happy to do so. 'It isn't as glamorous as motor racing,' she said when she'd finished, 'but I think it's important.'

'It is. Have you been doing it for long?'

Was he probing for her age? 'I've helped behind the scenes for years, but I've been working full-time since I left school at sixteen. I'm almost eighteen now.'

Her birthday was actually several months away but she hoped that *almost eighteen* sounded more mature and sophisticated than seventeen.

'I'm twenty-three,' he said.

It seemed to Alice that he was pointing out something he considered to be important, but she didn't know whether that was because he feared she might consider him too old for her or if he considered her too young for him.

Alice commented on the soup instead, hoping to convey the impression that age was unimportant to her. Was it significant to him, though? Alice couldn't tell.

He took her arm as they walked to the bus stop and again when he walked her home. 'I'm no longer free tonight – my sister is insisting on giving me dinner,' he said. 'My parents are expecting me to spend tomorrow with them before I set out for Oxford, but might we do this again when I'm next in London?'

'I'd like that.'

He smiled. 'Good.'

'Thank you for my lunch.'

'I'm sorry it was so late.'

Stepping forward, he kissed her cheek then waited until she'd reached her front door before waving and walking onwards. A kiss on the cheek meant what, exactly? Mere friendliness? Or something more? She hoped it was the start of something more.

Three weeks passed before he returned to London one Saturday. 'It's just a flying visit. I'm dining with investors tonight, but might I take you to tea this afternoon?'

This time he'd brought his car so he drove her into London's West End to take tea at Claridge's. Alice wore her prettiest dress but still felt gauche in such a smart hotel. 'You look lovely,' Daniel told her, but she couldn't decide if it was a romantic compliment or the sort of confidence booster he'd give to any young woman.

He made her laugh during their tea, and he seemed

to enjoy himself, too. But soon the tea was over and Daniel looked at his watch.

'You have to go,' she said.

'Unfortunately, yes. We're meeting for drinks before dinner and I'm representing the company so I can't be late.'

He drove her home and she hoped he might kiss her properly in the relative privacy of his car but, once again, all she received was a peck on the cheek. Alice told herself it was still early days in their relationship and she had no idea what was usual when a young man began walking out with a girl.

Over the next few months they visited London Zoo, saw *Underneath the Arches* at the cinema, and took the train to Kew Gardens. Each time Alice fell a little more in love with him, but his parting kisses continued to be mere pecks on her cheek. He liked her, certainly, but was that all?

Then a thought struck her. Perhaps he considered seventeen too young for kissing and was waiting for her to turn eighteen. He'd learned the date of her birthday by then, though, thankfully, he'd said nothing about the claim she'd made some months ago to be almost eighteen. Hopefully, he'd forgotten all about it. He was in Oxford on her birthday but sent a large bouquet of flowers with the message *Hope you have a lovely day, Daniel x* on the accompanying card.

Alice touched a fingertip to that kiss, hoping it had romantic intentions behind it, but when Daniel next came to London, the heavens opened as they walked home from tea and when they reached her house he urged her to 'get out of this horrible weather quickly'. It meant his kiss on her cheek was briefer than ever.

Would he have kissed her properly if it hadn't been raining? With an aching heart, Alice feared that he wouldn't have kissed her lips even if the sun had been blazing. She wanted romance but the suspicion that he wanted nothing more than companionship when he was at a loose end in London was hardening into certainty.

She was miserable over the next few weeks, but then one Sunday afternoon he knocked on her door with a small boy in tow. 'My nephew, Teddy,' he said, ruffling the boy's dark curls. 'Would you like to come to Highbury Fields to fly his new kite?'

Daniel smiled down at her and Alice felt the usual thrill of longing. It was unlikely that he'd wish to kiss her in front of Teddy, whatever his feelings for her, but perhaps he might still give her some sort of clue as to what those feelings were, so she'd know once and for all whether she should abandon hope.

'I'd like that,' she said, 'as long as Teddy doesn't mind?'

Teddy grinned to show he didn't mind at all.

He was a sweet little boy and kite-flying was fun, but while Daniel's eyes were soft when he looked at Alice she saw nothing in them to lead her away from the reluctant conclusion that he saw her as just an older version of his nephew – a young person whom it was fun to entertain.

She was feeling wretched as they set off for home. Caught up in her thoughts about Daniel, she had no inkling that the minutes were counting down to disaster. But so they were.

There was nothing to be gained now by speculating on how her life might have turned out if she hadn't gone to Highbury Fields that afternoon. Alice had no power to change the past. She could only make the most of the future, and she had a goal – to bring books to the men at Stratton House. On that thought an idea for getting hold of more books jumped into her mind.

CHAPTER SEVENTEEN

Alice

The journey wasn't long – less than ten miles – but as the bus trundled through villages and hamlets, stopping here and there for passengers to get on or off – it felt like a very long journey indeed. Alice supposed she'd grown impatient after the speed of London's underground trains.

Reaching her destination at last, she stepped down from the bus to find herself beside what looked to be a livestock market, although no livestock were being sold today. She couldn't come to St Albans without remembering that Daniel had been here visiting his godmother not long ago. Had he stood where she now stood? Had he—

Enough. She was here on business. She asked a passer-by for directions to a bookshop and a few minutes later sat in the cramped office of the manager of Murton's.

'Let me be sure I understand,' Mr Earnlow said, after he'd heard her proposal. 'You want Murton's to donate a number of books and supply others for you to sell on with no guarantee that they'll actually be sold?'

'I believe it's called sale or return.'

'But you're neither a retailer nor a charity?'

'No, though as I explained, the books are for servicemen who are in hospital recovering from injuries suffered while serving our country. There's no library or bookshop nearby so I want to take books into the hospital for patients to borrow or buy. With luck, the patients who buy books will then donate them so other patients can read them, too. I see it as a way of building up a library of books, with new titles being brought in regularly to keep the collection fresh.'

'You couldn't buy the books yourself and donate them or sell them on?'

Alice would love to do just that, but she needed her modest savings for things like birthday and Christmas gifts for her father as well as emergencies.

Mr Earnlow polished his glasses on a handkerchief. 'It's a commendable idea, but we're already in touch with the Red Cross about donating books to prisoners of war, even though we're worried about how the war will affect our business. Paper shortages, you see? Not to mention customers having less money for luxuries. We couldn't donate books to your venture, too. Neither could we risk making a loss on sales.'

'I understand.' Yet Alice's disappointment cut deeply.

'I can make a small donation to your stock,' he continued, relenting a little. He took a book from a cupboard. 'There's a slight tear in the jacket but it's perfectly readable.'

The book was *A History of Hertfordshire*. Hopefully, some patients would enjoy it, so Alice was glad to have it. 'Thank you. I'm sorry to have taken up your time.'

'I wish you good luck, Miss Lovell.'

Back outside she asked another passer-by if there was a second bookshop in town. She was directed to a smaller shop where she met with another polite refusal but emerged with a water-damaged copy of *Ivanhoe*.

To fill the time before her return bus was due, Alice walked down to the cathedral and tried to set her troubles aside by taking in the beauty of the stained-glass windows, gracious arches and rolling parkland. It was no use. Much as she admired her surroundings, her troubles crept back in – Daniel, the patients, her diminishing hopes for independence . . .

As far as the patients were concerned, Alice needed a fresh idea. As for her other problems, she could only hope that time would take the sting out of her longing for Daniel and help her to see a way to achieve independence.

She stretched her injured fingers carefully. She exercised them every day, as the surgeon had taught her, but typing at speed would never be possible. Which meant that returning to secretarial work would never be possible either.

What other skills did she have to offer? Alice was a good organizer and thought she was good with people too, Naomi Harrington excepted. There must be some sort of work that would utilize those skills and provide an income. But what?

Churchwood was too small to offer much in the way of opportunity. London offered the most scope, but perhaps here in St Albans there might be some chance of work. It was something to think about anyway, once her hand had healed a little more.

The return journey felt even longer but Alice arrived in Churchwood at last and got off the bus by the village green. She smiled when she saw Janet Collins walking towards her. 'Hello, Janet.'

'Oh, hello, love.' Janet spared her barely a glance as she passed.

Alice frowned. Surely Mrs Harrington hadn't . . . No, not everything in Churchwood was connected to Naomi Harrington. 'Janet!' Alice caught her up and touched her arm. 'Is something wrong?'

'I'm fine, love.'

'I don't wish to pry, but clearly you're not fine.'

Janet sighed. 'Nothing's happening in my family that isn't happening in thousands of families up and down the land, but it's hard to bear.'

Alice worked it out. 'Your son has been called up?'

'My Charlie. I knew it was likely, but I couldn't help hoping something would keep him at home – flat feet or another trivial condition. It isn't natural for a mother to want her child to be sick, but I'd have given anything for Charlie to have something just a little bit wrong with him so he'd fail the medical.'

'I'm sorry.'

'I suppose you think I'm unpatriotic.'

'I'm sure you love your country as much as anyone. It's only natural to love your son more.'

'I do. And I don't want to see my Charlie's name over there.' Janet gestured towards the village green and the memorial to the six Churchwood men who'd fallen in the 1914–18 war. 'It's bad enough seeing my brother's name on that lump of stone. Jack Marsh. He fell at Passchendaele. Just turned twenty-one, he was. My Charlie's even younger.'

'I'm not surprised you're worried.'

Janet put a hand on Alice's arm. 'Thanks for under-standing, dear. Not everyone does. When I think how many lives are going to be lost because of that tyrant,

Adolf Hitler, and his goose-stepping followers, I'd like to go over to Germany myself and strangle him.'

'I think a lot of people feel like that.'

'Well, I'd best get on. Don't worry about me, dear. I'm a little down today but I'll pull myself together. Not that I'll stop worrying about Charlie. I'll worry about him every day until he's home safe and sound, but we have to get on with life despite our worries, don't we? Especially in wartime.'

'We certainly do.' Movement on the far side of the green caught Alice's eye. It was the woman in the blue coat. 'Do you know that lady, Janet?'

'Edna Hall?'

'I've seen her walking by the lake.'

Janet nodded. 'Her Arthur loved to fish in that lake and Edna used to walk down to him with tea and sandwiches. He died not so long ago after forty years together so I expect she's taking comfort in her memories.'

'I'm afraid I rather jolted her out of her memories the first time I saw her.'

'Scurried away from you, did she? She's keeping herself to herself at the moment so she isn't welcoming visitors. She says she needs time to work her way through her grief, which is fair enough.'

'I'll be ready with a smile for whenever she feels like company.'

'That's the spirit.'

With that Janet walked on, briskly at first, but soon her shoulders drooped. Poor Janet. Poor Charlie, too.

CHAPTER EIGHTEEN

Naomi

Despite her best efforts to keep busy, the feeling that cracks were opening in the life Naomi had built for herself had persisted over the last few days. Whatever she did recently appeared to be the wrong thing.

She'd lain awake for much of Saturday night, and when her thoughts hadn't been turned to her unsuccessful dinner party, they'd been occupied by the question of whether she should do something about unintentionally sabotaging Alice Lovell's book appeal or leave the upset to blow over. She'd decided that doing nothing would not only be cowardly but would also leave the poor men at Stratton House without enough books to read. Naomi might not have the sort of forthright courage that had brought Alice to Foxfield, but there was still a little iron in her backbone.

Something had to be done, but what? Naomi had soon dismissed the idea of an apology or even an explanation of the misunderstanding. Either course would be tantamount to an admission that she'd been feeling hurt and that Marjorie had been spreading gossip. A subtle approach would surely get the job done just as well. Naomi had decided to ask Alice publicly if the book appeal had gone well and then say, 'I hope you received the books I donated? They were left at the cottage in a box.'

Those few words would signal her approval of the appeal clearly, and doubtless village gossip would soon spread the word that, contrary to earlier rumours, Naomi was happy for residents to donate their books.

The next morning's service at St Luke's had felt the best place to start and she'd arrived early in the hope of catching Alice as the congregation filed past on their way to their pews. But Alice had arrived only moments before the service began, slipping into a pew at the back. As soon as it ended Marjorie had let out a shriek because a button had fallen off her coat and rolled under the pew. By the time Naomi had retrieved the button and got outside, Alice was striding into the distance.

Despite lingering in the village yesterday and again this morning, she'd seen no sign of Alice. Tomorrow the next first-aid class would take place and, if Alice attended, Naomi would be able to speak to her then.

Despite having every intention of shielding Marjorie from blame as far as possible, further reflection persuaded Naomi that it would be impossible to protect her completely. People were bound to assume that Marjorie must have got things wrong because she so often *did* get them wrong. Deciding to warn her friend of her intention to declare her support for the book appeal in public, Naomi wrote a short note inviting her to visit and asked Suki to deliver it.

As always, Marjorie looked delighted to be at Foxfield. 'Only me invited today?' she asked, preening at what she clearly took to be a privilege.

'I thought we could go through the lists for the Red Cross parcels,' Naomi told her, planning to work up to the book appeal gradually in the hope that Marjorie would feel more relaxed and rational when the subject was broached.

They discussed the Red Cross parcels then Suki brought in tea. 'I know what would make a nice treat,' Naomi said, and fetched the chocolates that had been brought by the dinner guests Alexander had so despised.

Predictably, Marjorie's eyes widened. 'Chocolates? How kind!'

She took the strawberry cream. Marjorie always took the strawberry cream. She nibbled at it, relishing every tiny crumb.

'Have another,' Naomi invited, and Marjorie took a hazelnut praline.

'Something odd,' Naomi said then, hoping Marjorie had been softened up enough not to take offence. 'I heard a rumour that you told people they shouldn't give books to Miss Lovell's book appeal.'

The praline descended Marjorie's gullet with a gulp. 'A rumour? About me? Are people saying unkind things about me?'

'Not at all, though perhaps there's been a misunderstanding.'

Marjorie's breathing quickened and her face turned puce. 'I don't see how I can be to blame for anything.' The words burst out like sputtering fireworks.

'It isn't a question of blame. I'm just trying to get to the bottom of things.'

'I only repeated what you told me about not

getting involved in the book collecting. About leaving it to Alice Lovell and that awful Fletcher girl.'

'I didn't say I disapproved of the project.'

'But it's what you meant! You disapprove of both those girls!'

'I didn't intend—'

'Now you're blaming me!' Marjorie burst into tears. 'I've tried to be a good friend to you, Naomi. No one could be more loyal, and to be treated as though my feelings don't matter is—'

'Oh, for goodness' sake, stop being so dramatic!' Naomi hadn't slept well for several nights and her patience felt gossamer-thin. 'Can't we have a sensible conversation for once instead of launching into this sort of silliness?'

'You're calling my feelings silly?'

'I'm calling your behaviour silly.'

'I never knew you could be so cruel. Well, far be it from me to inflict my silly presence on you. I know when I'm not wanted.'

Marjorie rushed from the room and headed home crying, while Naomi sat back, weary from the encounter. Was there a more tedious woman than Marjorie in Churchwood? In the world, even?

But soon self-blame rushed in. Having known Marjorie for many years Naomi was well aware of her weaknesses – her foolishness and gossip-mongering especially. But Naomi was also aware of her friend's more admirable qualities, loyalty being one of them.

Marjorie's tears were exasperating but there was no doubt that she was genuinely upset – and would remain upset until the rift in their friendship was healed.

Naomi let half an hour pass then told Suki she was going out.

Marjorie lived in a small terraced cottage near the centre of the village. She'd been brought up in a fine country house with ponies in the paddock but her family fortunes had declined over time and now Marjorie, a spinster, was a woman of modest means. Looking up at this shabby little cottage, Naomi felt even worse for upsetting her.

Marjorie's eyes were red-rimmed and she was sniffling into a handkerchief when she opened the door. 'I hope you haven't come to—'

'I've come to apologize. May I come in?'

Looking mollified but still not completely thawed, Marjorie led the way into her sitting room. It hadn't changed in decades. The wallpaper featured faded roses on a green background. The sofa and armchair were a dull brown, and so too were the fireplace tiles, while the room's ornaments were mostly a collection of cheap pottery trinket boxes, which Marjorie had crammed into a glass-fronted display cabinet, the family heirlooms having long ago been sold.

'I'm sorry I upset you,' Naomi said, sitting on the sofa but keeping to the edge as the worn springs had a habit of swallowing a person whole. 'Clearly, I gave the wrong impression of my feelings about Miss Lovell's venture. Her idea of helping the men at Stratton House is a good one.'

Marjorie shrugged her bony shoulders. She didn't have it in her to meet Naomi halfway and accept some blame for the misunderstanding, but bridges were being rebuilt and for that Naomi was grateful.

Should she ask for help in undoing the damage

to Alice's project? Better not. Knowing Marjorie, she'd only suspect that she was being held responsible after all.

Naomi didn't stay long. Walking home, she reached Brimbles Lane and, feeling the sudden lure of impulse, turned into it.

Brimbles Farm was a good mile away and Naomi was unaccustomed to walking so far. Her shoes had sturdy heels but even so her feet began to ache and she felt herself growing breathless. Was this another sign of the change of life or was she simply out of condition?

Naomi wasn't sure why she was heading this way. She had no intention of speaking to Kate Fletcher or even being seen by her, but for some reason she wanted to observe her. From a distance.

Spotting the girl in one of the fields, Naomi lingered behind the hedgerow to watch as Kate hammered nails into a fence. Her tall, supple frame moved with easy, balanced grace but there was no doubt that the work was hard. As Alice had said, Kate didn't have an easy life. Perhaps Alice was right about her family treating her cruelly as well.

Naomi had thought herself safely hidden but apparently she'd been deluding herself as Kate stopped hammering, put a hand on a hip and stared in Naomi's direction. Glared, rather. Even over a distance Naomi could feel waves of hostility.

She wanted to scuttle away but made a show of looking at the sky as though she hadn't even noticed Kate. Then she turned and headed for home, wincing at the increasing discomfort in her feet.

She reached the lake and noticed Edna Hall on the

other bank, dressed in her distinctive blue coat and staring down at the water. Naomi was keen to be at home in her slippers but Edna had lost her husband not so long ago and a kind word wouldn't hurt. 'Good afternoon, Mrs Hall!' Naomi called. 'Cold today, isn't it?'

She waited for an answer but none came. Edna couldn't have heard. Relieved at being able to avoid a long chat, Naomi walked on.

She reached home at last, kicking off her shoes and rubbing her burning feet. Today had been productive, all things considered. Naomi had put a stop to Marjorie's gossip and paved the way for making a public show of support for the book appeal. All she needed now was for Alice to attend the first-aid class so Naomi could mention the book drive in front of a large group of Churchwood women.

Luck wasn't on Naomi's side, as Alice didn't attend. Should Naomi say something about the book appeal anyway? One look at her friend decided her against it. Marjorie was all helpfulness but still carried an air of hurt sensibility. Any mention of a misunderstanding might send her into floods of tears again. It would be better for Naomi to wait until she came face to face with Alice in a shop, hopefully when Marjorie wasn't present.

But despite lingering in the shops over the following days Naomi never seemed to call in at the same time as Alice. She pinned her hopes on the Sunday service again and this time was racing after Alice as the congregation filed out when Septimus Barnes called out, 'A word, Mrs Harrington, if you please?'

Vexed, Naomi turned back. 'Of course, Vicar.'

He waited until the last congregant had left then produced a poster from behind a bookcase. 'Might I have your opinion on this?'

It was similar to the poster Alice had put up for her first book appeal but with the date for receiving donations changed and with the addition of a banner announcing: *Modest prices paid for books if desired.*

Oh, heavens. Many doctors charged fat fees and were comfortably off but Naomi had seen no sign of wealth in the Lovells. In fact, she suspected Alice's funds were limited. It was terrible to think of her paying out money she couldn't afford to tempt people into parting with books they might have donated for free if Naomi had handled things better.

What was Naomi going to do now?

CHAPTER NINETEEN

Alice

Thank you for your letter, Daniel had written.

> *As always, I was delighted to receive it and pleased to hear that Audrey, Louisa and Constance are all laying well. Is there a 'Best Performing Hen' among them? If I were a betting man, I'd guess the honour would go to Constance as she's the fattest.*
>
> *I like to think of you collecting warm, fresh eggs for your breakfast. I hope you'll allow me an egg to eat when I'm next in England. Boiled with bread and butter would be wonderful. Only a scrape of butter, though. I know it's rationed.*
>
> *I haven't had a fresh egg in an age but it isn't all doom and gloom with food on this side of the Channel. A few of us had the good fortune to encounter a local couple who pressed a large cheese and a bottle of red wine on us. We drew lots for it and I won! Not that winning meant anything as naturally the cheese and wine were shared (and both were delicious), but it felt good to know that Lady Luck was smiling down on me.*

Alice had read the letter several times in the hours since it had been delivered that Monday morning and only the knowledge that she was expected at Stratton House made her put it away now.

'Who'd like to hear a story?' she asked when she arrived on Ward Two. Having no more books to circulate, she was determined to begin her visit in a way that might lift the men's moods rather than bring them down.

She read a story about a man who was lost in the jungle. With his life at risk from poisonous spiders and snakes as well as piranha fish, the story of poor Albert Spinks, reporter for a fictional newspaper, had the audience rapt.

Except for Jake Turner, who'd sighed loudly. Alice always spoke to him on her visits but was making no headway. 'How are you today?' only ever earned her looks that suggested her question was stupid, while the one time she'd asked, 'Can I fetch anything for you?' he'd replied with, 'A new pair of legs?'

'I'm sorry he's so miserable,' Stevie Meadows said as Jake was taken away for a therapy session. 'Don't take it personally. He's like that with everyone.'

Alice wanted to say that she understood why Jake was so miserable but she'd come by information about his broken engagement by chance and it wasn't her place to share it.

'I don't know what demons he's wrestling inside but I hope he gets the better of them,' Stevie continued. 'It must get on his nerves to have someone like me in the next bed.'

'Someone cheerful?' she asked.

Stevie grinned. 'I can't help seeing the sunny side of life, but I'm trying not to prattle on about it too much.'

How considerate he was.

His eyes took on a conspiratorial brightness. 'Let me show you the latest photo from Esme while Jake's away.'

He took it from an envelope and Alice saw again the pretty, fair-haired girl with the gentle smile.

'You can't tell from this photo, but she has the bluest eyes you could imagine. I'm thinking of a sapphire for the engagement ring. To match them, you see?'

'A sapphire sounds beautiful.'

'It'll have to be a small one – money's going to be tight – but Esme won't care about that. A simple ring and a simple wedding are all we want.'

Thoughts of Stevie's romance inevitably brought Alice's thoughts to Daniel as she walked home. She needed to steer clear of anything romantic in her reply to his letter. What might she write instead?

I was glad to hear that you're safe and well? Alice always began her letters in such a way. It probably bored him but she really was glad for any assurance that he was alive and uninjured – at the time of writing anyway. Besides, the word *glad* conveyed the sort of steady emotion a young woman might feel for anyone of her acquaintance. Alice steered clear of words like *joy* and *delight* in case they betrayed the romantic interest she was trying to hide.

What next? She decided on:

Constance is indeed the best performing hen when it comes to laying eggs, though Audrey and Louisa are pretty good, too. I don't have a favourite as there's something endearing about all three hens, from Audrey's way of stretching her neck when she looks around to Louisa's fastidiousness in avoiding mud.

174

Should she tell him she'd happily boil an egg for him when he was next on leave? Or would he interpret it as encouragement to visit? Alice would have to think about that. She might want nothing more than to see Daniel again but it wouldn't be good for her.

I was at the hospital today, she'd add, and she'd tell him about one or two of the stories she'd read on the wards. She might mention the nurses too. *I don't have a favourite hen but I can't help having favourite nurses. Most are friendly but there's one who's—*

But no. He might feel even sorrier for Alice if he knew one of the nurses wasn't particularly welcoming.

Hearing someone approach, she glanced up to see the smart woman with the dark-eyed children. She looked just as tense as on the first time their paths had crossed.

'How nice to see you all again,' Alice said, smiling, but the children only looked solemn while the woman's expression made it clear that it wasn't nice at all in her opinion. 'May I walk with you for a while?' Alice asked, despite the unpromising response. 'I'm new to the village. I don't know many people.'

This time the woman shrugged. 'It's a free country. At the moment. It won't be free if those blasted Germans invade.'

'They'll turn our lives upside down,' Alice agreed.

'Some of us have already had our lives turned upside down.' She turned to the children. 'Go and play, but don't go far and don't make nuisances of yourselves.'

'What are nui—' Speaking with an accent, the eldest girl stumbled over the word.

'Just be good.'

The girl beckoned to her brother and sister, and all three moved into the trees.

'I've heard that the children are refugees from Poland,' Alice said.

The woman fired up at that. 'You've *heard*, have you? People have been talking about me behind my back, I suppose. Gossiping.'

'Not at all. Someone said you'd done an admirable thing, taking in three children and moving to Churchwood to keep them safe.'

It was Janet who'd passed on the information one day when Alice had seen the elegant woman waiting to collect the children from school but standing apart from everyone else. 'Not what you'd call friendly,' Janet had added, though Alice didn't repeat that now.

'I didn't have much choice,' the woman said.

'The children are related to your husband, I believe?'

'His sister's kids. My Marek came from Poland ten years ago but the rest of his family stayed behind. They're Jewish, and you know what that means.'

'Jewish books burned, synagogues vandalized, businesses confiscated, children banned from schools . . . My father hates all discrimination but the ban on Jewish doctors practising in German hospitals particularly incensed him. He worked alongside a Jewish surgeon in the 1914 war and that surgeon saved the lives of countless German prisoners. To be repaid in such a barbaric fashion . . .'

'Hitler made it clear early last year that war would mean the extermination of the Jews in *all* of Europe, including Poland. Marek urged his family to flee, especially after Czechoslovakia was invaded. He thought Poland might be next but his father was sick after a heart attack and his mother suffered with leg problems. Anna – that's Marek's sister – wouldn't leave them. It wasn't until the invasion actually started that a family friend managed to sneak the children out of the country and bring them to England.'

'It must be awful for the family to have been torn apart.'

'Without a doubt. We were living in London when the children arrived, but Marek was worried the Germans might bomb the cities again, so here we are.'

'Your husband isn't with you?'

'If only! Marek was so incensed by what Germany was doing that he joined up as soon as Britain declared war. He's off fighting while I'm left with the kids.'

'Have you heard from their parents?'

'A few times, but it's getting harder to get letters through. Jews in Poland have to wear yellow stars or armbands now, and who knows what's going to happen next? It's terrifying, and I don't know what to say to the children when they ask about their parents and grandparents. I just tell them I hope they'll all see each other again soon.'

'Three children must be a handful at the best of times.'

'Yes, and these are far from being the best of times. The children don't speak English and I don't speak Polish. I might have been married to a Pole for eight years but Marek only spoke English over here.'

'You're learning each other's languages now?'

'The children are picking up English, and I'm trying to learn bits of Polish. But it isn't just the language that makes us different. I don't understand Jewish customs either. I'm not Jewish, and Marek isn't what you'd call a strict observer, so I've never learned much from him.'

'You can only do your best.' Alice gestured towards a rough seat that someone had made out of fallen logs to overlook the lake. Now they were nearing mid-February daffodil buds were poking through the soil like miniature spears. 'Shall we sit?'

'Why not? I'm May, by the way. May Janicki.'

'Alice Lovell.'

'The doctor's daughter.'

'Retired doctor.'

'I expect you think I'm a terrible person, not being all mumsy over the kids.'

'Children aren't for everyone.'

'They weren't for me. Marek agreed we'd concentrate on our business instead of having a family. We have a factory in the East End that makes clothes for women. Not for the fanciest stores in the West End, but for women who aren't rich but still want to be fashionable. I took pride in the designs and cutting, and made sure the quality of the sewing was excellent too. I saw it as a service to women – good clothes at affordable prices.'

'The coat you're wearing is gorgeous.'

'My design, and made in our factory. I was apprenticed to a tailor when I was fourteen and knew even then that I'd found my calling. I loved my work. But now . . .'

'You're in a small village living the sort of domestic life you never wanted.'

'Meanwhile our factory is making parachutes. I

178

know I'm a bad person. Not only unpatriotic, but cold too. Heartless, even.'

'I think you're heroic.'

'Full of resentment is nearer the truth.'

'But you've taken the children in anyway. You've given up your way of life to keep them safe. That's admirable.'

May still looked sceptical.

'Are they difficult children?' Alice asked. 'Aside from the language barrier?'

'Not really. There's no malice in them and they're well behaved most of the time. To be honest, I think they're a bit afraid of me. That's awful, isn't it? They must want the sort of hugs and kisses they got from their parents but I'm not . . . I'm just not made like that.'

'You're finding your way in unexpected circumstances. It'll take a while for things to settle. Not that you'll be here forever. The war will be over one day.'

'Not much sign of it so far. The last one went on for four years.'

'But in time . . .'

May looked bleak at the thought of how much time might have to pass before victory came. Or defeat.

'I found it easier to adjust once I found a friend,' Alice said. 'Kate Fletcher.'

'The farm girl who terrifies people?'

Alice laughed. 'That's because she won't be beaten down by Churchwood disapproval.'

'Churchwood disapproves of me, too. I've seen the looks and I've walked into shops to find conversations coming to a sudden halt.'

'Churchwood doesn't know you.'

'Because I've kept myself at a distance? Perhaps you're right. The thing is . . .' May hesitated then took a deep breath and said, 'The thing is, I'm ashamed. Here are three little kids dragged hundreds of miles from home to a strange country where they can't speak the language, and here am I resenting them. Who wouldn't disapprove of me?'

'Anyone who understands that this is a difficult situation. The important thing is that you're trying to make it work. I'd like to be your friend, if you'll have me?'

May swallowed and tears shimmered in her eyes. 'You're very kind.'

'I need friends, too, and so does Kate. We're all outsiders in one way or another. Not that I think we should remain outsiders. We can help each other to become accepted.'

'That won't be easy. Not from what I've seen of Churchwood. It's one of those set-in-its-ways places, and it's run by a dragon.'

'Mrs Harrington?'

'Hmm.'

'I'm ready for a fight if you are? Why don't you introduce me to the children? It must be hard, looking after them by yourself when you're unused to little ones. You could let me take them off your hands sometimes.'

'You'd do that?'

'That's what friends do, isn't it? Help each other?'

May smiled. 'I'm glad I met you, Alice Lovell.' Turning, she called to the children. 'Rosa! Samuel! Zofia!'

They came out of the bushes and Alice felt a pang

at the nervous looks on their young faces. 'This is Miss Lovell,' May said.

'Call me Alice. Would you like to come to my house one day?'

The children listened intently, working out what she was saying. 'Your house?' Rosa said.

'It's a cottage,' Alice explained, drawing a small house in the air. 'I'm trying to grow vegetables and I have chickens.' She mimed digging and eating, then made them laugh by pretending to be a chicken.

Rosa turned to her brother and sister and spoke quickly in Polish. The younger children smiled in response. 'We like to come,' she told Alice.

'Tomorrow?' Alice asked May. 'It'll give you time to yourself. Guilt-free time.'

'I'm not sure it'll be free of guilt but even some breathing space will be wonderful.'

Alice told her father about the invitation when she reached home. 'Perhaps I should have asked you before inviting three children. They may disturb your studies.'

'Don't worry about that. Those children need kindness. I'm sure they've been checked by a doctor already but it won't hurt for me to peek at them too. Just to observe. They won't know I'm doing it.'

'Thank you.'

'You're a kind girl, my dear.'

Alice felt tears well up. She appeared to be living on an emotional precipice these days but at least she could tell Daniel about May Janicki and the refugee children to help prove how busy and useful she was being.

A line from Daniel's letter floated into her mind. *It*

181

felt good to know that Lady Luck was smiling down on me. Hopefully, Lady Luck wouldn't decide that she'd been generous enough and turn away from him.

No, that was fanciful. Pushing it from her mind, Alice reached for the carrots.

CHAPTER TWENTY

Kate

Kate had done it again: rushed through the side gate of The Linnets only to come to an abrupt halt when she saw that Alice had visitors already. Children, this time. Three of them. Refugees from Poland, according to conversations Kate had overheard in the shops. They'd moved to the village with the most glamorous woman Churchwood had ever seen, though she appeared to be no more popular than Kate. Well, no, that wasn't quite true. No one ranked as low as a Fletcher in village circles.

Kate stood awkwardly while the children stared at her, doubtless thinking she looked like some sort of filthy oddity.

'Come in,' Alice beckoned, then made the introductions. 'This is my friend Kate. These are Rosa, Samuel and Zofia.'

Kate nodded at them. They simply stared back, though whether in shyness or disgust Kate had no way of knowing.

'I was just introducing them to the chickens,' Alice added. 'They were choosing favourites.'

Rosa chose Audrey, Samuel chose Constance and Zofia chose Louisa. 'Can you make chicken sounds?'

Alice asked them, and she tried to demonstrate what she meant by clucking.

'Kate?' she appealed. 'You must know chicken sounds.'

Oh, heck. Kate knew a lot about chickens but little of children. They were waiting for her to begin, though, and she didn't like to disappoint them after all they'd been through. She began to cluck and flap her arms like wings. She must have made a good job of it because the children laughed and tried to copy her.

'Can you walk like chickens?' Kate asked, demonstrating a stilt-legged walk that made them laugh even more.

'Me!' Samuel said, setting off around the garden in chicken mode. Rosa and Zofia followed.

'You good,' Samuel told Kate.

'Best chick hen,' agreed Rosa.

'What other animals do you know?' Kate asked. 'Cows?' She launched into a moo sound.

'*Krowa!*' Rosa translated, and all three children began to moo.

'Sheep?' Kate asked, making a baa sound.

'*Owca,*' Samuel said, and they all began to baa.

Kate took them through pigs, horses, cats and dogs, too.

'You're an excellent mimic,' Alice told her.

Little Zofia tugged at the bottom of Kate's jacket. '*Opowiedz historię,*' she said softly.

Kate had no idea what she meant.

'Story,' Rosa explained. 'Tell story?'

'Me?' Kate looked surprised.

'Shall I fetch a book?' Alice asked

'Yes, please. No, wait! Let's see if I can do without

one.' Kate thought for a moment, suggested they sit on one of the shabby bench seats, then began. 'Once upon a time there were three children.' She held up a hand and counted off three fingers. 'The eldest was about . . . Ooh, let's see . . .' She held the hand level with Rosa's head. 'This high. She was called Rosa.'

The real girl of that name smiled.

'The second was a boy. This high.' She indicated Samuel's height. 'He was called . . .?'

'Samuel!' the children shouted.

'The third child was another girl. Smaller, and called . . .?'

'Zofia!'

'One day, the children wanted eggs to eat.' Kate mimed finding, cooking and eating an egg. 'From . . .' She pointed to the chickens and made a clucking sound. 'But the chickens were feeling mean.' Her mouth turned down and she gestured for the children to turn their mouths down too. 'The chickens asked the other animals to help keep their eggs safe. First the cow came up and told the children, "Go home." ' She made a shooing-away movement. ' "No eggs for you today. Moo!" '

Again, the children copied the sound and action.

'The children turned around.' Kate drew a circle in the air. 'And they started to walk away. But then they came back to try again. Guess who jumped in front of them?'

'Sheep?' Rosa suggested.

'Horse?' Samuel said.

'Cat?' said Zofia.

'It was the pig. And what did he say?'

185

'Go home?' ventured Rosa, making the shooing-away movement.

'That's exactly what he said. "Go home! Oink! Oink! Oink!"'

The story continued with several animals driving the children back, then Kate said, 'The children needed an idea.' She pointed to her head and tried to look pensive. 'But what could they do?'

The children waited, wide-eyed, to hear what would happen next.

'Well,' Kate said, 'the children were hungry.' She rubbed her tummy and looked sad. 'Thinking the chickens might be hungry too, the children fetched some chicken food called grain.' She acted out filling a bucket and offering the grain to the chickens. ' "You give us your eggs and we'll give you this grain," they said. And what did the chickens say?'

'Yes!' the children chorused.

'Indeed they did. So the children scattered the grain and the chickens pecked it up.' She mimed the actions. 'Then, very carefully, the children took the eggs, boiled them, ate them and rubbed their tummies again, this time happily.'

'Good story,' Samuel approved.

'Thank you,' Rosa added.

Little Zofia beamed.

'Tell me how many daffodils you can find,' Alice suggested to the children, and they ran off down the garden in search of them. 'The men at Stratton House would love your way of telling stories,' Alice told Kate. 'You make them so real.'

'I'm sure you read stories just as well.'

'I hope I make a decent job of it, but you're excep-
tional.'

Kate shrugged. She'd enjoyed telling the story but
there was no way she could ever set foot inside Stratton House. She had neither the clothes nor the time
for it. 'They're nice kids,' she said, to change the
subject.

'Lovely,' Alice agreed. 'They're going through a
tough time so it's wonderful to see them smiling and
laughing. Their aunt isn't finding life easy. When I
collected the older two from school today someone
described May as haughty. I tried to explain that she
was simply finding her new life difficult and that
appearances can be deceiving but I don't know if I
made any difference. You should meet May, Kate.'

Hmm. Appearances *could* be deceiving – the clothes
Kate was forced to wear were evidence of that – but
they weren't always so. Naomi Harrington was a prime
example. And to think Kate had actually worried
about upsetting her! No, Kate was in no hurry to meet
May Janicki.

CHAPTER TWENTY-ONE

Naomi

Naomi could put it off no longer. Alice had missed another first-aid class yesterday so there'd been no chance to talk about the book appeal in front of her. But time was marching on and Naomi had decided that she shouldn't let Alice's absence stop her from mentioning the book appeal to others. The most important thing was to encourage people to donate their books, and though Naomi hated to think that Alice considered her a mean, spiteful woman, clearing her name over the first mix-up was a secondary concern. With luck, Alice would come to hear of Naomi's support via Churchwood gossip. If not . . . Well, Naomi would have to think of another way of smoothing things over.

She wrapped up warmly in her coat, wishing it was a suit of armour, then walked into the village to put things right. A glance through the grocer's window showed few customers inside. The Post Office looked busier. She smiled tightly as Mrs Hutchings emerged from its depths, then took a deep breath and stepped inside – only to wish she could step straight out again.

Marjorie was here. So too was Bert Makepiece. Could Naomi postpone her mission yet again to a day when she wouldn't have them in the audience? As though he'd looked straight into her mind and seen her hesitation, Bert sent her a hard stare. Then, doubtless to emphasize that he wouldn't be moving until she'd done the right thing, he leaned back against a wall, folded his arms across his bulging middle and waited for her to begin. It was all right for him. He was only concerned that a wrong should be righted. Naomi had to consider Marjorie's feelings too.

Joining the queue, Naomi wondered how she might begin but Bert coughed pointedly. His message was obvious: *Get on with it, woman.* Naomi glared at him but he merely stared back steadily. Why should his opinion matter to her? It shouldn't. It didn't. After all, she was Naomi Harrington of Foxfield while he was . . . well, not in her circle. But annoyingly he had right on his side on this occasion.

She took a deep breath and said loudly, 'I see Miss Lovell has put another poster up about books for the hospital. I haven't seen her to ask, but do any of you know if it's because she wasn't given many books after her first appeal?'

Faces turned towards her.

'I didn't manage to get there in person,' Naomi continued, her throat dry. 'I had a clash of commitments. But I had some books delivered to Miss Lovell at The Linnets.'

Looks of surprise passed between the women. 'You gave some books?' Mrs Hayes questioned. 'But we thought . . .'

Their gazes swivelled towards Marjorie, who promptly turned puce. Naomi knew tears would follow soon if she couldn't head them off. 'I believe there's been some sort of misunderstanding about how I feel,' she said. 'It was my fault for giving Marjorie the wrong impression. I actually think it's a marvellous idea to supply books to the patients at Stratton House. We owe those poor men a debt of gratitude. After all, they've been injured in the line of duty, trying to keep us safe from that dreadful Hitler man and his thugs.'

'Alice is offering to pay for books now,' Mrs Larkin said.

'Which is sweet of her, but we wouldn't dream of asking for money, would we? Churchwood is more generous than that.'

Naomi glanced at Bert but he didn't budge. Clearly, he was expecting more. She moistened her lips with her tongue, hoping she wasn't smudging her lipstick. 'Why don't we all go along to the Sunday School Hall on Saturday and surprise Miss Lovell with our books? I'm sure I can find a few more to give. I hope you'll all oblige me by passing the word along to others too. The more people who support the venture, the better.'

At last Bert let his arms drop and pushed away from the wall. 'I'll bid you ladies good day,' he said, and shambled to the door, putting his battered hat on as he went.

Relief floated through Naomi. She realized perspiration was beginning to cool in her armpits and under the front of her corset. Terribly unladylike.

Marjorie's face still bore purple blotches and she looked ready to crumple into tears. Sighing as she reconciled herself to the inevitable, Naomi bought some stamps that she didn't actually need then invited Marjorie to walk back to Foxfield for a cup of tea.

'They all blamed me,' Marjorie wailed as soon as they got outside.

'I went to some trouble to explain that I was the one at fault.'

'They still blamed me. Didn't you see the look Elsie Fuller gave me? I know what she was thinking: *Typical Marjorie. Can't get anything right.*'

'You're imagining it,' Naomi insisted, though she'd seen the look, too.

'As for Ada Hayes, I heard her sniff at me.'

'Only because she has a head cold.'

Goodness, this was exhausting. Naomi might have been at fault in giving her friend the ammunition to spread a rumour but she was serving her penance now. There'd be no getting rid of Marjorie for at least an hour, and there was every chance she'd keep up this self-pitying lament for weeks. Meanwhile, Bert Makepiece had gone home to the tranquillity of his market garden. Was he chuckling over Naomi's misfortune, having guessed how Marjorie would react, or was he simply feeling superior?

Two hours passed before Marjorie left and Naomi slumped back in her chair to recover from the wailing. Marjorie was her own worst enemy when it came to gossip. Had she been less eager to set tittle-tattle circulating, the problem with the book appeal would never have arisen.

But perhaps Naomi was being unfair. Marjorie was known throughout Churchwood as Naomi's closest ally and, even if she hadn't been so quick to gossip, people might have questioned her about Naomi's views on the book appeal anyway. And while Naomi hadn't actually voiced disapproval, she might well have given the impression of it, considering the way she'd been smarting from Alice Lovell's rejection.

No, Naomi's conscience was far from clear, and it smote her repeatedly on the days that followed. She still didn't cross paths with Alice but there was no doubt that the rumour mill was grinding.

'So sorry I misunderstood your intentions,' Mrs Lamb said in the grocer's shop. 'I should have known Marjorie would . . . Well, we all know Marjorie, don't we?'

'Of course I'll give a book or two now I know that you think it's a good idea,' said Miss Gibb. 'I should have asked your opinion instead of listening to Miss Plym.'

'Marjorie is a dear in many ways, but she's never been top of the class,' Mrs Webster opined.

Eventually Naomi found herself snapping back in defence of her friend. 'I don't know how many times I have to say it. If Marjorie misunderstood my feelings, it was because I didn't make them clear.'

'Oh, of course,' Mrs Webster said. 'I didn't mean . . . I haven't caused offence, have I? I'd hate to think I'd caused offence. I count you as a dear friend, and I so enjoy coming to Foxfield.'

That last comment struck another nerve. Was Naomi really a dear friend or courted only for her invitations to the best house in Churchwood? It was depressing to think the latter was more likely.

CHAPTER TWENTY-TWO

Alice

'So,' a new patient called Jonty O'Brian said, 'there's not much here by all accounts.'

'Churchwood is a village, not a town, so it's fairly small,' Alice admitted. 'There are shops, of course, mostly selling food and other necessities.'

'Two pubs selling beer, too.'

The longing in his voice made Alice smile. 'The Wheatsheaf and the Red Lion. I haven't been inside either of them so I can't describe them.'

'Rumour says one's rough and the other's respectable, but they're both as dull as a cloudy day in winter. I wouldn't mind how dull they were if I could put my lips to a pint of best bitter, though. Not much chance of that.'

Alice realized that Nurse Morgan was waiting to take her patient's temperature. 'Sorry. I'm in your way,' Alice said, stepping back from Jonty's bed.

Nurse Morgan smiled but it was nothing like the genuine smiles Alice received from the other nurses. 'I'll try to find a book for you soon,' Alice told Jonty.

Moving to the next bed, she spoke to the patient about the sort of book he wanted but remained aware of Nurse Morgan bustling around the ward.

'Take those tablets now, please,' she commanded

Stevie Meadows. 'You don't want me to have to fetch Matron.'

As if Stevie was any bother!

'Doctor's orders,' she told Andy Aynsworth, refusing him permission to walk to the bathroom.

With Timmy Foster she made a fuss about crumbs he'd spilt in his bed. 'You're a tough nut, Nurse,' Timmy commented. 'If I were a betting man, I'd put money on you being the eldest child who grew up bossing your little brothers and sisters.'

'You'd lose every penny,' she retorted. 'I've no brothers, and no sisters either.'

'Then you're making up for it by bossing us patients about.'

'I only boss patients who need it. Look at the state of this bed . . .'

Nurse Morgan had a brusque manner and Alice wasn't the only person to think so. 'That one needs a touch of your gentleness,' Timmy told Alice as the nurse bustled off again.

Alice smiled, but people had judged Kate and May Janicki unfairly and Alice didn't want to judge Ruth Morgan before she'd had a chance to get to know her. The nurse might be a different creature beneath that starched uniform.

May called at The Linnets during the afternoon. Rosa and Samuel were at school but May had brought little Zofia along. 'Come in,' Alice invited.

'We don't want to intrude. Zofia just wanted to bring you a picture she drew.'

'You won't be intruding if you come in out of the cold.'

May hesitated but clearly wanted company. Settling the matter, Alice stepped back to allow May and Zofia to enter. 'Give the door a shove when you close it,' Alice advised. 'It has a habit of sticking.'

She led the way into the dining room and admired Zofia's drawing of the chickens. 'It's excellent. Would you like to do some more drawing while Aunt May and I put the kettle on and fetch you some milk?'

Zofia nodded, climbing on to a chair as Alice took paper and crayons from a drawer. Leaving her engrossed with her small tongue peeping between her lips, Alice took May into the kitchen.

'Thanks again for looking after the children last week. I wish I could say I got all sorts of things done while they were with you,' May confided. She'd thanked Alice before, of course, but been unable to speak freely in the presence of the children.

'Instead, you sat and stared into space?'

'That's shameful, isn't it?'

'On the contrary, it's natural – a kind of shock at being suddenly alone again. Next time it won't feel so strange and you'll find yourself getting things done.'

'You've got a wise head on those slim shoulders, Alice Lovell.'

'Not really. It's just that I saw people who were going through all sorts of situations when my father was practising in London.'

May hesitated, and then said, 'You mentioned a next time?'

'Certainly. If it suits you?'

'It does, though I don't want to impose.'

'You won't be imposing if you leave them with me a couple of times each week.'

'I don't want the children to feel I'm getting rid of them either.'

'I'll make sure they don't feel like that,' Alice promised, glad to see that May was already looking calmer. Perhaps she was starting to open herself up to the possibility that she might find a way through this difficult period of her life after all.

'I'll ask if my friend Kate can come again. Did the children tell you about her?'

'Apparently, she told them a story and made it a lot of fun for them. Easy for them to understand, too, which is no mean feat given the language problems.'

'Kate is wonderful. I hope you'll meet her soon.'

'I'd like that.'

Alice smiled gratefully, though she'd expected no less. The question was whether Kate would like it.

'Has anyone offered to sell you their books?' Kate asked, calling in on one of her brief visits the following day.

'No one has mentioned selling books but two people have said they'll look out books for me and two more have told me they think that supplying books to the hospital is a good thing.'

'Quite a turnaround.'

'Mmm. I can't help wondering if it's Mrs Harrington's work. Perhaps she's changed her mind about the appeal.'

'Or perhaps someone has pointed out that she was hardly supporting the war effort with her previous attitude.'

'Who knows?' Alice said. She paused, and then added, 'May Janicki called yesterday. The children told her about the story you acted out for them. They loved it.'

'They're nice kids.'

'You're a nice person, too. May wants to meet you.'

Kate's expression turned stiff as though she was barricading herself behind it.

'Just because some people in Churchwood have judged you by your family, it doesn't follow that everyone will do the same,' Alice pointed out. '*I* like you. Daniel likes you. So does my father, and you know he usually hides away from people. May will like you, too, if you give her a chance.'

It was obvious that Kate didn't believe her. 'I barely have time to see you, let alone anyone else,' she said, falling back on her standard excuse. 'In fact, I need to get home now.'

Blast Ernie Fletcher and his awful boys for reducing Kate's self-esteem to dust. Alice was trying her best to build her friend's confidence by introducing her to people who might value her but it wasn't working because the Fletcher men had done too good a job. Watching Kate race home before her absence was discovered, Alice wished she could do more to help.

CHAPTER TWENTY-THREE

Naomi

Naomi stood at the sitting-room window and watched the Fletcher girl galloping up the lane towards Brimbles Farm. The girl never strolled, but that was because she never had time to stroll – if Alice Lovell were to be believed. Remembering her own walk to Brimbles Farm, Naomi felt tired at the thought of Kate rushing around. She had young legs and feet, of course – no creaky knees or bunions – but those clod-hopping boots couldn't be comfortable.

Naomi had noticed other people calling at The Linnets recently – the Jewish refugee children and their aunt. And yesterday, Naomi had seen Alice knocking on Janet Collins's door and handing over what looked to be a posy of primroses before being welcomed inside like a much-loved daughter. Had Naomi ever been invited into Janet's house? She couldn't remember receiving any such invitation. Not in more than twenty years.

Now Naomi had voiced her approval of the book appeal, others had begun to speak of Alice in warmer tones, too. 'I'm so glad you support what Miss Lovell's doing for the poor patients,' Mrs Hutchings had said. 'I only wish I had more books to give but we're not great readers in my house. We prefer newspapers and magazines.'

'It's the same in our house,' Mrs Giddins had said. 'Still, all credit to the girl.'

Naomi couldn't disagree. She didn't *want* to disagree. She understood the difference books would make to patients who would spend weeks – perhaps months – with no other source of entertainment. Even so, she still felt as though her life were being ploughed over like one of the fields at Brimbles Farm. Old certainties had been cut through and new *uncer*tainties had come to the surface.

It was strange how much time Naomi spent at this window these days. In the past, she'd looked out only occasionally to check on the weather and to give herself time to prepare to meet Alexander when he drew up in the car. Now she often found herself watching the comings and goings at The Linnets.

Of course, it was only possible to see who came and went because the trees and bushes that bordered the Foxfield gardens were still skeletal after their autumn shedding. Spring was approaching, though, and soon those trees and bushes would grow dense with new growth. Would Naomi feel more settled when that happened? Or would she feel even more excluded?

'Naomi, are you listening to me?' Marjorie was visiting again.

Naomi closed her eyes as she heaved a sigh and summoned her reserves of patience. 'Of course I'm listening, Marjorie.'

'Then you'll understand why I'm upset.'

Naomi didn't actually understand because her

mind had wandered from Marjorie's bleating complaints. 'You've no need to be upset,' Naomi said, returning to her chair and hoping she was saying the right thing.

'People will talk about me. They'll say it's because I've taken against Miss Lovell. Or because I'm mean.'

'You're not mean,' Naomi assured her, though Marjorie guarded her purse carefully and was happiest when Naomi picked up the bills. Not that Naomi objected; she understood that Marjorie's finances were meagre. But what on earth was Marjorie talking about?

'Mother and Father only left me a small number of books. They may not be worth much money but they have sentimental value. You do see that?'

Naomi began to feel a glimmer of insight.

'I couldn't give away a bible, could I?' Marjorie continued. 'What would Reverend Barnes say?'

'You've no books to give Miss Lovell,' Naomi stated, having hit upon the problem.

Marjorie looked puzzled. 'That's what I've been saying.'

'I was merely turning the matter over in my mind. I'm pleased to report that I have a solution.'

'Oh?' Marjorie sniffed and rummaged for a handkerchief.

'I've looked out several books. No one needs to know if I give some of them to you to take to the book appeal.'

Marjorie swallowed and wiped her red-rimmed eyes on a handkerchief. 'Thank you, Naomi. You're a true friend. But how will I get them home?'

Naomi clung to her patience with difficulty. 'In your basket.'

'Someone might see them.'

'Then I'll lend you a scarf to cover them.'

'So kind!'

'I'll fetch the scarf now.' Naomi fetched Marjorie's coat, too, hoping it would encourage her to leave.

'There,' she added a moment later, having arranged the scarf over two books.

'Thank you, Naomi.'

Naomi saw her friend to the door then returned to the window, though there was nothing to see except a blackbird with a worm in his beak, a final supper as dusk gathered and drew the light from the day.

A moment earlier she'd been desperate for Marjorie to leave but now she realized she'd only traded irritation for the sort of quietness that rang in the ears. Naomi took a final look at The Linnets and saw smoke rising from the chimney. It made the cottage look cosy and doubtless Alice was inside feeling hopeful about her book appeal.

Naomi decided she'd simply drop her books at the Sunday School Hall, express good wishes for the project and leave. There was no need to linger, especially if Kate Fletcher was there. Alice might not like Naomi but she'd be polite, which was more than could be said of her friend. That girl's glares could boil water faster than a stove.

Naomi pulled the curtains across the window and turned back into the room. The evening stretched ahead with only a solitary meal to look forward to because Alexander was staying in London. He was almost always staying in London these days.

Basil looked up from his basket. Ugly and faithful, he lumbered across to her. 'Let's have the wireless on, shall we?' she said. It would be company for both of them.

CHAPTER TWENTY-FOUR

Kate

'What's wrong with your foot?' Ernie demanded as Kate limped across the kitchen.

'I twisted it. These hand-me-down boots don't fit properly.'

'If you think I'm buying you new boots, you can forget it.'

'Have I said anything about new boots? *You* asked about my foot. *I* simply told you what had happened to it.'

'Humph.'

'Don't worry. I shan't be malingering. I can hobble around this place well enough, though I'll have to take Pete out in the trap to do some shopping tomorrow. I'm not walking two miles.'

She waited for Ernie's reply but none came. Taking his silence for begrudged agreement, she hopped to the stove and stabbed the potatoes that were boiling in a pan. The fork slid in easily. The potatoes were ready. 'Someone will have to carry the pan to the sink,' she called. 'I can't hop with heavy pans.'

Vinnie kicked Kenny's leg as though to say *You do it.*

'Fred can do it. He'll look fetching in a woman's apron,' Frank mocked, shoving Fred hard.

'Not half as fetching as you.' Fred shoved Frank in return.

Kate waited, then said, 'If no one helps, you won't get any dinner. Not that you deserve any, you bunch of animals.'

Kenny got up, cursing, and carried the pan to the sink to drain the water and dump the potatoes into a bowl.

'Someone needs to carry the stew,' Kate said.

Fred pushed Frank so hard that both he and his chair toppled over. 'I win!' Fred punched the air in victory.

Defeated but vowing revenge, Frank got off the floor and came to fetch the stew.

Kate limped around for the rest of the evening, standing on one foot as she washed the dinner dishes. She limped in the morning, too, as she made breakfast, washed dishes again then went out to see to the hens. No one objected when she put Pete into harness and set off for the village.

Turning out of Brimbles Lane on to Churchwood Way, she spotted Naomi Harrington returning from business in the village. Kate sent her a scowl, hoping her business hadn't been to sabotage Alice's book drive again.

Mrs Harrington gave no sign of having noticed except perhaps that her chin tilted up a little, probably in disgust.

Kate brought Pete to a halt outside the bakery. Getting down from the cart, she kept up the pantomime of an injured ankle. The chances of anyone noticing her and bothering to report the sighting back to her father and brothers were slight, but why take the risk?

No one commented on her injury in the bakery, though Kate was aware that at least two glances slid down to investigate it. With the exception of Alice, Kate doubted anyone in Churchwood would show concern for her health even if she walked in dripping blood.

'You were telling me about Abel,' Mrs Hutchings reminded Mrs Hayes, and Kate bought bread while half listening to an account of Abel's bronchitis.

She climbed back into the cart and nudged Pete on to the Sunday School Hall. The book appeal should have finished by now, but she waited several minutes to allow for any stragglers as she hoped to find Alice alone with only books at her side. A great pile of books.

'You're limping!' Alice said, concerned, as Kate entered. 'What happened?'

'Nothing happened.' Kate began walking normally again. 'I needed an excuse for coming out in the cart, that's all.'

'How clever of you. But it must have been annoying to go around limping.'

Kate shrugged. She was feeling awkward because that glamorous woman was here. May Janicki. Kate had been self-conscious about her appearance when she'd first met Alice, but while Alice was always neat and fresh and pretty, there was nothing grand about the flannel skirts, simple blouses and knitted cardigans she wore. May Janicki looked as though she'd stepped from the page of a fashion magazine – or so Kate imagined, never having looked through such a magazine. May was tall and slender like Kate, but there the resemblance ended. May's smooth, glossy hair was dressed in an immaculate French pleat, her face was enhanced by skilfully applied cosmetics and her coat must have cost a small fortune. Even her shoes, stockings and handbag were the picture of elegance.

'It's a pleasure to meet you,' May said politely when Alice introduced them.

Kate nodded, shuffled awkwardly, then turned back to Alice. 'Were you given many books?'

Alice gestured to a book-laden table. 'Nineteen,' she said, 'and only two duds among them.'

'Better than last time.'

'Much better. And no one asked for money except for an old chap who whispered, "How about sixpence?" behind Mrs Harrington's back.'

'*She* was here?'

'She gave some books and insisted she was donating them rather than selling them. Miss Plym gave two books as well but didn't know what to say when I asked if she'd enjoyed them so I suspect the books were Mrs Harrington's. A few people popped in to say they had no books to give but wished me well with the project.'

'Kate!' A cry went up from the back of the room where the Kovac children had been playing.

Kate looked round to see them running towards her, smiling. Rosa and Samuel came to a halt just in front of her but little Zofia kept on running and threw her arms around Kate's dirty breeches, looking up with shining, dark eyes. 'Nice chick hen story,' she said.

Oddly emotional all of a sudden, Kate smiled back

205

and touched the child's hair. How soft it was! 'I'm glad you liked it.'

What did glamorous May Janicki make of her youngest charge rubbing her cheek against dirty breeches? If May was cross, she hid it well.

'You tell more story?' Rosa asked.

'And do . . .' Samuel struggled to find the right word but flapped his arms like chicken wings to show he meant actions.

'Maybe one day,' Kate said, which committed no one to anything. She looked at Alice. 'We'd better get these books to the hospital.'

'Of course. I don't want to make you late.'

Kate helped Alice to pack the books into a box. They said goodbye to May and the children, Alice warmly and Kate a little gruffly.

'It was nice to meet you,' May said, but Kate supposed the woman was only being polite.

'You too,' Kate grunted, then heaved the box up and moved towards the door, not forgetting to limp as she got outside.

'It seems I misjudged Mrs Harrington,' Alice said as Pete pulled away from the kerb.

'Hmm.' If Naomi Harrington truly regretted sabotaging the first book drive, Kate was sorry she'd scowled at the woman earlier. But it seemed more likely that Churchwood's Queen Bee had only been thinking of her own reputation.

There was no sign of her in the Foxfield gardens when the cart drove past, but Kate forgot Mrs Harrington as they neared Brimbles Farm. Once again, she hoped to take Alice past without her being seen by any of the Fletcher men or there'd be harsh questions to answer.

No one saw them as far as Kate could judge. She continued to the hospital and pulled up near the steps, jumping down to carry the books to the door and then leaving Alice to summon help from the porter, a man she appeared to know.

'Thanks so much,' Alice said, climbing back into the cart. 'It would have taken me days to get all of the books to the hospital. Now the men won't have to wait to enjoy them.'

Kate was pleased she'd been able to help.

'Drop me here,' Alice suggested as they neared Brimbles Farm.

'Sure?' Kate didn't like to leave her friend with a long walk home, but time was ticking on.

'It's no trouble to walk from here,' Alice insisted. She paused, and then said, 'Now you've seen how nice May is, I hope you'll want to see more of her.'

'Perhaps,' Kate said, then changed the subject. 'I haven't finished reading *Jane Eyre* yet.'

'Don't rush it. Savour it.'

Kate brought the cart to a halt to let Alice climb down. They exchanged brief waves before Alice walked on and Kate turned the cart along the track to the farm.

Her thoughts turned brooding as she thought of Alice's growing friendship with May Janicki. Doubtless more friendships would follow as Alice settled deeper into village life. She deserved many friends, but where would that leave Kate? On the outside, of course. Uneducated and unpresentable, she wouldn't fit in with smart, clever people like May.

Alice's kindness would stop her from actually dropping Kate, but as her other friendships grew, her relationship with Kate would gradually wither to occasional waves and passing pleasantries.

Loneliness was nothing new to Kate, though. It was normal, in fact. It was the past few weeks that had been different. They'd brought light into the gloom, but she'd survived before and she'd survive again.

Kate's mood was foul over the rest of that Saturday and all through Sunday. If she wasn't snapping at her father and brothers, her manner towards them was surly. When the bad mood continued into Monday she decided to try to pick herself up by trying on her mother's old dresses in the hope of seeing a way to make them fit. But it was hopeless. Kate was too tall and too broad in the shoulders.

Devastated, she flung the dresses across her bedroom, only to cry in remorse and gather them back up. She folded them carefully and, kissing them, returned them to the drawer where she kept the other precious items that had belonged to her mother. It had been a pointless exercise. Had it been possible to adjust the dresses, she'd have done it years ago.

Her only solace lay in reading. What was it Alice had said when she'd lent her *Jane Eyre*? Something about Jane sharing some of Kate's qualities. Kate certainly identified with Jane as an unloved, rebellious child, but the grown-up Jane appeared to have considerably more patience than Kate could muster. It was a terrific story, though, and, desperate to escape her misery, Kate had taken to sneaking it downstairs in the pocket of her jacket and reading a page or two when she was alone in the kitchen, making meals or washing dishes.

Having come indoors to make cocoa now, she treated herself to a few more pages and gasped when Jane, at the very moment she was in church to marry Mr Rochester, learned that he already had a wife secreted in his attic – a poor woman who was afflicted in her mind but dangerous with it. Kate turned the page to read on but a hiss alerted her to the pan of milk she'd left on the stove boiling over. Putting the book down, she ran to rescue it, and at that moment Vinnie came in with Frank 'n' Fred.

More concerned about the book than the scalded milk, Kate couldn't decide what to do. Running to the book would only draw attention to it, but—

Too late. 'What's this?' Vinnie asked, picking the book up.

'Leave it alone. It isn't yours,' Kate cried.

'It isn't yours, either. So whose is it?' He sent her a nasty look and began to flick none too gently through the pages. 'Looks boring.'

'Give it back!'

Kate rushed over to snatch the book back before he damaged it but Vinnie called, 'Here, Fred. Catch this!'

The book flew through the air and Fred caught it, crushing the pages in his dirty hands. 'To me!' Frank called as Kate pivoted towards Fred, and so it went on, with the book passing roughly from brother to brother, pages falling out and scattering around the room.

Finally, Kate wrestled it from Vinnie but the book was ruined. 'Look what you've done!' Kate was devastated. 'You absolute—'

Ernie and Kenny walked in. 'Problem?' Ernie asked mildly.

'Kate's got a book,' Vinnie said.

'Whose book?'

'It doesn't matter whose book it is,' Kate argued. 'Vinnie and the twins have wrecked it!'

'Whose book?' Ernie repeated, and the hard glimmer in his eyes had Kate's breath catching in her throat.

Ernie wouldn't care about a damaged book. But he *would* care if he knew she had a friend.

'I found it,' Kate said.

'Found it where?'

'In the lane. Someone must have dropped it.'

'Who drops books in the lane?'

'I don't know! I didn't see. People who work at the hospital walk past on their way into the village. Perhaps it was one of them.'

Ernie stared at her and Kate willed herself not to blink first. Losing interest, Ernie headed for the table.

'If you don't know whose book it is, you won't need to return it,' Vinnie pointed out and with malicious pleasure he tore another page from the book, rolled it up and dipped the end in the fire so he could use it to light a cigarette.

Kate waited until they'd all left the room before she gathered up the remains of the book and wept bitter tears. What on earth was she going to tell her friend?

CHAPTER TWENTY-FIVE

Alice

'You've got a book for me?' Timmy Foster's eyes brightened.

'A choice of *The Call of the Wild* or *Murder on the Orient Express*,' Alice told him.

'I'll take the second one. If I read about a murder, maybe I won't want to commit one.'

'Bad day?' Alice asked.

'It's the boredom that gets to me. The frustration, too. My ma hasn't been well and I hate being unable to go and help out. She's a widow.'

'I'm sure she knows you'd help if you could. You've written to her to explain?'

'Yes, though she's not so good with reading. My sister will read the letter to her if she can get over there, but Sal's just had twins so she's struggling a bit. Her Alan is away in the navy.'

'I won't say try not to worry – that would be impossible – but I hope the book will take your mind off things for a while.'

'It will, miss, and it's kind of you to bring it. Breath of fresh air, you are.'

Alice smiled and moved on to give *The Call of the Wild* to Jonty O'Brian, whom she suspected would have preferred the Agatha Christie but was grateful for any book.

It had been a busy morning and Alice was glad when Nurse Carter mimed a tea-drinking gesture from the door and beckoned Alice to follow. Nurse Carter and her friend Nurse Evans were the two friendliest nurses in Stratton House. They were quick and efficient, too, and obvious favourites with the patients.

Alice moved into the corridor then turned into the small room where tea was made and teacups washed. Nurse Carter already had tea brewing. 'Get this down you,' she said, offering a cup to Alice.

'Thank you.'

The nurse leaned back against the cupboards for a breather, so Alice did likewise.

'What you're doing here . . . I think it's great,' Nurse Carter said. 'The patients always look forward to your visits. Even Jake Turner, and he's a miserable so-and-so if ever I saw one.'

'I suspect that being miserable is his way of protecting himself. A shell that keeps the world out and the fears in.'

'You could be right. He's always got his nose in one of those old seed catalogues you brought. I asked him if he was enjoying them yesterday and he flung the catalogue aside and said there was nothing else to do around here. But a few minutes later he had his nose buried in it again.'

Alice was glad to hear it. When she'd offered him a catalogue, he'd given one of his long-suffering sighs before reaching out to take one. 'Anything for a bit of peace,' he'd muttered, as though she'd been

212

nagging him, but Alice had suspected he'd wanted a catalogue all along.

'He's right when he said there's nothing else to do around here,' Nurse Carter said then.

'Jonty O'Brian said much the same, though he had pubs in mind. Is it dull for the nurses, too?'

'No dance hall, no cinema, no teashop, even,' Nurse Carter confirmed. 'I've been to St Albans and Hatfield on the bus but it's a long walk from here to the bus stop and the buses are slow. They don't run late, either.'

'I believe they've reduced the service due to the petrol shortages.'

'We spend most of our free time in the staff quarters sipping cocoa, darning stockings and writing letters home. What we'd really like is a change of scene. But we're better off than the patients. All we've got to complain about is boredom, but for them . . .'

'That's why you became a nurse,' Alice guessed. 'To help the patients.'

'It certainly was. Bored or not, I don't regret it. I always planned a career in military nursing. I had two aunts who were volunteer nurses in the 1914 war, serving in France and sleeping under canvas for some of the time. It was so cold in winter they had to sleep in coats and scarves. They saw terrible injuries, too. There were no antibiotics then so men could die of gangrene within days. Within hours sometimes. As for blood transfusions, they were pretty primitive and they didn't always work, even when attempted.'

'Medical care is better now.'

'Yes, but it can't save every life. And even those who

213

survive ... You've seen how some patients are suffering.'

'You're all doing your best.'

'We are. There'll be thousands of patients needing help before this war is over. Did you never think of nursing, Alice?'

'Yes, but I decided I'd be better suited to a job that meant I could organize things. Organize people, too. I expected to work for some sort of business but it hasn't quite gone to plan. Not yet, anyway.'

'You're enterprising. You'll find something eventually.'

Alice wished she could share Nurse Carter's confidence, but she wasn't going to dwell on her troubles now. Something else the nurse had said had sparked an idea.

'Penny for them,' Nurse Carter said, smiling because Alice's attention must have drifted off momentarily.

'Sorry. I was thinking about what you said about a change of scene. Would you like to come to tea at my house one day? It wouldn't be a grand tea but—'

'I'd love to come!'

'Nurse Evans, too. You're friends, aren't you?'

'Good friends. We trained together.'

'Let me know when you're both free.'

'Thank you, we will.' The nurse rinsed her cup and left it to drain. 'I'd better get back to work but I've enjoyed our chat, Miss Lovell.'

'Alice. My name is Alice.'

'I'm Barbara. Babs. Nurse Evans is Pauline.'

'I've enjoyed the chat, too. Don't worry about my cup. I'll wash it myself.'

It would be nice to enjoy more of Babs's and

Pauline's company. Their visit would also provide material for Alice's next letter to Daniel – more evidence that her life was just fine without him.

She'd just placed her cup on the draining board when someone entered the room behind her, coming to a halt and saying, 'Oh! Pardon me.'

Alice turned to see Nurse Morgan. 'Sorry. I didn't mean to invade your space. I'm just leaving.'

'I didn't know visitors were allowed in here.'

Oh dear. Nurse Morgan's tone was accusatory. Having no wish to get Babs Carter into trouble, Alice decided to fib. 'I popped in for a sip of water. I'm about to read a story to the patients and my throat was croaky.'

'Should you have come to a hospital if you're starting a cold? Some of the patients are vulnerable.'

'I don't have a cold, but water helps with reading out loud. I didn't realize the room was off limits to visitors.'

'I'm sure it isn't for me to tell you where you should and shouldn't go.' Nurse Morgan's smile was unpleasantly superior.

Alice had thought of inviting her to tea as well but decided she wouldn't this time. She needed to get to know the girl better first, though whether it would prove possible to find a way past her disdainful exterior remained to be seen. While Ruth was different to Kate in many ways, Kate used aggression as a shield and maybe Ruth's supercilious manner was a defence, too. As in Kate's case, perhaps a warm heart beat behind it.

Alice was glad when Kate called the following afternoon but saw immediately that something was wrong. 'What is it?'

Kate took a book from her jacket pocket and passed it over. It was Alice's copy of *Jane Eyre*, and it was ruined. Even so, Alice was relieved. 'Goodness, Kate, you scared me for a moment. I thought . . . Well, I thought something terrible had happened.'

'Something terrible *has* happened! I've ruined your book!'

Kate's misery tugged at Alice's heart. 'It's a pity the book is ruined but I doubt that you're responsible. Did your brothers do it?'

'Who else?' Kate said bitterly. 'I'm sorry.'

'No, *I'm* sorry. Sorry you have to live with such a bunch of selfish, mindless vandals.'

'I should never have let them get near the book. I don't have the money to replace it right now, but I'll replace it one day. Until then I'll try to make it up to you by digging your garden and—'

'The damage wasn't your fault so there's nothing to make up for. Come in, Kate. You're obviously upset.'

'I can't.' Kate gestured towards the lane. 'I've left the cart out there. I'm supposed to be shopping for beer.'

'At least let me fetch another book for you.'

'No! I mean, no, thank you. I can't risk it. Not now. I'm not sure they believed me when I said I found the book in the lane. Vinnie might search my room, and if he sees another book, he'll know I have a friend and I'll be kept on the farm.'

'Oh, Kate.' Alice touched her friend's arm but Kate stepped away, looking as though she might cry.

'I'll see you when I can get away again,' she said.

'Come for tea. I've invited two nurses from the

hospital. You'll like them and they'll like you. You deserve friends, Kate. I'll let you know when they're coming.'

'Bye,' Kate said, racing out to the lane but not quite quickly enough to hide the shimmer of tears in her eyes.

Alice burned with anger on her friend's behalf. Life wasn't fair. Alice knew that. But for Kate and the patients at the hospital, it was particularly unfair.

Kate called in twice over the days that followed but, obviously depressed, was more inclined to work in the garden than to talk. On both occasions Alice mentioned the nurses' visit but received barely a grunt in response. It was understandable that Kate couldn't commit to coming along but Alice sensed that her friend wouldn't attend even if she could get away. Neither would she agree to seeing more of May Janicki.

Alice wished again that she could hit upon some way of helping Kate but no new ideas occurred to her. She could only keep trying to build Kate's confidence bit by little bit and hope that one day it would make a difference.

CHAPTER TWENTY-SIX

Alice

Alice wished she could do more to help the patients too.

'Got any Sherlock Holmes stories yet?' Stevie Meadows asked. 'I love a mystery story.'

She'd managed to give him *Ivanhoe* but he'd finished it weeks ago. 'As soon as *The Hound of the Baskervilles* is returned I'll pass it on to you,' Alice promised.

'I know you will,' he said, smiling to show he wasn't nagging, but she still wished she didn't have to keep him waiting.

She took a deep breath then turned to Stevie's neighbour, the man Babs and Pauline called Private Misery. 'How are you?' she asked.

'Fine and dandy.' Jake Turner's voice dripped sarcasm.

Alice sighed and moved on to Jimmy Attercliffe, whose sight still hadn't returned. She read the letter he'd received from his parents that morning.

Dear Jimmy,
Thank you for your last letter. We've read it so many times we know it by heart. We hope you're keeping well and cheerful. Are you getting enough to eat? Are they airing your sheets?

We miss you badly, our Jimmy. The house hasn't been the same since you left, though we're battling along. We have to, don't we?

Cathy Gregg from number sixteen had her baby last week – a boy. I'm knitting a matinee coat for him . . .

The letter ended with expressions of love. 'Would you like me to write a reply?' Alice asked.

'Maybe tomorrow after I've thought of what to say. Could you read a story, though?'

More patients wanted a story so Alice read 'Lost in the Sahara' from *Your Fireside Friend.*

'That was a cracker,' someone called at the end.

Jake Turner shook his head as though the world was full of idiots who were easily pleased by nonsense.

It was time for Alice to leave but she lingered for a moment in the hope of making some headway with Ruth Morgan. 'It's been a busy day for you,' Alice said.

'I can't discuss patients with a visitor. Especially not a civilian visitor.'

'I was simply admiring the work you do.'

'Kind of you, I'm sure.' Ruth reinforced her insincerity with a sniff.

What a difficult girl she was. Babs Carter must have overheard Ruth's comment because she rolled her eyes from across the ward. But Alice wouldn't give up on Ruth any more than she'd give up on Jake Turner.

Babs and Pauline duly came to tea. 'It's just a sandwich, a scone and a cup of tea,' Alice warned, leading them into the dining room.

'Sounds lovely and, anyway, we'll enjoy just sitting and chatting,' Babs said.

Alice was pleased when her father came in to welcome the girls. She was always glad to introduce him to visitors as she didn't want him to withdraw from the world completely. If ever Alice got the chance to strike out independently, she wanted to know that he was part of the Churchwood community, even if he was only on the edge of it.

He stayed for a few minutes to talk about nursing and medical matters. 'Enjoy your tea,' he said then, taking his own tray into his study.

'This is delicious,' Babs declared, tucking into an egg sandwich. 'So fresh!'

Alice told them about the chickens and the vegetable patch.

'Hopefully rationing won't reduce us to gruel,' Babs joked. 'We need decent food when we're on our feet all day. Or all night, depending on our shift.'

They talked about London, too. 'We trained at Queen Alexandra's Hospital,' Babs said. 'It was a great place to work. We could use our free time to see the sights and visit the shops. Do you miss London, Alice?'

'Sometimes. My two friends from school – twins – left to live in Canada a year or so ago, but I still enjoyed exploring museums and art galleries.'

'I liked walking by the river,' Babs said.

'Yes, and calling in at a Lyons' Corner House for cheese on toast,' Pauline agreed. 'The London shops are wonderful, too.'

'Selfridge's bargain basement!' Babs cried.

'Churchwood has its compensations, though,' Alice suggested.

'Like meeting us?' Babs joked.

'I know what Alice means,' Pauline said. 'My parents are glad I'm here. They think I'll be safer than in London when the bombing starts.'

Babs and Pauline had skills that would hold them in good stead wherever they went – unlike Alice. But she wasn't going to let worry about the future spoil her afternoon. 'Have another sandwich,' she urged.

Alice hadn't expected to see Kate but was still disappointed when she didn't appear. No one needed friends more than Kate but the thought of sitting here in her hand-me-down men's clothing had obviously been too mortifying for her to contemplate.

'We'd better head back to Stratton House,' Babs said eventually. 'Would it be cheeky to say I hope we can visit again?'

'I'd take it as a compliment.'

'We'll see you at Stratton House in the meantime. You're making such a difference to the men.'

Pauline nodded. 'They often ask if you're coming.'

'I'll visit tomorrow. Hopefully, I'll have *The Hound of the Baskervilles* for Stevie Meadows,' Alice said.

'Lovely boy,' Babs approved.

Miraculously, Alice arrived to find that one of the patients had finished reading that very book. 'Might I have it now?' another patient asked.

'Next time. I've already promised it to someone who's been waiting a while.'

'Right you are, miss.'

Alice took the book straight to Stevie Meadows but his bed was empty. Ruth Morgan was stripping it, in fact.

'Is Private Meadows in therapy?' Alice asked.

'Suspected blood clot to the lungs,' Ruth told her. 'He died unexpectedly.'

Alice felt as though her breath had been punched from her body. 'Died?'

'It happens, I'm afraid.'

Alice stared at the empty bed; then she stumbled from the ward, along the corridor and out through the front door where she sank down on the steps. How was it possible that a young man so full of sweetness, courage and hope should be struck down so cruelly and swiftly?

Poor Stevie. He'd never read *The Hound of the Baskervilles* now. Neither would he marry pretty Esme, the girl he'd loved for almost all of his life, and she'd never bear his golden-haired children. As for Stevie's family, their house would never again be the same happy place it had once been. His mother wouldn't feed her beloved son dumplings, and neither would his father see him eat the rhubarb he'd grown especially for a fruit crumble. The jumper his grandmother was knitting for him would be set aside and his sisters would cry at being unable to treat their lovely brother to fish and chips and a film. Alice wept for the sheer, wasteful tragedy of it all.

Someone sat beside her. Tom, the porter. 'You've heard about the lad?' he guessed.

Alice nodded. She wiped her eyes on the back of her hand but more tears came and Tom passed her a handkerchief. 'It was so unexpected,' she managed to say.

'Death can be like that. I saw a lot of it when I was fighting in the last war. Young men – hale, hearty and full of promise – struck down in an instant. It's right to grieve for those lost lives, and we mustn't run away from the grief. We should use it. Look out there and tell me what you see.' He gestured away from the house.

Alice blinked to clear the blurriness from her eyes. 'Trees, shrubs, grass, cows . . .'

'In other words?'

'Life going on and new life beginning.'

There were buds of soft, pliant growth on the trees and daffodils showed yellow like bold pioneers braving the winter frosts and paving the way for more flowers to follow. Birds sang cheerily, energized by the approaching spring, and day by day the sun would rise higher in the sky, its rays gaining strength and ushering in vigour and opportunity.

'Use your grief, Alice. Use it to feed your determination to make life as good as it can be for the chaps who remain. For everyone, in fact.'

She nodded slowly. 'I'm not running away. I'm just . . .'

'Taking a moment to adjust. We all need moments like those.'

They sat for a few minutes longer and then went back inside. Alice washed her face in the cloakroom, took a bracing breath and returned to Stevie's ward.

The mood was sombre. Little was being said, and in the few conversations that were taking place, voices were hushed. Even Jake Turner took his medication from Pauline in silence without as much as a sigh or an eye roll. Had Stevie's death put Jake's own problems into perspective or merely reinforced his belief that all life had to offer was disappointment?

It was too soon to judge, but for her own part, Alice planned to take Tom's advice and help the patients draw every scrap of enjoyment from their lives. She couldn't do much, but she could find more books for them. Somehow.

A picture of Kate's sad face floated into her mind and Alice determined to make life as good as it could be for her friends, too.

CHAPTER TWENTY-SEVEN

Naomi

'I understand,' Naomi told Alexander when he called to let her know he'd be staying in London over the weekend. Again. He'd been gone for more than a week. 'You needn't worry about me. I'm keeping busy, as always.'

'Good. Well, I'll—'

'I've been thinking about Alice Lovell's book appeal. You remember Alice Lovell? The doctor's daughter?'

'What about her?' Alexander sounded bored, but, if Naomi couldn't see her husband, she wanted at least to talk to him.

'Her second book drive received some support but I'm sure she still needs more books and if the hospital expands . . .'

'What are you trying to say?'

'I'm thinking of donating money so she can buy new books.'

'For heaven's sake, Naomi! We don't have unlimited funds and who knows what sort of dent this war will make in our finances.'

'I don't mean a large donation.'

'Do as you see fit but this war has barely started yet and our investments may suffer. It's a time for conserving money, not handing it out on lame-duck projects.'

'Hardly a—'

'I have to go. I have a client waiting.'

'When will you be home next?'

'I don't know.'

'I hope you can make it soon. Goodbye, Alexander. I miss you.'

But the call had ended.

Naomi replaced the telephone receiver and stared down at it, fighting against the suspicion that Alexander wasn't missing her at all. He was a busy man. Clients had always made heavy demands on his time and now the war was adding challenges. After all, it must be hard to advise on investments when the war was making it difficult to predict which companies offered the best long-term rewards and which were in danger of sinking.

He'd misunderstood her about the donation, though. She didn't have hundreds of pounds in mind. Just five or ten pounds that would enable Alice to buy some modern books to complement the older books she'd received.

But giving money was a sensitive subject even without Alexander's opposition. For one thing, Alice hadn't actually asked for money. And for another, Naomi feared that offering it might be seen as another attempt to push her way into Alice's project. The thought of the resentment – the hostility, even – that might come her way made Naomi shudder. No, she wouldn't offer a donation just yet.

The book project was an excellent cause, though. Naomi pitied the men who must be lying in their hospital beds or shuffling around the wards with little to occupy them. Doubtless they could chat to each other, but it didn't follow that they found their companions congenial hour after hour, day after day, week after week . . . Books offered escape and interest as well as filling time.

The thought of filling time had Naomi looking around her sitting room. Another empty evening lay ahead of her. Perhaps she could look at her bookcase again to identify any other books she could donate to the hospital.

The front of the bookcase displayed the books her father had bought when trying to launch himself into society. They were large leather-bound tomes on Britain's grand houses, art, antiques, birds, butterflies and other flora and fauna. He'd done little more than poke his nose into them before arranging them so as to catch the eyes of visitors, who were supposed to feel impressed.

Some of the patients might find them interesting but their sheer size and weight made them impractical for patients who were trying to read in bed or in an armchair. These books needed to be studied at a desk.

Behind them were Naomi's novels but as she leafed through them she knew she'd be too embarrassed to offer such torrid romances to the hospital.

Might she send away to Murton's bookshop in St Albans for *modern books to the value of £10* or similar? But no. It would still feel like a badly contrived attempt to push in and take over.

Out of ideas, she settled down with one of the torrid romances and tried not to draw comparisons between the passionate Florian of the book and the brisk, even abrupt, man Naomi had married. Florian was an invention. Alexander was a flesh-and-blood man and, as such, he had his flaws like everyone else. After all, Naomi herself hardly measured up to Florian's love interest in the story, the fair-haired, slender and achingly beautiful Marianne.

Naomi fair-haired, slender and achingly beautiful? Hardly.

With a cook, maid, daily cleaning woman and gardener to do her bidding, Naomi had no need to walk into the village every day but on most days she walked there anyway. 'Stretching my legs,' she'd say, thinking that she'd be more bulldog-like than ever if she took no exercise.

Besides, there was company to be found in the shops and passers-by. People to organize and encourage by example, such as by buying a little something for a Red Cross parcel. She could issue invitations too: 'Come for luncheon next week,' or, 'Do come for tea.'

As always these days, Naomi looked towards The Linnets as she left the house the next morning. No one arrived or left as Naomi approached but Alice was doubtless busy doing something or seeing someone.

Naomi had almost reached the shops when rapid footsteps sounded behind her. A glance over her shoulder showed Alice drawing near. How was it that, even as she was hastening along the pavement in her unremarkable grey coat, Alice managed to look quietly dignified? 'Good morning, Mrs Harrington,' she said.

'Miss Lovell.'

Alice slowed down to walk in step with Naomi, as though she felt politeness required it. As the older woman – a woman of substance, too – Naomi thought she should have the upper hand but it always deserted her when Alice was near. Chiding herself for being a fool for feeling so gauche, Naomi said, 'I was glad to see your book appeal being supported.'

'Thank you for your contributions. The books are at the hospital now and being enjoyed by the patients. Forgive me if I've guessed incorrectly, but are you the person who left a box of books at my door the first time I appealed for reading material? If so, I'd like to thank you for those, too.'

Naomi felt pleased. 'I only hope they're proving welcome.'

'Very much so.'

'Do you have enough books now?'

'Not nearly, but—'

But what? Naomi didn't get to find out because Alice broke off as Marjorie hastened across the road towards them.

'Miss Plym.' Alice nodded at her then continued on to the baker's shop.

Moments later she swept past again with a loaf of bread in her basket. Listening with only half an ear to Marjorie's prattle, Naomi wondered what purpose was drawing Alice home so briskly.

Belatedly, Naomi realized Marjorie was asking what had brought her to the village today. 'Just stretching my legs, though I think I'll call in to the grocer's.'

'Buying something for dear Alexander?'

'Not today.' Alexander dined out when he was in

London, and if he wanted something light he had food delivered to the flat by Fortnum & Mason – pâté, fine cheeses and Gentlemen's Relish. At home ... Well, who knew when he'd be home again?

Naomi bought two tins of pilchards for the Red Cross parcels before she managed to shake off Marjorie and turn towards home. The shops soon gave way to cottages, their gardens bright with early flowers. William Treloar's daffodils were looking particularly fine but then he was Churchwood's keenest gardener. His shed door was open and Naomi could see tools inside along with a watering can, bottles of this and that, and something half hidden beneath an ancient brown blanket.

She only realized she'd stopped to look when Mr Treloar appeared from behind the shed and stood watching her with a frown that suggested he was wondering what on earth she was doing. 'Good morning, Mr Treloar,' Naomi called. 'Please don't let me disturb you. I just stopped to catch my breath.'

She smiled awkwardly and continued on her way, taking with her the beginnings of an idea. She'd think long and hard about what, if anything, to do with it before she mentioned it to anyone else, though.

CHAPTER TWENTY-EIGHT

Kate

Kate had much to be thankful for. She knew that. Looking out across the farmland, she could see beauty in the pearly white of the sky and the rays of sunshine that lit up the buds on trees and bushes. The worst of the winter had passed. Days could still be chilly and nights could still be cold but even the frosts scattered the world in diamond-like crystals and made the air so crisp and clear that the moon's craters showed in smudges of blue.

Kate had health and vigour, too, which was more than could be said for those of the country's soldiers, sailors and airmen who were facing devastating injuries or sickness from inhospitable climates and conditions.

For the time being, she also had a friend in Alice, but Kate's fear of receding into the background of Alice's life was growing. First there'd been May Janicki and now there were those nurses. It was only to be expected that Alice would have more in common with educated, professional people like them than with ignorant Kate who'd barely been to school. But it was still going to hurt.

She uprooted two turnips to use in a stew and shook them forcefully to dislodge earth and vent her frustration. Movement caught on the edge of her vision. If this was Vinnie come to pick a fight, he could—

It wasn't Vinnie. When Kate saw who was approaching, she felt as shocked as if she'd been punched in the gut. No, no, no!

She glanced around desperately, relieved to see that none of the Fletcher men were in sight. Then she hastened to meet Alice. 'You shouldn't be here!' she cried. 'I'm sorry if that sounds rude, but if anyone sees you, I'll—'

'It can't go on, Kate.'

She imagined Alice meant the cruelty, the bullying, the controlling of Kate's life. But her friend didn't understand. 'It's lovely that you care, Alice, but there's nothing you can do to change things. The best way you can help is to leave before anyone—'

'Got a visitor, have we?' Ernie had rounded a corner.

Kate cursed inside her head while doing some quick thinking. 'She's looking for a book she lost in the lane.'

'Is that so?'

'Actually, I'm here to see you, Mr Fletcher,' Alice said, and Kate groaned despairingly. 'You *are* Mr Fletcher?' Alice added.

'Maybe I am. Maybe I'm not. What's it to you?'

'I think we should talk inside.'

'We'll talk here.' Kenny, Vinnie, Frank and Fred all appeared and lined up with their father, feet apart and arms crossed in stances that Kate knew were intended to be intimidating.

'Don't do this, Alice,' Kate murmured. 'Please.'

Alice was tiny next to the Fletcher men, but she met their stares without flinching. 'Inside,' she said, and, without waiting for an invitation, she walked to the kitchen door and stepped into the house.

'What the . . .?' Ernie began, then hastened after her.

Kate followed only to be jostled aside so her brothers could enter first.

By the time Kate got inside, Alice was standing with her back to the shabby old dresser, facing the Fletcher men with her chin tilted high.

'Now look here, Miss Whatever-your-name-is,' Ernie said. 'We don't take kindly to people taking liberties on our land.'

'Really? I thought you were all too familiar with taking liberties, Mr Fletcher.'

'Eh? What's this about?'

Kate shook her head warningly but Alice was looking at Ernie. 'It's about the way you treat your daughter.'

'That's no business of yours.'

'On the contrary, it's the business of anyone who hates bullying. It's my business in particular because your daughter is my friend.'

Ernie turned to Kate with fury in his eyes. 'I knew you were lying about that book.'

'If Kate lied, it's because you gave her no choice,' Alice argued. 'You use her as a skivvy and allow her no clothes, no money and no life of her own.'

'She'll do her duty. No more, no less. And if you come round here again, I'll—'

'What, Mr Fletcher? Bully me too?'

'I've every right to turf trespassers off my land.'

'You've no right to manhandle them. Touch me and I'll report you to the police. I'm a respectable doctor's daughter. You and your sons are known in Churchwood as a pack of uncouth brawlers. There can't be much doubt about which of us will be believed.'

'Get out.'

'When I'm ready. You're not only unfair and unkind, Mr Fletcher, you're also stupid.'

Kate sucked in breath and so did her brothers. 'You can't say that!' Vinnie stepped forward with his hands bunched into fists.

Alice didn't even spare him a glance. Her attention remained on Ernie. 'You're stupid because you don't realize that the more you try to crush Kate, the more likely she is to leave. You may think that she has nowhere else to go, and that might have been true once, but it isn't true any more. Kate can come to me the moment her life here becomes intolerable. I'll help her to find work and independence.'

'Who's going to employ *her*?' Vinnie mocked.

'It may have escaped your notice but there's a war on. That means there's plenty of work for young women like Kate. Not in this village perhaps, but there are lots of other places, and some of them aren't far from here. Hatfield, for one. That's where de Havilland's make aircraft and I imagine they'll be glad to employ someone like Kate. She doesn't need you, Mr Fletcher. But you need her.'

Ernie's venom spilt over. 'You little—'

'Don't you dare!' Kate cried.

What was she thinking, standing here and letting Alice fight her corner? Without a penny to her name, Kate had believed herself to be powerless. But with Alice helping her, she had choices. Not easy ones, but still . . . choices.

'Stop acting like a thug,' Kate told Ernie. 'Do you want me to stay or do you want me to leave?'

'Your place is here.'

'That's not what I asked.'

'You can please yourself what you do.'

'Very well. Alice, if you wouldn't mind waiting while I fetch my—'

'All right!' Ernie snarled. 'You should stay. It's your duty to look after—'

'I don't need a lesson on duty. Not from a man who's failed in his duty as a father. If I stay, it'll be on my terms.'

'What do you mean, *terms*?'

'I want money.'

Skinflint Ernie blanched.

'Every week. Ten shillings.'

'Are you mad?'

'Take it or leave it.'

'One shilling. You get bed and board, too.'

Kate snorted. 'This place is a dump and the only reason anyone gets bed and board is because I do the cooking, cleaning and washing. Five shillings, and that's my final offer.'

Ernie turned back to Alice. 'See what trouble you've caused?'

'I'd say a revolution on Kate's part was long over-due,' Alice taunted.

'You've turned her into a harpy.'

'On the contrary, Kate is magnificent.'

'Well?' Kate demanded. 'What about the five shillings?'

'Two shillings. And you'd better earn them.'

'I *already* earn them. And I'll have the first week's wages now, please.'

'You'll get 'em when the boys get theirs.'

'They got theirs yesterday so I'll have mine today.' Kate marched across the room for Ernie's cash box and thrust it towards him.

Cursing, Ernie dug in his pocket for the key. He sat at the table and twisted sideways as he opened the box to shield the contents from prying eyes. Counting out two shillings, he slammed the coins on the table and gave them a rough push in Kate's direction.

She picked them up and held them tight. 'Money was only the first term. I have another.'

Ernie looked even more outraged.

'I want time to see Alice.'

'I'm not paying you to go gallivanting.'

'You're paying me to work, and I *will* work. Hard. Just not all of the time. Is that agreed?'

He waved a hand as though he couldn't bear to talk to her for a minute longer.

'I think that's satisfactory enough for now,' Alice said. 'You won't forget what I said about Kate having friends to help her? I hope I won't hear that you've gone back on this agreement, because if I do . . .'

'You've said your piece. Now get out of my house.'

'That will be a pleasure. I'm sure you have a lot to do now you can't treat your daughter as a skivvy. Good day to you all.' Alice smiled around at the Fletcher boys.

They all looked towards Ernie, who'd thrown himself into a chair, looking sulky.

'Ernie!' Vinnie protested. 'You're not going to let Kate—'

'Oh, shut up,' Ernie told him. 'Or do *you* want to keep house for the rest of us?'

Vinnie was silenced.

Alice swept from the room, sending Kate a wink.

Kate followed her into the farmyard, feeling stunned. 'I don't know what to say, except thank you.'

'You managed the negotiations all by yourself. I only gave you a nudge.'

'More than a nudge,' Kate said, but Alice only shrugged.

'You have two shillings. It's a beginning. I hope to see more of you now, and maybe you can meet May and the nurses next time they come to tea.'

Once again, the mention of Alice's new friends sent thoughts darting through Kate's mind like tiny, poisoned arrows telling her she wouldn't fit in with them. 'Maybe,' she said.

Alice stepped forward and folded Kate's tall frame into a hug. 'Stay strong,' she said. 'And hold your father to the terms he agreed.'

'I will.'

Alice walked off and Kate squared her shoulders, ready to go back inside and face what was certain to be jeering hostility from her family. But she had every intention of staying strong; jeering hostility was nothing new to her. Even if it worsened, it was a small price to pay for some money of her own. She jiggled today's coins in her hand, her heart beating faster at what they represented: hope for a better life.

The first thing on Kate's shopping list was going to be soap; the second a copy of *Jane Eyre* to give to Alice to replace the copy Vinnie had ruined. After that, she'd save for clothes. She needed everything from underwear to shoes so kitting herself out was likely to take months, but she'd manage it in the end – unless Ernie stopped paying or gave her so much work she barely had time to breathe let alone leave the farm to see her friend.

Had Alice really meant that Kate could abandon home and go to The Linnets for help, or had she merely been bluffing? Kate hoped she'd never have to put it to the test.

CHAPTER TWENTY-NINE

Alice

Two days passed and there was no sign of Kate. Alice tried not to worry. While it was possible that the Fletcher men had reacted to Alice's interference with spite and perhaps even violence – God forbid that her friend was nursing bruises – it was equally possible that Kate was simply labouring hard on the farm to demonstrate her intention of holding to her end of the bargain. After all, now spring was rousing the world into new life, the work must be increasing. Alice saw no sign of Kate when passing Brimbles Farm on her walks to and from the hospital, but Kate was surely too brave and enterprising to let herself be trapped. With luck, she'd visit soon.

Other demands were keeping Alice busy in the meantime.

The mood at Stratton House had moved on from shock to sad acceptance of Stevie's death, but Alice had been unable to prevent a foolish superstition from entering her mind – that the more she helped the patients at Stratton House, the more fate would smile kindly on Daniel and keep him safe. She knew it was ridiculous but she couldn't shake it off.

She made no mention of Stevie's death in her next letter to Daniel, though it was hard to resist the urge to pour her heart on to the pages. She knew instinctively that he'd write back the very words that would soothe her, but she needed to keep him at a distance and avoid complicating a situation that was difficult enough already.

This time she wrote about the Kovac children mixing up words when they'd told May that Samuel had fallen on the bomb – much to her consternation. They'd meant to say he'd fallen on his bum. Alice also wrote about her confrontation with the Fletcher men because surely that would help him to understand that she was far from helpless.

My father and I both continue well, she wrote at the end. Did Daniel make light of his feelings when he wrote too? He always wrote cheerfully but it must be grim to be away from home, loved ones and the career he'd built. To be facing an uncertain future too, knowing that his life could end prematurely as poor Stevie's had. An urge to comfort Daniel overwhelmed her suddenly and she added, *I hate to think that you're suffering over there. Please let me know how you really are.*

She'd folded the letter and put it into an envelope when someone knocked on the door: May and little Zofia. 'Is this a bad time? I'm interrupting your letter writing,' May said.

'I'd just finished.'

Zofia wanted to see the chickens so they moved into the garden.

'I've still had no news from the family in Poland,' May confided when Zofia was out of earshot. 'It's been ages since they last got a letter through.'

'The children must be missing their parents dreadfully.'

'They cry sometimes. I'm trying to get better at dealing with that sort of thing, but hugs and cuddles don't come naturally.'

'You weren't given them as a child?'

'I was brought up in an orphanage.'

'I'm sorry. I didn't realize.'

'How could you?'

'What happened to your parents?'

'I never knew my father. My mother was just a kid herself when she had me. She died of tuberculosis when I was two.'

'That must have been tough.'

'I don't remember her, to be honest. I hated the orphanage but refused to be beaten down by it. I decided it would make me strong instead, so I made vows to myself.' She counted them off on her fingers. 'I'd always earn my own living and never be poor. I'd always wear attractive clothes because we had to share clothes in the orphanage. And I'd always keep my hair looking nice because our hair was cropped short when nits were going around. I told my Marek about my vows and he agreed I should stick to them. But now . . .' May wrinkled her nose. 'Self-pity is ugly, isn't it? But I'm fighting it and feeling more relaxed with the children.'

'I can see you are.'

'You're helping by taking them off my hands sometimes. I don't feel so . . . crowded, and that means I don't feel so sharp. They're lovely kids, actually.'

'And you're taking excellent care of them.'

'I'm trying.'

'Succeeding.'

May didn't stay long as she had to collect Rosa and

Samuel from school. 'Shall I post your letter on the way?' she asked.

Alice hesitated. She wasn't sure she'd done the right thing in imploring Daniel to tell her about his feelings. It might come across as intimate when what she really needed was to keep her letters impersonal. 'Thanks, but a walk to the pillar box will do me good.'

She could leave the letter unposted if her doubts continued.

They walked into the village together, then went their separate ways. Alice moved towards the red pillar box, took the letter from her bag and held it to the opening. Should she? Shouldn't she?

'Good afternoon, Miss Lovell.' Naomi Harrington spoke from behind her.

Alice was so startled she dropped the letter – into the pillar box. She wanted to cry out and snatch it back, but retrieving it was impossible. Fighting to get a grip on herself, she turned and realized she must be flushed because Mrs Harrington added, 'I'm sorry if I took you by surprise.'

Alice attempted a smile. 'I was away with the fairies, wondering if there was something I'd forgotten to write in my letter,' she fibbed, and was relieved when Mrs Harrington gave no sign of disbelieving her.

'I'm glad our paths have crossed, Miss Lovell. I was looking through some of my things earlier with a view to giving away those I no longer need when it occurred to me that you might be planning some sort of bring-and-buy sale to raise funds for books. If that's the case, I'll gladly put my unwanted items aside until you're ready for them.'

'I hadn't thought of a bring-and-buy sale but it's a wonderful idea,' Alice admitted, struck by it. 'Many people might have items they'll be willing to donate. Or if they can't afford to donate them, they might be willing to sell them and share the sales proceeds with the book appeal.'

Her imagination began to take flight. 'Some people might offer services instead of items. Cooking, babysitting, gardening ... So many possibilities! Thank you, Mrs Harrington. If you'd like to help to organize—'

'Oh, no.' The older woman stepped back as though distancing herself from the idea. 'I'm too busy to take on another commitment.'

'I understand. But if you change your mind . . .'

'Good day, Miss Lovell.' Mrs Harrington was already walking away.

What a woman of contradictions she was – bossy and snobbish, yet generous and perhaps sensitive, too, beneath the surface. Was she really too busy to get involved? Or had Alice and Kate left a wound behind when they'd rejected her earlier offer of help? If the latter, it was particularly kind of her to share the fundraising idea.

Unable to do anything about her letter, though still fearing she'd made a big mistake, Alice tried to fill her thoughts with the bring-and-buy sale as she walked home. Deciding that her first step should be to test the idea on others, she was pleased to reach The Linnets and see Kate approaching. Surely there was a new bounce in Kate's step?

'You look well,' Alice said.

'I *am* well,' Kate confirmed before her face

registered surprise. 'Have you been thinking I might *not* be well?'

'It crossed my mind that your father and brothers might be vindictive after I'd left.'

'They've been horrible. But they're always horrible so I can cope with it. I'm sorry you've been worried, though. If I'd realized, I'd have visited earlier.'

'Instead, you've been proving that your work won't suffer by the agreement.'

'I don't want to give Ernie any excuse for going back on it.'

'Sensible,' Alice agreed. 'Come inside. I want to know your thoughts on something.'

They settled indoors and Alice explained the idea for the sale.

'It's a wonderful idea,' Kate agreed.

'You're willing to take part?'

'Me?' Kate looked taken aback. 'I've nothing to give.'

'You could give a service. Gardening, perhaps. An hour's work in someone's garden must be worth something to someone.'

'Maybe.' Kate sounded uncertain. 'As long as the person who buys it knows that I'll be doing the gardening.' Clearly, she didn't want to turn up at someone's door only to be told that Fletchers weren't welcome on the premises.

'Of course.'

After Kate left Alice decided to go and speak to Babs Carter. 'It's a terrific idea,' Babs said. 'I can give some shoes. They were a gift but they're too small for me. I'll ask the other nurses if they can donate a few things, too.'

'Even small items will be welcome. Pennies and six-pences add up.'

May Janicki was enthusiastic, too. 'I can offer to make up a dress or a skirt. There must be plenty of fabric remnants hanging around the factory. I'll have them sent to me.'

Janet Collins was equally keen. 'With a range of prices there'll be something for everyone. I'll look through my cupboards to see what I can spare, and you can put me down for minding children as well. Betty can work magic with a darning needle so she can offer mending. That may interest some of the men. Have you spoken to Bert Makepiece?'

'Not yet.'

'He'll give something, I'm sure. Eggs, vegetables . . .'

'He's a kind man.'

The event needed a venue and the Sunday School Hall offered the only possibility. Reverend Barnes smiled benignly when Alice approached him for per-mission. 'What does Mrs Harrington think of the project?'

'It was Mrs Harrington who gave me the idea for it.'

'Perhaps I'll have a little word with her, just to be sure.'

'And if she confirms her support?'

'Then you have my permission to proceed.'

Alice was particularly relieved to be able to focus on the sale because by this time Daniel's reply had arrived, the speed of it implying that he'd jumped on her show of tenderness and wasted no time in writing back.

Dearest Alice, he'd begun, having only addressed her as *Dear Alice* in the past.

That's my girl! he'd written next. *I can picture you braving Brimbles Farm like a magnificent glowing angel. It's in your nature to try to make things right for people no matter what it costs you.*

If only she really was his girl! But what a fool she'd been to let him think he could consider her as his.

He'd gone on to tell her that he'd laughed at her story about the Kovac children; then he'd continued with:

It's lovely of you to be so concerned about me. Physically, I'm as fit as a butcher's dog, as the saying goes. Being an officer keeps me busy too as I have men to organize and look after. It goes without saying that I'd rather be at home, but I could never shirk my duty and everything you tell me about the little Kovac children – everything I hear about the situation in Europe generally – convinces me that this war is essential for justice and decency. The men help to keep me cheerful as there are some great jokers among them. I like to think about life after the war ends too.

I know you haven't travelled much yet but there are so many places I'd like to take you to see, from the Highlands of Scotland to the rugged coastline of Cornwall, not to mention places overseas. I can picture us walking along beaches as gulls soar overhead, exploring woods with secret streams, and toasting our toes before log fires in country inns.

Alice had groaned inside when reading that. Not only did it cross a line from mere friendship, it also felt like tempting fate to be making plans while a war was raging.

Finally, he'd changed the way he signed off his letter from *Fond regards* to *With love.*

Desperate to reinstate some distance, she'd written straight back, addressing him simply as *Dear Daniel.*

I'm glad to hear you're keeping well. Something funny happened at the hospital today. A few of the more able men played a joke on the nurses by swapping beds . . .

She'd signed off *Best wishes,* determined to keep her letters light-hearted from now on.

It was time to leave for Stratton House. Not caring that it was raining hard, Alice set off, thinking about the books she'd buy if the sale proved successful, and also hoping for more funny stories to relate to Daniel.

'Rotten weather today,' she commented to Tom, the porter.

She put her umbrella into the stand with other dripping brollies. Turning, she was surprised to see that he'd got to his feet and come out from behind the desk, his expression grave.

'Are you all right, Tom? You look—'

'I'm sorry, Alice, but I've been instructed not to let you in.'

'Visitors aren't allowed today?' And after she'd walked all this way in the rain! Her thoughts turned to Stevie Meadows. 'There hasn't been another tragedy?'

'Nothing like that.'

'Some sort of visitation then? Are the bigwigs here?'

'I'm not sure what's going on,' Tom said.

'Then I'll come back tomorrow and hope for better luck.'

'The thing is, Alice, my instructions are to keep you out.'

'Permanently?' Alice was shocked.

He read from a note. '*Under no circumstances is Miss Lovell to be allowed on to the premises until further notice.*'

The mention of her name made the order sound personal. 'I haven't done anything wrong, have I?'

'I can't imagine so.'

'Have I been named because I'm the only visitor?'

'I wish I could give you an answer, but no one is telling me anything.'

It occurred to her that he might get into trouble for standing here chatting. 'I'll leave now, but I hope this is only a temporary problem.'

'So do I. Your visits do the patients so much good.'

He looked upset so Alice touched his arm by way of reassurance. Then she reclaimed her umbrella and stepped back into the rain, her emotions reeling.

CHAPTER THIRTY

Alice

'You can't have done anything wrong,' Kate insisted.

Apparently, she'd seen Alice walking home from the hospital yesterday and waved, only to realize that Alice hadn't even looked in her direction. It wasn't like her and, worried, Kate had rushed through her work today to carve out enough time to come and find out if something was amiss.

'Not deliberately, but perhaps without realizing . . .'

'You're not the sort of clod who goes around crashing into sensitive matters like an army tank. You're discreet, and you care. About the patients. About the nurses. About everyone.'

The banishment still made Alice feel like some sort of criminal.

The feeling persisted when she walked into the village for bread the following morning, so she didn't linger. She was hoping that a note might come from the hospital – from Babs or Pauline, if not from anyone official – but no such note had yet arrived.

'No hospital visit today?' her father asked when she took a cup of tea to him.

'Not today.'

He stared at her then gestured her to sit. 'What's wrong?'

Not wanting to worry him, Alice had mentioned nothing about her banishment from the hospital but, seeing he was worried anyway, she told him what had happened.

'They're probably just tightening security,' he suggested.

'I wish I knew for sure. I hate not knowing if I'm being blamed for something.'

'I can't imagine you're being blamed for anything. You're such a force for good.'

Alice smiled, touched by his obvious affection, though still feeling desperately unhappy. 'At least I can still supply the patients with books.'

'That's the spirit.'

She'd settled down to create a new poster for the bring-and-buy sale when she was surprised by a knock on the cottage door. A glance at the grandfather clock showed that it was past nine o'clock, late for a visit.

She opened the door while holding the blackout curtain in place to minimize escaping light. 'Matron!'

'I'm sorry to call at such an unsocial hour. I've been on duty and wanted to keep my visit private. May I come in?'

'Of course!' Alice led the way into the dining room. 'Let me take your coat . . .' She hung it in the hall, popped her head around her father's study door to let him know who'd called, then returned to Matron. 'Can I offer you tea?'

'I'm afraid I can't stay. As you may have guessed, I'm here about the events at the hospital. After all you've done for the patients, I think you're entitled to an explanation.'

'I'd certainly welcome one.'

'You must have had an anxious couple of days.'

'I've been wondering if I'm to blame in some way.'

'You're not. The problem is . . . delicate, which is why I've come to see you privately.'

'Meaning you shouldn't be here and you shouldn't be giving me an explanation?'

'I haven't been prohibited from talking to you. I judged it prudent not to risk prohibition by seeking permission.'

Clever Matron.

'What I have to say must go no further, though. Apparently, there's been a breach of security. Someone has been supplying confidential information to the enemy.'

Alice's eyes widened. 'Not me!'

'I don't know what sort of information is involved except that it's of a general nature. I imagine that means information about the numbers and movement of our troops, weapons, training . . .'

'The sort of information someone could garner by chatting to patients,' Alice guessed.

'Each conversation sounding harmless enough . . .'

'Until the pieces are fitted together like a jigsaw puzzle and a picture emerges.'

'Quite so. As I said, I'm not aware that anything particularly compromising was disclosed, but military intelligence want to tighten things up to stop information from being leaked in the future.'

'So I'm banished.'

'For the moment. I've argued that the good you do far outweighs the risk of letting you loose on the patients. I've even suggested that you might be willing for the military intelligence people to look into your background.'

'I am. My father served as a doctor to the troops during the first war and I've never worked for anyone else.'

'Unfortunately, the suggestion wasn't accepted. It's the patients who'll suffer most, of course.'

'I can still supply them with books. Some of us are planning a fundraiser so—'

'I'm afraid that won't be possible either. I was told books might be used for sending coded messages. You know the sort of thing – letters or words circled lightly in pencil. Put them together and you've got a sentence.'

'Can't the books stay at the hospital? They couldn't be used for spreading information then.'

'At the moment I've been told that no donated books are allowed but I'm fighting the decision. It's against the patients' interests.'

'Perhaps I won't cancel the fundraiser yet. Just in case you manage to win the argument.'

'I'm afraid all signs point to failure.'

'Even so . . . What shall I say if people ask why I'm no longer visiting the hospital?'

Matron thought about it. 'Perhaps you might mention that security at Stratton House is being tightened generally as a precaution.' She got to her feet. 'I'm sorry to be the bearer of bad news.'

'It isn't your fault.'

'It's the traitor's fault,' Matron said firmly. 'My apologies again for calling at an unsociable hour.'

'Are you walking back to the hospital alone?'

'I am, but I have a stout heart and a torch to guide

me. Thank you for everything you've done for the patients. It's made a difference. Goodnight, my dear.'

They found Alice's father waiting in the hall, his coat on and a scarf wrapped around his neck because the nights were still cool. 'Allow me to see you safely back to Stratton House, Matron,' he said.

'No need, Dr Lovell.'

'Forgive me if I disagree. I need some exercise anyway. Alice tells me I spend too long hunched over books so a walk will do me good.'

They set off together and Alice waited impatiently for her father's return, keen to discuss the situation with him but worried that the prohibition on talking about it extended even to him. She was relieved to learn that Matron had confided in him, too.

'It's a real shame,' he said. 'Patients need care for their minds and souls as well as their bodies. Books and visitors make an important contribution to their wellbeing. Unfortunately, it's out of your power to change the situation, but let's hope Matron's powers of persuasion win the day eventually. Meanwhile, it's a case of wait and see, and the waiting may go on for some time.'

Janet Collins called the following morning. 'Can't stop. I just want you to know that Betty is more than happy to donate an hour's mending to the fundraiser. She's also got some lovely lavender bags to give. Twelve of them, so they should raise at least a couple of shillings. Must dash now. I've got the grandchildren coming.'

Oh, heavens. It wasn't right to leave good people like Janet rushing around for a fundraiser that might never happen, but when was the right time to cancel?

Evening brought more visitors: Babs and Pauline.

'It's lovely to see you, but are you allowed to be here?' Alice asked.

'Probably not,' Babs answered. 'But no one's actually told us we can't visit.'

Alice led them into the dining room but when she went into the kitchen to make tea they followed. 'Sorry if we're taking liberties,' Babs said, 'but we want to know that you're all right.'

'I'm fine,' Alice assured them. 'Well, perhaps not fine, but coping.'

'Whatever information was passed to the enemy, we know it didn't come from you.'

Alice smiled. 'It's sweet of you to say so.'

'We know our opinions make no difference, but we want you back at the hospital and so do the patients. They've been complaining that it isn't right to keep you away.'

Alice was touched. 'I'd love to come back, but how can I prove I'm innocent?'

'That's partly why we're here. We think the only way to prove that *you* didn't share the secrets is to find out who *did* share them.'

'Unmask the traitor? Goodness. Have you any idea who it might be?'

'Not yet. But let's talk about it. The kettle's boiled, by the way.'

Alice had been too distracted to notice. She made the tea, took a cup in to her father then returned to the kitchen to find Babs and Pauline sitting at the little table.

'We've made ourselves at home,' Babs said. 'We hope you don't mind?'

'Of course not.' Alice sat. 'Where do we start?'

'It has to be someone who has access to the patients,' Babs began. 'That means doctors, nurses . . .'

'Cleaners,' Pauline added. 'Possibly kitchen staff and administrators too. They don't see much of the patients, but perhaps they pick up bits of information here and there.'

'It's difficult to speculate when we know so little about the information that was shared,' Alice said. 'At least, I don't know much.'

'Neither do we,' Pauline told her. 'That makes it hard to narrow down who might have had access to it.'

'Let's begin with some questions,' Alice suggested. 'Why would anyone betray their country?'

'Because their loyalties lie with a different country,' Babs offered, clearly having considered the question already. 'The only staff member with a foreign-sounding name is a doctor called Isaac Goldstein but he's Jewish. Given the way the Germans are treating people of his faith, we can't imagine he'd wish to help them.'

'Unless he's being blackmailed,' Alice pointed out. 'Betraying his country to protect family members in Germany?'

'Or in one of the countries Germany has invaded.' They all considered that for a moment.

'We'll look out for signs of strain,' Babs said.

'Do you know of anyone else with foreign connections?' Alice asked.

'That's something I'm trying to find out,' Pauline told her. 'My grandparents came from Czechoslovakia so I'm going around telling people I'm worried about distant cousins who still live there. I'm hoping if I share information about my family, others will share information about theirs.'

'Or look shifty,' Babs put in.

'Or triumphant about the progress Germany and her allies are making in the war,' Pauline finished.

'Don't risk getting into trouble,' Alice cautioned, before continuing with, 'Why else might someone betray their country?'

'Because they resent what their country has done to them,' Pauline suggested. 'One way or another, all of the patients have been injured in the service of their country.'

'Do any of them appear to be nursing a grievance?' Alice asked.

'There's Jake Turner,' Babs said, echoing Alice's own thoughts. 'His injuries are life-changing.'

'Apparently, his sweetheart abandoned him,' Alice confided. 'I heard his parents talking about it. All the other things he loved have been taken from him, too. His work, his hobbies . . .'

'He's a bitter man, then. He can't leave hospital premises, so he'd have needed help to get information out of Stratton House.'

'Unless he posted it.'

Babs nodded. 'Coded messages. Matron told us they were the reason given for banning book donations.'

'Jake did seem interested in the old seed catalogues I brought,' Alice said. 'He might have posted one with a code inside, pretending he was sending it to show the plants he'd like to see in his garden once he's finally discharged home.'

'Do you remember how many catalogues you

brought in?' Pauline asked. 'We can count up how many are still in the hospital and work out if any are missing.'

'Seven or eight, I think, but I can't be sure.'

Pauline nodded thoughtfully. 'We can't do anything about any catalogues that have already been sent out but we can count up how many are left in case any go missing in future.'

'The catalogues won't actually need to leave the hospital if Jake has an accomplice,' Babs pointed out. 'Jake could pass the catalogues to someone inside the hospital – a therapist, perhaps – who could then return them with the codes rubbed out.'

'Let's watch out for Jake taking the catalogues off the ward and keep an eye on the catalogues generally as they might show signs of having been used to pass messages. Incomplete rubbings-out . . . That sort of thing.'

'If Jake has an accomplice, he might not need the catalogues at all. He could whisper secrets straight into his accomplice's ear,' Alice said, and a moment of silence followed in which she guessed they were all thinking that, in a hospital inhabited by dozens of staff and patients, the possibilities for espionage were numerous while the chances of unmasking the traitor were tiny.

Despite that, Alice was thrilled that Babs and Pauline cared enough to go to so much trouble to try to clear her name. Well, not clear her name exactly. If Alice had been a suspect the authorities would surely have hauled her off for an interview. Even so, she still felt tainted by her banishment and unmasking the real traitor would enable her to hold her head up high again. The patients would also benefit because surely then books – if not Alice herself – would be welcome in the hospital.

'Are there any more reasons why someone might turn traitor?' Alice asked.

'Blackmail needn't be limited to protecting family members,' Babs replied. 'Gambling problems, love affairs, stolen money, stolen drugs . . . People can be blackmailed over all sorts of things. We should look out for anyone who appears particularly worried or jumpy.'

'Or living above their means,' Pauline added. 'If we can't identify who's being blackmailed, we may be able to identify the person who's doing the blackmailing. Of course, someone might sell secrets without being blackmailed if they're being paid enough for them.'

'I'm sorry all the hard work is down to you two,' Alice said.

'Let's meet again when we've something to share,' Pauline said, getting up. 'It might mean another cloak-and-dagger visit under cover of night but I don't see an alternative.'

'Just take care,' Alice urged again.

She showed the nurses to the door and within seconds they were swallowed up by darkness.

Days passed. And no news came from Stratton House. Babs and Pauline were clever and enterprising, but two busy nurses were hardly a fair challenge to people who might be highly trained in espionage. Alice's disappointment still cut deeply.

Daniel's latest letter – another one he'd wasted no

time in sending – hadn't helped her mood. She'd been hugely relieved to know he'd been well at the time of writing but her attempt to reinstate some distance had failed. *Dearest Alice,* he'd written again.

The next section had been lighter-hearted:

We've had an addition to our company over the last few days – we've been adopted by a dog. Terrier blood in his background, I think, though mixed with a dozen other varieties. We're calling him Oswald for no particular reason and we've discovered he has a taste for army-issue corned beef.

But after writing a little more about Oswald's antics Daniel had added:

It's too soon for me to hope to be granted leave but I can't wait to see England again, and to see you too. Do write back soon with all your news. It feels like the sun has come out when your letters arrive, even if it's raining.
With love,
Daniel x

Of course, Alice could write back and tell him in no uncertain terms that he was making a mistake if he thought they had a future together because she didn't love him and never could. It would be a lie, but did that matter if it achieved what her more tactful attempts to put him off were failing to achieve?

She asked herself why she hadn't told him long ago that she didn't want him. Alice supposed it had taken time for her to realize what he intended, and after the penny finally dropped it had felt kinder to hope that time and distance would do the job of changing his mind, especially if she gave him no encouragement to think of her as anything except a friend.

It hadn't worked, though, so was bluntness the best way forward? Alice still couldn't think so. Not in a letter that Daniel would receive while he was away at the war. He might feel upset and helpless. He might be distracted when what he needed was to focus on staying alive. Perhaps when he next had leave and she could talk to him face to face to gauge the impact of her words it would feel like the right time to explain that they had no future. Until then she'd continue to write impersonally in the hope that he'd get the hint that she wanted nothing closer. In her reply, she wrote:

I held an Easter Egg hunt for Rosa, Samuel and Zofia in the garden. It was terrific fun. I only had hard-boiled eggs instead of chocolate ones but the children still enjoyed it. They painted faces on the shells then ate the eggs.

The garden is still a little wild apart from the vegetable patch but I love seeing flowers emerge. So far we've had snowdrops, daffodils and primroses. It looks as though we're going to have bluebells and tulips, too . . .

Should she mention her banishment from Stratton House? If she stopped writing about her hospital visits, then sooner or later he'd ask why and take her earlier silence on the subject to mean she was upset. The last thing she needed was for Daniel to feel even sorrier for her. She decided to drop the subject into the middle of her letter as though it was of no great importance. *Security at the hospital has been tightened so I won't be going there any more. It means I've more time for seeing friends and looking after things at home.*

Surely that was casual enough? She wrote a few more lines then ended the letter with *Best wishes* and walked into the village to post it.

Several Churchwood residents were out and about, and after three of them made enthusiastic comments about the bring-and-buy sale, Alice knew it wasn't fair to keep them dangling. It was time to cancel it.

CHAPTER THIRTY-ONE

Kate

'It's a crying shame,' Kate said when she called in on Alice and heard that the sale was to be cancelled.

'I can't let people waste time preparing for something that isn't going to take place.'

'You're sure the situation at the hospital won't change?'

'Not completely sure. But I can't let things drag on indefinitely.'

'What will you tell people?'

'The same as I told you. Security at the hospital has been tightened. It's the truth.'

Kate's instincts stirred suddenly. 'But it isn't the whole truth, is it? Good grief, the security hasn't actually been breached, has it?'

'Hush!' They were in Alice's garden but she still glanced around as though fearing they might be overheard by someone in the lane. 'I don't know details.'

'But there's been a breach.'

'You mustn't tell anyone, Kate. I was only told in strictest confidence and I don't know any details.'

'Who would I tell? But no one could think *you* were responsible?'

'I think I'm a casualty of the tightening-up rather than a suspect. At least, I hope so.'

Kate wished there was something she could do to help, but what? She burned with outrage at the shabby way poor Alice had been treated. National security was important, but couldn't the hospital have treated her with more kindness? Kate pitied the patients who'd miss out on her friend's visits, too.

'I'll come back soon,' she promised because, as ever, work on the farm was calling. She was entitled to time off under her agreement with Ernie but was anxious to prove that he wasn't losing anything from it. Except for the two shillings a week, of course.

Frank 'n' Fred were in the field next to Brimbles Lane as Kate drew near. As usual, they were spending more time joking with each other than working but that was a good thing as it meant she was able to duck down behind the hedgerow and sneak past them. After another furtive look around, she glided through the orchard and then, satisfied that she was safe, strode towards the farmhouse.

A gust of wind blew tendrils of hair into her eyes. Reaching up to push them away, Kate thought she saw a flicker of movement behind the window of her bedroom. She stopped to stare but didn't see it again. It must have been a trick of light. Unless . . .

She broke into a run, threw the kitchen door open and raced upstairs without bothering to remove her boots. Vinnie was on the landing. 'What were you doing in my room?' Kate demanded.

'Why should I have been in your room?'

Because he wanted her money.

She pushed past him and stared down at the door handle. 'It's dirty.'

'So? *You're* dirty.'

'My hands are clean.'

'The rest of you isn't.'

Kate muttered a disgusted sound, walked into the room and closed the door behind her. Looking around, she could see no obvious sign of Vinnie's presence but she could sense it. She wanted to check if her money was still in its hiding place but suspected that Vinnie was hovering outside the door, listening for sounds that might signal the hiding place's location.

'Vinnie!' Ernie called. 'Get down here. There's work to be done.'

Vinnie cursed, but clattered down the uncarpeted stairs in his boots. Kate waited by the window until she saw him out in the yard, then crouched down and reached for the paper bag of coins she'd hidden beneath the chest of drawers.

Heart beating fast, she teased the bag out and heaved a mighty sigh when she saw that her money was intact. For now. But it wouldn't be long before it was found.

Kate tipped the coins into a sock and tied the end. Then she wrapped a scarf around her middle, tucked the sock into it and pulled her shirt over the bulky mess. It wasn't an ideal solution to keeping her money safe but it was the best she could do in an emergency.

Later that evening, she tore a strip of cloth from the rag pile, sewed the sock to it and tied the fabric around her waist. Better, though it was awful that she had to hide her hard-earned money to keep it from being stolen by people who were supposed to love her.

She kept the makeshift belt under her pillow when she got into bed and as she thought over the day her thoughts returned to Alice and the cancelled bring-and-buy sale.

Hopefully, most people would sympathize, but Kate knew all too well that there was a mean, gossipy side to Churchwood. Might some people think Alice must have done something wrong to be banished from the hospital? It wasn't as though she could give much of an explanation.

Kate wouldn't put it past Marjorie Plym to start the rumours flying. As for Naomi Harrington, she might be only too willing to crow in triumph at Alice's downfall after the snub she'd been dealt. Well, she'd have Kate to answer to if she did.

CHAPTER THIRTY-TWO

Naomi

'Cancelled?' Naomi felt blank with surprise. 'But why?'

Strangely, Alice's cheeks turned pink. 'Apparently, the hospital isn't allowing visitors or book donations any more.'

'Not allowing . . .?'

'I wanted to tell you personally because you gave me the idea for the sale. I didn't want you to feel that I thought badly of it.'

'I see,' Naomi said, though she didn't see. Not really. 'What reason did the hospital give?'

The colour in Alice's cheeks deepened. 'I believe the decision was something to do with security. I must go back in now, but I'm glad I caught you.'

Alice had rushed out of The Linnets just as Naomi had been returning from the village. She hadn't been wearing a coat and the day was cold.

'Thank you for telling me,' Naomi said, and continued onwards feeling flat.

Reaching home, she sat down to think about what she'd just heard. Alice had looked embarrassed as well as upset. Was there more to the hospital's decision than she'd disclosed?

Naomi could understand that the hospital might not want civilians wandering about amongst men who had information that could be useful to the enemy, but refusing to allow books on the premises was surely an overreaction – unless books had been implicated in some sort of security breach? Had Alice been implicated, too? It would explain her awkwardness.

But Naomi wouldn't judge Alice prematurely. She was beginning to suspect that she'd been too swift to judge people in the past and she didn't want to make another mistake. She'd keep an open mind instead.

She picked up her list of items for the Red Cross parcels to review how it was progressing but the flat feeling turned into restlessness and she couldn't settle. Tossing the list aside, she got up and paced the room.

Being confined to Churchwood must be getting on Naomi's nerves. In the past she'd had the use of the Daimler when Alexander was likely to remain in London for several days together. Instead of driving it himself, he'd allow Sykes, the gardener, to drive him into town then return with the car so Naomi could be taken to charity committee meetings and other engagements with women in her social circle. The petrol situation had put an end to that.

Speaking on the telephone was a poor substitute for getting out and about. Besides, the women in her circle weren't exactly close friends and it was hard to imagine ringing any of them just to chat. Were any of them missing her? Had any of them even given her a moment's thought? Naomi winced as the answers came back to her: probably not. Her life had long been busy, busy, busy, but, while people doubtless appreciated her involvement and invitations, it was humbling – hurtful, too – to think that few people would seek her out if she had nothing to offer except herself.

Was all this soul-searching a sign of boredom, war-time, the change of life or all three? Naomi didn't know but it made her uncomfortable. Unhappy, even. Perhaps a change of scene would help. She couldn't travel by car, but there were trains.

Alexander didn't welcome telephone calls while he was working, but surely he wouldn't object to a call from his wife now they were spending so little time together?

'What is it?' he asked.

'I'm thinking of coming up to town for a day or two.'

'What for?'

'To see you, of course. We could take in the theatre or a nice dinner. I haven't been to London for months. I can take the bus to St Albans then pick up the train.'

Alexander didn't answer and Naomi swallowed. Was someone listening in at the exchange? Unable to bear the thought of a witness to this one-sided conversation, Naomi brought the silence to an end. 'If it isn't a good time for a visit . . .'

'I'm busy, and with the war on it wouldn't be prudent to neglect my work.'

'Another time, then.'

'Goodbye, Naomi.' She could hear him talking to his secretary even as he put the telephone down. 'The Walters file, please, Miss Seymour . . .'

Naomi put her telephone down, too, regretting that she'd made the call because it had only made her feel worse.

She realized someone was approaching along the drive. Marjorie. Now here was someone who did value Naomi's friendship. Yes, Marjorie enjoyed feeling that her frequent visits to Foxfield elevated her status in the village, but she was also the person most likely to remain a friend if fortune suddenly snatched away Foxfield and the rest of Naomi's wealth.

She might get on Naomi's nerves sometimes – often, in fact – but still deserved to have her loyalty and affection returned.

'I'm glad I caught you at home,' Marjorie said as Suki showed her into the sitting room. 'Have you heard that Alice Lovell has cancelled her bring-and-buy sale?'

'She told me so this morning. It's a pity.'

'Did she tell you the reason?'

'Something to do with tightened security. It's wartime. These things happen.'

'I suppose so,' Marjorie acknowledged. 'You don't thing Alice did anything wrong?'

Naomi paused before answering. She didn't want to judge Alice unfairly but neither did she want to be found to be in the wrong should it emerge that Alice had in fact done something wrong. 'I've no way of knowing so I'm keeping an open mind.'

Marjorie nodded, looking disappointed because there'd be nothing juicy for her to say when she was out and about in the village.

Feeling warm towards her friend despite her gossip-mongering tendencies – and who didn't have their flaws? – Naomi rubbed her hands together and smiled. 'I'm in the mood for a glass of sherry,' she announced. 'Want one?'

Marjorie turned pink with pleasure. 'Oh, what a treat! Yes, please!'

CHAPTER THIRTY-THREE

Alice

'I'm sorry we haven't called for so long,' Babs said as Alice led her into the cottage. 'Pauline is on duty but we didn't want to keep you waiting.'

'It's good of you to come at all. Let me take your coat.'

'Best not. It's just a quick call to tell you—'

Alice held her breath, hoping for news. Good news.

'There's nothing to tell you, really,' Babs continued, 'but we want you to know we're still trying.'

Alice's disappointment was intense but she forced a smile. 'I'm grateful, but—'

'You don't want us to get into trouble. We *want* to keep trying, though, for everyone's sakes. Yours, ours, the patients' and even the country's. If there's a spy at Stratton House we want to expose him. Or her.'

'I had to cancel the bring-and-buy sale,' Alice said.

'We heard. With luck it isn't cancelled but only postponed.'

'Let's hope so.'

'Stay strong, Alice. One of us will call again, and hopefully we'll have better news.'

Babs peered through the door to be sure the coast was clear.

'My father will walk you back to the hospital,' Alice said.

'I'm less likely to be seen if I'm alone.' Babs drew Alice into a hug and slipped back into the night.

More days passed but there was no further visit and Alice couldn't help feeling low. The whole of Churchwood appeared to be sorry that the bring-and-buy sale was cancelled. 'It would have been a bit of excitement for a worthy cause,' one resident said. 'Now we're just back to the daily grind.'

On Wednesday Alice was walking to the shops when Mr Makepiece stopped his truck beside her and leaned through the open window. 'Shame about Stratton House, young Alice, but I'm sure you'll find another way to do good in this village. It's in your nature.'

'You're very kind,' Alice told him.

'Just telling the truth as I see it.'

Alice still felt as though the world she'd been building for herself had crumbled into dust. Her visits to Stratton House, and her mission to improve the lives of the patients, had given her a purpose. Without it she was like a boat adrift on the sea.

Back at home she found a letter from Daniel had arrived.

Dearest Alice,

I was so sorry to hear that you're no longer allowed to visit the hospital. I've no doubt in my mind that you were a great boon to the patients and I know how much it meant to you to be able to help them. If I'm ever in hospital, nothing will cheer me more than the sight of your sweet face.

It's at times like this that I find it frustrating to be so far away because I wish I could be there to comfort you.

271

*Duty calls so I can't write more now but I want to get this
letter in the post to you urgently. I'll write again soon.
With love,
Daniel x*

So much for pretending she wasn't unduly upset by
the banishment. And how like Daniel to see through
her words to her true feelings.

Alice blinked tears away then read the letter again.
Dearest Alice . . . cheer . . . sweet . . . comfort . . . With love . . .
And that kiss . . .

How was it possible that he understood her so well?

'I wonder if I did a selfish thing in moving us here
to Churchwood.'

Alice whirled around to see her father standing
behind her and felt a pang of dismay at the worry in
his face. She blinked again to clear more tears before
they could add to his distress. 'Don't say that! You've
worked hard all your life and you deserve your retirement. Churchwood is giving you everything you
need – peace, quietness, the chance to study . . .'

'But it isn't giving *you* everything you need, Alice.'

Before she could deny it, he was speaking again.

'It became obvious to me back in '38, if not before,
that war was on the horizon and London might become
a dangerous place to live. I couldn't face another war
head on, and I thought we'd both be safer living somewhere quieter. But perhaps I should have delayed the
move until you'd settled to something new. New job,
new friends . . .'

Alice hugged him. 'You wanted the best for both of
us, and I *like* Churchwood.'

'It offers no opportunities to you.'

'It might not suit me forever, but it's a good place to be right now,' she insisted. 'The people are lovely. Most of them. And perhaps I'll find a job nearby when my hand is stronger.'

Her father looked unconvinced.

'I'm out of sorts because of the hospital situation,' Alice admitted. 'But I'll get over it. The chickens, the house and garden all keep me busy, and I've more friends here than I had in London after Clare and Elizabeth moved to Canada.'

'But is it enough? Chatting with friends is all very well, but you have a good head on your shoulders. You need stimulation for your brain.'

'I'll find a way to get it. Stratton House may not have worked out, but there'll be other opportunities.'

'I hope so. But if you ever decide Churchwood isn't the right place for you, tell me and we'll think about moving somewhere else.'

'I will.'

'Promise me, Alice.'

'I promise,' she said, but the last thing she wanted was to spoil the retirement her father had spent so many years anticipating, especially as she wasn't sure he could afford the costs of another move.

She needed to lift her mood but the future loomed over her like a shadow. Her father was right. She needed stimulation and purpose. But she had no clearer idea of how she might achieve them than when she'd first come to Churchwood. She could only pretend to be happy and hope that true happiness would catch up with her soon.

She wrote back to Daniel, trying once again to restore the light, friendly tone.

Dear Daniel,

It was kind of you to be concerned about me but there's really no need. I'm sorry if I gave the impression of being in low spirits because I'm fine. I did enjoy being with the patients at Stratton House but walking two miles each day was rather a bind and I need to spend more time tending the vegetable patch if I'm to make a success of it. All meat is rationed now and who knows what will be next? I want to ensure we have a good supply of vegetables and eggs, too.

On the subject of eggs, Audrey, Constance and Louisa must have had a scare last night because they suddenly began squawking. I suspect a fox was nearby. Luckily, they were safe in their coop but I need to be careful . . .

She wrote a little more then signed off with: *Best wishes, Alice.*

No expression of love and no kiss either, though her heart was bursting with them, and before she dropped the letter into her bag the next morning, she couldn't help whispering, 'Stay safe, Daniel Irvine.'

'I'm going to post a letter,' she called to her father. 'I shan't be long.'

Opening the door, she stepped outside – and came to a sudden halt as a surprise awaited her. It wasn't the answer to her problems – not nearly – but it certainly gave her a boost.

CHAPTER THIRTY-FOUR

Kate

'There's something you need to see,' Alice said when Kate arrived at The Linnets. She looked excited.

'You've had a letter from the hospital? You're allowed back into Stratton House?'

'It's nothing like that. There!'

Propped up against the shed was a bicycle. Not new, but clean and cared for. 'Read the label,' Alice instructed.

A stout brown card had been tied to the handle-bars. *For Kate Fletcher*, it read.

'Alice, you shouldn't have!' How amazingly generous of Alice to buy a bicycle for Kate, even a second-hand one. But Alice needed all her money for her future.

'I didn't buy it,' Alice told her.

Kate was confused. 'Then where did it come from?'

'Your guess is as good as mine. I opened the door this morning and here it was. At first I thought my father had arranged it so I could see more of you, but he knew nothing about it either.'

'There wasn't a note?'

'Only the label, which suggests your well-wisher wants to remain anonymous.'

'I can't imagine who that well-wisher might be.' After all, Alice was Kate's only friend.

'Maybe you'll find out one day. Meanwhile, just enjoy having a bicycle. Have you ever ridden one?'

'No. Have you?'

'Not for years.'

'Let's try it.' Kate wheeled the bicycle into the lane. 'You go first, Alice. Explain what you do.'

'The knack is to keep moving so raise the pedal and push down on it quickly as you set off. If you stay still, you'll fall over.'

Alice demonstrated, wobbling only a little. 'Your turn,' she said then.

Kate got herself into position on the bicycle, raised the pedal and pushed down hard. She didn't quite manage to get a foot on the other pedal so came to a halt before she fell. At her second attempt she fared better.

'Wonderful!' Alice cried. 'Watch out for that tree, though!'

Kate had been too busy concentrating on her feet to pay attention to her steering. Narrowly missing the tree, she crashed into a bush instead but her only injury was a scratched forehead. Setting off again, she managed to steer as well as to pedal. Within ten minutes she was riding up and down the lane with just a scraped shin added to her injuries.

'You're a natural,' Alice told her. 'This bicycle will cut the time you spend getting here by . . . what? Ten minutes?'

'At least ten minutes each way,' Kate said. It would mean she could come more often and for longer.

But there was a problem. Ernie or one of her brothers would love to get their hands on the bicycle to either ride it or sell it. 'I need to think of a safe place to keep it.'

'It was left with this.' Alice fetched a chain and padlock. 'You'll still need to hide the key.'

Kate would keep it in her money belt. 'You'll tell me if you find out where it came from?'

'Of course. Unless I'm sworn to secrecy.'

Alice's gaze switched suddenly to a space behind Kate. Turning to see what had caught Alice's attention, Kate saw widowed Mrs Hall walking along the lane in her blue coat.

'Good morning, Mrs Hall,' Alice called.

The older woman walked straight past them. Reaching Churchwood Way, she turned towards the village.

'Charming!' Kate declared, feeling the burn of bitterness. 'I hope it wasn't my presence that made her ignore you.'

'I've only ever had wary looks and an unwilling nod from her.'

'More than I've ever had.' Unwilling to waste her thoughts on someone so rude, Kate turned her attention back to the bicycle. 'I'm going to try some tighter turns.'

She pushed off again and attempted to turn without taking up the entire width of the lane. After several tries she'd narrowed the turning space she needed by around half. 'This is fun,' she said, but Alice wasn't listening. Instead, she was frowning.

'What's the matter?' Kate asked. 'You're not upset about being snubbed by Mrs Hall?'

'I'm worried about her. I'd swear she never even saw us.'

277

Kate thought back to the look on the woman's face. Perhaps it had been odd. She'd looked strained, yet determined. But determined to do what? Kate felt a stir of unease. 'We should check on her.'

They set off after Mrs Hall but she was already out of sight. 'Do you know where she lives?' Kate asked.

'Woodcutter Row, I think.'

Janet lived in Woodcutter Row. Alice knocked on her door. 'Edna's at number twenty,' Janet told them. 'The house with the aspidistra in the window. Is there a problem?'

'I just want a word with her.'

No one answered Alice's knock on the door of number twenty so she knocked again. Still no answer.

'She might be shopping,' Kate pointed out, but Mrs Hall hadn't looked to be in a shopping mood. 'Letter box,' Kate suggested then.

Alice bent over, pushed the letter box open and peered into the hall. 'I can't see her.'

She called through the opening. 'Mrs Hall? Could you come to the door? Just for a moment?'

Silence.

'Back door?' Kate asked.

A narrow passage opened between Mrs Hall's house and her neighbour's property. Passing through a gate into Mrs Hall's rear garden, they approached the kitchen door. There was still no answer when Alice knocked. Kate looked through the window – and shock rippled through her. 'We need to get inside,' she gasped. '*Now*.'

The door was locked. 'Stand aside,' Kate instructed.

Raising her boot, she stamped on the door. Once, twice . . . On the third stamp the door burst open.

Mrs Hall was lying on the floor with her head in the gas oven.

'Open the window!' Alice called as she turned the gas off, grabbed a tea towel and used it as a pillow while she eased the unconscious Mrs Hall's head on to the floor.

The smell of gas was strong. If a spark caught it . . . 'We should get her outside,' Kate said.

Together, they got Mrs Hall into the garden then Kate ran back into the house for the blue coat, which she placed over Mrs Hall to keep her warm. 'Could you fetch my father?' Alice asked.

Kate raced away. Reaching The Linnets, she didn't bother to knock but launched herself through the back door and headed straight to Dr Lovell's study. 'You need to come!'

He rose from his chair looking frightened. 'Alice . . .'

'She's fine, but another woman . . . Edna Hall . . . We found her with her head in the gas oven.'

Galvanized into action, Dr Lovell grabbed a medical bag from under the desk. He might have retired but clearly liked to stay prepared for emergencies. He snatched his coat and a blanket from the hall cupboard then followed Kate at speed to Woodcutter Row where he got down on his knees beside the barely conscious woman. 'Good afternoon, Mrs Hall. I'm Dr Lovell. You've had a bit of a turn and I'm just looking you over.' He checked her pulse and her breathing.

Kate realized a small crowd had gathered at the gate. Miss Plym was at the front. 'Shall I telephone the police?' she asked. Suicide was a crime, of course.

Dr Lovell fixed her with a stare. 'This woman is unwell. The police have nothing to do here.'

Miss Plym flushed.

'I think she needs to go to hospital, however,' he said to the crowd. 'An ambulance might take some time. Does anyone have a car or other vehicle?'

Blank looks were exchanged.

'I'll find one,' Kate offered.

She pushed through the crowd and returned a few minutes later. 'The grocer was out in his van but his wife telephoned Bert Makepiece. He's coming in his truck.'

Soon the rumble of the truck could be heard. Then Mr Makepiece's deep voice reached them from beyond the gate. 'If you wouldn't mind standing aside, ladies . . .?'

He came in and crouched down beside Mrs Hall. 'Got yourself in a pickle, eh, Edna? Don't worry. We'll soon have you right again.'

He looked to Dr Lovell for instructions, and the doctor turned to the crowd. 'I don't think we need to keep any of you from going about your business,' he said.

Marjorie Plym in particular looked disappointed, but then appeared struck by an idea. 'Naomi needs to hear about this. I'll go and tell her.' She hurried off to spread the news and the other onlookers drifted away, too, except for one woman, who approached.

'I'm Hilda Roberts from next door. I knew Edna had taken her Arthur's death hard but I never dreamt . . . If there's anything I can do to help, please tell me.'

'We'll let you know,' Alice assured her, because this neighbour looked genuinely concerned.

Hilda nodded and left them. Mr Makepiece looked

280

at the door. 'I'll be along to mend that broken lock later,' he said.

Gently, he and the doctor carried Mrs Hall to the truck and drove off. 'Is the hospital far?' Alice asked Kate. 'I only know of Stratton House.'

'Bert Makepiece will know the best place to take her. Poor woman.'

'I should have realized something was wrong long ago. She looked troubled every time I saw her.'

'You couldn't know *how* troubled she was. *You* hardly knew her, but other people must have known her for years. Like that neighbour. If there's blame to be laid, it shouldn't be put at your door but at Churchwood's.'

'We all failed,' Alice insisted. 'Thanks for helping. No one could have fetched my father or organized a vehicle faster. I'm going to stay until Mr Makepiece returns but there's no need for you to stay, too.'

Kate hesitated. She didn't like to leave Alice but neither did she wish to give Ernie and her brothers the chance to accuse her of shirking.

'Go, Kate. There's nothing more you can do.'

'All right. I'll try to call at the cottage later, to hear how Mrs Hall is getting on.'

Alice managed a smile. 'Come on your bicycle.'

Kate smiled too and then raced away.

Vinnie was in the farmyard when Kate cycled up. 'Where did you get that?' he demanded. He couldn't even ask a question without sounding spiteful.

'None of your business.'

'Taken to thieving, have you?'

'Don't judge me by your standards, Vinnie.'

'I hope Ernie didn't pay for it.'

'Afraid he might be giving me more money than you?' Kate taunted.

'If he is . . .' Vinnie stomped away and Kate guessed he was going to their father to demand more money for himself.

She wheeled the bicycle into the barn and locked it to a wooden post.

'What's this?' Ernie said from the open door.

'A bicycle.'

'Don't get lippy with me, girl. Whose is it?'

Should she admit it was hers? Better not. A chain and padlock wouldn't keep it safe from Ernie and the boys if they knew no consequences would arise from hacksawing through the chain. Besides, Kate didn't know for sure that it was a gift rather than a loan. 'I've borrowed it,' she said.

'Who from?'

'Someone who wishes to remain anonymous.'

'Some man? You'd better not be misbehaving, girl.'

Kate laughed. 'You think a man would look at me in these clothes?'

Ernie grunted in a way she took to be acceptance of her point. 'I still want to know whose it is.'

'I want a lot of things. It doesn't mean I get them. All you need to know is that the person who loaned me the bicycle will be very angry indeed if any harm comes to it.'

With that, Kate walked past Ernie and crossed the yard to the house.

CHAPTER THIRTY-FIVE

Alice

It had been kind of Kate to acquit Alice of blame for failing to help Mrs Hall but Alice couldn't let herself off the hook so easily. Even so, she'd been struck by what Kate had said about Churchwood being responsible.

Alice was still relatively new to the village, but she could see that, despite the kind hearts of many of its residents, the village didn't always pull together to look after its own. Edna Hall had slipped through the net of care. Janet Collins appeared to be carrying her family worries alone. May Janicki hadn't been welcomed as warmly as she might have been, and poor Kate had received the harshest treatment of all.

The April morning was cool and the gas must have dissipated by now so Alice went inside to close the window. It was a small house, comprising a kitchen at the back and a sitting room at the front, but there were signs that happiness had lived here once. A sofa with twin indentations showed where Mrs Hall and her husband had sat side by side. Photographs recorded their togetherness through the years, while embroidered chair backs and a hand-made rag rug spoke of cosiness and pride.

Alice imagined the rooms had once glowed with

polish and care but now there was dust on the surfaces and ash dulled the hearth rug. The aspidistra was wilting in its brass pot and another plant had died, its leaves crumbling when Alice touched them.

Moving back into the kitchen, she hesitated, feeling like an intruder, then opened cupboards to see little food inside. Mrs Hall deserved her privacy, but clearly she also needed help.

Alice set to work, dusting, sweeping and beating the rug outside in the garden. As ever, her injured hand made her slow, but the house was looking considerably better by the time her father and Mr Makepiece returned, even if she hadn't achieved a thorough clean. 'They're keeping Mrs Hall in for a day or two,' her father said.

'What did you tell them?'

'That I understood she was feeling low after the death of her husband and might have grown absent-minded with the gas.'

It was a clever explanation that would ensure Mrs Hall's emotional condition received attention while protecting her from investigation by the police.

'I'll get along home,' her father said.

'I'll stay to help here.'

Mr Makepiece studied the broken door. 'That's lucky. The lock's fine. It just needs more screws to hold it in place.' He'd brought a toolbox in from his truck and soon the door was as good as new.

'I'm going to take a key so I can come back and get the house ready for Mrs Hall's return,' Alice said, having located the key in a pottery bowl as she cleaned.

'Good idea. The hospital will telephone me when she's coming home and I'll pass word to your father.

They'll also let the doctor in Barton know. He looks after Churchwood folk, though he isn't a patch on your father. Come on. I'll drop you at the cottage.'

They drove the short distance to Alice's home. 'You did well today, young Alice, and so did your friend,' Mr Makepiece said. 'That girl is cut from different cloth to the rest of the Fletchers. Quality cloth. But Churchwood . . .' He shook his head in disappointment. 'We're a village, not a city full of strangers. We should be doing better.'

CHAPTER THIRTY-SIX

Naomi

The Post Office was buzzing with conversation when Naomi walked in. 'What's happened?' she asked.

'There you are, Naomi!' Marjorie turned from the group that was holding court around her. 'I went straight to Foxfield to tell you all about it, but Suki said you were out.'

'I was taking a walk.' Naomi's unsettled mood had continued and she'd hoped a walk might shake it off. Unfortunately, the walk had made no difference.

'Well,' Marjorie said, relishing her role as the oracle of important news, 'Edna Hall is in hospital. We were *told* it was an accident but some of us know better. We could smell the gas coming from her kitchen and the lock on her door was hanging loose as though she'd tried to stop people from rushing in to rescue her.'

Edna Hall had tried to gas herself? Emotion rushed in on Naomi – shock, concern, guilt and, finally, dismay at the way Marjorie was speaking about the poor woman. 'You can't possibly know the facts, Marjorie. You're spreading gossip based on guesses.'

'I wouldn't dream of gossiping, Naomi!'

'Humph,' Naomi said, but who was she to criticize when she'd been at fault, too?

Everyone in Churchwood knew that the death of Edna's husband had been a blow to her. But Naomi had also seen Edna staring down at the lake. Thinking back, it had been odd behaviour from a woman who'd always been a homebody. Perhaps she'd been contemplating putting an end to things even then. Naomi should have made time for her instead of thinking of her own needs.

Edna, May, Kate . . . Naomi had done little to help any of them. 'Edna has been taken to hospital, you say?'

'That's what Dr Lovell intended. He sent us away, though, so we don't know what happened.' Marjorie let out a small sniff of outrage at having been expelled from the scene of the drama.

'That was very proper of him,' Naomi countered. 'I can't imagine Edna would have appreciated an audience while she was feeling so vulnerable. I for one am sorry about letting poor Edna down.'

'How were you to know what Edna was planning?'

'I don't know that she planned anything, and neither do you,' Naomi reminded Marjorie. 'But I knew she'd taken the loss of her husband badly, so it isn't to be wondered at if she grew distracted and left the gas on by mistake. I should have kept a closer eye on her.'

'But you're always so busy.'

'It's a question of priorities, Marjorie. Unfortunately, I can't change the past, but I'll be keeping a closer eye on her from now on.'

'You'll let me help? Please let me help!'

Naomi sighed at the thought of Marjorie fluttering around Edna. She'd give the woman no peace and doubtless she'd pass on everything she saw and heard to anyone who cared to listen. 'You can be sure I'll include you if I think you can be useful.'

'We could go to Foxfield now and make plans.'

'I think it needs careful thought first.'

'We could think about it together.'

'Not today, but thank you for the offer.'

Marjorie looked crestfallen. She was missing out on a Foxfield tea and perhaps another chocolate.

Naomi stayed firm, though, and a few minutes later she knocked on the door of The Linnets.

'I'm sorry to trouble you,' she said when Alice answered. 'I'm here about Mrs Hall. Not, I hasten to add, to ask about things she might prefer to keep private, but to ask you to let me know if there's anything I might do to help her. She's in hospital, I believe?'

'Please come in, Mrs Harrington.'

'It's good of you to invite me, but I won't take up your time.'

'Mrs Hall is indeed in hospital,' Alice confirmed.

'Would you let me know when she's coming home? I imagine you might hear about her progress through your father. I don't wish to interfere or to pry into Mrs Hall's private concerns, but if it would be useful to her, I'd like to ensure that her house is ready for her – clean and tidy, with a fire laid and food in the pantry.'

'That's kind of you, Mrs Harrington.'

'I'd offer to collect her in the car but the petrol restriction means that won't be possible. If there's anything else I can do . . .?'

'I'll let you know if I hear of anything.'

'Thank you. Good day, Miss Lovell. My regards to your father.' Naomi forced a goodbye smile and scurried away.

She was too upset to talk now – upset about what Edna must have suffered, and upset about her own negligence in failing to realize that Edna needed help.

Not so long ago, Naomi had congratulated herself on making the village a better place. Now her life was being exposed as a shallow and vain illusion.

Naomi didn't venture into the village the following morning but by afternoon concern that Marjorie might still be spreading gossip about Edna drove Naomi out to put a stop to it. Sure enough, Marjorie was outside the grocer's shop with a rapt audience of two other women. Naomi never got to hear what she was saying because Marjorie saw her approaching and broke off suddenly, but her cheeks turned tell-tale pink.

'We've been hearing about Edna Hall,' Mrs Larkin said.

'Yes, she was taken ill yesterday.'

'Taken ill?'

'That's right.'

Mrs Larkin gave Marjorie a sidelong look of mistrust then turned back to Naomi. 'We heard something about a gas oven.'

'I believe the flame blew out and Edna didn't notice.'

'So nothing much happened?'

The woman's attitude appalled Naomi. 'Something most definitely happened. Edna Hall was taken ill. Fortunately, Alice Lovell and Kate Fletcher happened to call at the house and fetched Dr Lovell. If they hadn't done so, Mrs Hall might have been in a much worse condition.'

Mrs Larkin gave Marjorie another long look then

walked away, taking her friend, Mrs Blackstock, with her.

'I don't understand,' Marjorie said then. 'What you just said isn't—'

'You need to learn to respect other people's privacy, Marjorie.'

'But the truth—'

'Counts for far less than kindness.'

'You mean we should lie?'

'I mean kindness comes first. Especially when we don't know the facts.'

'But when we do know the facts—'

'Kindness still comes first.'

Marjorie's face took on the look of a chastised child.

Naomi sighed. 'I have some chocolates left. Would you like to help me finish them?'

Marjorie beamed.

'I was just coming to see you,' Alice said as Naomi walked out through the Foxfield gates the following Monday. 'Mrs Hall is coming home on Wednesday. Mr Makepiece and my father are collecting her and she's going to stay with Janet Collins for a day or two. Just until she settles down.'

'Has Janet Collins got room?'

'She's made room. A team of us have got Mrs Hall's house and garden ready for when she moves back in.'

'There's nothing I can do?' Naomi was disappointed.

'I hope you won't consider this an imposition, but Mrs Hall's stock of coal is low and, even though we've moved into April, the nights are cold.'

'I'll be glad to provide her with coal. Anything else? Don't be coy, Miss Lovell. I want to help.'

'Food,' Alice said. 'Perhaps some tins of soup?'

'I'll go to the grocer's now. I'll buy soup and a few more things besides. Where should they be delivered?'

'I think Janet's house would be best.'

Naomi heard a familiar rumble and knew without looking that it came from Bert Makepiece's truck. Unwilling to put herself through more criticism from that insufferable man, she hastened away and was relieved to hear him pull up beside Alice.

Naomi managed to buy soup, pilchards, jam, a pot of meat paste and a few other bits, and arranged for them to be delivered to Janet Collins's house. Emerging from the grocer's she stiffened when she saw Bert Makepiece coming towards her, having parked his truck at the kerb. 'Morning, Mrs H.,' he said, and his nod suggested he knew what she'd been doing and actually approved of it. Not that Naomi needed his approbation.

She set off for home only to find herself regretting that all she'd been asked to contribute towards Edna Hall's comfort was money. Janet Collins and others had all worked together to give time and care.

CHAPTER THIRTY-SEVEN

Alice

Saving Edna boosted the reputations of both Alice and Kate in Churchwood circles. 'No one has thrown their arms around me, but two people smiled in the baker's and one woman actually said "Well done",' Kate reported.

'Progress,' Alice agreed.

Wednesday came and, at Edna's request, Alice waited at Janet's house to welcome her home. 'I did a foolish thing,' Edna confided. 'Losing Arthur blinded me to what else was good in my life. I couldn't see beyond my grief but now . . .'

'You *can* see?'

'I'll always miss my Arthur but I have a life to lead here before I'm reunited with him in the hereafter. Thank you for making that possible, Miss Lovell.'

'Please call me Alice.'

'Thank you, Alice. I'd like to thank your friend, too, if she can spare the time to visit.'

Kate duly visited the next day but looked awkward sitting beside Edna, shifting her long legs around as though she didn't know what to do with them. Undeterred, Edna took hold of Kate's hand. 'I was as guilty as everyone else in turning my nose up at you, but I was wrong. Your family may be . . . Well, we know what your family is like. But you're different, and it's to your credit that you're a good person when you've had such an upbringing.'

'Even Mrs Harrington has visited,' Edna told Alice after moving back into her own home the following day. 'Fancy that! A grand lady sitting in my little parlour with her feet on a rug I made from rags.'

'She was as worried about you as the rest of us,' Alice said.

'I didn't know whether to curtsey,' Edna admitted, and the thought of it made them both laugh.

Alice didn't laugh when she walked into the Post Office on Saturday morning to see Nurse Morgan ahead of her in the queue. She tensed then, reminding herself that the security breach wasn't her fault, stepped forward with a smile. 'Good morning, Nurse Morgan.'

Ruth glanced around and her eyes widened as though she couldn't believe Alice wasn't sitting in jail on a charge of treason.

Bracing herself for a snub, Alice asked, 'I hope you're keeping well?'

Ruth's gaze slid down to the letters Alice was holding. Did Ruth suspect that one of them might contain military secrets? Two were bill payments but the third was a letter to Daniel at his forces address. She held up all three letters. 'I've been writing to a friend who's serving overseas. You?'

'Me?' The question appeared to startle her. 'I've been writing to my brother.'

She briefly flashed the letter before Alice's eyes,

giving her time to register only the name on the envelope and the fact that the address was in London. 'Your brother isn't in the forces?'

Ruth blushed. 'No.'

Was she worried that Alice might think he was shirking his duty and leaving the dangerous work to others? 'Many people are contributing to the war effort in all sorts of ways,' Alice pointed out. 'Look at the farmers and the people who are keeping the country going in factories and transport. You're all doing a splendid job at the hospital, too.'

'The sooner this awful war is over, the better,' Ruth said. 'It's splitting families and sweethearts, and bringing grief to so many people.'

'The sooner the better,' Alice agreed.

Ruth had reached the front of the queue. 'How can I help?' Mr Johnson asked.

Ruth bought stamps but honoured Alice with a nod as she left the shop.

Alice went about her shopping and then called in at the cobbler's to collect some shoes that were being mended. 'I hope you're satisfied with the job I've done?' Mr Corbett said. 'Hexton's leather soles are the best, in my opinion.'

'Thank you, they look perfectly satisfactory.' She handed over some coins and waited for her change.

Then she gasped with sudden shock as her mind caught up with what she'd seen and heard – or thought she'd seen and heard.

'If you're not happy . . .' Mr Corbett began, and Alice roused herself to reassure him.

'I'm more than happy. Thank you, Mr Corbett.'

She took her change and headed home, deep in

thought as she cast her mind back several weeks. Was she remembering correctly? Alice couldn't be certain, but she felt sure enough of her memory to determine that something needed to be done. In fact, she was desperate for something to be done. But the people she needed to see were Babs and Pauline, and Alice had no way of getting a message to them that wouldn't risk getting them into trouble. She'd have to wait until they visited again, but who knew when that might be?

Waiting was going to be agony.

CHAPTER THIRTY-EIGHT

Kate

Every morning Kate went to the barn feeling appre-
hensive, and then slumped in relief when she saw
that the bicycle was still undamaged and chained to
its pillar.

Not that the Fletcher men had accepted Kate's gift
quietly. She caught Ernie staring at her with those
weasel's eyes sometimes and guessed he was speculating about the bicycle's owner. Once she came upon
Vinnie trying to open the padlock with a collection of
old keys. And every few days Fred or Frank, or both of
them, would beg to borrow the bicycle. 'We won't let
it come to harm,' they'd say.

But even if they started out with good intentions
they'd fight about it or lark around once they'd got
some beer in their bellies. The bicycle would be broken or – worse – end up in the lake.

Mostly Kate used it to visit Alice, though today she
went further afield because she spotted Kenny hiding
behind a tree in the lane. Glancing back, she saw him
signal to Vinnie to indicate the direction she'd taken.
They were obviously hoping she would reveal the
identity of her mysterious benefactor.

She cycled on to confound them and reached the
village of Barton. It was only a handful of miles from

Churchwood but the visit still felt like an adventure. Kate had never been on a bus or train, and she'd never travelled further than Churchwood's outer limits as far as she could remember. Short as it was, the visit to Barton cheered her. With an income of only two shillings a week, the prospect of leaving the farm to forge a different life felt almost as remote as ever. But not quite. She'd made a start, and from small beginnings . . .

She was cycling past the Churchwood shops when Alice waved her to a stop. 'Do you have time to talk?' she asked. She looked agitated.

'Has something happened?'

'I'm not sure. I'd like your opinion. But not here.' Alice glanced around as though fearing she might be overheard. 'Can you come to the cottage?'

Five minutes later they reached The Linnets and sat on the old garden chairs Alice had dragged from the shed and cleaned up now the days were growing warmer.

Kate listened as Alice told her about her encounter with Nurse Morgan two days earlier. 'Do you think I'm making too much of it?' Alice asked.

'You can't be sure it's significant, but you can't be sure it's *in*significant either. It needs investigating.'

'That's what I think, but I'll have to wait for Babs and Pauline to visit.'

'Waiting is awful in situations like this.'

'Dreadful.'

That evening Kate stood at her bedroom window and saw two torches in the lane, directed downwards to minimize the light in these blacked-out times. She hoped they were heading for Alice and The Linnets.

CHAPTER THIRTY-NINE

Alice

'Thank goodness,' Alice said as she opened the door to Babs and Pauline.

'That's a lovely welcome but I'm afraid we don't have any news,' Babs answered. 'We're only calling to let you know you haven't been forgotten.'

'I have news for *you*,' Alice told them. 'At least I think I have.'

'Do tell,' Babs urged, as they settled in the dining room.

'I hope I'm not doing someone a grave injustice.'

'Just tell us and then we can decide if there's an injustice or not.'

'I was in the Post Office on Saturday morning,' Alice explained. 'Ruth Morgan was there, sending a letter to her brother.'

'And?' Babs looked mystified. Pauline, too.

'If memory serves me correctly, I once heard her tell a patient that she hadn't any brothers or sisters. I know it's a big leap from lying about a brother to passing secrets, but—'

'It's an inconsistency,' Pauline said.

'Suspicious,' Babs added.

'Of course, Ruth might simply be the sort of person who likes to guard her privacy,' Alice said. 'She might have pretended to have no brothers and sisters so no one would ask about them.'

'Did you see the letter?' Babs asked.

'Briefly. I saw the name – *Mr R. Morgan* – and London in the address, but that's all.'

'Ruth is from Wales, but there's no reason why she shouldn't have a brother in London.'

'I asked if her brother was in the forces. She said not – and seemed embarrassed by it.'

'Which could be another reason for keeping quiet about him to the patients,' Pauline reasoned. 'They might not take kindly to hearing about a man they believe to be a shirker.'

'On the other hand, Mr R. Morgan might not exist,' Babs said. 'We don't know what's going on, if anything, so we need to proceed with caution.'

'Proceed how?' Alice asked.

'If Ruth is sending letters, she might be receiving letters, too.'

'You're going to search her room?' Alice was shocked. 'Oh, Babs! What if you're caught? You'll lose your jobs. Don't put yourselves at risk for my sake.'

'We'll be careful,' Babs promised. 'Besides, finding the real traitor will help the patients and the country, too.'

With that Alice had to be content, but she was left waiting for news again. It was unbearable.

Two days later, Babs visited alone. 'I managed to get into Ruth's room with Pauline keeping a lookout,' she reported, 'but the only letters I found were from her mum. Either Mr R. Morgan isn't writing back or she's destroying his letters – unless she's hiding them somewhere else.'

'So there's nothing to be done?'

'I didn't say that.' Babs grinned wickedly. 'We have a plan, and it involves you, Alice.'

'Well?' Alice asked Kate after explaining the plan to her.

'I can see how it *could* work.'

'But you don't think it *will* work.' Alice couldn't blame Kate for having doubts. She had so many of her own.

'It's going to need some luck, that's all.'

'A *lot* of luck.' The plan would be like a game of Snakes and Ladders – with numerous rolls of the dice and hazards.

'Even if the plan fails, you might learn something helpful,' Kate suggested.

'If I haven't been arrested,' Alice joked, though nerves soon wiped the smile from her face.

Anxiety kept Alice awake into the small hours on Saturday, but she still woke early and was ready long before she needed to be.

Spring was in full force, the sun bathing the village in a golden glow of warmth and promise. Alice's coat was too warm for the weather but she needed its large pockets. Time and again she patted them to ensure her letters were safe, not yet knowing which one she'd need – if either. *Stamped letter in the right-hand pocket,* she recited silently. *Unstamped letter in the left.*

As the sun rose higher, she opened her bedroom window and leaned out to listen for voices in the lane.

She wished she'd asked Babs to talk loudly when approaching the cottage. The trees and shrubs that had been skeletal in winter were now lush with green growth and passers-by would be harder to spot.

An hour ticked by and Alice began to wonder if the plan had failed before it had even started. But then she heard an 'Ouch!' followed by, 'Hang on! I've got a stone in my shoe!'

Clever Babs, giving Alice notice that she and Ruth were nearby. Alice closed the window, called goodbye to her father and left the cottage by the side gate just as Babs and Ruth approached.

'Good morning,' Babs called, doing a terrific job of looking surprised by Alice's appearance.

Alice faked surprise, too. 'Oh, hello. Are you walking into the village? You won't mind if I join you?'

''Course not,' Babs replied, sending Alice a private wink.

Ruth was already looking as though she hadn't taken kindly to having Babs's presence foisted on to her. Now Alice was being foisted on to her, too, and Ruth's downturned mouth took on an even more resentful cast.

Either Ruth was nervous about passing secrets in the presence of bystanders or she simply preferred to be alone.

'Lovely day, isn't it?' Alice said as they walked along. 'I think I've made a mistake in wearing a warm jacket, but it was cooler when I went out to collect the eggs earlier.'

'At least you live nearby so haven't far to walk,' Babs pointed out. 'The hospital is so far away, there's plenty of time for the weather to change even on a walk to the village. Rain can turn to sunshine or sunshine can turn to rain.'

'No rain today, thank goodness.'

The conversation was intended to fill the time and persuade Ruth that nothing was amiss. Ruth contributed nothing to it. Was she too tense? Too afraid even? Or merely disgusted that Babs should chat so casually with a girl who'd been banished from Stratton House on security grounds?

Babs's enquiries had established that Ruth always walked to the village pillar box on Saturday mornings unless she was working. 'If she's passing secrets, it would make sense for her to post her letters in the village. Less risky than using the Stratton House posting box.'

The plan had two alternative elements to it. At the very least Alice and Babs wanted a closer look at Ruth's letter so they could learn the full address of Mr R. Morgan. Babs would then ask friends in London to try to find out more about him.

If possible, though, they hoped to engineer a slight accident so Ruth's letter could be exchanged for one of the letters in Alice's pockets. That way they could take the letter away and read it.

'Can you remember what sort of envelope she used for the letter you saw?' Babs had asked.

'Plain cream, I think. I have some that are similar. At first glance anyway.'

'Then you need to write one out to Mr R. Morgan in London. You'll have to make up the rest of the address and hope that Ruth doesn't notice.'

To help Alice with copying Ruth's handwriting, Babs had produced a note Ruth had pinned to the nurses' bathroom at Stratton House. *It would be*

302

appreciated if you could all leave enough hot water for those of us on late duty. If we use just a little in our baths, there should be enough for everyone. Thank you, Ruth Morgan.

Not knowing whether Ruth's letter would be stamped, Alice had written two envelopes, one with a stamp and one without.

They reached the village but Ruth walked straight past the pillar box. Was this because she had no letter to post today? If so, the plan had come to nothing.

But a moment later it was back in business. 'I'm going in here,' Ruth said, and walked into the Post Office.

Alice and Babs followed. There was a small queue of two customers and Ruth joined it. Frustratingly, she didn't take a letter from her bag.

'I'd like a postal order for five shillings, please,' she said, when it was her turn to be served.

Alice and Babs exchanged looks. Perhaps Ruth wasn't here to post a letter after all.

'And two stamps,' she added.

At last, she dug in her bag for her purse and two envelopes, which she placed on the counter. The topmost one was addressed to a Mrs Morgan in Wales and appeared to be a greetings card. Perhaps the postal order was a birthday gift for Ruth's mother.

A corner of a second envelope peeped out from beneath it. Was it addressed to Mr R. Morgan? How was Alice to find out? And how was she ever going to get hold of it?

Ruth managed to slip the postal order into the greetings card envelope, seal the flap then add stamps to both envelopes, all while keeping the address on the second one hidden.

Alice nodded at Babs to suggest that, if they were going to take action, it should be now. Babs nodded back then, shrieking, clutched her eye and stumbled forward, barging into Ruth in the process. Alice reached out as though to help her friend and swept Ruth's purse and envelopes to the floor. Coins scattered in all directions.

'Ruth, help me!' Babs cried.

'In a moment. I'll just—'

'I'll pick up your things,' Alice said. 'You help Babs as you're the nurse.'

Ruth cast an agonized look across the floor. Was she searching for her envelopes? Babs let out another cry to divert Ruth's attention and Alice crouched down to retrieve the scattered possessions.

'What is it, Barbara?' Ruth asked, obviously annoyed.

'My eye! My eye!'

Alice picked up Ruth's purse, which had landed close by, then looked around for the envelopes. The greetings card had come to rest near Babs. Where was the other one?

There! But as Alice scrambled towards it, a pair of feet in sensible but expensive-looking shoes stepped across her path. Alice's gaze travelled up past stocking-clad legs and a tweed suit to meet the grave, accusing stare of Naomi Harrington. Unable to stop herself, Alice blushed.

Without a word, Mrs Harrington picked the envelope up and slipped it into her bag. 'I'll return when you're not so busy, Mr Johnson,' she called, then left the shop.

For a moment Alice stared after her in shock. Then, heart racing with worry, she collected the coins, returned them to Ruth's purse and, to hide the fact that the other letter was missing, dropped the greetings card into the shop's internal posting box.

Ruth was still tending to Babs. 'I can't see anything. If you'd hold still, I might—'

Alice nudged Babs, who promptly stopped making a fuss. 'Actually, I think I've blinked away whatever was hurting me.'

She blinked a few times for dramatic effect then dabbed at her eye with a handkerchief.

'Your purse,' Alice said, holding it out to Ruth. 'I'm pretty sure I collected all of the coins.'

'My letters?' Clearly, they were of more concern.

'I posted them for you.'

Looking alarmed, Ruth glanced at the posting box and appeared to be considering if it might be possible to retrieve them. But she must have decided that a fuss would only arouse suspicion because she muttered a resentful, 'Thank you.'

Babs sent Alice a triumphant look that turned to dismay when Alice gave a small shake of her head. Babs's gaze was full of questions but this wasn't the time to discuss what had gone wrong.

'Actually, I've promised to call in on someone,' Alice said, hastening towards the door. 'It was nice to see you both.'

Mrs Harrington was heading towards Foxfield but she paused to look around and send Alice another hard stare. Was it an instruction to Alice to follow? When Mrs Harrington continued walking, Alice set off after her.

CHAPTER FORTY

Naomi

Alice's light footsteps soon brought her level with Naomi. 'Mrs Harrington, I—'

'You'll oblige me by waiting until we're inside before you explain yourself, Miss Lovell.'

'Of course.' Alice sounded chastened. As well she should.

Naomi had never been more shocked because she'd begun to see Alice Lovell as a force for good in Churchwood. She felt foolish, too, because it seemed she might have been taken in by the girl's pretence of integrity. But it was possible that the girl had an explanation for what had happened and it was the wish to find this out that had stopped Naomi from handing the envelope straight back to its owner or involving the police.

Suki must have noticed their approach because she opened the door and helped them off with their coats. 'Would Madam like—'

'I'll ring if I need anything, Suki.'

Naomi led the way into the sitting room. 'Please sit, Miss Lovell,' she said, too agitated to sit herself.

Alice sat, as neat in her movements as ever but clearly upset. No wonder, if her true self had been exposed. 'Mrs Harrington, I'm here because you appeared to want to speak to me about something.'

'Please don't insult my intelligence by trying to bluff your way out of the situation, Miss Lovell. You know what I saw – or appeared to see: two young women engineering a fake accident in order to get their hands on another young woman's money.'

'No!' Alice cried. 'We didn't want Ruth's *money*. We're not thieves!'

'Then you wanted her post.' Naomi opened her bag, took out the envelope and saw Alice swallow.

'Interfering with someone's post is a serious issue,' Alice admitted. 'But the reason we wanted the letter wasn't frivolous or nosy or spiteful. We had genuine concerns.'

'I hardly think it could be a matter of life or death, Miss Lovell.'

'Actually, it might be.'

Naomi blinked. Was Alice making fun of her? 'This is not the time for flippant theatricals.'

'I'm not exaggerating.'

Something in Alice's expression caused Naomi's anger to falter. Perhaps there really was more to this incident than appearances suggested. 'Start at the beginning and tell me the whole story,' she said, finally sitting in her usual armchair.

Alice did so.

Naomi was silent for a moment; then she stared at the envelope. 'You planned to steam this open?'

'Then glue the flap down again and post it with no harm done if it really is an innocent letter to a brother.'

'And if it isn't innocent?'

'We'd have taken it to the hospital matron. She'd know how to report it to an appropriate authority.'

Naomi got up and walked to the window, thinking hard. Decision made, she pulled the bell near the fireplace and a moment later Suki appeared. 'I'd like a kettle of boiling water, please.'

The maid looked confused. 'A kettle with tea things?'

'Just a kettle for now.'

Alice waited for the maid to leave. 'You're going to open the envelope?'

'Reprehensible in normal circumstances, but I agree these circumstances are far from normal. If it's opened here, I might be useful as a witness.'

'Thank you.'

The kettle must already have been boiling – doubtless in anticipation of Naomi ringing for tea – because Suki brought it straight away.

'That'll be all, thank you,' Naomi told her. Then she looked at Alice. 'I've never done anything as underhand as this before. I suppose I hold the flap up to the steam and hope it weakens the gum?'

'I haven't done this before either, but I believe that's the theory. Would you prefer me to do it? I don't want you to scald your fingers.'

'I'll be careful.'

It didn't take long to loosen the gum enough for Naomi to ease the flap open. Drawing the letter out, she began to read.

Dear Ralph,

The week has been quiet but I hope some of the things I've seen and heard might be useful to the cause. A corporal from the West Staffordshire Regiment told me his platoon had suffered problems with a batch of rifles.

308

Apparently, they wouldn't fire properly . . . Another
private, also from the West Staffordshires, told me that
his superior officer – Major Morley – was believed to
have been promoted beyond his capabilities. He might
be a weak link in the chain of command . . . A corporal
told me that his brother is on a submarine somewhere
off the coast of Ireland. He didn't say where . . .

Naomi felt colour draining from her face and finished the letter with a hand clutched to her chest. 'You were right.' She passed the letter over for Alice to read.

None of the revelations appeared to be of great significance. At least not in this letter. But over time letters like this might paint a picture of how the Allies were faring in the war and perhaps even what they were planning, especially if similar reports were coming from other parts of the country.

'It makes me wonder how many more traitors are in our midst,' Naomi said. 'The young woman who wrote this looked so ordinary in the Post Office. Almost *wholesome*. And she's a nurse at the hospital? Looking after British servicemen?'

'The very people she's betraying.'

Naomi shook her head then tried to gather her thoughts. 'I need to take the letter to Stratton House.'

'Of course.' Alice handed it back. 'The person you saw helping me is Barbara Carter. She's a nurse too. Her colleague, Pauline Evans, also helped.'

'I misjudged you, Miss Lovell. I apologize.'

'Barbara and I acted strangely. You were right to be suspicious. I'm just glad you gave me a chance to explain.'

'I try to be fair. Now, let me offer you tea . . .'

'Thank you, but I need to see Barbara. She'll be worried.'

'You'll ensure your friends don't let Ruth Morgan know she's been found out? She shouldn't be given a chance to escape justice and neither should the traitor who's going by the name of Ralph Morgan. They should both face justice and I'm sure the authorities will want to question them about the contents of previous letters.'

'Of course.'

They walked to the door. 'You know of no reason why Ruth Morgan should have betrayed her country?' Naomi asked.

'None, but I've only spoken to her a few times and never in private. You'll let me know what happens?'

'I'll do my best.'

Alice nodded and Naomi went back inside to change into more comfortable shoes. Putting her coat back on, she set off on the two-mile walk to Stratton House.

CHAPTER FORTY-ONE

Alice

There was no sign of Babs in the street or at The Linnets. No sign of Ruth Morgan either. Alice supposed they must have returned to the hospital as Babs was due to go on duty and perhaps Ruth was working, too. Doubtless Babs was desperate for news, but Alice had no way of getting it to her.

For the rest of the morning thoughts of Ruth's betrayal circulated round Alice's mind along with the faces of the patients at Stratton House, some no more than boys. Sweet boys, mostly, yet Ruth had betrayed them just as she'd betrayed other men who might die as a result of her treachery. Men like darling Daniel. Alice shuddered at the thought.

She tried to keep busy but her powers of concentration had deserted her.

A little after midday Kate cycled down from the farm. 'Well?' she asked.

Alice told her what had happened and saw Kate's eyes widen. 'Mrs Harrington picked up the letter?'

'I was worried sick at first, but it might turn out to be for the best as she's more likely to be taken seriously.'

'Let's hope so. And let's hope you're allowed back into the hospital.'

311

'I'm not getting my hopes up about that,' Alice said, but the truth was that her hopes were high despite her efforts to keep them in check.

When Kate left to go into the village Alice accompanied her outside; then she glanced across at Foxfield, wondering how Mrs Harrington was faring at the hospital. Turning to go back indoors, she paused when she saw Mrs Harrington coming down the lane, her laboured gait suggesting that she was troubled by her feet.

She reached Alice and paused to catch her breath and wipe perspiration from her face with a handkerchief. 'I saw the matron,' she said then. 'Miss Peters. Sensible sort of woman, though naturally shocked and vexed when she read the letter. She called Nurse Morgan an unintelligent fool. Not that she treated the matter lightly. On the contrary, she assured me that she'd waste no time in reporting it to the authorities. She couldn't promise to let us know the outcome as it's a security issue, but whatever happens we've done our duty.'

'You've had a trying day, Mrs Harrington. Come in and rest for a while.' An idea had been building in Alice's head and she wanted her neighbour's opinion on it.

'Thank you, but I need to get home.'

Alice couldn't argue with a woman who was obviously fatigued. The conversation she had in mind would have to wait for another time.

It was a day for visitors; Pauline appeared later that afternoon, desperate to know what had happened. 'I only snatched a quick word with Babs but she told me the plan went disastrously wrong. Now Stratton House is abuzz with tension again and I can't find out why. Do you think Babs and I are in trouble?'

Alice told the story for a second time.

'So we were right,' Pauline said, amazed but thoughtful. 'I never warmed to Ruth but I didn't expect this of her.'

'You'll let me know if you hear more? It's hard being cut off from things down here in the village.'

'We nurses can be cut off from security stuff even if it's going on under our noses, but we'll do our best.'

Alice would have to wait for news, but how she hated the delay.

No word came the following morning. Or the following afternoon. But after dusk had fallen on Sunday there was a knock on the door.

'This cottage is becoming as busy as our Highbury house,' Alice's father commented.

'You don't mind?' Were her visitors disturbing his peace?

'I'm not complaining, my dear. You've exposed something important.'

Alice had told him what had happened. Now he shook his head wonderingly. 'Churchwood looked so quiet and peaceful when I first saw it. I would never have expected it to be the scene of such dramas, but I suppose every place contains a mix of good and bad people. Human nature in all shapes and sizes.'

He moved into his study, and Alice opened the door. 'Matron!'

'I thought it only fair to come and fill you in on

313

developments as you were instrumental in exposing Nurse Morgan's treachery.'

They settled in the dining room. 'Ruth has been arrested,' Matron confided, 'but I managed to speak to her before she was taken away. Foolish, deluded girl! It seems she betrayed her country for love. Or rather the illusion of love. She was involved with a German chap called Karl before the war. When the war separated them she was desperate for peace to come quickly so she could be reunited with him.'

'But to betray British servicemen . . .'

'Karl persuaded her that Germany was certain to be victorious, and the sooner the war ended, the better for all concerned. He put her in touch with her London accomplice, who's been arrested too. In her distorted way, she convinced herself that she was helping to avoid casualties.'

'A German victory could never be better for all concerned. What about Jewish people?' Alice was thinking of the Kovac children whose parents were who knew where.

'She told me I shouldn't believe all the stories I read in the newspapers and hear on the wireless because they're exaggerated or invented as anti-German propaganda.'

'She must know the war started with German aggression.'

'That's an inconvenient truth, which she chooses to ignore. Ruth's mind has been focused on a rosy future with Karl and she's regarded anything that stood in the way of that dream as an obstacle to be eliminated. She's been naïve and selfish, but there'll be no rosy future with Karl, and she'll pay a heavy price.'

'What sort of price, do you think?'

'Hopefully not the ultimate one. I deplore what Ruth has done, and I've long struggled with her smugness, but I wouldn't wish that on her. A prison sentence, though . . . I'm sure she'll be facing prison. You've proved you're on the side of King and country, Alice, and I've urged that you be allowed back into Stratton House, but I'm afraid it's a case of wait and see what the authorities decide.'

More waiting.

The following morning Alice made two visits. The first was to Brimbles Farm. Alice didn't go to the farmhouse as she saw nothing to be gained by antagonizing the Fletcher men further. She simply walked along Brimbles Lane in the hope of seeing Kate in one of the fields and was delighted when her hope was fulfilled.

They waved to each other then Kate galloped over. 'Any news from the hospital?'

Alice brought her up to date.

'It's the patients who'll suffer if you're not allowed back.'

Alice couldn't disagree, but there was something else she wished to discuss.

'Goodness,' Kate said, after Alice explained what she had in mind. 'No one could call you unambitious!'

'I can't do it by myself. I need a team. You, I hope. May and Janet too.' Alice hesitated. 'I'm also going to ask Mrs Harrington.'

Kate made a scornful sound. 'She won't want to be in the same room as me.'

'I suspect there might be a nice person hidden beneath the surface, so I'd like to give her a chance. But tell me what you think of the project?'

Kate grinned. 'I think it's wonderful!'

The second visit was to Foxfield. Alice began by telling Mrs Harrington about Matron's visit.

'What that nurse did was appalling, but she's ruined her life and that's sad for her family as well as for her,' Mrs Harrington said.

Alice thought of the postal order Ruth had sent to her mother. It was likely to be the last gift Mrs Morgan would receive from her daughter for many years. The Morgans would have to bear the shame of a traitor in the family, too. 'Changing the subject, I have an idea I'd like to discuss if you can spare me another few minutes?'

Mrs Harrington's expression turned wary. 'I hardly think I'm the right person to . . .'

'Please,' Alice added.

'Really, I don't feel . . . Oh, very well.'

Alice outlined her plan.

'A bookshop?' Mrs Harrington questioned.

'A bookshop and so much more. A place to buy books, certainly, but also to borrow them, read newspapers and magazines, hear stories being read, listen to talks about all sorts of things and simply chat over cups of tea. A relaxed sort of place, for children and adults alike, that'll bring the community together. It seems to me that some Churchwood people struggle at times. Poor Mrs Hall is an obvious one, but there's also Kate, May Janicki and the little refugee children. Even Janet Collins is worried about her Charlie and I'm sure there are others. If we bring people together, we'll get to know each other better instead of making assumptions and judgements. We'll notice each other's struggles, too, or have a better chance of hearing about them. And we'll be able to help.'

'My word, Miss Lovell. No one could call you unambitious.'

'That's what Kate said, but it isn't just about me. It's about all of us. If we're allowed, we might involve the hospital staff and patients too.'

'How would such a venture be funded? Books and the rest of it will cost money.'

'I'm hoping that people will buy books for themselves and as gifts for each other and that some of those books will be donated back to be loaned to other readers. That way we'll keep the supply of books coming, especially if we share the resources between the hospital and the village. I'm also hoping that those people who can afford it will be willing to donate a few pennies each time they come so we can pay for newspapers and things like that as well as more books. They might donate when they come to special events, too. Then there's fundraising. Like your bring-and-buy sale idea.'

Alice's head was overflowing with possibilities. She was sure the bookshop could help to bring the community together and, while it wasn't her first concern, it would give her a sense of personal purpose too. The experience she gained might even hold her in good stead when she came to look for paid work. It might help Kate find other work, too, as it would show she'd been involved in more than just farming.

'You appear to have thought it all out without my help,' Mrs Harrington commented.

'Only the initial idea. Your support will be invaluable.'

'I wish the venture well, Miss Lovell, but we both know the saying about too many cooks.'

'They spoil the broth,' Alice finished. 'But a group of people working as equals needn't spoil anything. We could create something special. Something valuable.'

'As I said, I wish the venture well, but my time is already fully committed.'

Mrs Harrington got to her feet, doubtless a hint that Alice had outstayed her welcome.

'If you should change your mind . . .'

Mrs Harrington smiled tightly, and Alice guessed a change of heart was unlikely. Ah, well. She would have to make the bookshop happen without her neighbour's help.

CHAPTER FORTY-TWO

Kate

'That wasn't kind of her,' Kate said, when she heard of Mrs Harrington's refusal to help.

'She wished us well,' Alice pointed out. 'That's something.'

'Humph.' As far as Kate was concerned, Mrs Harrington's refusal was typical. Being Alice's project, the bookshop wouldn't shine enough glory on the woman who regarded herself as Queen Bee of Churchwood.

'*You're* still willing to help?' Alice asked.

'I'll do what I can,' Kate said, though the thought of working alongside other Churchwood residents jangled her up in awkwardness.

Kate's role in helping Edna Hall might have thawed Churchwood's opinion of her a little, but memories could be short while tongues and eyes could be cruel. At least she wouldn't have to endure Naomi Harrington's scorn.

'We could revive the bring-and-buy sale idea to raise funds,' Alice continued. 'Of course, I'll need to persuade Reverend Barnes to let us use the Sunday School Hall. Not just for the sale but for the bookshop as well – there's nowhere else for it.'

'He should be all in favour of a project that'll help his parishioners.'

'Let's hope so.'

Kate had ridden the bicycle down to The Linnets. She was a confident and quick rider now, which meant she could see Alice often, even if her visits were short.

Her thoughts were on the bookshop as she cycled home. Kate was in favour of the good it would do but wished a few more weeks could have passed before Alice had been struck by the idea. More time would have meant more money in the pouch that sat snugly against Kate's stomach – maybe enough for her to kit herself out in the sort of clothes that would make her less of an oddity. Alice might insist that clothes didn't matter, but years of being looked down on had taken a toll on Kate, and the thought of mixing with Alice's new friends in her farmer's hand-me-downs filled her with dread. Still, Alice's plans might take time to get started.

Another thought tiptoed into Kate's head. It was the same selfish thought she'd had before and Kate hated herself for allowing it entry. Not that she was *allowing* it exactly, as the thought had a life of its own. *With all the new friends Alice is making, she won't have much time for you*, it whispered, leaving behind a pang of loneliness. Alice was her only friend, after all.

Searching for something else to think about, Kate turned her mind to the bicycle and her mysterious benefactor. Ruling out Alice and Dr Lovell, there was only one other candidate as far as Kate could see, and she was trying to decide whether she should thank him. It felt ungrateful to stay silent. On the other hand, he might not be pleased if she ignored his preference for anonymity.

Kate was still debating the matter when she wheeled the bicycle into the barn and reached under the hay bale for the chain and padlock she'd hidden earlier.

They were gone.

CHAPTER FORTY-THREE

Naomi

Not Bert Makepiece again! Naomi heard his truck rumbling along the road behind her and quickened her pace in the hope of reaching the shops before he drew level. They had no business with each other but that hadn't stopped him from taking Naomi to task before and she wasn't in the mood for him to do it again now.

Unfortunately, she was wearing her newer shoes, and as they hadn't yet adjusted to her feet, they were making her wince.

The truck slowed beside her, and Bert looked out through the open window. 'Looks as though you're wearing someone else's shoes today, Mrs H.'

'I hardly think you're the person to criticize anyone's appearance, Mr Makepiece.' His shirt collar was fraying and his jacket was limp with age. Doubtless there'd be string or twine holding some other part of his clothing in place.

'I put comfort before other considerations.'

'If you mean vanity, Mr Makepiece, just say so.'

He grinned. 'I was trying to be polite.'

'A polite man wouldn't have commented on my shoes at all.'

'Not moving in your refined circles, I don't know

these things.' Annoyingly, Bert continued driving at her side. 'I hear young Alice has plans to start a bookshop.'

'Apparently so.'

'Sounds like a good idea to me.'

'I agree – and told her so.' He had no grounds for criticizing Naomi today.

'I also heard you knocked her down when she asked for help.'

'*Knocked her* . . .? What a wild way of speaking! I merely pointed out that my time is already fully committed.'

'To what?'

'I beg your pardon?'

'You said your time is fully committed. I asked, to what?'

'I don't have to account for my time to you, Mr Makepiece.'

'You don't *want* to account for it because you can't. You have plenty of time.'

Insufferable man!

'Seems to me that Churchwood folk should start pulling together before there's another Edna,' he said.

The mention of poor Edna Hall made Naomi swallow. Edna appeared to be much better now Churchwood had rallied around her, but if Alice and Kate hadn't found her that day . . .

Naomi reached the cobbler's shop and dived through the door, calling, 'Good day to you, Mr Makepiece.'

'How can I help you today?' the cobbler asked.

Naomi had no idea. She'd only come in for

sanctuary. 'I'd like a tin of brown shoe polish, please, Mr Corbett.'

She had no need of shoe polish but perhaps she could include it in a Red Cross parcel or give it to Marjorie, who was always grateful to be spared the necessity of spending her own meagre funds.

Naomi paid for the polish, slipped it into her handbag and moved to the door. Was it safe to emerge? It wasn't possible to see all the way down the street from the inside of the shop, but it would look odd if she lingered.

She stepped outside and was relieved to see no sign of Bert. But the urge to be out and about had left her. She'd come into the village for the same reason she'd worn her new shoes – to lift her mood. Thanks to Bert, it hadn't worked.

Naomi was impressed by everything she'd heard about the bookshop, but the memory of being snubbed before had lodged in her mind like a malevolent imp, insisting that Alice's invitation to help now was motivated only by guilt over that earlier rejection. Naomi would be there on sufferance, and while she was sure Alice and her friends would be polite to her face, it would be a different story behind her back. Picturing grimaces, sighs and rolling eyes, Naomi felt an echo of the humiliation that had dogged her youth when her father had tried to buy his way into a society that despised him. Naomi wouldn't put herself through that sort of mortification again.

Even so, Edna Hall's near-tragedy had shaken Naomi and she was eager to ensure that no one else in Churchwood suffered such desperation. Was there something she could do to support the bookshop without getting closely involved in it? Naomi decided that yes, there was.

That afternoon she hovered in the Foxfield gardens. With luck, any observers would assume she was giving Basil an airing. Secretly, she was keeping an eye out for Alice. An hour passed before Naomi noticed movement by the cottage. Peering through the leaves of the hedgerow, she saw her quarry and hastened to the Foxfield entrance gates, trying to appear nonchalant as Alice passed by on the other side of the lane.

'Good morning, Mrs Harrington,' Alice said.

Naomi answered with what she hoped was a gracious smile. She let Alice take a step further, then, as though it were an afterthought, said, 'Actually, Miss Lovell, something occurred to me about your bookshop.'

'Oh?' Alice had turned back.

'I can't get involved, as you know, but I assume you wish to use the Sunday School Hall so might it help if I mention the bookshop to Reverend Barnes? Put a good word in for it? Of course, if you've already spoken to him, there's no need for me to—'

'Actually, there's every need.' Alice's smile managed to be both sweet and wry. 'I *have* spoken to him, but he said the matter would need careful consideration. He asked what *you* thought of the project, too.'

Six months ago, Naomi would have been pleased to hear that her opinion mattered. These days, she suspected the vicar was more influenced by her status and hospitality than respect for her personally. 'I'll tell him I'm in favour.'

'Thank you.' Alice sounded heartfelt. 'We'd like a Saturday for the bring-and-buy sale. That was your wonderful idea, if you remember? We're hoping it'll raise the funds we need to buy books and newspapers. As for the bookshop itself, we're thinking of two or three days each week and one or two evenings.'

'I'll pass that on.'

Naomi returned to the house feeling she'd managed the situation well.

But the feeling didn't last. What if her intervention made no difference? Septimus Barnes had sought Naomi's opinion, but there might be stronger influences at work – church rules that forbade the use of the hall for the sort of bookshop Alice had in mind, perhaps.

Thinking back over the years, Naomi could remember the hall being used for only a limited number of purposes: Sunday School classes; parish meetings; the first-aid and nursing courses; and occasional gatherings for weddings, christenings and funerals.

Hoping there were no rules in place to thwart the bookshop, she tried to take an optimistic view and imagined herself delivering happy news. She felt a glow of satisfaction but only momentarily because a different picture came into her mind: Alice and her friends laughing as they made their plans over cups of tea while Naomi merely delivered her news and walked away again. It made her feel like a stranger passing by a window and glimpsing happiness on the other side.

But enough of maudlin moods! Keeping busy was the thing. Naomi went to congratulate her gardener on his display of tulips.

CHAPTER FORTY-FOUR

Kate

The trouble with living on a farm was that there were hundreds – no, thousands – of possible hiding places, from ploughed fields to sacks of potatoes. Kate searched the barn first but if the chain and padlock were still there, they were hidden well. A search of the other outbuildings proved fruitless, too.

She'd kept the bicycle with her as she searched, but now that she had to go indoors to prepare the mid-afternoon tea, she dragged it upstairs and wedged it into the narrow space between her bed and the window to make it harder to steal.

The padlock and chain wouldn't have kept the bicycle safe from a determined thief armed with a hacksaw, but without them, it would be easier for Vinnie to steal it himself and blame the loss on a passing scoundrel. Or perhaps he'd simply wanted to put temptation in the way of Frank 'n' Fred so they'd take it out on one of their destructive larks. How spiteful he was!

Stomping downstairs again, Kate set to work.

'Thank you, dear sister,' Vinnie mocked as she dumped a plate of bread and butter on the table.

'I know you took it.'

'Took what?'

'The chain and padlock for my bicycle.'

'Wasn't me,' Vinnie denied, but he grinned, revealing the gaps where he was missing teeth.

Kenny began to talk to Ernie about a problem with the tractor while the twins challenged each other to a drinking competition at the Wheatsheaf. Kate and her problem were no longer of interest. She stood by the window, burning with anger. 'By the way,' she said, 'no one's getting any dinner until my chain and padlock are returned. In perfect condition.'

'That's not fair!' Frank complained. 'We didn't take the blasted things! Did we, Fred?'

'No, we didn't. Tell her, Ernie. Tell her to make the dinner.'

'Make the dinner,' Ernie instructed, 'or there'll be no wages for you this week.'

'What about my chain and padlock?'

Ernie looked at Vinnie. 'Give them back.'

'Haven't got them,' Vinnie insisted, doubtless knowing that, while Ernie wouldn't care whether Vinnie gave them back or not, he really would withhold Kate's wages if she didn't cook dinner.

The injustice made Kate's anger blaze even hotter.

The Fletcher men slurped their tea then went back to work but soon the twins returned, exchanging the cunning glances of conspirators. 'How much is it worth to you, this chain and padlock?' Fred asked.

'You want me to give you money in return for telling me about Vinnie's hiding place?'

'Two shillings,' Frank said.

'That's a whole week's wages! If I'm going to lose two shillings, I may as well lose it by refusing to cook the dinner.'

'You'd still have to buy another padlock and chain,' Fred pointed out. 'Paying us two shillings will save you money.'

Kate fumed silently.

'All right, one shilling,' Frank said.

'Sixpence,' Kate bargained.

The twins glanced at each other. 'Sixpence,' they agreed, then Fred added, 'Each.'

How could they be so vile to their only sister? 'Sixpence each but I won't pay until you've told me the hiding place.'

'The long grass behind the chicken coop. Now pay up.'

Kate paid them then rushed outside. But there was no chain in the grass behind the chicken coop. No padlock, either. She looked towards the farmyard and saw the twins bent over in laughter.

She ran at them but had barely grabbed hold of Fred's arm before Frank pulled her away, keeping hold of her until she stopped fighting.

'You're disgusting!' she told them.

'Yeah,' Fred agreed. 'But we're also sixpence richer than we were five minutes ago.'

'That's sixpence each,' Frank reminded her.

They walked off, laughing.

Kate ran inside and threw herself into a chair. It felt weak to cry but tears flowed anyway. The bicycle had given her a sense of freedom over the weeks she'd had it but it wasn't fair to her benefactor to let it be stolen – something that was bound to happen sooner or later. She'd have to return it to him. Tonight, while it was still in her possession.

Getting up, she crossed to the sink, splashed cold

water on her face and dried herself on the rag she kept in her pocket as a handkerchief. She was hanging the rag on a hook to dry when something in the yard caught her eye through the window – a glint of silver overhanging the gutter of the barn.

Heartbeat quickening, she rushed to the barn for a ladder, climbed up and found the chain and padlock. Vinnie must have tossed them up there and not bothered to check that they were completely hidden.

Lesson learned. Next time she took the bicycle out she'd wrap the chain and padlock around her middle for safekeeping.

Next time? She wouldn't return the bicycle to her benefactor just yet. That was a good thing. But she'd lost a shilling from her savings and that was bad. Even without that loss she'd be struggling to pay for a new outfit any time soon. Could she face meeting with Alice's friends while dressed in her filthy men's clothes and smelling of the farm? The thought made her feel sick.

CHAPTER FORTY-FIVE

Alice

I'm enjoying seeing some sunshine, Daniel had written. *I hope there's sunshine over Churchwood, too.*

There was indeed sunshine over Churchwood. Alice loved to see how it gilded everything in gold, but sunshine could do nothing about the unease that slid inside her like shifting sand.

The news from the war was concerning. The last few weeks had seen Germany invade both Norway and Denmark. Norway was fighting on but Denmark had surrendered within hours. Which country would Germany invade next and what was it all going to mean for Daniel?

He continued to write in an openly affectionate way while Alice tried to keep her tone less and less personal, though she hated the thought that, if something terrible happened to him, the last words he'd have received from her would have been cool. Not indifferent exactly, but hardly overflowing with warmth.

Being busy might have helped to occupy her thoughts but she'd heard nothing from the hospital and the bookshop project had come to a halt because Reverend Barnes had taken to his bed with a stomach complaint so Mrs Harrington had been unable to ask him for permission to use the hall. Until he gave his blessing, Alice was reluctant to take her plans any further.

She explained her reasons when her small team of helpers met at The Linnets – Kate, May, Janet and also Bert Makepiece, who'd stepped forward as a volunteer. 'We let people down when we cancelled the bring-and-buy sale the first time. I suggest we don't mention that we're trying to revive it until we're sure it can go ahead. Maybe we shouldn't mention the bookshop, either. People might lose confidence in our ideas if we disappoint them again.'

No one disagreed, though they were all frustrated. Kate had sat in a corner, saying little, and she bolted the moment the meeting finished.

'You worry about her,' May said to Alice.

'I wish she could see herself as I do – as clever, brave and kind.'

'I'm beginning to see her that way, too. As for everyone else, well, it would help if she didn't frighten them by scowling so much. Mind you, who am I to criticize when I did more than a bit of scowling when I first came to Churchwood?'

'You seem happier now.'

'I won't pretend I find life easy. I miss London and my old job, and I'm worried about Marek. But I'm adjusting, and yes, I'm happier. Mostly that's down to you.'

'Hardly.'

'It's true. I was in shock when I first moved here. I was outraged to have the life I'd worked so hard to build snatched away, and I was out of my depth with the children. Lonely, too. You've eased the loneliness and helped me to see that while I've lost in some ways, I've gained in others.'

'The children?'

'I'm ashamed of the way I resented them.' May looked as though the memory was making her wince inside. 'Their little lives had changed far more drastically than mine. I always knew that, but I couldn't seem to move past my own situation.'

'You just needed some thinking space.'

'Which you gave me. You offered friendship at a time when I despised myself. Now I can see how amazing the children are. Rosa is caring and wise beyond her years. Samuel should go on the stage because he's so funny. And Zofia couldn't be sweeter.'

'You'll miss them when they return home.'

'I will, but I'll be glad for their sakes.' May paused; then she added gravely, 'If it ever happens. I still haven't heard from their parents.'

'These are worrying times.'

'We need our bookshop to help us get through them, so here's hoping Reverend Barnes returns soon.'

Two days later, Alice was passing an upstairs window when she saw Mrs Harrington cross the lane to The Linnets and pause. Was she hesitating because she had bad news for Alice? Or simply catching her breath before walking on?

As though reaching a decision, Mrs Harrington squared her shoulders, passed through the cottage gate and knocked on the door.

CHAPTER FORTY-SIX

Kate

'Where do you think you're going?' Ernie demanded as Kate got ready to leave the farm.

'Into the village.'

'There's work to be done.'

'And I was up at the crack of dawn to do my share of it.'

'We need help in Five Acre Field. You can go into the village later.'

'I need to go now. I'll help when I get back.'

Kate would actually have preferred to stay on the farm today. But Alice was her friend and Kate wouldn't let her down.

She arrived at the Sunday School Hall as late as she dared, and Alice greeted her with a smile. 'I'm so glad you made it!'

Kate looked around her. 'You've been busy.'

The hall was laid out with long trestle tables on one side of the room. Here they had placed the items that were being offered for sale – shoes, toys, a hand-bag, a hat, a watering can and more. The other side of the room contained smaller tables with chairs behind them where the people who were offering services would sit so they could talk to potential buyers.

May was placing signs on the smaller tables. Kate read those nearest to her.

Janet Collins: three hours of babysitting. One shilling.

May Janicki: dressmaking (dress, blouse or skirt). Five shillings.

Bert Makepiece: Digging for Victory: a lesson, with seeds included. Two shillings.

Kate's sign was on a front table: *Kate Fletcher: two hours of gardening. One shilling.* Alice had suggested that gardening justified a higher price but Kate wasn't comfortable with asking for more money. She wasn't comfortable with asking for any.

'I'll just have a look around,' Kate said, and managed to swap her sign for someone else's to give herself a table at the back where she'd be less conspicuous.

Kate had been delighted for Alice – and the village – to hear that Reverend Barnes had finally given permission for the bring-and-buy sale and, more cautiously, the bookshop, too. 'Let's say I approve in principle,' he'd apparently said. 'As long as it's well managed and the hall is looked after.'

Alice had wasted no time in calling her team together for another meeting and just one week later here they were, about to begin the sale. 'I don't see why we need to delay it when we only have to revive our earlier plans,' she'd said.

'Will Mrs Harrington be helping?' Bert had asked.

'She's already helped by speaking to Reverend Barnes and she's promised to donate something to the sale, but she still won't join our team.'

Kate was secretly glad. May, Janet and Bert all tried to make Kate feel comfortable, but Naomi Harrington would be awful.

'Let's go over things one last time,' Alice suggested now. 'Everything is priced but we need to write down which items we sell and how much they raise so we can pay those people who are only donating part of the proceeds. If people are buying a service, they need to understand exactly what's been offered and when it can be delivered. Everybody ready?'

She was met with an answering cry of 'Yes!'

'Good luck,' Alice called, and they all took their places.

Kate slouched in her chair with her arms crossed over her middle, trying to look as though she couldn't care less if people ignored her service. Indifference had to look less embarrassing than desperation.

She was surprised when quite a crowd rushed in, clearly in search of bargains. Marjorie Plym was at the front but came to a dithering halt, looking overwhelmed by the choices she faced. Naomi Harrington followed but stood alone and aloof, her chin tilted high. She'd donated a handbag and two bottles of sherry, but it was hard to imagine what she'd actually buy. Bert's fishing rod? Cyril Moorcroft's old tankard? Kate almost giggled at the thought. Perhaps Mrs Harrington would buy something to pass on to a servant as there could be nothing she—

'I was here first!'

'No, I was!'

Mrs Hutchings and Mrs Hayes met in front of Kate and blocked her view.

'I have the bigger garden,' Mrs Hutchings pointed out.

'But I have a bad back so need more help,' countered Mrs Hayes.

Bert turned from his table, looking amused. 'Now, now, ladies. You'll give young Kate a poor opinion of you if you don't act civilized.'

What had Kate to— Good grief. Were they arguing over who could buy *her* service?

'You must have seen that I got here first, Miss Fletcher,' Mrs Hutchings appealed.

'The girl isn't blind. She knows I got here first,' argued Mrs Hayes.

'Erm . . .' Kate mumbled, then Bert intervened again.

'There's a solution to this dispute if young Kate's feeling generous.'

'What's that?' the women chorused.

'She could help both of you if she can spare the time. How about it, Kate?'

'Please,' Mrs Hutchings said.

'I'd be grateful,' Mrs Hayes added.

Kate was bemused. 'Well, yes. All right.' She'd raised two shillings for the cause and she hadn't expected to raise anything!

Two more people bought Kate's service, doubling her fundraising, even though she couldn't promise to help them for a couple of weeks.

'Don't look so stunned,' Bert told her, in between dealing with his own customers. 'You should have more confidence in yourself.'

Kate wasn't sure about that, but it felt like the right time to bring up the bicycle. 'I'm sorry if the gift was supposed to be anonymous, but I want you to know I appreciate the bicycle. It's made a big difference to—'

'Wasn't me who gave it to you.'

'Wasn't . . .' Kate was thrown off balance. 'Then who did?'

Bert's eyes signalled that Kate should look to her left. She did so and met the gaze of Naomi Harrington, who, judging by her flustered expression, had heard every word.

As Kate stared at her in disbelief, Mrs Harrington turned as though to leave.

'If you run away, folk'll hear me calling to you all over the hall, Mrs H.,' Bert said.

'I'll thank you to respect my private business, Mr Makepiece,' she told him, turning back.

'Afraid to show you have a heart?'

'Don't be ridiculous.'

'Did you really give me the bicycle?' Kate was thunderstruck.

Mrs Harrington made a dismissive gesture. 'It wasn't being used.'

'It was your bicycle?'

'Well, no.'

'She bought it from William Treloar,' Bert said, and Mrs Harrington looked annoyed.

'Mr Treloar should learn to respect people's private business, too.'

'Oh, he didn't volunteer the information. I teased the story out of him when I saw him giving the bike a good cleaning.'

Mrs Harrington had actually paid out money. On Kate. A girl she disliked intensely. It was too odd for words.

'Looks like everyone's happy now,' Bert said. 'William's got some money in his pocket. Kate's got a means of getting around quickly. And you've done a good turn, Mrs H.'

Mrs Harrington looked far from happy. She looked as though she wanted to murder Bert.

'It's great to see this little fundraiser doing well, isn't it?' Bert continued blithely. 'I think we should all do our best to help the bookshop along. Are you doing your best, Mrs H.?'

'I'm here, aren't I?'

'Yes, but you could do more. You could join the organizing team.'

'I'll have you know I'm a busy—'

'That's settled, then. Welcome aboard, Mrs H.'

CHAPTER FORTY-SEVEN

Naomi

Having left the bring-and-buy sale feeling all of a dither over Bert Makepiece's interference, Naomi had thought of little else all through the rest of that Saturday and all through Sunday also. Now it was Monday morning and she still couldn't decide what to do. It was all very well for Bert to steer her on to the bookshop team like a farmer herding cattle. He wasn't in charge of it and neither had he considered the feelings of the other team members.

Doubtless Alice would be polite, but the thought of her listening patiently to Naomi's views only to side-step them as tactfully as possible was excruciating. As for Kate Fletcher, her stunned reaction to the gift of the bicycle had shown how she felt about Naomi. Clearly, it hadn't even crossed Kate's mind that Naomi could be thoughtful.

At least Kate wouldn't be returning the bicycle, which was a relief. Naomi had got up that morning to find that a note had been pushed through her door very early. The handwriting was neat but unfamiliar. Naomi opened it and saw with some surprise that it was signed *Kate Fletcher*.

Dear Mrs Harrington,
Thank you for the gift of the bicycle. It will be useful to
me and I appreciate it.
Yours sincerely . . .

It was far from gushing with gratitude, yet Naomi understood that it would have cost Kate some effort to thank a woman she obviously despised. Might the bicycle be an olive branch of peace? A spindly branch, perhaps, but a beginning? Naomi hoped so but it didn't follow that Kate would welcome working side by side with a woman who'd always looked down on her.

Why *had* Naomi looked down on her? The Fletcher men were uncouth, but Mary Fletcher had been decent enough as far as Naomi could remember. Why hadn't Naomi given Mary's daughter a chance? Kate had always been wild and hostile, but she'd been a child. As an adult, Naomi should have made allowances for the girl's unfortunate upbringing.

Looking back, Naomi supposed she'd been too busy trying to outrun her own insecurities to spare sympathy for the wayward daughter of such an unpleasant man as Ernie Fletcher. It had been easier to tar them with the same brush. Naomi felt ashamed of herself now.

She'd got the idea of buying the bicycle for Kate the day she'd seen it half hidden in William Treloar's shed. He hadn't ridden it in years as far as Naomi was aware, yet there was Kate running up and down Brimbles Lane in dire need of transport.

Naomi's motives in wanting to help were mixed.

She'd come to feel pity for the girl's dreadful situation, guilt over her own failure to recognize that situation and even more guilt over the way she'd treated Kate. Naomi also knew all too well the scalding humiliation of being looked down upon by others.

But it would never have done for her simply to buy the bicycle and present it to Kate. The girl might have reacted with scorn, and Naomi quaked at the thought of it.

Then the idea for the bring-and-buy sale had drifted into her head. If numerous Churchwood residents were busy clearing out their homes to find things to donate or sell, it would be easier for Naomi to make her gift anonymously. The funds raised would benefit the hospital patients, too.

But then the sale had been cancelled and, disappointed, Naomi had approached Mr Treloar directly, agreed a price for the bicycle and arranged for him to deliver it to Kate via The Linnets under cover of darkness and in complete confidence. All had gone well – until Bert Makepiece had spoiled it. Irritating man! It would have been a pity if Kate had rejected the bicycle out of pride.

Now there was a word: *pride*. Doubtless Bert would assume that, if Naomi refused to join the bookshop team, it would be due to wounded pride because she was used to being in charge. It was true that her pride would sting if she found herself unwanted. But she'd also be hurt.

It wasn't only the likely reactions of Alice and Kate that troubled Naomi. There was also May Janicki. Naomi hadn't exactly gone out of her way to welcome her to the village, so why should May welcome Naomi on to the team? Then there was Janet Collins. They'd known each other for years but never as equals. Naomi had given the orders and Janet had followed them.

Naomi's arrival on the team might cause an exodus, each of the others bowing out under one pretext or another. Even if they stayed, their enjoyment in the project might wither.

Restless, Naomi went to the sitting-room window and peered out. Then she turned from the window, wondering how her life could have changed from well ordered to *dis*ordered in a matter of mere months. Was it the arrival of Alice Lovell or the changes in Naomi's own body that had worked the difference? Both, perhaps.

Then again, had her life been as well ordered as she'd liked to think? Or had she closed her eyes to cracks and fault lines?

Impatient with her brooding, Naomi picked up the telephone and asked the exchange to put her through to Alexander's office. Miss Seymour, his starched and efficient secretary, was first on the line but soon Naomi was speaking to Alexander. 'What is it?' he asked. 'Is there a problem?'

'Nothing like that. I'm just ringing to see how you are and whether you've thought any more about my coming to London for a day or two.'

'Naomi, I'm working.'

'Yes, but you spend so little time at home and—'

'I need to prepare for a meeting.'

'You can't work all of the time.'

'Naomi, have you any idea what our lifestyle costs us?'

'I'm sure it's expensive, but perhaps the time has come to have a think about our priorities.'

Alexander's impatience escalated to irritability. 'The middle of the working day is hardly the time for that sort of discussion.'

'Next time you're home, then.'

'Goodbye, Naomi.'

'Alexander, I—'

Too late. Alexander had rung off.

It really hadn't been a convenient time to call, but his comment about their style of living struck her as a little harsh. Foxfield was large and needed staff to run it, but Churchwood wasn't an expensive place to live compared to London. And while Naomi wore good quality clothes, she hardly had a vast collection, and she kept them for years. Beauty parlours and expensive hairdressers had rarely featured in her diary, and she'd never been the sort of woman to loll about drinking champagne or cocktails. As for jewellery, she hadn't had a new piece in an age.

Alexander spent more on clothes, having a taste for beautifully cut suits, bespoke shirts and handmade shoes. He took satisfaction in keeping a Daimler as his motor car too, and enjoyed membership of several expensive golf clubs. He also dined out often and treated Fortnum & Mason as a corner shop for delicacies. Making a favourable impression on clients was only part of it. The fact was that Alexander enjoyed wealth.

Well, why not? It would be hypocritical of her to find fault with that enjoyment; hadn't she too used her wealth and the standing it gave her to stake out her own position in the village and beyond it? Once again, Naomi thought about the women who'd been part of her social circle before it had been fractured

344

by the war and petrol shortage. They might only be acquaintances but reconnecting with one or two of them might still lift her from this unsettled mood.

She consulted her address book, picked up the telephone and asked the exchange to connect her to Lara Frobisher, a woman she'd met at charity events and occasional dinners.

'Naomi!' Lara said. 'How are you, my dear?'

'Well enough, thank you, though I'm not getting out as much as I'd like.'

'Thank goodness for trains. I pop up to town two or three times a week these days. We stay at the flat, so it saves Giles the bother of taking the train home each night. Bunty and Lawrence Cavendish were up last week – we went to the Velvet Slipper Club and danced like the giddy young things we used to be. Such a scream! We're dining with Fenella and Piers tonight. You know Fenella and Piers? No? Oh, well. You must persuade your dashing Alexander to bring you up to town soon. We need to have fun with this miserable war going on. Must rush now or I'll miss my train . . .'

Naomi ended the call feeling she'd been watching a film or a play instead of speaking to a real person. Clearly, Lara's life was far more glamorous than hers. Not that Naomi was jealous. She didn't *want* to live a glamorous life. As she'd said to Alexander, she wanted to review their priorities because the sort of life she craved was . . . Oh, what were the words? Honest? Yes. Solid? That too. And above all warm-hearted.

Quite how that might translate into day-to-day life was something she couldn't yet picture but she'd give it some thought and who knew? If Alexander was willing to pause his busy schedule and consider a different way of living too, perhaps it might bring them closer together.

The morning moved on and another note was pushed through the door, this time from Alice.

Dear Mrs Harrington,
Mr Makepiece tells me you're considering joining the bookshop team after all. How wonderful! We're meeting at The Linnets at two thirty this afternoon to discuss our next steps and I hope you'll be able to come along, if only to try us out.
Best wishes,
Alice Lovell

Should Naomi attend or plead another commitment? She decided on the middle ground. She'd attend one meeting but make it clear that she might be unable to spare the time for others so she'd have an excuse to fall back on if the first meeting proved intolerable.

Despite that plan, she still found it difficult to summon her courage when the time came to set out. Haunted by the scorn of the past, she was full of agonizing uncertainty.

Movement on the drive caught her eye as she stood at the sitting-room window. Bert Makepiece. Driven into a sudden panic, she considered inventing a headache but she'd left it too late. Suki would think it strange as Naomi had said nothing about an indisposition earlier.

'Hello, young Suki,' Naomi heard Bert say. 'I thought I'd walk Mrs H. over to The Linnets.'

Walk her over? Frogmarch her was what he meant.

'Thank you, Suki.' Naomi swept into the hall, doing her best to appear as dignified as a galleon in full sail.

'Your carriage awaits,' he said, holding his arm out for her to take.

Pretending she hadn't noticed, Naomi strode outside, spoiling the effect by slipping slightly on the gravel; soon rectified but still a blow to her fragile self-possession.

'Glad to see you're in fine fettle,' Bert said, as they walked down the drive. 'No sudden headache. No grit in the eye. All good.'

Naomi sent him a glare.

As soon as Alice opened the cottage door, Naomi launched into her escape plan. 'I happen to be free today but may not manage future meetings due to my other commitments. I hope that's acceptable, but if you'd rather I didn't—'

'Whatever time you give will be welcome,' Alice told her.

The others were already in the dining room, a small room fitted out with furniture that was too big for the space available but still managed to look cosy. 'Mrs Harrington is joining us today,' Alice announced.

Kate Fletcher was there, scowling as always, but with an uncertain look in her eyes when she glanced at Naomi. May Janicki was there, too, her hair and dress immaculate. She gave Naomi a small smile, but Naomi suspected she was reserving judgement. Janet Collins's smile was friendlier, or at least appeared to be. Naomi hoped her presence wasn't making Janet feel awkward, like a soldier in the presence of a senior officer.

Bert pulled a chair out for Naomi then sat beside her.

Alice distributed glasses of barley water and beamed around the room. 'The bring-and-buy sale raised a magnificent eleven pounds,' she announced, to cries of 'Wonderful!' and 'My goodness!'

'It's a great start,' Alice continued. 'We'll be able to buy a modest selection of books to sell on or lend, and also pay for regular newspapers, magazines and comics for a while. Thanks to Mrs Harrington, we have the use of the hall, too. All we need to do now is work out how to launch the bookshop and publicize it.'

Something had been overlooked. Naomi opened her mouth to point it out but subsided again, fearing she was pushing herself forward. A quiet word with Alice later might be better.

'What is it?' Alice asked.

'Nothing important.'

'All opinions are welcome here. If there's something we've forgotten, the sooner we know about it the better.'

Bert Makepiece gave Naomi a look that said, *Spit it out, woman.*

'Blackout curtains,' Naomi said. 'The hall isn't used in the evenings so it only has blackout paper pinned up as a precaution and it isn't very effective. Of course, you may have considered this already.'

'We haven't and it's an excellent point,' Alice said.

'Curtains will be expensive,' Janet observed. 'I paid two shillings and sixpence per yard when the blackout order first went out, but I hear the price has gone up to three and eleven.'

May nodded. 'The price of everything is going up.'

'Actually, I may have a solution,' Alice said. 'The people who bought our London house didn't want all of the curtains we'd had fitted so we brought them with us. Some have been put up here but there are others.'

She excused herself, and then returned a moment later with her arms full of black curtains. 'We could remake these to fit the hall.'

'That's a job for me,' May said.

'I'll help, too,' Janet offered.

They agreed to visit the hall with Bert, who'd measure the windows.

The rest of the meeting passed in a similar spirit of cooperation. Alice was notionally in charge, but mostly she simply encouraged ideas and comments from everyone else. Differing opinions were discussed but no one appeared to feel small if an opposing opinion was accepted. The important thing was the community bookshop.

Naomi said little but agreed to continue to liaise with Septimus Barnes. She also found herself agreeing to telephone Murton's bookshop to request a book catalogue and draw up a list of recommended purchases for consideration when the team next got together. Clearly, she'd have to return at least once. The meeting ended and everyone said goodbye, except that Kate and Naomi simply exchanged awkward nods. A truce? Naomi hoped so.

She went home to telephone Murton's then headed out again straight to the vicarage to inform Septimus Barnes of the outcome of the meeting. 'I feel better knowing the project is in your safe hands,' he said.

'It was in safe hands before,' Naomi pointed out.

Murton's sent the book catalogue out that same day and she spent hours poring over it. The budget was modest so she was careful to ensure her recommendations included books for children as well as adults, and covered a variety of interests.

She was nervous when they met again that same week and she was invited to talk about her recommendations. Her mouth felt dry but she took a deep breath and got the words out. A discussion followed in which *The Inimitable Jeeves* was preferred to Naomi's suggestion of *A Passage to India*, but the sky didn't fall in just because Naomi's recommendations weren't accepted in full. The effort she'd put into making them was clearly appreciated.

She went home feeling exhausted but relieved. Also, rather satisfied. She'd enjoyed herself, and everyone had appeared to assume that she'd return next time. Even Kate Fletcher had made a gruff attempt to talk as they made their way outside. 'The bike,' she'd said. 'It's good.'

Progress indeed.

CHAPTER FORTY-EIGHT

Alice

*Coming soon: The Churchwood Bookshop
(in the Sunday School Hall)
for adults and children alike.*

*Buy books, borrow books, read newspapers,
magazines and comics, or simply chat with
friends over cups of tea.*

*Hear stories read out loud and talks on a variety
of subjects (ideas welcome).*

Help bring Churchwood together.

*For more information, please speak to Janet
Collins, Kate Fletcher, Naomi Harrington, May
Janicki, Alice Lovell or Bert Makepiece.*

Alice stood back and surveyed the poster she'd made. It was bright. She hoped it was cheerful. And most of all she hoped it would succeed in rousing interest. At this stage she was merely giving a flavour of what would be on offer. Specifics would follow once they'd heard people's thoughts on the sort of get-togethers they'd find most useful or enjoyable.

It was in the hope of encouraging people to talk

about the bookshop that she'd added names to the bottom of the poster. Kate had shifted uneasily when she'd seen her name, doubtless thinking that no one would wish to talk to her. But Alice hadn't wanted to exclude her and had listed the names in alphabetical order to show that team members were equally important.

The preparations were going well. Bert had measured the hall windows and both May and Janet were busy making the curtains on their sewing machines. Naomi had sent off for the agreed selection of books, and more books would be ordered over time using the money raised by selling those first books or through other fundraising. Naomi had also written to a county newspaper appealing for donations and had been delighted when parcels of books had started to arrive. Meanwhile, Alice had spoken to Mr Johnson at the Post Office about supplies of newspapers, magazines and comics.

'We'll definitely be along,' Babs and Pauline had told Alice. They were visiting her openly now.

'Everyone's welcome, so do tell your friends.'

To the team Alice said, 'I think we should launch the bookshop with a special event. A party.'

'What a lovely idea,' May said.

Bert and Janet agreed. Naomi agreed, too, but also looked thoughtful as though a party had sent her mind travelling in an interesting direction.

Unsurprisingly, Kate looked horrified at the thought of mixing with the entire village, but Alice would do her best to talk her into attending.

The party was fixed for the afternoon of the first day of June.

'I might ask my husband to come, if that's all right?' Naomi asked Alice as they parted.

'The more the merrier,' Alice told her.

It was a relief to be able to write to Daniel about something positive. She set out to entertain him with bookshop news and stories from the preparations, including an account of the day she'd run into an old Churchwood resident, Jonah Kerrigan, in the bakery.

'What's this bookshop business I keep hearing about?' he'd asked.

Alice had explained it to him.

He'd frowned and shaken his head. 'Books are dangerous, in my opinion. They give a person ideas and overtax the brain. Resting the brain . . . that's the thing for me. But I'm all for feeding the stomach, and if you're offering biscuits with the tea, I'll be along.'

But, while the bookshop was looking promising, the war news was even graver. On 10 May, Belgium, the Netherlands and Luxembourg all came under attack and the first German bombs to fall on British soil landed on Kent. It wasn't a sustained bombing but a foretaste of what was likely to come. On that same evening Prime Minister Neville Chamberlain resigned after British troops failed to liberate Norway from German occupation. Many people thought his response to the war had been disastrous.

The following Monday the new Prime Minister, Winston Churchill, made his first speech to parliament:

'I have nothing to offer but blood, toil, tears and sweat. We have before us an ordeal of the most grievous kind. We have before us many, many long months of struggle and of suffering. You ask, what is our policy? I will say: it is to wage war, by sea, land and air, with all our might and with all the strength that God can give us; to wage war against a monstrous tyranny, never surpassed in the dark, lamentable catalogue of human crime. That is our policy. You ask, what is our aim? I can answer in one word: It is victory, victory at all costs, victory in spite of all terror, victory, however long and hard the road may be; for without victory, there is no survival.'

The following day the Netherlands surrendered and the day after that a German armoured division entered northern France.

Daniel was in France, though Alice didn't know in which part of the country. She'd been worried about him since the day he'd left England but now her sickly dread that he might be injured – or worse – was almost constant. Even as she smiled and laughed and talked about the bookshop, anxiety squeezed like a fist inside her. With a German victory looking increasingly likely, groups of Local Defence Volunteers began to form.

When no reply to her letter came after more than a week, Alice's tension mounted. More days passed and still no letter came. Daniel might be too busy to write, of course, or perhaps he was caught up in troop movements that made it difficult for him to receive post or send it. There was no reason to fear the worst. Even so, she found herself writing again and urging him to take care, only to tear the letter up. She'd already made one mistake in writing too intimately. It would be madness to make another when a letter might arrive from him any day.

CHAPTER FORTY-NINE

Kate

A party! Could there be anything more likely to make Kate feel uncomfortable? A hall full of people dressed up in their Sunday best . . . Chatter, laughter, dancing . . .

Dancing! Kate didn't know how to dance. Not that anyone would ask her to be their partner. She'd be the awkward fool leaning against the wall or hiding in a corner.

'You *will* come?' Alice had asked. 'We want you there.'

We? Alice, May, Janet and Bert might want her there, but Naomi Harrington?

The gift of the bicycle still puzzled Kate. 'What shall I do?' she'd asked Alice at the bring-and-buy sale.

'Write a note to thank her then get on with enjoying the freedom the bicycle gives you.'

'I should accept it, then?'

'Of course. Why not?'

'You don't think it would be hypocritical of me? I haven't exactly been complimentary about Mrs Harrington.'

'She hasn't exactly been complimentary about you. But that was in the past when you didn't know each other. Now you're beginning to see each other's good qualities.'

Did Naomi Harrington have good qualities? Clearly, she did, and not just her generosity. She'd mostly dropped her bossy and superior manner. She listened to others, and when she made suggestions of her own she did so almost humbly.

Naomi Harrington humble? Surely that was a step too far. Perhaps not, though. Alice had often said that people had hidden depths and Kate had to admit that she herself was one of them. After all, there was more to her than the scowls and anger she'd hidden behind for most of her life.

Even Alice had layers to her life that she kept private, not least her friendship with Daniel Irvine. Not once had Alice mentioned that she loved him but she looked stricken whenever Kate asked how he was faring in the war, which rather gave it away.

Despite all that, the thought of a party where she'd be on show to patients and staff from the hospital as well as Churchwood residents made Kate want to run for the hills. Her awful clothes, her lack of social graces . . .

'If you're worried about what to wear,' Alice had said one day, 'I can help to—'

'I'll be fine.'

'Sure? Because May will—'

'Quite sure.' Kate was tired of being a charity case.

'It doesn't matter what you wear anyway,' Alice insisted.

Which was easy for her to say. Alice always looked neat and attractive.

At home in her bedroom, Kate counted her savings. She now had a little more than a pound, but was that enough to buy shoes and underwear as well as a dress? Kate doubted it, and she seethed when she thought of the shilling she'd lost to the twins. Doubtless they'd spent it at the Wheatsheaf.

Still, nothing ventured, nothing gained. If she took the bus to somewhere like St Albans, she might pick up some things in a sale. They needn't be fancy. In fact, she'd much prefer to blend into the background than to stand out in the crowd. If she found something suitable to wear, she *might* go to the party, though she wasn't going to commit to anything yet.

Kate knew that Alice or May would happily accompany her to St Albans, but they were busy running their homes and preparing for the party. Kate already felt her contribution to the bookshop was less than theirs.

Alice was doing the most, of course. She was a natural leader. Had she been an officer in the army, the troops would have followed her faithfully. She never tried to dominate; instead, she invited views and listened to everyone.

At the same time, she was alert to every change of expression. 'What is it, Kate?' she asked at the next meeting, and Kate cringed at the sudden attention.

She thought of pretending to be stifling a cough but then chided herself for a fool. Everyone else contributed ideas and comments. Kate shouldn't sit there like an empty hand puppet. 'I was just thinking that if small children are going to be coming to the bookshop, it might be helpful to have some toys to keep them entertained.' She shrugged to suggest it wasn't much of an idea and it wouldn't matter if the others opposed it.

'I think it's an excellent idea,' a voice said.

Naomi Harrington's voice. Who'd have thought it? Kate's gaze met hers momentarily in an uneasy truce.

The others agreed, too. 'Any thoughts on how we might get hold of some toys, Kate?' Alice asked then.

Kate's cheeks already felt warm. 'Could you appeal for them on the poster?' she asked, and breathed out in relief when the others agreed with this way forward, too.

'I can speak to Reverend Barnes about placing a box in the hall for people to put donated toys in,' Mrs Harrington offered.

'And I can give the toys a good wash,' Janet said.

'Something else, Kate?' Alice asked then.

Oh, heavens. 'You might also think about having a rug or two for children to sit on as they play.'

Naomi offered to donate one rug and it was agreed that an appeal for others should be added to the poster, too.

Of course, it didn't mean that people would actually donate toys *or* rugs but Kate was pleasantly surprised to find that, over the coming days, Janet's box began to fill with rattles, puzzles, teddy bears, dolls, building bricks and an ancient hobby horse. 'Shame it's broken,' Janet commented when the horse's head flopped loose.

Kate inspected it. 'I can mend this.' Years of making and mending on a farm run by a skinflint had its uses.

She found herself roped in to wash some of the toys at Janet's house, too. It was a tiny terraced house but wonderfully neat, clean and cosy. Everything in Janet's house was cherished, the people most of all.

Kate met Janet's husband and two of her grandchildren and was struck by the love they all shared. Number eleven Woodcutter Row was a sanctuary rather than a battleground.

'I've heard you're wonderful at telling stories,' Janet said. 'If you can spare five minutes, perhaps you could read to these two?'

Kate read a story about a twinkling star and the children listened with rapt attention. How nice it was to see their eyes grow large with fascination and feel their little bodies close to hers.

Returning to Brimbles Farm was like entering a cold, hostile world. Might she escape it one day? She counted her money again and decided to wait until closer to the party before she attempted to buy a dress. She'd have another week's wages by then, though she feared it still wouldn't be enough.

CHAPTER FIFTY

Alice

Alice walked on to Ward One with Matron only to come to a sudden halt as the patients broke into a round of applause.

'Welcome back, Alice,' someone called.

'About time,' shouted someone else.

There were cheers, too, and a cry of, 'Get over here and read us a story!'

Matron smiled. 'Didn't I say you'd been missed?'

'This is quite a welcome.'

'I was worried you might not have the time to visit us any more, now you're organizing the village bookshop.'

'I want to be here.'

The note Matron had dropped through Alice's door had been brief but considerate.

Dear Alice,
I'm delighted to inform you that permission has been given for you to resume your visits to the hospital – if this is what you'd like. I'll understand if you feel the way you were treated has soured the idea of visiting again, or if you no longer have time to visit due to your other commitments. I'm posting this note through your letter box rather than calling at The Linnets in person to avoid putting you on the spot, and to give you thinking time.

Hoping to see you soon, in the village if not the hospital.
Best wishes,
Marion Peters

'The way I see it, the hospital visits and the book-shop could be two parts of the same project, sharing books and other resources,' Alice said now.

'Sounds interesting. I'd like to hear more but I don't think the men are taking kindly to us standing here chatting – they're keen to have you to themselves again.'

Alice glanced around at the expectant faces. Matron was right.

'Let's talk before you go home,' Matron said.

She patted Alice's arm encouragingly then walked away, and Alice went to greet the patients, chatting with those who were familiar and meeting those who were new. She read a story about an adventure in the Arctic, promised she'd be back to read and write letters another day, then moved on to see the patients in Ward Two – there was one patient she was particularly keen to see.

She received a similar reception there. After chatting to a few of the men she approached Jake Turner, who was sitting in a wheelchair. 'How are you, Private Turner?' she asked. Ever since Ruth's betrayal had been unmasked, Alice had been feeling guilty for having suspected Jake of treachery.

He studied her for what felt like a long time. 'Hmm,' he finally said. Then he appeared to remember her question. 'I'm tickety-boo, thanks.'

Was he being sarcastic? Probably. 'I've a book for you, if you want it?'

'Trying to cheer me up?'

Trying to make up for thinking badly of him, actually. Not that she could admit it; Ruth Morgan's treachery was a secret she couldn't share. 'A book might help to pass the time.'

He held out a hand and she passed him *Kidnapped*. He looked at the title then nodded in a way that implied the conversation was over.

Alice moved on, passing Babs, who winked and said, 'Good to see you back.'

'It's good to be here.'

Alice called at Matron's office before she left and explained more about her idea for the village bookshop. 'Sharing books between the village and the hospital will mean more choice for everyone. The staff from here will be welcome at the bookshop events and perhaps some of the more able-bodied patients might like to visit, too.'

'I'm sure they would.'

'We're arranging a launch party for a week on Saturday – the first of June – and it would be lovely if some of your staff and patients joined us.'

'I'll do my best to get a group of us along. The doctors will need to approve it, of course, and I'll need to look into the transport situation, but in principle . . .'

'Excellent,' Alice said.

She spent a few minutes catching up with Tom, the porter; then she headed outside, turning when she heard the sound of crunching gravel. Jake Turner was approaching in his wheelchair. He must have let himself out through the ward's French windows.

'You thought it was me,' he said, fixing her with a challenging look.

Alice grew wary. She'd understood that the patients knew nothing of what had happened with Ruth and didn't want to be tricked into blurting out secrets. 'Thought what was you?'

'I lost my legs, not my brains. One day you're here and everything seems to be fine. The next day you're gone and this place is abuzz with tension. Then those nurses you're friendly with start looking at me suspiciously. Next thing that Welsh nurse is whisked away and your nurses are giving me apologetic looks instead. Now you're back and giving me the same sort of look. Something was going on behind the scenes. Something to do with security. And you and your friends thought I was involved.'

Alice said nothing because what could she say?

'I asked for it, I suppose, being a miserable so-and-so. First time anyone's thought I might be a spy, though.' His granite face cracked in what she realized was the Jake Turner version of a smile. Then he laughed. Actually laughed.

Alice found herself warming to the wry humour glinting in his eyes.

'Fact is, I'm not cut from the same cloth as saints and heroes,' he admitted. 'I've had some setbacks and I haven't taken them well. I was a carpenter and I loved everything about it, from the smell and texture of the wood to the way I could turn it into things of strength and beauty. When this first happened' – he gestured to his missing legs – 'I thought I'd never work with wood again, though I'm beginning to think of ways I might still manage some woodwork along with other things that were important to me. Like getting out on the moors.'

'That's wonderful.' And what about the girl who'd abandoned him? Had she re-entered Jake's life and brought about this change of attitude?

'You're wondering about romance,' he guessed shrewdly. 'I had a girl but it didn't work out. I was sore about it at first, coming on top of my other setbacks, but the fact is we didn't have what it took to weather the storms of life, so Judy did us both a favour by breaking things off.'

It wasn't pride talking. Jake came across as sincere.

'Anyways,' he said, 'I want you to know there's no hard feelings about suspecting me.'

He began to turn.

'Do you need any—'

'No help, thanks. The sooner I get used to this blasted wheelchair, the better.'

He set off back to the ward, calling, 'Thanks for the book!'

Alice walked home feeling pleased, but when she reached the cottage and sat down with a newspaper, worry pinched at her stomach. The news from the war was even worse. Germany was occupying Brussels, having also invaded Luxembourg and the Netherlands. German troops had broken through French defences and were cutting a swathe across the country, forcing many British troops into retreat. And a letter from Daniel was now long overdue.

'Not looking good across the Channel, is it?' Alice heard Godfrey Michaels comment as the congregation filed out of St Luke's that last Sunday in May. 'I've heard thousands of our chaps are being swept towards the coast.'

'Dunkirk, apparently,' Mr Randall said. 'Let's hope they don't get trapped there – they'll be sitting ducks for enemy gunfire.'

Once again raw fear clutched Alice's heart in its talons. Not knowing Daniel's whereabouts . . . not knowing if he was safe, afraid, injured or even worse was torture.

Thankfully, May's husband was safe, being back in England for some sort of signals training. Janet was anxious, though; her Charlie was in France and she hadn't heard from him. Alice spotted Janet leaving the church and smiled encouragingly at her, hoping it would also buck up her own spirits. She couldn't afford to sink into a low mood with the bookshop party scheduled for Saturday.

'It's good to have something to look forward to in the middle of so much gloom,' one woman told her.

'I can't wait,' another said.

'It'll do so much good,' said a third. 'It's a chance to put on a bit of lipstick, too. I haven't done that in a while.'

'I hear there's going to be food,' old Humphrey Guscott said. 'I'm happy to turn out for food.'

'Fish paste sandwiches are my favourite,' Don Walker replied.

'Mine, too,' Humphrey said. 'Just don't ask me to dance.'

It was the same at the hospital when Alice visited the following day. There was an atmosphere of deep concern over the war, mixed with excitement amongst those patients who were well enough to join the party.

'Will there be beer?' one asked.

'And a gramophone?' asked another. 'I may only have one leg but put a Glenn Miller record on and I'll be up there on my crutches.'

'Apparently, Dr Marwood is lending a gramophone and a stack of records,' Alice told them. Dr Marwood was a new doctor at the hospital and all in favour of his patients enjoying themselves as much as possible. 'And yes, there'll be beer.'

'I just can't wait to escape this hospital for a few hours,' said another.

'The party is causing quite a stir,' Matron told Alice as she moved between the two wards.

'It isn't the only stir around here,' Alice observed, because Stratton House was bustling with even more activity than usual.

'We're preparing to open another ward.'

Which meant that more casualties were expected. Alice must have looked stricken because Matron smiled sympathetically. 'You and I are powerless to influence the progress of the war so we need to concentrate on what we *can* do.'

'Which is to help make the lives of the patients better.'

'Easy to say but hard to accomplish,' Matron admitted. 'But we have to try.'

Alice smiled and sketched a mock salute. 'Yes, Matron.'

She kept the smile in place through the rest of her visit but it faded as she walked along the corridor to make her way outside.

'Got some news for you, Alice,' Tom the porter said as she was leaving.

Not worse news! But Tom's eyes were bright. 'I spoke to my sister on the telephone last night. She's married to a fisherman, and he's been asked to sail over to Dunkirk to help get British troops off the beaches there. The water near the land is too shallow for the big boats to get close, so they need the little boats to ferry the troops out to them and bring some of the chaps back home, too. He was setting out from Ramsgate this morning. Lots of boats are going over – fishing boats, lifeboats, yachts and even pleasure steamers. We may save our army yet.'

Was Daniel amongst those waiting on the beaches? It was wonderful to hear that there was hope of rescue. But how many men would be saved and how many would be taken prisoner or perish in the meantime? It chilled Alice to think of the troops lined up on the sand amid German gunfire from land and air.

Tuesday passed in a mix of activity and agony. Alice heard nothing from Daniel. Neither did she hear anything more about the attempt to rescue troops. The lack of information stretched her nerves almost to breaking point.

On Wednesday, she was in the baker's when Mrs Phillips rushed in. 'Have you heard?' she asked.

'Heard what?'

'Someone told me Belgium has surrendered.'

That would be devastating for the Belgians and would also release more German troops to attack the British and French. Time was surely running out for the British men still trapped at Dunkirk.

Dazed and anxious, Alice bought bread and then hastened home, where she found her father standing by the wireless, looking grave. 'Is it true?' she asked. 'Has Belgium surrendered?'

'It's true, all right.'

'What will happen next?'

'I imagine Germany's plan is to overrun France and invade Britain. But don't despair, my dear. If your friend Tom is right, thousands of our chaps are being evacuated, and if we save enough, our army can regroup to fight another day.'

If. It was all so uncertain. And would Daniel be among the saved?

CHAPTER FIFTY-ONE

Naomi

'I enjoyed it,' Naomi had told Alexander over the telephone after attending her second bookshop team meeting.

'They're nice people,' she'd said after the third meeting when he was actually on one of his increasingly rare visits home. 'Different from the people we usually get to know in social settings. Not grand or eager to appear clever. But decent and sometimes funny, too. I'd like you to meet them.'

Naomi had been struck by the laughter, warmth and camaraderie the group shared. They cared about each other and were always concerned to know if there was news of Janet's son, Charlie, and the young man who was Alice's former neighbour but whom everyone appeared to suspect of being rather more. Not that they said so, but Naomi was getting better at reading faces and hearing words that went unspoken. It was sobering to realize that the reason she was getting better was because she was listening and watching more than in the past when – as Bert had put it – she'd jumped into situations with her boots on and barked orders.

The most wonderful thing was that the team was growing visibly more relaxed around her. Even Kate

Fletcher's wariness was easing off. Perhaps Bert had helped with that. At the third meeting he'd called her Mrs Harrington very pointedly on several occasions. Everyone else used Christian names. 'Call me Naomi,' she'd finally said, and Bert had rolled his eyes as though thanking the Almighty that she'd cottoned on at last.

At another meeting, May had nudged her in the ribs as they were talking through their plans and said, 'Isn't that right, Naomi?'

Then Janet had touched Naomi's arm and said, 'Look after yourself,' as they parted.

Small and simple human contacts but they'd felt warm and cosy.

If Alexander would surround himself with people like these, he might see that there was pleasure – even joy – to be found in a simpler, less expensive life that would relieve the pressure on him to work so hard and enable them to spend more time together.

But he'd said nothing in reply to her comment about meeting them.

'You'll be home for my birthday?' she'd asked him then.

He'd murmured something about his presence depending on work commitments.

'Please try to come home.'

'I don't want your drippy friend Marjorie or that tedious vicar here.'

'I'm not planning on a dinner. My birthday is on the same day as the bookshop party. I don't want to steal the bookshop's thunder so I'm not telling anyone that it's my birthday, but I'd like you to come to the party and meet my new friends.'

'In the Sunday School Hall?' Alexander had sneered.

'Hardly the Ritz, I know. But the party will be fun, Alexander. Fun!'

His look had suggested he thought she'd taken leave of her senses.

'It will make me happy if you come,' she'd finished.

CHAPTER FIFTY-TWO

Kate

With the party fixed for Saturday, Kate had planned to go dress shopping in St Albans on Monday and worked especially hard through the weekend to justify the time off. But fate had intervened in the shape of Ernie announcing an overhaul to the barn roof, which had begun to leak. May was a prime growing month and the rest of the farm couldn't be neglected, so while Vinnie and the twins toiled in the fields, Kate was required to join Ernie and Kenny in the barn.

Tuesday was spent the same way. By Wednesday afternoon the barn was completed but shops often closed early on Wednesdays. Kate didn't want to risk venturing out – and incurring bus fare – only to find that no shops were open. She'd never get away with taking a second day off. She decided on Thursday for her shopping trip, hoping she wasn't leaving it too late.

The bus had worked its way through other villages before reaching Churchwood, so when Kate boarded it was already half full of strangers. In unison, the gazes of the nearest two women swept her up and down. Also in unison, their mouths turned down in disapproval. Then a child's voice piped up with, 'Mummy, why is that lady wearing funny clothes?'

'Shush, darling. And stop staring. It's rude,' the child's mother answered, but by then all of the passengers had been alerted to the presence of an oddity, and more faces turned in Kate's direction.

Cheeks burning with anger and shame, Kate flung herself into an empty seat and stared resolutely out of the window. She'd gone to considerable trouble to clean herself up, washing her hair and ensuring the braid was neat, wearing a clean shirt that was patched only where it wouldn't show, and brushing as much mud as possible from her jacket, breeches and boots. Clearly, she'd wasted her time.

She avoided all eye contact when she got off the bus and stood uncertainly on what appeared to be one of the main streets in the city. She'd thought she might ask for directions to a shop that sold modestly priced dresses but, having no wish to speak to anyone now, she set off along one side of the street then crossed the road and made her way down the other side.

A small shop called Elizabeth's looked likely to be the cheapest. Kate approached the door only to stand aside as a woman came out. The woman's eyebrows shot up when she saw Kate. Boiling with humiliation, Kate stomped away again, raging against the smug superiority of people who had no insight into her circumstances.

In time, her footsteps came to a halt. She'd given up too easily.

Kate returned to Elizabeth's and looked in the window again. Movement inside the shop caught her eye and she saw that two shop assistants had their heads together. From the glances they sent in her direction, Kate guessed they were talking about her. Asking for help from these two was impossible. How they'd sneer at her men's underwear and lack of a brassiere.

She stomped off again but forced herself to turn into Murton's bookshop, glaring so hard at a woman who dared to give her an outraged look that the woman scuttled away. '*Jane Eyre*, please,' Kate told the assistant.

She bought the copy he offered together with another book that they hadn't had enough money to buy for the bookshop out of the bring-and-buy funds. Then she headed for the bus stop thinking it would be a long time before she returned to St Albans.

The walk back to Brimbles Farm took her past The Linnets so Kate knocked on the door and handed the books over when Alice answered.

'How lovely, but you shouldn't have spent your money, Kate.' Alice looked concerned. 'You especially shouldn't have spent your money on replacing my ancient copy of *Jane Eyre*.'

'I wanted to replace it.'

'I hope you bought something for yourself if you went shopping.'

Kate knew Alice meant something to wear at the party, though she could see, too, that Alice suspected there hadn't been enough money for an outfit as well as books.

Kate gave what she hoped was a casual shrug. 'I've decided not to bother with a dress. It isn't as though I'm likely to wear it again.'

'You're still coming to the party?'

It was hard to keep up a front of indifference with those kind eyes upon her. 'I might have to work.'

'Oh, Kate! What happened? Was someone unkind?'

Kate's throat tightened and she was sure her face must be red from the effort of holding back tears. 'No one said a word to me, kind or unkind.'

'But you still felt judged.'

'I'm not the sort of person who dresses up and goes to parties anyway, so it doesn't matter.'

'Of course it matters. I wish I'd known you were going shopping. I'd have come with you.'

'I'm not a child.' Kate regretted her sharpness the moment she'd spoken. No one could be a dearer friend than Alice.

There was a moment of silence, then Alice said, 'I don't care if you wear a potato sack. You deserve to be at the party and I *want* you to be there. Naomi, May, Bert and countless others will feel the same. Come in for a moment. Let's talk.'

Kate swallowed, her eyes burning with gathering tears. 'I need to get home. You know what it's like on the farm.'

'The work never stops. But it *should* stop sometimes, and the party is one of those times. I really hope—'

Kate had already raced away.

CHAPTER FIFTY-THREE

Alice

The knocking on the cottage door that Friday morning sounded urgent. Alice threw down the tea towel she was using to dry dishes and rushed to the door. 'Janet!' she said.

'I didn't think you'd mind me calling. Not when I've had news.' Tears spilt from Janet's eyes.

Oh, no. 'Charlie . . .?'

'He's safe,' Janet said. 'Sorry about these stupid tears. I didn't mean to frighten you. It's the relief, you see?'

Alice did see. 'This is wonderful news. When did you hear?'

'Just a few minutes ago. By telegram. Charlie arrived in Dover this morning. He's on a train now, heading to an army base somewhere, so I won't get to see him yet. But he's alive. In good health and spirits, too.'

Alice folded Janet into a hug. 'I couldn't be more pleased for you.'

'I wanted you to know because you've been kind when things have got on top of me.'

'We've helped each other.' She squeezed Janet's shoulders then released her. 'Now we have the bookshop to bring the community together, I hope we'll hear about everyone who's going through difficult times.'

'You've a good heart inside you, Alice. But what about your friend, Daniel? Any news of him?'

Alice's smile withered but she forced it into a stiff replica of its former self. 'Not yet.'

'Hopefully soon.'

Janet left and Alice went back inside, picking up the tea towel only to stare into space. Any telegram giving news of Daniel would go his parents, not Alice. If he survived, she might hear from him eventually. If he didn't – Alice blew out air to steady herself – she might learn of it only from a list of casualties in a newspaper.

The thought was unbearable. 'You're welcome to use my telephone whenever you like,' Naomi had said a few days earlier. 'It'll give you more privacy than the telephone in the Post Office.'

She'd meant it as a way for Alice to speak to Daniel if he returned, or so Alice assumed. But perhaps she wouldn't object if it was used for a slightly different purpose. Alice crossed the lane to Foxfield and found Naomi at home. 'Might I use your telephone to call my friend's parents?'

'You're wondering if Daniel's out on those beaches,' Naomi guessed. 'Of course you can use the telephone. I need to speak to Cook anyway.'

Naomi melted away and Alice picked up the telephone, asking the exchange to connect her to the Irvines. Moments later, the voice of Daniel's mother came down the line. 'Hello?'

'I'm sorry to disturb you, Mrs Irvine. I'm Alice Lovell. I used to live—'

'I remember you.'

Of course she did. Daniel had been distraught after Alice's accident. His mother had probably comforted him. She'd sent Alice flowers, too. 'I'm wondering if there's news of Daniel?'

'We haven't heard from him, I'm afraid. We suspect he's one of the poor chaps awaiting rescue from France but we don't know that for sure.'

'Apparently, hundreds of small boats are helping in the rescue now.'

'So we've heard, but it's a worrying time even so. Every time there's a knock on the door or the telephone rings . . .'

Their nerves must have leapt into a frenzy at Alice's call. 'I'm sorry I'm disturbing you now. But if it wouldn't be too much trouble, would you mind letting me know when you have news of Daniel? I'm concerned. As a friend, I mean.'

'That's sweet of you, Alice.'

She gave them Naomi's telephone number and her own address. 'I won't keep you any longer.' She might be blocking other calls. 'I hope there's good news soon.'

Naomi returned a few minutes later. 'Did you manage to get through?'

'Yes, but they hadn't any news. I hope you don't mind, but I gave your number as a way of contacting me.'

'It's no trouble at all. Daniel sounds like a special young man.'

Alice knew Naomi was hinting at a closer relationship than old friends and neighbours, a suspicion that all of Alice's friends appeared to share. 'He is

378

special, but there's nothing of a romantic nature between us.'

Naomi nodded but looked unconvinced. 'I looked out that old bunting,' she said, changing the subject. 'Let me know what you think.'

She opened a box and brought out strings of brightly coloured pennants.

'It's perfect,' Alice told her. 'If there's enough, we can hang it in the garden as well as the hall.'

'Let's keep our fingers crossed for good weather.'

'Our toes, too.'

Sick dread might have taken up residence in Alice's stomach, but there was work to be done.

CHAPTER FIFTY-FOUR

Kate

'Someone's in a mood,' Vinnie said gleefully as Kate banged the lunchtime tureen of soup on to the table.

'That's what living among pigs does to a person,' she snapped.

'Ideas above your station, that's your problem.'

'Any half-decent person would have ideas above you, Vinnie, with your spite and slyness and—'

Oh, what was the point? She walked to the window and stared broodingly out at the farmyard. Behind her she could hear her father and brothers scrabbling for the food she'd cooked. Why did they have to be such animals? No wonder people sneered at Kate.

Sick of her family, and sick of her thoughts, she turned from the window and took her place at the table. Vinnie lunged for the last potato, stuck it with his fork and waved it in front of her face. 'Want this?' he asked. Then he shoved it into his mouth, laughing so hard that spittle spurted out between his open lips.

'You're pathetic,' Kate told him, reaching for vegetables instead.

Her mood continued into the afternoon. She scowled at the chickens, slammed the barn door and kicked the water trough in the farmyard for the simple reason that she needed to kick something.

She wasn't entirely surprised to see Alice walking up from the lane but wished she hadn't bothered. 'I haven't changed my mind about the party, if that's why you're here,' Kate told her.

'That's a pity. I think you'd enjoy being amongst friends.'

'I wouldn't feel comfortable.'

'But—'

'Do you *want* me to feel uncomfortable?'

Alice looked shocked. 'Of course not. But if people judge you for an appearance you can't help, the problem is theirs, not yours. It means they're shallow and uncaring, and you're worth ten of them. Anyway, if you're worried about clothes, I'm sure we can—'

'Stop nagging, Alice. It isn't helping.' Kate hated the thought of being a charity case.

'I'm sorry.' Alice paused, and when Kate continued her sweeping, said, 'I can see you're busy so—'

'Goodbye, Alice. I hope the party goes well.'

Alice looked disappointed. Hurt too. She nodded slowly, turned and walked away. Kate watched her go then threw the broom across the yard in frustration. Could she have been any unkinder to a dear friend, who only wanted Kate's happiness?

Kate felt an urge to race after her and put things right between them. She *would* put things right, but the best way to avoid another argument was surely to wait until after the party. Kate's conscience still sat on her shoulder like an accusing spectre, and she couldn't dislodge it no matter how busy she kept herself.

That evening, Kate sat down to some mending while listening to the wireless Kenny had finally bought, doubtless in a dodgy deal at the Wheatsheaf.

The news came on, the announcer's voice grave as he talked about the many thousands of British troops still awaiting rescue from the Dunkirk beaches. Was Alice's Daniel amongst them?

Poor Alice must be worried sick. Yet she was doing everything she could to make a success of the party and bookshop because Alice was brave. The soldiers at Dunkirk and in Stratton House were brave, too. And here was Kate, skulking on the farm for fear of encountering a few disapproving looks.

What was it Alice had said? *If people judge you for an appearance you can't help, the problem is theirs, not yours. It means they're shallow and uncaring, and you're worth ten of them.* Easy to say, of course.

CHAPTER FIFTY-FIVE

Naomi

'Happy birthday, madam!' Suki said, bringing a tray into the breakfast room. As well as the tea things, the tray bore several greetings cards and small gifts.

She'd wished Naomi a happy birthday earlier so this repetition was doubtless intended to remind Alexander.

'Oh,' he said. 'Yes.'

He got up and left the room, returning with an envelope and a gift, which he placed beside Naomi. 'Happy birthday.'

Sitting back down, he drank some coffee, showing no interest as Naomi opened his card and gift. The card bore a picture of flowers; the gift was a silk scarf in pink, a colour she didn't favour but his secretary wouldn't know that.

'Buy something suitable, will you?' he'd have asked Miss Seymour.

'Gift-wrapped, sir?'

'Of course.' As if he'd go to the trouble of wrapping it himself!

'Shall I buy a card as well?'

'Certainly.'

He'd probably spared them no more than a glance when they'd been presented for his approval and simply picked up a pen to write *Regards, Alexander* on the card.

Regards, Alexander. After more than a quarter of a century of marriage. No expression of love and no kiss beside his name.

'Very nice,' Naomi told him, and Alexander grunted something she didn't catch.

She turned to her other cards and gifts. Three cards were from outside Churchwood, the senders people she'd once considered important because they shared the same social circle. Another was from Marjorie, who'd also given talcum powder. The final card was from the staff, who'd given a small china hedgehog to replace one Naomi had broken some months ago. It was a thoughtful gift because she'd had the original since childhood and been fond of it.

She didn't bother showing either gift to Alexander. He'd consider one to be boring and the other to be vulgar.

Setting them aside, she poured herself some tea, reflecting that her birthday had started early and finished early since she'd told both Marjorie and Suki to mention it to no one else. Today was about the bookshop.

'It really would be lovely if you came to the party, Alexander,' she reminded him.

'I'm busy. Charles Anderson is collecting me. We're playing golf then he's dropping me in London.'

'He has petrol?'

'He's been given a three-gallon coupon.'

Had he really been given it? Or had he bought it in some sort of black-market transaction?

Getting up, she crossed to the window and stared

sightlessly into the garden, her thoughts turned inwards as she examined her feelings. Her efforts to persuade Alexander to spend more time with her had failed. Was she disappointed? Certainly. Was she surprised? No, actually. She'd made those efforts sincerely, wanting to bring at least a little warmth into their marriage, and for a while she'd found her imagination taking flight over what she might achieve. But testing her feelings now – her calmness, her acceptance of the situation – she knew she'd made them more in hope than expectation, a last-ditch attempt to improve their relationship before she accepted that it would never succeed because Alexander didn't love her and never had.

She thought back to the evening when they'd first met and he'd claimed ignorance of her name and situation. It had been a pretence, an elaborate pantomime enacted by a man who had no capital of his own and wanted hers.

Naomi's wealth had bought Foxfield, as well as the London flat, and the income from what remained of her investments meant they could live well, too. For Alexander, the marriage had simply been a trade – she'd provided wealth (though not half as much as he'd hoped) while he'd provided the status of his name and occasional appearances.

Her feelings had been different. She'd been dazzled by his debonair good looks, flattered by his appearance of charm and enormously grateful for the way he'd rescued her from social embarrassment and loneliness. She'd believed herself in love and been eager for their marriage to thrive. And over the years she'd done everything she could to make Alexander happy. She'd seen to his comforts, made few demands of her own and tolerated his absences in the hope that one day he could take his foot off the pedal of his career and spend more time with her, especially if there should be a child or two.

Did she still love him? What she felt now was sadness, not devastation, so no, her love for him hadn't survived his coldness towards her. A year or so ago, she'd have struggled to admit that fact because without even the pretence of a happy marriage, what would she have had?

But she'd changed since then. She'd discovered more rewarding values and more rewarding friends. As a result, her confidence had grown and she could face the truth head on. Yes, it was a pity – perhaps even a small tragedy – that Alexander didn't want even a friendship with her, but there it was.

So what of the future? Naomi looked ahead and saw that Alexander would have his life while she'd have hers, and only occasionally would they come together to greet the world as a couple. It wasn't the future she'd imagined when they'd married, but Naomi would cope with it. There was relief to be found in an end to pretence and, thanks to her new friends, she could even be happy.

Alexander reared up from his newspaper suddenly. 'What on earth . . .?' The low rumble of a rackety old engine announced that someone was coming up the drive. He hastened to the window to see a battered truck come to a halt on the gravel. 'What a nerve, bringing that heap of junk *here*!'

'Don't concern yourself,' Naomi told him. 'The driver has business with me, not you.'

She went out to the hall and opened the door as Bert swung his bulky frame out of his truck and ambled towards her. 'Thought you might like a lift to save your feet for dancing later,' he said.

'I doubt that I'll dance, Mr Makepiece.'

'Too old, are you? Too respectable? There's no such thing, in my book.'

'So you'll be dancing the Lindy Hop or whatever the young people call dances these days?'

'Hopping may be a bit ambitious given that I'm no lightweight, but I'll enjoy myself doing what I can. Dancing celebrates life, and that's what today is all about. Making lives better.'

'I'll celebrate as a spectator.'

'You need to live, not watch other folk living, Mrs H.'

He waited for her to fetch her coat and handbag, then carried the box of bunting to the back of the truck where he deposited it beside several ladders and a toolbox.

'Need a nudge up?' he asked, opening the passenger door for her.

'Certainly not.' The thought of Bert Makepiece *nudging* her sizeable posterior into the truck couldn't be borne.

Naomi started to scramble up, but it was no easy feat for someone of her substantial build. Someone whose snug skirt wasn't designed for gymnastics, either.

'Get on with it, woman,' Bert said, and boosted her up with his shoulder.

She sat on the bench seat feeling flustered and unsure whether to thank him or take him to task. Either way, he was likely to increase her humiliation by laughing at her. Bert said nothing about it when he walked around the truck and heaved himself into the driver's seat so she decided that she too would say nothing.

He started the engine then patted the dashboard. 'I hope you don't mind me polluting the immaculate drive of Foxfield with this trusty old elephant.'

He was mocking her, of course. 'As long as you're not shedding old nails and rust,' Naomi shot back, and his grizzled face creased in a grin.

'Perhaps you could call for Alice,' Naomi suggested, then realized that with three of them in the truck, she might become squashed up against Bert. It would be a cross worth bearing if it helped Alice, but Naomi's dignity smarted at the thought of it.

'Young 'un's gone on ahead already,' Bert told her.

Naomi felt relieved. But concerned for Alice, too. 'Has she—'

'Heard from young Daniel? Not yet.'

Poor Alice.

The truck rumbled into the village. 'Glorious weather,' Naomi commented; the sun was shining and Churchwood looked bright and expectant.

Alice, May and Janet were already busy inside. Alice looked round as Naomi and Bert entered. 'Here comes the cavalry!' she said, and the welcome gave Naomi a warm feeling inside, though she noticed that Alice's pretty face looked wan with worry.

'What would you like us to do?' Bert asked.

'You've brought the bunting?'

Bert held up the box.

'Perhaps you wouldn't mind putting it up?'

'Just show me where you want it.'

'Perhaps Naomi could show you?'

Naomi was suddenly uncertain. 'I'm not sure what your thoughts are, Alice.'

'This is *our* bookshop and *our* party, not just mine. I'm sure you'll make a brilliant job of the decorations.'

Naomi felt another burst of warmth.

'Want some help?' Janet asked, and Naomi smiled at her.

'Yes, please!'

Bert fetched a ladder and they set to work, hanging several strings of merry bunting inside, then throwing open the double doors at the back of the hall to hang more bunting in the garden. 'Here, ladies?' Bert asked, holding some bunting up to tree branch.

'Yes, I think so,' Naomi told him.

'Actually, I wonder if the next branch up might be better,' Janet suggested.

He moved the string.

'You're right,' Naomi admitted.

Afterwards, Janet offered to make tea and Naomi took the chance to have a quiet word with Alice. 'No Kate?'

Disappointment passed like a shadow across Alice's face. 'Not yet. I'm just hoping she'll change her mind.'

Poor Alice had two friends to worry about. Naomi reached out to squeeze her shoulder and Alice smiled gratefully. Human contact. So lovely!

'Tea up!' Janet announced, approaching with a tray.

'I brought biscuits,' Naomi said, taking them from her bag.

'Just what we all need,' Janet told her.

Soon after, Dr Marwood from the hospital arrived with a gramophone and a box of records. Janet gave him a cup of tea, too.

Then Marjorie appeared. 'I've come to help,' she said. 'If I'm needed?' She looked unsure of herself, as though she feared Naomi might prefer her new friends to her loyal follower of old.

'Of course you're needed,' Naomi said, squeezing her shoulder, too. 'Let me pour you a cup of tea.'

'That string looks loose,' Bert said, eyeing up some bunting.

He brought in his ladder and climbed it – and the twine that was holding up his trousers snapped. As his trousers began to slide earthwards, Naomi laughed as loudly and freely as anyone.

Then the door opened, and they all turned to see who'd arrived.

CHAPTER FIFTY-SIX

Kate

'I'm only here to help with the preparations,' Kate said as she walked into the hall and saw everyone staring at her. 'I'm not coming to the party.'

She wanted to make that crystal clear and she kept her manner brisk in the hope of dissuading anyone from trying to change her mind. 'What do you want me to do first?'

'Have a cup of tea,' Alice said. 'It's lovely to see you.'

Kate drank her tea but didn't sit, eager to get started so she could leave again. She'd slept little last night and woken despising herself for letting Alice and the others down. Helping with the preparations was Kate's way of appeasing her conscience, without committing herself to the public shame of appearing at the party itself.

'Right,' Kate said, putting her empty cup down. 'Shall I arrange some tables?'

Physical work came naturally to her and for the next hour she laid out tables and chairs as Alice directed. She shinned up a ladder to help put up a banner outside the hall, too. Music played in the background and the Kovac children ran around excitedly, but Kate resisted the merry mood, afraid it would weaken the strict control she was keeping on her emotions and perhaps even make her cry.

'All done, I think,' Alice said eventually.

'Time to go home and change,' May agreed.

Kate rubbed her hands down the front of her breeches. 'Good luck, everyone. I hope the party goes well. I'll see you in a day or two.'

She turned to the door but May got there first and blocked the way. 'You're not going home, Kate Fletcher. We've changed your name to Cinderella and you're coming to the ball.'

'But—'

'We're your fairy godmothers and we have everything ready for you. Please don't argue. If you don't like the way we transform you, you're welcome to undo our work and go home. But you've nothing to lose by seeing what we have in mind.'

Kate had her pride to lose.

Ever perceptive, Alice seemed to understand how Kate was feeling, and she said, 'I see friendship as a team. Each person has different needs and different things to contribute at different times. I was desperately lonely when I came to Churchwood. Unhappy, too. Your friendship helped to change that.'

'It was the same for me,' May said. 'You were one of the people who helped me to settle in, and you've been great with the kids. They adore you.'

Naomi had something to say, too. 'You and I haven't always seen eye to eye, Kate. That's an understatement, I know. But you helped me to take a long, hard look at myself and I think I'm a better – certainly a happier – person as a result. Go with Alice and May. See what they have in mind. I'm heading home now but I hope to see you later.'

Kate watched her go.

'Think of it as an adventure,' Bert suggested, then followed Naomi through the door.

Janet winked at Kate in passing and even Marjorie sent Kate a small but encouraging smile.

'Well?' Alice asked.

'All right, but I hope you haven't anything too drastic in mind.'

'Kids, we're leaving!' May called.

May's house was small but neat. Stylish, too, with beautifully arranged flowers, and curtains and cushions she'd probably made herself. 'What do you want me to do?' Kate asked from the door, embarrassed to walk in wearing her old farming clothes.

'Kick those hideous boots off before you tread mud everywhere, then come upstairs.'

By the time Kate reached the bathroom – a proper bathroom! What joy! – May had the water running into the bath. 'I've put in a drop of the fragrant oil I've been eking out. You'll find soap, shampoo and a razor in there, too.'

'A razor?'

'For your legs and armpits, if you'd like to try the smooth look. There's plenty of towels and a dressing gown you can borrow. Come out when you're ready.'

For a moment Kate was tempted to flee. She'd been a scarecrow for too long to feel comfortable any other way.

But she didn't feel comfortable as a scarecrow, either. Far from it.

'Don't take all day!' May yelled through the door.

Kate stripped off her clothes and folded them into a pile, picking up the clumps of dried mud that fell to

393

the floor and placing them in a bin. Climbing into the bath, she sank back into the hot, scented water. Oh, the bliss! She closed her eyes to savour the ecstasy then released her hair from its braid and let it float in the water like mermaids' hair. Double bliss!

She wallowed for a while longer then soaped herself and shampooed her hair, revelling in more gorgeous scents. Should she try the razor? Why not? She used it carefully, nicking herself only once and rinsing the blood away before it could stain May's towels. She put on the dressing gown – so soft! – and studied herself in the mirror. Her cheeks were pink and her eyes were bright.

Someone knocked on the door. 'Ready?' Alice's voice.

Kate stepped on to the landing. 'What torture have you planned for me next?' she asked but Alice's smile showed that she knew Kate had found the bathroom session far from torturous.

Alice led her into a bedroom where May waited, ready to steer Kate into a chair. Unwinding the towel from Kate's head, May combed the tangles from her hair. 'Gorgeous,' she declared as she set to work with a hair dryer. 'Far too gorgeous to be hidden away in a braid.'

When Kate's hair was dry, May cajoled her into clean underwear, including a brassiere. 'Feels strange,' Kate said, never having worn one before.

'Looks good, though. Petticoat next.'

Kate reached out and touched the fabric. 'Is this silk?'

'Rayon. It's artificial silk – much cheaper to produce so we don't have to be rich to enjoy it. They've invented other fabrics, too. Like nylon. Wonderful for stockings, though they're in short supply. I doubt we'll be able to buy them before the war is over. Luckily your legs are brown from the sun, so you don't need any.'

'On hot days I wear some old breeches that I cut into shorts,' Kate explained. 'Sometimes I kick my boots off and peel vegetables out in the farmyard.'

'Little did you know how useful that would be. Now for some shoes.'

May produced several pairs for Kate to try on.

'So many!' Kate couldn't remember having ever worn anything but boots, and they were always second-hand, if not third-hand.

'I liked to be fashionable when I lived in London,' May explained. 'These red ones may be too narrow.'

'Ouch, yes.'

'These should be better. You can adjust the strap.'

They were smart shoes in dark green leather with heels that made Kate feel she was likely to tip over when she stood. 'How can anyone walk in these?'

'These are low heels. Stand tall. Lift your chin. There. Now try walking and remember, you're not on an army route march so take it slowly. Elegantly.'

'Elegant? Me?' But Kate tried and earned a nod of approval.

'Now for the dress. Close your eyes, Kate.'

Kate did as she was bid and felt the caress of fabric falling over her like a soft waterfall. May's fingers fastened the buttons at the back. 'Can I open my eyes now?' Kate asked.

'Not yet.' May combed Kate's hair, then slid something on to her head – an Alice band? – to hold the hair from her face. 'Keep your eyes closed while I move you to the mirror . . . Now you can open them.'

Kate steeled herself to hide her ingratitude if she looked ridiculous. But the mirror showed she looked far from ridiculous.

'You're very beautiful,' Alice told her.

'Stunning,' May agreed.

Kate wouldn't call herself beautiful *or* stunning but what she saw was . . . well, fascinating. The dress was patterned in shades of green, russet and bronze that did wonders for her chestnut hair, dark eyes and clear skin. The design – slim-fitting with a belted waist – did equal wonders for her figure. 'I don't know what to say.'

' "Thank you, Fairy Godmothers" will be just fine,' May said.

Kate looked in the mirror again and had to gulp down her emotions. This wasn't the Kate Fletcher of old, oppressed and bullied by her uncouth family. This was a young woman with a lifetime of possibilities before her.

'Thank you,' she said, but it emerged as little more than a throaty whisper.

CHAPTER FIFTY-SEVEN

Naomi

May opened her door with a smile. 'Come in,' she invited, and Naomi stepped into the house to find an atmosphere of expectation and excitement, even if Alice's brightness was dimmed by worry over her young man.

Naomi gave a small shake of her head to signal to Alice that no telephone call had come from Daniel's parents.

Alice nodded; then she swallowed and said, 'We've been playing at Cinderella.'

Naomi turned to see Kate looking self-conscious but utterly lovely.

'You're spectacular,' Naomi told her.

'All May's work.' Kate shrugged, but she'd coloured up with pleasure at the compliment.

'You all look lovely,' Naomi said then.

May was even more elegant than usual in a simple but beautifully cut dress in the colour Naomi believed was called burnt orange, while Alice was delightfully pretty in a blue dress with lemon collar and buttons. 'Ten shillings in Selfridge's bargain basement when I lived in London,' she confided.

'Worth twice as much,' Naomi said, because the gentle colours flattered Alice's soft, golden prettiness.

'And what can I say about you three?' Naomi turned to the children. 'Rosa and Zofia, you're as enchanting as princesses. Samuel, you're as handsome as a prince.'

May beamed at them proudly then turned back to Naomi. 'You're looking rather smart yourself.'

Naomi was wearing a navy-blue dress that was decorated with white polka dots. 'You don't think I'm too frivolous?'

'We're going to a party!' May told her. 'There's no such thing as too frivolous. Besides, your dress is smart. All you need is a tweak or two, if I might just . . .' She indicated a chair.

'You don't want to waste time on an old thing like me.'

'You're in the prime of life and my time won't be wasted. Now sit!'

Naomi sat and a cape was placed around her neck. May's deft fingers unpinned Naomi's pleat and picked up a brush. Naomi couldn't see what she was doing but she certainly wasn't scraping her hair back tightly.

'Now for your face,' May announced.

She used some sort of cold cream to wipe away the cosmetics Naomi had applied then got busy with her own box of tricks.

'What do you think?' May asked when she'd finished.

Naomi took the mirror May was offering. 'Oh, heavens.'

May had teased Naomi's hair into waves and pinned it back only loosely while the cosmetics were much subtler than Naomi's rather brutal red lipstick and rouge. The effect was soft and feminine, and Naomi felt tears springing up.

'No crying!' May ordered. 'Everyone ready?' she asked. 'Then let's get to the party!'

'I'll catch you up,' Alice said as they made their way outside May's neat little house.

None of them needed to ask why. She was going home to check if any news of Daniel had reached the cottage. The rest of them headed for the Sunday School Hall, pausing outside it to look up at the banner that been put up that morning. *The Churchwood Bookshop – All Welcome.*

'Looks wonderful,' Kate said.

Inside, three long trestle tables had been laid out along one side of the room to hold the food and drink. Small tables and chairs were dotted around so people could sit. Brightly coloured bunting hung from the ceiling beams, while flowers and greenery from Churchwood gardens decorated the tables and window ledges.

The double doors at the back of the hall stood open, revealing the sunny garden where there were more tables and chairs, and space for dancing. Bert had placed the gramophone just by the doors so music would be heard inside and out. The box of records was on the table beside it.

'Shall we get into the party spirit?' May asked, heading towards the gramophone. 'How about "Puttin' On The Ritz"?'

She set the record playing and danced along as they began to set out their own contributions to the party feast.

399

When Alice arrived, they all stopped and stared at her. 'No news yet,' she told them.

'Hopefully soon,' Naomi said, touched by the way Alice's wan face broke into a smile despite everything.

More people arrived, with Janet leading the way. Soon the trestle tables were packed with bottles, jugs, sandwiches, pies, sausage rolls, salads and, for dessert, scones, biscuits, strawberries and raspberries. Milk was placed in the kitchen because no party would be complete without tea. Gradually the feast extended out across the tables. 'Mmm,' Bert said, adding more salads and a bowl of boiled eggs.

His fingers crept towards a sausage roll.

'Hands off until later,' Naomi told him.

Janet and Betty covered the feast with clean white tablecloths to keep it fresh.

Soon the hall was bustling with chatter, music and the sort of on-the-spot jigging that warmed people up for proper dancing later.

The hospital party arrived – Matron, Babs, Pauline, Dr Marwood and more than a dozen patients, including some in wheelchairs. 'This is a sight for sore eyes,' one patient said.

'What a treat to stare at something other than hospital walls,' agreed another.

Every guest was welcomed and given something to drink. Beer was favourite with the patients. 'Nectar!' one declared, while Janet's fruit punch proved popular with Matron and the nurses.

'It's fruit, and a little something to give it a boost,' Janet confided, winking, then whispered, 'Sherry.'

Even Archibald Lovell came along. 'I had to see

what my lovely daughter has been up to,' he explained, and Alice hugged him.

Once everyone had arrived, Septimus Barnes clapped his hands for attention. 'It's a pleasure to stand here and see so many happy faces. When our dear Mrs Harrington first told me about this book-shop scheme, little did I realize how ambitious the project was. I should have known better – Mrs Har-rington has long been a force for good in Churchwood. Please join me in showing your appreciation in time-honoured tradition.'

He began to clap his hands, but Naomi moved towards him saying, 'Wait!'

The applause died out again.

'It's kind of Reverend Barnes to single me out,' she told the crowd, 'but I think we all know that the book-shop wasn't my idea. It was Alice Lovell's. Alice may have lived amongst us for only a few months but we were blessed the day she came to Churchwood because she's making such a difference. Alice, please come and share your ideas for the bookshop's future.'

Kate nudged Alice forward.

'Goodness,' Alice said. 'I've never made a speech before, but here goes. The bookshop may have been my idea, but it wouldn't have been possible without the help of so many people – Naomi, Kate, May, Janet, Bert and every last one of you. We're calling it a book-shop but, as you'll know if you read the poster, it'll be much more than that. Certainly, there'll be books to buy and books to borrow. A modest collection to begin with, but we hope to keep adding to it as our fundraising continues. As well as books there'll be

401

newspapers and magazines like *Woman's Weekly, My Weekly* and the *People's Friend.* Comics for children, too – *Beano,* the *Dandy* . . . You'll be able to read them with a cup of tea while you chat to friends because we won't be requiring silence like a public library.'

Naomi scanned the crowd and was glad to see that people were smiling.

'We'll also be offering story times,' Alice continued. 'Sometimes for little ones and sometimes for not-so-little ones. There'll be talks on all sorts of things as well. May will talk about how to be stylish on a budget in wartime. Bert will talk about Digging for Victory. Dr Marwood from the hospital will talk about music and dancing – letting you have a dance, too, I'm sure. And who knows? Maybe someone will come along and talk about beer.'

A cheer went up from the patients.

'No one needs to worry that they can't afford to come,' Alice said. 'There'll be no fee unless you want to buy a book. Donations will be both voluntary and anonymous. We'll have a plate in the vestibule rather than here in the main hall. Whether you support the bookshop by donating a few pennies here and there or by giving jam, lavender bags or anything else we can raffle, your contributions will be welcome. And let's not forget that lending a listening ear to friends is valuable, too.'

Alice paused. 'I think I've talked enough. To give you a taste of what's going to be on offer, let's listen to a story – one I think we can all learn from. Kate, would you read it to us?'

Kate looked surprised. Alarmed, even. They'd all read and approved the story in advance but, clearly, she hadn't expected to be the one to read it out loud. But she glanced around and must have seen only encouragement because she took a deep breath and said, 'I'll be glad to.'

Naomi was delighted to see her gaining in confidence.

Kate walked forward shyly, took the seat Bert had placed for her and breathed in again as though to steady her nerves. 'Today's story is one of Aesop's Fables,' she announced, and told the tale of a great big lion who was woken by a teeny, tiny mouse.

' "The lion was cross at being woken and opened its mouth to eat the mouse. But the mouse persuaded the lion to let him live on the grounds that he might be useful to the lion one day. The lion didn't believe it – in fact he laughed at the very idea – but he let the mouse go free anyway. Later the lion was caught in a hunter's trap. The little mouse chewed through the rope that was holding the trap closed and set the lion free." '

'Was the mouse right about being useful?' Kate asked the audience.

'Yes!' everyone chorused.

Alice stepped forward again. 'Now who can tell me the message of that story?'

Hands shot up.

'Rosa?' Alice invited.

'All persons can be kind.'

'Exactly. We can all help each other because all of us – from the smallest to the biggest – have something to offer. Thank you, Kate. You read beautifully.'

There was a round of applause. Kate blushed but

looked all the lovelier for it. She got up and joined Alice, and they whispered together.

'Mrs Harrington – Naomi – wanted to blend into the shadows a few minutes ago,' Kate said then, 'but she needs to come into the light again because, for her, today is particularly special. It's her birthday!'

What? To Naomi's amazement Janet walked out of the kitchen holding a cake on which candles blazed.

'Happy birthday to you . . .' everyone sang, following it with 'For she's a jolly good fellow'.

Three cheers went up – hip, hip, hurray!

'My word,' Naomi said, blushing as brightly as Kate. 'My word.'

'Don't dither, woman,' Bert called. 'Those candles need blowing out.'

'Don't forget to make a wish,' Alice said.

Naomi leaned towards the cake. What should she wish for? That she could salvage her marriage, after all? No, she wouldn't waste a wish on Alexander.

'Fallen asleep over there?' Bert demanded.

I wish health and happiness for my friends, Naomi uttered inside her head. *For Alice's Daniel, too.*

Taking a deep breath, she blew the candles out. 'It's a large cake as well as a beautiful one, so there should be enough for everyone,' she said.

Bert walked over and gave her a nod of approval. 'This is quite a celebration, particularly for you,' he said as people started to help themselves to food.

'Another year older.'

'I wasn't thinking of your birthday.'

'The bookshop—'

'I wasn't thinking of that, either.'

'Ah.' He was thinking that she'd changed as a

person. And he was right. 'You don't know anything about my life before I came to Churchwood, do you?' she asked him.

'Not a thing.'

She told him about her father and Tuggs Tonics. 'I've never told anyone about my past before,' she said once she'd finished. 'Not in more than a quarter of a century. There'll be no more putting on airs for me. I've found ... honesty. And friends. Real friends.'

'I hope you count me amongst them, Mrs H.,' Bert said.

'It's Naomi, as you know very well.'

'I do. But I'll still call you Mrs H. sometimes. Just to keep you on your toes in case you're ever tempted to get high and mighty again.'

'There's not much chance of that with you around, Mr M.'

He chuckled. 'Fetching dress,' he said then.

'You're looking rather smart yourself. No string belt, I see.'

'Braces instead. Red ones, too. Do you think I'm turning into a man-about-town dandy?'

'I'd put the chances of that at close to zero,' Naomi said, laughing, then excused herself to thank Alice and Janet for the cake.

'Such a fuss for an old thing like me,' she said. 'But who told you it was my birthday?'

'A little bird,' Alice answered, and Naomi guessed that Marjorie was responsible.

'How was such a splendid cake possible? So much butter and sugar!'

'Lots of people contributed,' Alice told her. 'An

ounce here and there added up and we had ingredients left over to make more cakes for today's tea.'

'I'm grateful,' Naomi said. 'I think – no, I *know* – that I've never had a happier birthday than this.' She swallowed as emotion threatened to overwhelm her. 'Thank you.'

Her eye was caught by someone standing in the open doorway. 'It looks as though you're going to have a wonderful day, too, Alice,' she said.

CHAPTER FIFTY-EIGHT

Alice

Alice turned – and gasped. For a moment she couldn't move. Then she set off towards Daniel on legs that felt stiff and awkward, as though the tempest of emotion sweeping through her was robbing them of function. Reaching him, she battled the urge to throw herself on his chest and weep for the sheer joy of seeing him, alive and well even if clearly exhausted.

'When did you get back?' she asked.

'Crack of dawn this morning.'

'From Dunkirk?'

'After several days on the beaches. We were put on a train to London and then another train to Bedford. Which isn't so far from here. I showered, shaved and changed – all three desperately needed – then got a pass from my senior officer, scrounged the loan of a motorbike and here I am. It's wonderful to see you, Alice.'

'You too.' She dashed away tears, laughing to show they were ridiculous. 'Sorry. It's just that I've been hearing such terrible stories.'

'My parents told me you'd telephoned.' He paused, and then added in a softer, hopeful voice, 'You were worried?'

'Of course I was worried.'

'I'm sorry,' he said, but a speculative gleam had entered his eyes.

It made Alice try to reel her emotions back in. 'How did you know I was here?'

'I heard music as I rode through the village. When you weren't at the cottage I left the motorbike in your garden and walked back to investigate. I appear to be an uninvited guest at a party, though.' He looked around as though half expecting to be asked to leave.

'This is a community celebration and you're more than welcome. Come and say hello to Kate. You remember Kate?'

'Of course.'

'She's been transformed.' Alice gestured towards Kate, who was dancing with Dr Marwood, her long chestnut hair swinging out beside her and her smile wide.

Kate had shaken her head and put up a defensive hand when the doctor first approached her, but he'd said something to make her laugh and perhaps the fact that he was middle-aged and married had reassured her because a moment later she'd allowed him to lead her towards the dance floor. Once there, she'd stood awkwardly for a moment; then, encouraged by the doctor, she'd begun to move, picking up the steps with ease and natural grace.

'Goodness. I'd call her an ugly duckling changed into a swan except that she's always been beautiful,' Daniel said. 'It was the old clothes that let her down.'

Daniel spoke like a man who was pleased rather than attracted, so Alice felt no jealousy. Not that she had any right to feel jealous, but she was only human.

'Come and meet some of the others,' Alice suggested.

'Unless you're tired?' Daniel must need to rest after his ordeal. To gather his thoughts in peace and quiet.

'I'm not tired,' he insisted. 'Not now I've seen you. Please lead on.'

She took him to her father first. Archibald Lovell got to his feet and shook Daniel's hand enthusiastically. 'Welcome home, son. It's a real pleasure to see you.'

'I'm glad to be here, though I'm surprised you're at a party, sir.'

'Churchwood has a way of growing on a person. But sit down.' He glanced over his shoulder. 'Someone fetch this man a drink. He's newly back from Dunkirk.'

Daniel sat and Alice's father asked him about his evacuation. 'But don't feel you *have* to talk about it. Sometimes we need time to process these things first.'

'Have the news reports been full of Dunkirk?'

'Not until Thursday evening but we'd heard rumours.'

'I was proud of the way my fellow soldiers behaved. I queued on the Mole – a long jetty made of concrete – and we scattered every time German aircraft flew over. But afterwards we queued up again in the same order as before. No one tried to get ahead of anyone else.'

'Those Messerschmitt aircraft sound deadly.'

'Messerschmitts, Stukas, Heinkels . . . The RAF did their best to fight them off, though. The new Spitfires are incredible, but they couldn't save every man.'

'It's a terrible thing to see men fall.'

'Nothing worse,' Daniel agreed. 'I felt for the men who were hit and I feel for the men who'll be left behind as prisoners of war. Many thousands of us got away, though. Tanks and artillery had to be abandoned, of course, but my impression is that enough of us were saved to fight again once we've reorganized.'

'That's good to hear. But enough war talk. This is a party.'

Kate arrived with Daniel's drink. 'Remember me?' she asked.

'How could I forget?'

'You can call me Cinderella from now on, seeing as Alice and our friend May decided I should come to the ball appropriately dressed.'

'I imagine there's no shortage of Prince Charmings who want to dance with you.'

'I wouldn't say that,' Kate told him, looking self-conscious but also happy. 'I'm glad you've made it home safely. Alice has been worried.'

Naomi came next. 'It's a pleasure to meet you at last,' she told him.

'Likewise. I hear you've been invaluable in making this bookshop actually happen.'

'Alice deserves most of the credit,' Naomi said. She paused, and then added, 'She's been worried about you.'

Daniel slid another thoughtful look in Alice's direction. 'You should eat,' she said. 'Come and choose something.'

'Sounds great, though I may not do justice to it. Food supplies were a little wanting in my last days in France and it's amazing how quickly the stomach shrinks.'

Janet came over as they reached the food tables. 'So you're Daniel,' she said. 'Welcome home. My son Charlie made it home, too.'

'Have you managed to see him?'

'Not yet. I can't wait to hug him, though a hug from his mum will probably embarrass him. Knowing he's safe . . . that's the main thing.'

'I was lucky in being sent not far from here and getting permission to come today.'

'It's lovely that you were able to put Alice out of her misery. She's been so worried. Enjoy the food.'

Janet moved away to be caught by Marjorie Plym. 'That's Alice's young man, isn't it?' Marjorie asked loudly, and Alice lost no time in steering Daniel away to sit at one of the outside tables.

They weren't alone for long. Babs and Pauline came to be introduced and Matron soon followed. All three mentioned how worried Alice had been.

Daniel spent time with some of the patients, too, as they were eager to hear the war news from a man who'd been involved as recently as the previous day.

'Alice has done wonders for us chaps at the hospital,' one said, and the others agreed.

'Breath of fresh air, she is,' one added.

Someone put 'Moonlight Serenade' on the gramophone and Daniel smiled. 'I hope you chaps will excuse us. I'd like to dance with the belle of the ball.'

He took Alice's hand and led her towards the other dancers. Then he turned and took her in his arms. Alice groaned inside at the sheer bliss of having the man she loved so close. She could feel the warmth of his body and filled her nostrils with the clean scent of him. Just this once, she told herself. Just this once . . .

His breath ruffled her hair – his lips must be so close! – and she closed her eyes to savour it. But in time the song came to an end. Daniel drew back just a little and smiled down at her, his dark eyes intense. 'Alice, you must know how I feel about you.'

'Don't.' She stepped away from him. 'Please don't.'

He looked stricken. 'Is my love so unwelcome?'

If only he really did feel love for her. Simple love, uncomplicated by guilt and pity. 'It's . . . I just . . .'

'Do you need more time? Is that it?'

Alice's throat was so tight she felt as though the very life was being choked from her. Tears stabbed her eyes like fiery needles. 'I do care for you. But not in the way you think. You're my friend. A dear friend. But that's where it begins and ends. I'm sorry if it disappoints you.'

'Disappoints me? Alice, it devastates me.'

'I'm sorry,' she said again.

He rubbed a hand over his face. 'You don't think your feelings can grow if—'

'I don't. I'm sorry.'

'So you said.'

'If I could change things, I would.' She'd go back in time to the fateful day of the accident and stop it from happening. It wouldn't have taken much to avert disaster – a little more attention on an excited boy, a speedier appreciation of approaching danger, a swifter reaction . . . Then Alice and Daniel could have explored what, if anything, was between them without the spectre of responsibility casting its shadow.

Instead little Teddy had spotted a dog across the road and run towards it as a horse and cart came along at a clip. Both Alice and Daniel had raced after him but Alice had been faster to see what was happening and reached Teddy first. She'd grabbed hold of him and, turning, pushed him to safety just before the horse collided with her and knocked her to the ground. At that stage the damage had been slight, but the panicked horse had reared up then brought his front hooves down hard, one of them landing on her hand and grinding it between the unyielding surface of the road and the lacerating metal of his horseshoe.

But there was no profit in thinking of what might have been. There was only reality.

'I understand,' Daniel said. 'I'm sorry, too, though for a different reason.'

'I'll always be fond of you.'

Daniel winced at that.

'I wish you happy, Daniel, but you wouldn't be happy with me. This way, you're free to find true happiness with someone else. You may not have found the right girl yet, but you will. I'm sure of it.'

'I thought I'd found the right girl in you, Alice.' He stared down at the ground for a moment, then heaved breath into his lungs and looked up again. 'I think it best if I leave now. Exhaustion is catching up with me and you have a party to enjoy.'

He stepped forward and kissed her cheek. 'Be happy, Alice. Know that I'll always—' He broke off and shook his head. 'No, best not.'

With that he turned and walked away down the path that led from the garden to the road. Alice watched him go; then she hastened round to the other side of the hall to weep in private.

CHAPTER FIFTY-NINE

Naomi

'Right,' Bert said. 'Enough talking. Let's see you on your feet, woman.'

'Dancing? Oh, no. Don't let me stop you, but dancing isn't for me.'

'Dancing is for everyone. It isn't a competition. Who cares if you look like a ballerina or a lumbering hippo as long as you enjoy it?'

Naomi glanced over at the dancers, who were clearly having fun. Why not join them? 'I warn you I'm more of a lumbering hippo,' she said, getting up.

'My toes can take a crushing. They've had tools dropped on them often enough.'

Naomi still felt self-conscious as they walked to the edge of the dancing area.

'You're not going to your execution,' Bert told her.

He stretched to put his arm around her waist. 'I'm no sylph,' she said.

'Neither am I. Let's get on with it.'

Almost immediately Naomi trod on his toe.

'It's had worse than that and survived to tell the tale,' Bert said. 'Now come on. Loosen up.'

Naomi did enjoy herself, despite getting hot and bothered by the unfamiliar exercise. She feared there might even be a sheen of unladylike perspiration on her upper lip but it didn't seem to matter. Not today.

Kate glided past, looking lovely in the doctor's arms. 'Beautiful girl, that,' Bert said.

'She is,' Naomi agreed, and Bert nodded approval.

And where was Alice? Naomi had seen her dancing earlier but couldn't see her now.

Kate glided close again. 'Have you seen Alice?' Naomi asked, hoping to hear that she'd gone for a quiet chat with the man she clearly loved and who equally clearly loved her.

'I expect she's with Daniel,' Kate told her, and they exchanged warm, pleased smiles.

Bert spun Naomi outside and she gave herself up to the dancing. What fun it was, even if Bert's description of a lumbering hippo fitted her perfectly.

But then a voice interrupted. 'Oi!' it called. 'You in the spotty dress.'

Naomi looked round to see one of the patients in a wheelchair beneath an apple tree.

'I think his wheels might be stuck,' she told Bert.

They approached him together. It was Jake Turner, the man whom Alice had once suspected of being the hospital spy. 'Are you deaf?' he demanded. 'I've been calling for ages.'

'We didn't hear above the music. Do you need helping inside?'

'I need you to find Alice.'

'Can it wait? She's with a rather dear friend at the moment.'

'But she isn't. That's my point. Her chap went off looking like all his hopes had ended. And she went off looking like she was crumpling into pieces.'

Naomi's pleasure in the day suddenly dissolved. 'I'll find her,' she said, hastening off.

She caught hold of Kate's arm, apologized to her partner, and pulled her aside. 'We've got to find Alice. Whatever happened with Daniel, it isn't what we hoped.'

Kate frowned. 'You look for her here. I'll run to The Linnets.'

But at that moment Alice walked around from the side of the hall and stood watching the dancers, her back straight but her lovely face pale.

Naomi's heart squeezed. Poor, poor Alice! She walked over with Kate at her side and placed a comforting hand on Alice's arm. 'Would it help to talk about it?'

Alice's eyes shimmered. 'Thank you, but there's nothing to say.'

'Daniel . . .'

'He left. He couldn't stay for long.'

'But you love him,' Kate said bluntly.

Alice looked as though she was about to deny it but seemed to realize she wouldn't be believed. 'I do . . . care for him. But some things aren't meant to be.'

'He loves you, too,' Naomi pointed out.

'I'm afraid you're mistaken. Daniel's feelings are complicated.'

'I don't understand,' Kate said.

'Me neither,' Naomi admitted.

'Coming through!' someone called.

CHAPTER SIXTY

Alice

Alice looked round to see Jake Turner in his wheel-chair. 'What's all this nonsense?' he demanded.

'Do you have a problem?' she asked, wishing she could be left alone for a moment. Wishing she could go home, in fact, so she could throw herself on to her bed and bury her face in her pillow.

'It's you who has the problem. One minute you're dancing with your young man. The next minute you're both looking devastated. Why? What happened?'

'Nothing happened.'

Jake sighed impatiently while Kate and Naomi exchanged worried looks. None of them believed her for the simple reason that it wasn't true.

'Please stop pitying me,' Alice said. 'I can't bear to be pitied.'

Kate and Naomi exchanged more looks, this time of bafflement, but Jake gave Alice a thoughtful stare, then said, 'I think I know.'

'Whatever you're thinking, please keep it to yourself.'

'It needs saying, Alice, love. Leaving aside the fact that I'm moody and miserable – which would put any-one off me – do you think the only reason a woman could ever consider wedding me is if she pities me because I've lost my legs?'

'Of course not!' Alice was horrified.

'Why should it be any different for you just because something tore into your hand and left a few scars behind?'

'You don't understand.'

'Explain then.'

'It isn't the injury itself that's the problem but how I got it. It was an accident but Daniel blames himself for it. He's trying to atone for his guilt.'

'By courting you? Doesn't sound likely to me. Besides, I saw the way he looked at you and you looked at him. Me and my Judy never looked at each other like that because we never really loved each other. But you and that chap . . . I know love when I see it and that was it. Oh, your man may feel guilt and who knows what else, but none of that takes away from the fact that he loves you.'

'But he only showed an interest in me – a romantic interest, I mean – after the accident.'

'So he made a mess of his timing. Maybe it was nearly losing you that woke him up to the idea of loving you. Or maybe there was some other reason he held back before. Have you talked to him about it?'

'Well . . . no.'

'Then you've let your sensitivity or however else you want to describe it lead you straight down Wrong Conclusion Alley and blind you to a truth. It couldn't be more obvious to the rest of us. That chap is head over heels in love with you.'

'Jake's right,' Kate said.

'One hundred per cent,' Naomi agreed.

'Never seen a man so smitten,' added Bert, who'd come to join them.

'The question now is, what are you going to do about it?' Jake asked.

A frenzy of thoughts tumbled round Alice's head. Jake and the others might be wrong about Daniel, but wasn't it cowardly not even to try to find out if they were right? She'd be risking her pride but surely it was worth that risk to discover for sure how he felt?

There was something else. The idea of him being sent back to the war not knowing that she loved him was suddenly unbearable, and if she didn't tell him today, she might never get another chance. 'I need to find Daniel.'

'The truck's outside,' Bert said. 'Let's go.'

'Yes, go!' Kate urged.

Alice snatched her friends into quick hugs, then kissed Jake's cheek.

'Get away with you,' he said. 'You're wasting time.'

'Daniel left his motorcycle at the cottage,' Alice explained, racing round to the front of the building with Bert. 'He'll have walked back for it.'

'Then let's—'

Too late. As they reached the street, they could hear the sound of a motorcycle disappearing into the distance. Alice was distraught, but Bert was undaunted.

'We'll take a shortcut to the main road,' he said, making for the truck. 'Hop in, girl.'

He drove at speed towards Brimbles Lane, turned along it then took a half-hidden track just past Brimbles Farm. 'This might be rough,' he warned as the truck bounced and rattled over rocks, roots, fallen branches and sun-baked ruts of earth. A tree branch slapped the windscreen. More branches scraped the truck's sides and there was an awful bang as the truck fell into a hollow like a ship careering down the far side of a wave. Bert kept his foot to the pedal.

'I only hope we're in time,' he said when they burst on to the road at last.

He screeched to a halt and Alice leapt out of the truck to survey the road in both directions. Nothing. Daniel had been too quick for them.

Or had he? Alice's ears picked up a faint phut-phutting sound. Praying that it was Daniel's motorcycle, she ran into the middle of the road and waved her arms.

A motorcycle rounded a curve and veered on to the grass verge to avoid hitting her. Leaping off, the rider kicked the support stand into place, ripped off his helmet and goggles and rushed towards her. 'Alice! Darling! Are you all right? You're not hurt?' He took her by the shoulders, raking his gaze up and down as though checking her for injuries.

'I'm fine,' she assured him. Physically, she was absolutely fine. But emotionally . . . 'I couldn't let you leave without telling you I love you.'

Daniel reared back a little. 'Love me? You mean the sort of love a person feels for a friend?' His expression was agonized, as though he didn't dare to hope.

'I mean the sort of love a woman feels for a man.'

He moistened his lips. Looked down at the ground then back at Alice. 'You're not just saying that because I'll have to return to the war?'

'I'm in love with you, Daniel. The war has nothing to do with it.'

He sucked in air before drawing her to his chest.

'My God, you've no idea how I've longed to hear you say that.'

'I'll say it again if you like?' Joy was fizzing through her veins. 'I love you, Daniel Irvine. With all of my heart.'

He let out a whoop then swung her off her feet and round in a circle. Releasing her again, he drew back to study her face, 'I love you, too, Alice Lovell. With all of *my* heart.'

It was Alice's turn to hesitate. 'You're not just saying that because you feel sorry for me?'

'Sorry for you? Alice, I've loved you from the moment we met in that bookshop. At first I told myself I was making too much of a chance meeting, especially as I was about to go to America. But when I saw you again I knew I hadn't exaggerated that first impression. You made my soul dance.'

'I thought you regarded me like an amusing sister or cousin.'

'Hardly. But you were young – just seventeen to my twenty-three – and I didn't want to scare you away. That's why I took things slowly. Then the accident happened. You were as sweet and polite as ever but . . . distant. I thought you blamed me for what happened. Why not? I blamed myself. After all, I'd been watching your lovely face instead of keeping a careful enough eye on Teddy. I'd been trying to decide if you were ready for romance or if I should give you more time.'

'I didn't know that. I'd begun to think you just weren't interested in me. It wasn't until after the accident that you began to behave as though you might want more than friendship, but I thought that you weren't being romantic as much as . . . practical. By then it was clear that I was going to struggle to work for a while so I thought you'd decided to provide for me because I couldn't provide for myself. I thought you were sacrificing your own happiness out of guilt.'

'I do feel guilty, but I also feel many other things. Admiration, longing, respect, desire ... In short, love. Being with you would never have been a sacrifice. It would always have been a joy. But I have wondered if my role in the accident meant I'd lost my chance with you. It seems we've both jumped to false conclusions.'

'Instead of talking,' Alice agreed.

'Do you think we need to talk more before you commit to me? By commitment I mean marriage. There's nothing I want more than that. Will you marry me, Alice?'

'I hope we'll talk for hours in the future. But for now, I think we've said enough.'

'Meaning?'

'Of course I'll marry you!' Alice threw her arms around his neck and kissed him.

Daniel kissed her back. Soundly. And it was delicious.

'I don't have a ring yet,' he said. 'But I'd like to announce our engagement to the world before you have a chance to change your mind. There's a perfectly good party taking place in Churchwood right now. I know it's a bookshop celebration, but do you think anyone will mind if we borrow it for a moment?'

'I don't think they'll mind at all.'

'Then what are we waiting for?' He grinned, released her, then jogged to where Bert was waiting in the truck.

'Back to the party?' Bert asked, smiling.

'Back to the party,' Daniel confirmed. He helped Alice climb into the truck and then ran to his motorcycle.

'I think we'll take the proper road,' Bert told Alice. 'This old truck has been challenged enough for one day.' He set off with Daniel following.

'Still there, is he?' Bert joked when Alice kept looking back.

'He is, and he's not a figment of my imagination.'

'A dream come true, then?'

'The best dream possible.'

They parked outside the Sunday School Hall and headed inside. Bert walked straight up to Dr Marwood and must have asked him to pause the music because quietness descended. 'I'm sorry to interrupt the party,' Bert said, 'but I hope you'll forgive me when I ask Alice and her young man to step forward and share their news.'

Daniel took Alice's hand and led her to Bert's side. 'I'm proud, delighted and ecstatic to announce that this wonderful girl' – he sent Alice a glowing look – 'has agreed to become my wife.'

'Well, thank goodness for that!' Kate drawled and, walking over, she kissed Alice's cheek.

Naomi followed, then May, then Janet, and then a whole crowd of well-wishers came forward to give hugs, kisses and congratulations.

Alice's father was amongst them. He kissed her proudly then shook Daniel's hand. 'Congratulations, dear boy. You've found the most priceless of diamonds in my daughter.'

'I know it, sir.'

Drinks were passed around for a toast, and, as Alice looked at the people who'd become her friends, she felt a burst of extraordinary happiness.

Doubtless there'd be more trials and tribulations to face – there was a war on, after all – but for this moment in time Churchwood and its people were content. And when adversity swept down again, the bookshop would be there to support them with love and care.

Acknowledgements

This book may have my name on the cover but actually it has involved a collaboration with some amazing people. Special thanks go to my incredibly helpful editor, Alice Rodgers, and the fantastic team at Transworld, and to super-agent Kate Nash and the wonderful team at the Kate Nash Literary Agency. It's a privilege to have such wise, creative and all-round lovely people on my side.

Friendship is important in this book and I'd like to thank my own friends for being so supportive and fun. Whether we're talking writing in the V&A café or drinking wine in a hot tub, it's great to spend time with you all.

Finally, I'd like to thank my daughters, who never stop believing in me.

If you enjoyed *The Wartime Bookshop*, don't miss the second book in the series . . .

Land Girls at the Wartime Bookshop

Catch up with **Alice**, **Kate** and **Naomi** as the war intensifies and the bookshop comes under threat. Can Churchwood band together to keep their beloved bookshop going?

Available for pre-order now.
eBook and paperback out in summer 2023.

And look out for . . .

Christmas at the Wartime Bookshop

Available for pre-order now.
eBook and paperback out for Christmas 2023.